Count
to
a Thousand

Caroline Goldberg Igra

Mandolin Publishing

Cover Design: Imri Zertal
Typesetting: Optume Technologies
Author photo: dboardmanphoto.com

ISBN: 978-965-92668-0-7

1 3 5 7 9 8 6 4 2

For my father

Part One

Chapter 1

Not my son.

Victoria gripped the steering wheel of the car with all her strength, watching her fingers turn white as they emptied of blood. She raised her gaze to meet the double-decker train appearing beneath the overpass and approaching the station.

Not my beautiful boy.

Tears pooled in the corner of her eyes. She wiped them away as she glanced in the rearview mirror. Her eyes looked spooked, tired. Foreign. She wondered how they would have looked if things had gone differently, if it had been her child lying in Rambam Hospital with shrapnel in his head. She sat up a bit straighter in the seat and raised her chin. She had to pull herself together, and quickly. Dwelling on what might have been wouldn't help her or Ben. She mustn't show how scared she'd been, how terrified she still was. He didn't need to deal with her fear on top of everything else he had on his plate.

Ben is fine. My Ben is fine.

It had been only ten days since he'd last been home, but to Victoria it felt like a lifetime. Since he'd begun his military service she *always* wanted him home. It didn't matter how much laundry he dragged in with him or the typhoon he'd leave behind when he headed back to the base. She cherished every minute.

Soldiers began to flood out of the station's exit: young men and women dressed in green, white or khaki, lugging heavy bags, and all, in unison, eagerly seeking their ride. Here in Israel every week's end was a kind of celebration: a homecoming.

Victoria didn't spot Ben among the first wave exiting the station, and her eyes began to blur, a different picture beginning to form in her head: a young man lying in a hospital bed unconscious, head wrapped in a bandage, family gathered around. Complete silence. *Was that the scene?* That other boy, the one from Ben's high school class, the one who'd been injured last night in the sniper fire on the northern border, was that what his morning looked like? Clinging to life while his pained family joined in prayer?

She looked at the clock on the dashboard but didn't register the time. Instead, she envisioned a day ticker. How many of the give or take thousand days of Ben's army service had already passed? How many lay ahead? Maybe 850? It was far too many. She couldn't bear it.

Again her inner eye returned to the vision of that young boy, and she wondered whether an official representative from the military had notified his parents. *What if I were to receive such a call? Could I simply not answer? And what if I didn't? How would I know?* That last thought was the only one she could answer. She knew she'd feel it, no question whatsoever. She was certain she'd know if something happened to her golden boy, if there was a chance he was lost and wouldn't come home.

A wave of nausea passed through her and she felt like she might throw up. She held on to the steering wheel as if it could keep her afloat, a kind of anchor, and tried to pull herself together, sitting up straighter in her seat, looking out the windshield and searching for a spot on the horizon that would steady her nerves and return her balance. And that's when she saw him, ducking under the exit gateway, gun gripped in his left hand, his heavy duffle bag slung over his right shoulder. She was overcome with a flush of relief and gratitude. *Here's my boy.*

She watched as he searched for her, his eyes scanning the endless rows of cars waiting in the lot. In that handful of seconds she acknowledged the fact that he was no longer her little boy. Over there stood a handsome young man on the brink of a life that had very little to do with her. She sighed and popped out of the car, calling out to him.

"Hi, sweetheart!"

A few heads turned at Victoria's words. In the midst of a sea of Hebrew greetings, her English one stuck out. She ignored their gazes and opened her arms to receive him.

"Mommy."

He reached her side, moved his gun out of the way, swinging it behind him, leaned over and caught her in a tight embrace. She loved this. Ever since he'd begun his military service he'd resumed the occasional usage of the term "mommy," so militantly discarded during his adolescence. She couldn't get enough of hearing it. Every time was as good as the first.

She wrapped her arms around his broad back, holding him close. He let her. This was a change as well. Not only the hug but the lingering; those extra few seconds he stayed in place, allowing her to hold on. She knew his reciprocation was genuine, as much for him as for her. He obviously needed this little bit of home.

There had been a noticeable shift since those first weeks in service, when he was establishing his newfound independence. Over the last few months he'd become a bit clingier, obviously happy to come home and be pampered. She really didn't know what went on during most of his week, save the few details he shared, but she understood it was both physically and emotionally taxing. It must be, to warrant the new attitude in his greetings, one of almost relief. She'd expected that to be her territory alone and was continually shocked to find it was his as well.

In some ways Ben's re-entries resembled her own after she'd officially left home for college. The minute she'd spot her parents she'd run to the car, hugging them eagerly, letting them into a space she'd so carefully protected as her own back in high school. Of course that shift in attitude had been brief, and soon enough she'd break the embrace, end that moment of intimacy with all the dependency it implied, keen to return to her newly acquired adulthood.

Yet Ben seemed to relish whatever she had to offer, his grip on her a blatant expression of need. They lingered for another moment, hung on a bit longer, prolonging the embrace. She didn't want to let him go. She had him, right here, right now. The image of that boy up in Haifa flashed through her head. She didn't want to think that she could have lost him. It simply wasn't possible. She wondered if he was thinking the very same thing.

"How are you sweetie?"

"I'm okay."

That's what she needed to hear. That's always what she needed to hear. Those were the words that enabled her to function, to breathe – to somehow survive his service. Her boy was okay.

He released his grip and swung his bag off his back. It fell heavily into the trunk of the car with a loud thud.

"What's in there? Barbells?" It was an old joke, but he laughed to indulge her. "This is nothing Mom. You should see our battle gear. So far we've been trained to carry 25 percent of our body weight but I'm told the eventual goal is 60. And in wartime the sky's the limit."

She couldn't imagine it. This weekend bag seemed heavy enough. How could her baby take on such a crushing load? His strong back was a far stretch from the soft, pearly white surface she'd tickled at bath time years earlier; she'd never foreseen it lugging such a burden.

"Mommy." His tone had changed; it was more ominous. "What about Omer?"

He retreated to the passenger side of the car, opened the door and climbed in. Victoria was one step ahead of him, already sitting behind the wheel. She hesitated before answering.

"He's stable."

"But..." He understood that her response was too short, its terseness revealing a longer story, a complicated one. He waited for her to continue.

"I don't know a lot, Ben. There are so many rumors. I understand the doctors are hesitant to remove the shrapnel."

"Where's it lodged?"

"Somewhere in his head."

They both fell silent as Victoria pulled out of the parking lot and onto the main road in front of the station. She searched for something to say, words that might assuage his fears. She didn't want him to be afraid; to consider, for a minute, that this could be him. But she figured he already had, more than once.

"I understand they're hopeful."

Ben gazed away from her, out the passenger side window. She couldn't begin to imagine what was going through his head. She reached over and patted his leg. "I know someone who's close with the family. She's been up to Rambam to sit with them. I'll check in with her later and find out what's going on as of today, okay?"

More silence. It was unbearable. She needed to move forward, shake off this terror. She couldn't deal with what could have been, so she changed the subject, starting out gently. "Ben, sweetie, tell me about your week. Didn't you have some kind of navigation exercise?"

He didn't answer immediately but she noticed him begin to relax, stretching his legs forward and sinking back into the cushy car seat.

"It was a tough week." He sounded grim, as if determinedly trying to make the transition from the scene playing out in his head of his friend lying in the hospital, to the conversation in the car. She wondered what it felt like to know you're okay when something terrible has happened to someone else in the same position. Maybe that burden was as great as the physical weight Ben carried daily.

The car filled up with a silence so thick it felt almost suffocating. She waited patiently, eager to hear whatever he had to tell, eager to move beyond the threat of what might have been.

"So," he began, clearing his throat. "We started with a trek from the Carmel Mountains west toward the sea." His voice sounded almost neutral, forcibly unaffected. She figured it was anything but.

He's trying to suppress the fear.

She wanted to help him deal with the unbearable, or at least tuck it away for a few moments and concentrate on the here and now, the good. "So, that terrain was familiar to you," she paused to glance over at him, making eye contact in an effort to keep him in *his* story instead of returning to that of his friend.

"Exactly. I felt right at home." He shifted his gun off his lap and checked that he'd buckled his seat belt. He sunk into silence again.

Victoria needed to get him to the other side.

"Familiarity is always comforting. It wasn't as bad as you'd expected?"

"Actually, it was worse." He looked over at her and smiled. She caught a glint of light in his eyes, a glimmer of his life force shining through.

He continued in a more engaged tone. "The thing is…the trek started at midnight, in total darkness. We weren't allowed to use any form of GPS, and we had to cover the fifteen-kilometer distance as fast as possible."

"Were you near Beit Oren? Was it that kind of very steep terrain?"

"Even worse, Mom. You can't imagine."

Victoria started to relax. Ben's mood had begun to lift; it had become almost lively, energized by the topic and finally freeing itself from under the heavy cloud of anxiety and sadness that had weighed it down at the start of the ride.

"We had head lamps strapped on, you know, the kind that wrap around? But mine dropped and flickered out. I couldn't find it in the darkness. I wasted a lot of time groping around the brambles."

He stretched his hands out over the dashboard to show her the cuts and scratches. She winced.

"Ooh, they look awful." She paused. "Oh God, I just had a thought. Were there snakes?"

"Snakes…other crawling creatures. You name it. I was desperate to find that head lamp."

"And did you?"

"No. I never did." He shook his head to emphasize the futility he'd felt. "I ended up radioing back to the company command. I really couldn't move even one step forward without it. They brought me another one."

"Great." She breathed a sigh of relief. Even a story about an event in the past could evoke concern.

They continued along the road, only ten minutes from home. Victoria settled back in her seat, enjoying his story, absorbing his presence and savoring these precious minutes alone. Guy was waiting at home. He'd no doubt question Ben further, dig into the horror Victoria was eager to avoid. This was a father's prerogative. She'd never dare. It was enough to deal with the thought of what it might be like not to have even these singular moments, these mundane exchanges. She pushed that unwelcome concept out of her mind, it was too painful to bear, and focused on his words. In a few minutes he would step back into the house and be thrust into a world of simple pleasures, on the phone connecting with friends, eventually heading out to meet some of them as she loaded the laundry. These few minutes here in the car: this was an opportunity not to be missed.

Ben jiggled his leg, bouncing it rhythmically against the side of the seat well. He wanted to get home. Get on the phone. Figure out what was up with Omer. What it all meant. The news had spread quickly yesterday. He'd received it from a number of sources the minute he'd turned his phone back on. Networks were so quick to report the worst. It had put a cap on the euphoria he'd felt finishing his navigational unit.

This was all anyone was talking about, yet no one really knew anything. There was no prognosis. Not yet. He felt deeply on edge, disturbed, yet at the same time desperate to shrug it off. He didn't want to focus on it anymore, couldn't. He couldn't let himself worry about what might have been, or even, what could be. Seeing his mother's concerned face at the train station had brought back the distress he'd felt upon learning the news, his awareness of how close loss could come.

He was relieved when he realized she didn't want to talk about it either. In any case, what was there to say? He couldn't begin to express what he felt, let alone handle what had gone through his mind when he'd first heard. He was more than delighted to switch the subject to something safer, with less potential for pain. As hard as it was for him, he knew it was tenfold for her. She didn't have the protective emotional shell that came from being born into a conflict. Her barely suppressed hysteria could only escalate his own distress.

"The thing is," he continued his story about this latest training unit, clinging to normalcy, "I basically had to run the entire exercise. We weren't permitted to do it at a nice, normal, strolling pace. That would have been almost fun."

"And precisely which trail was that? One we've hiked before?"

"No. In fact that was part of the challenge. There wasn't really a trail. We each had to create our own path and find our way, coping with the hilly and rocky terrain, billy-goat style."

His mother glanced over at him, her lips opening wide into a smile. "Billy-goat style?"

"Grandma used to use that phrase. Seems to fit." He smiled. "You know, it was great. I mean, it was hard, it was definitely hard, but it was great too. And the best part was emerging from the woods and running through the fields, that last section that leads to the beach, to the sea. That was incredible! Just knowing I'd made it. I was home!"

He was overwhelmed with exhaustion but simultaneously jittery, no doubt a combination of nerves and physical stress. He tried to slow his leg a bit, tried to let his own words calm him. He'd been so excited yesterday, so thankful to finally complete yet another major component of his special training. This particular test, known as "Mountain to Sea," had been crazy terrifying, but he'd passed with honors. He'd been one of the first in his platoon to get to the water. Back at the base they'd pronounced him officially able to find himself out of any hole – orient himself to any given location. He placed his left hand on his thigh, forcibly slowing the jiggle, willing himself to soak up the calm of the car interior, an extension of home.

His eyes shifted outward, toward the passing vehicles; all those lives moving forward. The border attack had complicated everything, even the usual pleasure of a weekend off. He felt burdened by his own well-being, wasn't sure if it was okay to simply be happy. He looked over and caught his mom glancing at his leg. He knew his jiggling drove her nuts. How many times had he set the dishes clattering with his leg banging against the kitchen table? He knew she wouldn't be able to restrain herself much longer and almost laughed out loud when she finally took one hand off of the steering wheel, reached out and gently laid it on his thigh. She really couldn't take it.

"That's amazing, sweetie. What an accomplishment!"

Her hand lingered where it lay, now motionless. "I'm so proud of you, Ben" she added quietly.

He looked down at her hand and concentrated on remaining as still as possible. He didn't mind her touch; truth be told, he craved it. He flipped over his hands, looking at the cuts and scratches he'd picked up this week. Some of them were pretty deep. He admired them one by one, evidence of what he'd succeeded in overcoming. *Not bad.* He nodded his head once in self-affirmation.

And then, as if that moment of reflection had opened the possibility for other sensations, his nose picked up a foul smell, his own foul smell! As if on cue, he heard his mother sniff once or twice in response. He smiled, relieved by yet another shift in their exchange, this time to something amusing.

"I know. It's bad, right? Do you have anything?"

She nodded her head in affirmation. "In fact, I do."

He followed her hand as it dipped into the seat compartment between them and emerged with a tiny sample bottle of ladies' perfume. He grabbed it and, without a moment's hesitation, sprayed it everywhere he could think of: on his neck, down by his ankles, under his arms, behind his knees and under his shirt. He couldn't get enough. He never thought he'd be so happy to smell like a bouquet of flowers.

Ben handed the bottle back to his mom and they both laughed. It was empty. There was a pause as they appreciated the hilarity of the situation and then laughed again. Suddenly everything felt normal, and even if it wasn't to last for long, normal was an enormous relief. Soon enough he'd be out with his boys, going over the details of the attack, talking about Omer's injuries; each one would offer his assessment of what should have gone down, what might now be. This wasn't a subject he wanted to examine with his mother.

"Next week we have Krav Maga."

"Like what you did with Patricia back in elementary school?"

"No, Mom. That was judo. And that was a game. This isn't a game."

He bit his lip. He hadn't meant to lash out at her. He knew this was hard for her, knew she'd have preferred him to take a desk job instead of insisting on a combat assignment. Every now and then he'd see that look in her eyes, the one that managed to seem simultaneously disappointed, scared and proud; the one that would flash through his mind when training got difficult, when he had to remind himself that he'd chosen this path. *What was it about mothers and intuition?* Despite her continued distress over his decision to purposefully pursue a dangerous path, he recognized she'd made a conscious effort to play it cool. She didn't needle him on the phone, never bemoaned the harder details and was always there to hear whatever he wanted to share, assuming the role he allowed her without pushing for more. She was, no question, one of the best parts of coming home.

Sealed in a cloud of sweet fragrance, dizzy with exhaustion and wired nerves, he vaguely heard her rambling on. "Krav Maga pops up here and there in contemporary American lit, always replete with a young woman looking to be empowered and a handsome, macho Israeli instructor."

He laughed out loud, his brief reverie broken. "Leave it to an Israeli. We've really cornered the market on martial arts over the last few years. So much for the Japanese." He paused and then added, "I'm not sure your heroine would survive our classes. They're pretty down and dirty. Try to imagine doing push-ups on your fists! I'm warped enough to like them."

Ben reached both his arms behind him, his movement constricted by the seat belt, and pushed his back into an arch. He needed to stretch out and relieve that nagging pain. He looked out the window and gauged that they'd be home in only a few minutes. He'd take care of it then. He looked over at his mother, hesitating to mention it; he didn't want to add to her continual worries. Unfortunately this one was relatively obvious. "It doesn't hurt that much, just kind of a throbbing here and there."

He anticipated her expression before meeting her concerned eyes as they entered their street.

"Lower back pain? Be careful. That can develop into a real issue."

He smiled to reassure her. "Don't worry, Mom."

They pulled into the driveway and Ben popped out of the car, grabbing his heavy duffle from the trunk and heading into the house. Maybe Jon and Maia would be home. He'd hurl his bag at his brother, give him a little taste of the future; find a way to tease his sister, make her squirm. He couldn't wait to have a hot shower, maybe stretch out in bed for a few minutes before he met his boys. Home was definitely the best.

Victoria remained in the car, enjoying the hermetic silence. She folded her arms over the steering wheel and rested her head, lulled by the purring engine. She adored every moment Ben was home. Each time he stepped back into her life, into the cocoon of their home, felt like a reprieve – a deep exhalation, as if she'd been holding her breath during the interim.

She couldn't get enough of these weekend visits, never tired of watching Ben sleep in his bed – almost willing him back to infancy. The relief of having him home, seeing him let down his guard, relax, maybe even stop wiggling that nervous leg, went beyond satisfying to euphoric. A quick recognition of the relative quiet Israel had enjoyed since Operation Pillar of Defense immediately calmed her. How ironic that at the time, eighteen months earlier, it had seemed more an inconvenience than a threat – lasting a brief handful of days. But she would never forget its date, November 2012. An errant missile had somehow made its way to Tel Aviv causing the sudden cancellation of her big birthday bash. The concept of her son being part of the action, one of those mobilized to protect the citizens along the border, was abstract – an idea she preferred to keep in the distant future.

Victoria stilled the engine, leaned back on the headrest a moment and then stepped out of the car, just in time to catch a whirl of jeans, a patch of blond hair and the bright glint of the sun reflected in a pair of polarized sunglasses. Ben had burst out of the house and was sprinting toward his car. He was off and running, probably on his way to meet his friends at the local hummus joint. She wondered if he'd had time to shower, smiling at the recollection of all that perfume.

She closed the car door firmly and made her way up the path to the house. Ben's move into Greater Israel, the one outside their little lives in small-town Caesarea, had been no less complex than hers decades earlier. There had been that first phone call; the one received six hours after he'd left the house, his military service limited to a bus ride and a new uniform.

"*Hem kulam tembelim.*" She'd been taken aback. First, it was the Hebrew. He never spoke Hebrew with her. Maybe it was the surroundings. She'd imagined him standing in the processing center among hundreds of other young men. He probably didn't want to seem different, project any sense that he wasn't just like the others. But it wasn't just that. She'd understood the words he'd spoken but they had made no sense. She was more focused on the fact that her baby had just begun his military career. He seemed to be completely somewhere else.

"What are you talking about? Who?"

"Everyone. They're all idiots." He'd repeated himself in English, obviously wanting to make sure that she'd understood.

She'd never forget that perplexing conversation. Later that same evening, when she'd discussed it with Guy, he'd actually laughed, dismissing it as an expected part of Ben's enlightenment: the army a great equalizer that exposed the overly sheltered younger population to the diversity of the country. Victoria had felt confused. Hurling these innocent children into a great war machine was more than enough to swallow, maybe even too much for a mother to get used to. It was difficult to comprehend that on top of it all, this whole episode might actually be educational, that it might teach him something about accepting others.

But only one week later the tide had turned. She'd received a call proving that Guy had known exactly what he was talking about. Ben had regaled her with tales of his new friends and their adventures as fresh inductees. His tone had been exuberant and enthusiastic, his adaptation to this new world necessarily quicker than hers. She would need to struggle to keep up.

She entered the house and headed straight for the laundry room. There it was: two meters of green. Her son had stripped off every single vestige of the army and her job was to turn it all around, cleaned, folded and ready for repacking, by Sunday morning. Time to roll up her sleeves and dig in. This should be the worst evil.

Chapter 2

"No."

"No?"

Victoria shook her head. "No, I don't mean *no*; I mean yes! Of course, yes! But how?"

"What do you mean 'How?' What's so complicated?"

Minutes ago, this morning had been like any other. She and Guy had been sitting at the kitchen table drinking coffee, spooning up warm bites of oatmeal, leafing through the morning paper. And then…and then everything that was as it was, safe and stable, usual, had tilted over on its side. Now everything felt different. Even the oatmeal had lost its taste, seemed flatter.

Victoria hadn't expected any of this. Or maybe she had. It was clear that at some point they were going to have to decide whether they were going to go for broke, give this love story a happy ending, or at least, the kind of ending people expected. Being in love, being crazy in love, meant eventually dealing with what came next.

But their story was so complicated. Complicated and at the same time, very much not so complicated. In some ways it was the classic story: two people had met, fallen in love, couldn't get enough of one another, couldn't bear to be apart. And then? Well, in the storybooks they lived happily ever after, together. And in some, they eventually married. But from the beginning, Victoria hadn't seen this being the end, their end. There were too many considerations, too many reasons not to look toward that expected conclusion; foremost was the fear that it wouldn't come to fruition. And that, she couldn't bear.

She pushed away from the table, jumped out of her chair and plopped herself into Guy's lap. She wrapped her arms around his neck and pulled his head close to her in a tight embrace.

"I don't see how this can work."

He snapped his head back and looked straight at her, his hands threading through her hair, his blue eyes deep emotional wells. This direct, no-nonsense appeal always struck her to the bone. *How can I say no?* Guy was someone she could depend on. He would stand by her side and love her, forever. One look into his eyes told her this was the case and she knew that counted more than anything.

"Vicki, I love you. I want to spend the rest of my life with you. As far as I'm concerned the rest isn't important – only details." He pulled her head down towards his and met her lips with his own, sealing his vow with a warm, cushiony kiss.

Victoria's head spun. This was what she wanted, what she'd always wanted; the kind of passion she'd yearned for from time immemorial. The last two years with Guy had been indescribable – like a dream; strolling through streets hand in hand, sitting at coffee shops and talking for hours on end. Every time she looked up, his eyes were right there on her; the touch of his hand, his lips or even just his arm brushing against hers, had become a part of her everyday life, as essential as air.

Yet, at the same time, she'd always somehow thought it would stay just that: a dream. She'd never had any expectation that it would turn into something real, altering the nuts and bolts of her life. She had a full life in New York. He lived in Israel. Although they'd alluded to more along the way, the possibility that their worlds could come together, that they could have a future, the real happily-ever-after had heretofore remained unspoken. She really couldn't imagine herself in Israel. For her, it had always been just a place to visit, the Jewish homeland she'd always support, but usually from a safe distance. She preferred a life without ripples and couldn't imagine living in such a hotbed. The politics, the wars, the hardships. None of this appealed.

"I can't." She pulled herself back from his intoxicating kiss. "I can't possibly move to Israel."

"Why not? Tell me. Why can't you? It's merely another place. It's the place you belong. You can't imagine how much you'll love living there."

Victoria's eyes locked on his again. He made it sound so simple, so easy, and maybe even more significantly, so romantic. Who wouldn't say yes to romantic? Was there anything to consider at all? *What's holding me back?*

Her mind raced to their trip last summer.

It had been market day, her first time at Mahane Yehuda – the ultimate souk. She and Guy had whisked by a number of circular hanging racks stuffed to the gills, overflowing with clothing. It was impossible to actually get a good look at the items for sale; they were squeezed together so tightly that pulling one out for examination was impossible. A crush of individuals was lined up to take advantage of the bargain prices: two shirts for 15 shekels, a pair of slacks for 25. Guy had pulled her through the slender gap between the racks and crowds of shoppers to a wider corridor of wall-to-wall food stands stretching as far as the eye could see.

"Hold on tight." He'd squeezed her hand tightly.

Could it get better than this?

Victoria's excitement had grown by the moment. This was it. This was what she'd been looking forward to. Before her was the ancient world she'd adored studying back in school and had made an effort to discover in multiple pockets of Europe over the years – Live and Technicolor. She hadn't been able to get enough of the scene before her and had yanked sharply on Guy's arm to bring him to a halt. Their eyes met and his sparkled. He'd understood.

To the left were stalls lined with enormous square metal trays measuring one meter in either direction. Almonds, thousands of them, were splayed out loose for the customers, not sealed tightly into vacuum-packed bags as she was used to finding them at the supermarket in New York. Right at hand were freshly opened walnuts, pine nuts glistening like pearls in the sunlight that managed to infiltrate the market despite the metal roofing, Brazil nuts and both pumpkin and sunflower seeds. Their sheer quantity, displayed by the thousands, was overwhelming. She paused at a smaller bin of peanuts, still in their shells, taking a moment to take in their aroma. "Why so few?"

"Peanuts are more of an American taste."

She frowned. "Who doesn't like peanuts?"

He laughed and squeezed her hand again. "I totally agree." He entwined his fingers with hers and gave her a slight tug. "Hang on. We've only just begun."

"But Guy. Aren't we going to buy some?"

"Soon. I want you to see it all first, take it in."

Progressing primarily by gently nudging people aside, those clusters of individuals shouting to get the attention of the attendants in charge of weighing and selling the nuts on the far side of the stalls, they'd passed onward to the fruit section. The tans and browns and beiges, the various shades of white, in the nut section, blossomed, within seconds, into a multicolor tapestry. She'd gasped with surprise. This was too much. She'd never seen anything like it. "Oh Guy! This is magnificent!"

Lining both sides of this corridor were the same enormous trays she'd noted in the nut section, this time filled with pre-packed baskets overflowing with fruit. There were apples, green, red, yellow and a shade of rose; oranges threatening to burst out of their rinds, like those perfect ones her parents had ordered by the carton from Florida each winter; grapes, purple and green, big and succulent, and tiny ones, like miniature, juicy beads; melons of all size; and then, to her complete delight, figs.

"What are these beauties? Guy, are these figs?" She pulled him over to the bin and reached in. "I must have some. I've only ever seen the dried variety. Look how they're popping out of their skin! They are simply gorgeous!"

Guy exchanged words, and then shekels, with the seller, then passed her the bag. She gripped it in her left hand and gingerly reached in with the other to grasp the topmost fig, certain the slightest squeeze would leave her fingers covered in juice. She raised it to her mouth and took a bite. Her eyes closed. Nothing could have prepared her for this, for the extraordinary sweetness and pleasure in this one small purple package. She opened her eyes and looked directly into Guy's face. Tiny, almost dancing, wrinkles formed at the outer edges of his eyes, the corners of his mouth reached upward.

"Soooo good. A fig. I can't believe how good this is." She took another bite. He reached down and kissed a spot near her mouth, licking up some of the juice left there.

"The best." His eyes twinkled. "Come on. There's even more ahead."

Still gripping the sticky fig she'd let him steer her by the elbow through the rest of the market, taking it all in, the wealth of Israeli produce. Bright red tomatoes; red peppers with taut, glistening skins that seemed almost impenetrable; halved watermelons, their pink insides beckoning invitingly; mangoes and guavas stacked in impossibly high towers, threatening to cascade onto the ground in an avalanche of color.

There were baskets of apricots, orange and brown in hue, spiky pineapples, ugly brown kiwi whose lush green insides lurked just beneath the surface, bunches of bananas piled high in an unruly heap. At the end of the passage there were enormous bins of dried herbs that attendants dispensed by the scoop, as well as dried fruits whose variety extended well beyond the offerings she'd become accustomed to on American market shelves. She picked up a long, brown, desiccated specimen marked by three tiny bumps, passing it to Guy.

"What is this?"

"It's a carob. A kind of natural chocolate. It falls from trees."

The vender said something to them and gestured for her to take a bite. She looked toward Guy to see if she'd understood correctly. "Yes. He wants you to try it! Break it open like this first." He took it out of her hand and bent it in two until it snapped. The carob seeds rolled into his hand and he offered her the remaining pod.

She picked it up between thumb and forefinger. "You know, it's not all that appealing looking."

He'd laughed. "Try it."

She took a tiny bite, chewing on the very tip of the pod, and then a larger one. She worked the tough skin of the carob with her teeth, trying to coax out the flavor. "It's not as good as chocolate."

"True enough. But if you're looking for a natural alternative, this is it."

"I'll stick with my figs. I don't think you'll be able to top them." She looked back into the bag, tempted to have another.

"Just wait and see. There's so much more to discover." He pulled aside a strand of hair that had gotten stuck onto her sticky cheek, tucked it behind her ear and leaned in close, kissing her on the lips. "You simply can't imagine."

Victoria had been afraid she'd melt, then and there.

How much better could this get?

Yet sitting in the calm of her apartment, nestled into the comfort of her chosen life, something inside her resisted. It couldn't be done. "My career. I've worked so hard. I don't have anything there. I don't even speak the language. I can't start from scratch." She'd spent a decade developing a career in journalism and had only recently been assigned to the Weekend department, an encouraging step up from her position as stringer. Pitching this promising beginning for a romantic notion was crazy. Guy kissed her again and then pulled his head back and laughed. "You're moving to the country where everyone starts from scratch; it's simply the norm. There are plenty of opportunities for you in Israel. Just think about it as a new angle. Don't journalists love angles? What could be more interesting than on-site reports on life in the Holy Land from the viewpoint of a new immigrant? This move could actually make your career!"

He sounded so certain and she had no doubt he was. She considered his words for a moment, the idea of stepping into an underexploited niche appealed tremendously. All of a sudden she could almost see a door opening before her. Her mind quickly considered the possibilities, beginning to grasp that this could actually be a brilliant move.

Victoria pushed off Guy's lap and moved across the room to the window. She looked outside at the jumble of rooftops, windows, bricks and glass. She was so unsure. What would it be like not to be here?

"But what about all this?" She whispered, her breath leaving a circle of moisture on the pane of glass.

He laughed again and joined her side. "You must be kidding. Who would choose the chaos of the city with its noxious smells and unrelenting noise over a cozy, peaceful spot along the Mediterranean Sea? Do you know what it's like to live in a climate conducive to actually breathing? One where you can go outside all year round, where you'll never need a winter coat and gloves. Remember the South of France? You always said you'd love to live there. Well, now you will…kind of, in a manner of speaking. It'll merely be another version of the same fantasy." He gestured dismissively at the jumble of buildings outside. "You don't need this."

She looked over at him and tried to soak up some of his confidence, his certainty that this was the right next step, that this new life would suit her. *How does he know?* She wanted to share his conviction. Saying no to this man, the one who embodied everything she'd ever dreamed about, the one from the fairy tales, was going to be impossible.

Maybe it was enough: the love, the passion, the "over the moon" feeling that hadn't lessened in the two years since they'd met. And if all that wasn't enough, what exactly did she want? Two years of heaven held enormous potential for future smooth sailing. She sighed heavily, her mind racing. She was running out of reasons, reasons why it was impossible, why it made any difference at all whether she lived in Manhattan, Philadelphia, Israel or Timbuktu for that matter, when it was clear that they needed to stay together, to hang on to the unique treasure they'd discovered in one another. *Why not go for the fairy-tale ending?*

The skies darkened quite suddenly, shutting out much of the bright light that had flooded into the apartment earlier in the conversation. She pressed herself closer to the window, watching that first mark of moisture grow and migrate in all directions, interfering with her ability to see through the glass. She gazed upward toward the heavy clouds moving in from the West. She couldn't imagine how she'd break this to her parents. They'd guided her toward one future and this wasn't it. Crossing the world and moving to Israel was way off their radar and would definitely meet with their disapproval. She raised her hands and pressed both palms to the glass, feeling the chill of the morning outside. Guy moved directly behind her and wrapped his arms around her waist, kissed her neck. His warmth was overwhelming. Maybe this was enough. It definitely felt so.

Victoria took in the city before her, eyes wide open, careful not to blink. If she wanted this – and yes, she most definitely wanted this – she would have to stand firm before her family, her friends, everything she had right here in New York. She would need to present her plan as a fait accompli. If even one glimmer of doubt appeared they'd all take the opportunity to chip away at this dream, pull the fragile carpet of certainty out from under her, pressure her to cave.

She swiveled around and met Guy's embrace, carefully tucking her head under his chin and holding him firmly, this time as if for dear life. Choosing to give up what she knew, to take a chance on the unknown, meant handing him the reins to her future. *"I have everything here Guy."* Her voice was quiet now, almost a whisper. He tightened his arms around her and pulled her in even closer, molding his chest to her own. "And you're going to have even more there. You're going to fall in love with Israel just like you've fallen in love with me. There's no question about it. We're going to have a beautiful family, and our children will grow up in the sunshine. It's not only a dream."

Tucked securely into his embrace, swaddled in the warm haze of his enticing words and strong arms, Victoria believed that anything was possible. Her heart began to beat faster, excited at the prospect of what lay ahead. This life, this new life, the one she was racing for at high speed, was going to be beautiful.

Chapter 3

"You'll never find your place. There's nothing there for you."

Victoria ignored her mother's words, pushing them to the far reaches of her mind, and focused on the purpose of this visit. Today was all about paperwork; in particular, having her parents co-sign a legal document pertaining to her aliyah. It wasn't such a big deal, or at least it shouldn't have been, but the tension in the room, nothing to do with the crinkly document in triplicate lying on her father's desk, was thick.

On her way over to his office an hour earlier she hadn't anticipated such a serious encounter. After all, this wasn't goodbye. The farewell dinner they'd arranged was still weeks away. And although she knew that her parents weren't thrilled with her decision, or rather, better said, were very unhappy about it, it was no longer a new subject. They'd gone over it time and again; an endless number of conversations had been devoted to enumerating the multiple minuses, emphasizing their conviction that it was a disastrous mistake.

This morning had started out just fine. She'd been on her way to cross one more item off the long list of things she needed to get done in preparation for her departure. The ball was rolling nicely.

Yet the minute she'd crossed the threshold of her father's office, her jovial mood had vanished. It was obvious she'd interrupted something. Her parents had stopped speaking as the door swung open, and her brother's presence signaled some unexpected game was in play.

Victoria didn't respond to her mother's comment, but she didn't let up.

"You're sure this is what you want?"

Victoria looked away from her father and brother, ostensibly busying themselves with the details of the paperwork on the desk, and gazed over at her mother. She seemed especially relaxed today, obviously convinced that in the end she wouldn't go through with her planned move to Israel, certain she'd eventually decide to stay. Victoria sighed out loud, tired of this subject, tired of everyone making such a big deal of this plan. She was eager to escape what was turning out to be some kind of intervention.

"Yes, Mom. We've gone over this again and again."

Her mother scooted her chair a bit closer to Victoria's and laid her hand lightly on her daughter's arm, one finger tracing a path from shoulder to wrist. Her caress was light, intoxicating. Victoria had loved it when she'd tickled her that way as a child. Triggering this memory now was particularly powerful, crumbling just a bit of her resolve.

"You know this makes it real." The distance between them closed by the caress, her mother's words trickled into her ear, managing to tug at her heart.

Victoria felt herself soften, her throat suddenly blocked, and she swallowed hard. "Mom, it's been real for over a year. You simply haven't wanted to deal with it."

The tickling stopped, but her mother's effort to somehow change her course continued. "I still don't understand. And I'm certain you don't as well. You're giving up so much, so many things that you love."

Victoria's eyes clouded for a moment. She'd known that chucking one life for another wasn't going to be easy, but she hadn't imagined it being quite this painful. She looked from one member of her family to the other, realizing how difficult it must be for them to stand aside and watch her go. She moved her chair an inch to the side, gaining a bit of distance in order to fortify herself.

"I'm certain I'll find new things to love as well, and really, it's not all that far away. Now you'll have a reason to visit." Matter of fact was the safest path.

Her mother was unrelenting, set on fulfilling some preconceived mission. "I told you about Emily Sondheim? Right? That she moved back? She was so devoted, such a part of the land, a real trailblazer. She raised the children in Jerusalem during difficult times. And then," she paused for dramatic effect, "one by one they left." She leaned forward, searching to make eye contact. "Now she's come back home as well."

There was something about the way she emphasized the word "home." Victoria felt something snap inside her. "Mom, please. This isn't helping. I'm going. It's decided. This whole family summit is ridiculous. There's no point. There's nothing more to say."

"She had a beautiful house in Abu Tor, just outside of the city walls. She held special evenings featuring intellectuals from all over, a kind of Salon. It was all so impressive. I attended one once, during a mission visit. She always seemed to be an exemplar of successful expat life in Jerusalem, but I guess," she paused to look up at her husband as if to emphasize the inevitable, "I guess, things weren't exactly as they seemed. In the end, she found it too difficult to live there. She's settled in Nashville." Another pause and then, "Imagine."

Victoria smiled in relief. Finally there was an opportunity to alleviate the gloomy mood in the room. "Wait, you'd rather I moved to Nashville? Aren't Jewish parents supposed to support their children's interest in Israel? Did I miss something somewhere?"

Her mother sighed. "It's not about Nashville and it's certainly not about Israel."

Victoria didn't give her a chance to continue. "Look Mom, I really don't remember her. I have a vague visual recollection of the house itself: super-thick stone walls painted white, everything white, Turkish throw rugs, low-set couches, tiny glasses of mint tea on miniature footstool tables, but otherwise…I don't know what her life has to do with mine."

"The differences were too vast to bridge."

"But here, you said it. She had this wonderful group of intellectuals, educated individuals with interesting ideas and thoughts. Who's to say that I won't find the same? Why are you so convinced that I won't find people just like me? That there won't be a fit?"

"Vicki, this simply isn't your destiny."

That was it. She'd had enough. Victoria stood up and moved over to the other side of the desk, joining her father and brother. "What's the hold up here? *Please* just sign so we can all move on with our day." *And our lives.* Victoria was losing patience. She'd had enough of this line of argument.

But her mother wouldn't let up. She couldn't. She'd obviously decided that this might be the last chance she'd have to stop this runaway train. She continued to harp on the cultural differences. Although Victoria understood what she was getting at, knew she'd have to adapt, knew this new life wasn't going to be exactly like her old one, she couldn't imagine it was going to be *that* big of a change. *How could it be?*

She loved Guy. She couldn't live without him. Living with him meant moving across the world. That was the bottom line. And yes, it was a big deal, a very big deal. She was terrified of what lay ahead. She and Guy had talked about it, more than once. But he'd promised to be there, he'd promised to help pave the way, to make it easier for her. He'd also promised to love her, forever. *Wasn't that enough?* It would have to be.

She grasped the cuff of her father's suit jacket and reached up to whisper in his ear, "Daddy, it's going to be fine." Her father busied himself with the papers spread across his desk, lining them up as if to signify conviction, or maybe, resignation, and met her gaze just a moment before looking away. She knew he was trying to maintain neutrality, to distance himself from the emotional intensity of the moment. He hadn't spoken much during this meeting but she could guess at what he was thinking. She was thinking the same. Leaving her father was difficult. If her mother had concentrated on this aspect of the whole business she might have gotten somewhere.

"You'll come visit *all* the time. I'll come home. This doesn't mean anything. It's just another place."

His eyes, for the most part blocked from her view with heavy lashes, looked so very solemn. She wasn't used to this from him. For a moment she felt just a bit less sure, a bit less confident. She quickly shook it off. *No, this is what I want.* She disengaged, physically removing herself from his side and moving back to the other side of the desk. She handed him the pen. "Let's get this show on the road. Come on. Time to rip off that band-aid. You're all being so melodramatic."

Her mother joined her at the massive desk. "We just want you to be happy."

Victoria raised her eyes and looked from one parent to the other, suddenly warmed by their presence instead of threatened. This was her family, her sanctuary, the only people in the world who'd always had her back. Victoria knew they'd always be there for her, that it really didn't matter where she chose to put down roots. She didn't understand why they seemed to be bracing themselves for some terrible eventuality. *What could be so bad?*

"And somewhere on the East Coast would have been more convenient." Victoria was startled by her brother's voice. He'd been so quiet, so careful not to take sides, not to add one more voice to an already stressful situation. It was obvious he didn't understand what she was doing, couldn't imagine moving elsewhere within the country let alone halfway across the world. He was so comfortable with where he was. Lately she'd come to understand that he respected her resolve, cognizant of how much strength it took to even consider such a bold move, let alone put it into play.

The corners of her mouth drew even farther apart as she smiled, appreciating this attempt at levity. She figured he was equally desperate to get on with this whole macabre ceremony and continue his day.

"You probably envision me riding a camel. Remember when we did that back in the '60s? Nice, or not so much actually. Pretty uncomfortable. Made for a good picture." Her eyes brightened at his smile. "Don't worry. As far as I understand, everything's a lot more First World. I won't be living in a tent."

"I'd actually like to see you live in a tent." They both laughed. Victoria was thankful for his cheery demeanor, anything to break the tension in the room and that terribly distracting look of sadness in her father's eyes. She just wanted this to be over. She buckled down, firmed up her posture and focused on the "why," the reason for this momentous move, purposefully skirting those fears and concerns regarding the "how."

"What about your friends?" Her mother just could not let this go. A cloying tone had entered her voice and she looked a lot less confident than she had when Victoria had first entered the room.

Now quite desperate to derail Victoria's plans, she seemed prepared to throw herself on the tracks. Victoria was unfazed.

"What about them? We'll still be in touch. Remember, there's the telephone."

"It won't be the same."

"No. And I'll miss things: birthdays, weddings, and parties. But Mom, I'm going to meet a lot of people. Think how I'll be able to broaden my world." She edged a bit closer to her, actually leaning into her mother and feeling the warmth of her arm before hooking her elbow in an unexpected embrace. "Mom, this is exactly what all those trips abroad were about. You never wanted me to walk around with blinders. This is your dream. I'm just realizing it."

There was silence in the room. Victoria knew she'd struck a nerve. It was her mother, and not herself, who was fascinated by other cultures, studying up on each one before every family trip, making such an effort to learn some of the native language. Victoria had simply picked up where she'd left off, taking the reins firmly in hand. The tension in her mother's body just moments earlier seemed to dissipate a bit, and there was a noticeable shift in mood within the room. Victoria had the feeling that maybe, just maybe, they could do this together.

As if this was precisely what he'd been waiting for, that sign of entente, her father grasped his pen in hand and signed the papers; a few scrawls here and there, followed by her mother's, and it was done. She was one step closer to making this leap. Although relieved, Victoria felt somewhat deflated. Her parents' acquiescence clearly stemmed from defeat rather than enthusiasm. This was her team, and they'd stand behind her forever, but each step forward would be taken alone.

Chapter 4

"It's done, Mom. You can't undo it."

Victoria held the letter from the army in her hand, glanced at the official stamp on the signature at the bottom and furrowed her brow.

"How did this come about? Where did you even come up with the idea?"

Ben loomed tall before her, steady and determined. It was hard to remember that he was still in high school, still dealing with the last throes of adolescence. Yet there was no hint of that in his determined face, nor his sturdy body. When had he become a man?

"Mom. I told you along the way. I told you I wasn't interested in being in Intelligence."

"But you went to all of the interviews! You were considering it. I know you were considering it!"

Victoria felt things were spinning out of control. She glanced down at the page in her hand. The words swam, snaking across the piece of paper in big loopy waves, but couldn't have been clearer: *This letter serves to confirm that you have disqualified yourself from the Intelligence Corps.*

She turned away from Ben and looked out the kitchen window. *How is it that everything always seems so calm out there when in here, inside my nest, what's supposed to be my comfort zone, everything's crumbling to pieces?*

"Ben." She tried to assume some kind of reasonable tone. She was afraid she might start to yell, or worse, cry. That wasn't going to get her anywhere.

"Ben." Repeating his name was somehow calming. At this point anything would help. "Why did you sign off without consulting us first? You have no idea what you've done."

Victoria turned to Guy. He'd been standing in the doorway since Ben came in with this letter, since he'd dropped this bombshell of an announcement. "And you?" Now her tone wasn't as even. "You're very quiet. Did you have something to do with this?"

Guy took a step toward her and reached out his hand, letting it drop just short of her arm. Offering a hug wasn't going to work.

"It's okay. This isn't a big deal. You knew Ben didn't want to be in Intelligence. The fact that he gave up his spot isn't such a surprise." He glanced at Ben. "I really can't imagine you sitting behind a desk. At your age I wouldn't have chosen such a boring option either." He paused. "In fact, I didn't."

Victoria crumpled the letter, waved it in Guy's direction and then threw it sideways, onto the kitchen table.

"You said we shouldn't get involved. That's exactly what you said. And now I understand that you were involved from the start. All that talk about your days in the Golani Brigade: the camaraderie, the guys, the weapons, and the heat. You made it sound like a movie set. Did you ever tell him about the losses?" She felt tears well up and willed them away. She needed to make a point. "How is this okay?"

"That's not fair." Guy took another step in her direction.

She stepped away from him. "This is all your fault. You got me into this. This wasn't my story. My life wasn't supposed to be this!" She felt her temper rising, her face reddening. She knew she'd stepped over a line, gotten into territory she was meant to steer clear of, had been avoiding for decades, like a mine field.

Guy recoiled and then turned to Ben.

"*Anachnu ga'im b'cha*. We are proud of you." He reached up to touch his shoulder.

Victoria turned away. She couldn't bare it, couldn't imagine being proud of such a foolish decision. She couldn't stand behind Guy's words this time – not in this context. This was the one eventuality for which she hadn't been prepared, an aspect of her decision to move to Israel decades earlier that she refused to accept. She wasn't willing to sacrifice her son to any cause whatsoever, no matter great or small.

As the two began to speak of technicalities, the different combat units Ben should consider, the arduous tests he would have to undergo in order to be accepted into one of the more elite units, her mind shifted to an entirely different scene, one far more dusty and chaotic than that playing out in her kitchen.

She saw masses of men in green, all moving. There were rivers of them, an endless flow working its way through unknown terrain, negotiating the dense and convoluted alleys of an urban area. Their faces were completely covered in camouflage makeup, their weapons raised in alert, tense with the potential of imminent peril, the inevitability of an attack. A deafening explosion broke the silence. She squeezed her eyes closed, shutting out the bright light coming through the kitchen window, desperate to disperse the clouds of dust raised by the immensity of the blast, trying to make sense of what had happened, shutting out the instant sense of obliteration.

The movement that had gone before, the men working their way through, around and between their target, the building they were clearing, all that animation, was stilled. The silence of the scene was as deafening as the explosion that had preceded it. Victoria's eyes darted everywhere, frantically searching among the mess of rubble and bodies. In her mind she scuttled among the detritus, stopping momentarily to search for proof that her son was not part of this, moving on the minute she realized that the size, or coloring, one feature or the whole, didn't add up to Ben.

She was halfway through the platoon that had been hit, heartened by the fact that she hadn't yet found him. She quickened her pace as a great relief began to set in. He'd escaped. He wasn't here. *She*, in fact, had escaped. Her breathing became more regular, less disturbed by choked gasps. She approached the end of the destruction, completing her examination of the scene. She could feel it, she was just about home free and then...and then, from where there'd been nothing, that blessed nothing, there was quite definitely something. Her attention had been drawn to one minuscule detail among the dust, the uprooted bricks and the shrubbery; one single element among the jumble of boots and clothing, the fragments of their weaponry. And it was then that she actually felt her heart stop, simply stop beating. She held her breath, wishing to have it wrong, desperately trying to pull herself out of this trance, to claw her way back to a reality with which she could cope. She began to convince herself that she'd been wrong. Her angle was bad. She didn't have a clear view.

But the horror wouldn't be stayed, and she knew deep down that were she to extend her finger, it would fit perfectly in the small cleft that crowned that gaping mouth before meeting that small upturned nose she'd first encountered on an early ultrasound. The latch of a door in her mind slammed shut. This was it. The moment she'd dreaded since forever. There was another horrific sound, this one of an ear-splitting vacuum. Her heart, in fact, hadn't stopped beating at all, but instead, was frantically pounding. She felt her whole body convulse with a wracking sob. Her worst nightmare, it was here.

"Mommy."

She became frantic. It was Ben. She didn't understand. He couldn't possibly call her. He was gone.

"Mommy." She opened her eyes. Ben was beside her at the kitchen sink, grabbing at her arm and turning on the spigot. She was confused, relieved. Oh, so relieved. Here was Ben, *her* Ben – right here beside her in the kitchen. She closed her eyes and opened them again, shook her head vigorously, shaking off the horrid place she'd been.

"Where were you?" She stared down at his hands, watched as he busied himself wrapping up her finger with a towel, staunching the trickle of blood. "How did that break? You were just standing here. Dad and I were chatting. Hey! Mom."

With his words she raised her eyes and met his, those gorgeous blue eyes, the ones that had first gazed up at her minutes after his birth as he lay swaddled on her chest, the ones that sparkled as he crossed the finish line of his first race, the ones that released tears of frustration when his grandfather left this life far too early without any advance notice. Today they were wide open and full of light, bright with expectation. Victoria didn't want to go back to that wretchedly dark place, was desperate to stay in the here and now.

She focused on Ben's confident moves, the manner in which he took care of her without flinching. Maybe it didn't have to be the way she'd imagined it. Maybe there was an entirely different picture, another reality waiting just ahead. Ben's eyes burned with anticipation and a desperate plea for her to let him get on with it, to stop worrying and let him live his life. This child of hers was moving on to another stage, one that would leave no room for her mothering. She didn't have a choice but to step aside and watch him move forward. If she didn't hop on board, she'd completely miss the ride and, after venturing to where it was blacker than black, she dare not turn her back for a moment.

Chapter 5

Victoria shifted her body to the right and reached down into the dark well in front of the passenger seat, straining to lift the heavy cake plate. She gripped the chilled bottle of wine in her left hand and pushed the car door open with her left elbow. *I can handle this.* She got out slowly, fearful that one of the items would crash to the ground, teetering a bit on the high wedges she'd chosen in an effort to convince herself that this was an actual social gathering, not simply an informal get-together, basically in her backyard. But after one wobbly step away from the car she regretted the decision. This wasn't going to work after all. She leaned back onto the heavy car door, slamming it shut with her backside. She'd have to take this one step at a time. She steadied herself in preparation for the trip up the steep flight of stairs to Evie's front door, contributions to this evening's soirée firmly in hand and feet planted firmly for leverage. *No teetering!*

A quick glance to the right and the left, an assessment of the other cars parked along the street, made clear that none of her friends had arrived. *Oh hell! First to arrive, as always.* With a sigh of exasperation she laid the bottle of wine down flat on the hood of the car, beside the wipers, and carefully placed the cake plate on the roof of the car. She had a few extra minutes; she might as well take advantage of this rare opportunity to take a deep breath and let the calm of the neighborhood seep in.

This evening was meant to be a kind of breather, a respite after the fright of the last few days. She was desperate to put all that behind her, forbid its possibility and deny it entry. Ben had returned to the base after the weekend with nary a glance behind; business as usual. His friend's condition had stabilized, but there was still no prognosis. Although his situation had been the focus of much conversation over the past days, Ben's trajectory continued forward. Victoria was a little bit slower to pick up the pieces, finding herself staring at her son now and then over the course of the weekend, trying to figure out how this was affecting him, what it all meant. In the end she'd had to satisfy herself with the fact of his presence, the liveliness and energy he brought to their home, and tuck the unmentionable away into a back corner of her mind.

The quiet of this street, so typical of those in her neighborhood, acted as a balm, a comforting salve for what ailed her. She wiggled her toes a bit within the wedges, trying to get the blood flowing, and leaned back onto the car with arms akimbo. One more clement evening spent with her best friends, a deserved prize for managing to survive the last few days. She glanced to her left, following the tree-lined slate sidewalk as it passed a row of large, single-family dwellings and snaked down toward a cul-de-sac. She took in the various versions of the cube, each house representing one more attempt at an "exclusive" adaptation of the all-too-popular Bauhaus style.

This was her reality, her port of call. This suburban transformation of what otherwise might have been one large pile of sand was her home. Evie's street looked very much like her own, each one part of a mini-cluster branching off a main thoroughfare that stretched from one end of the town to the other;

the neighborhoods lined up, one after the other, like pearls on a string. The houses espoused an architectural style she liked to call Mediterranean Dry, each one linear and undecorated, tilted at an angle meant to exploit the dramatic effect of the sun, and painted one or another shade of white.

It hadn't taken long for her to understand that much of Israel was painted white. In fact, it was pretty much the unofficial national color. Her town was no different, most of the houses sticking to the theme with an occasional risky stab at cream, beige, tan or some alternative version of sand. While accurately reflecting the ground it had replaced, that shifting pile of talc that stood for a foundation, it was just this side of boring. Victoria missed the red bricks and honey-toned wood she'd grown up with, that ever-present trace of America's revolutionary timber beginnings. Her "season" had always been autumn – the falling leaves of New England representing her happy place, her comfort zone. Life in Israel, most firmly lodged in summer, was something she'd never get used to.

Her eyes followed the line of cars parked along the street, a range of family-friendly vehicles for the most part – nothing too flashy but each dazzlingly clean. People here seemed to live at the local car wash, even heading out in rain storms to make sure their vehicles were sparkling and dirt-free, desperate to rid themselves of the omnipresent thin coating of sand. And of course, as if there'd been some unwritten contract with the local architects, they too were primarily white. *What a boring palette!*

She squinched her toes and adjusted her weight on the car door, smiling at the memory of the first car she'd purchased as a new citizen. She'd wanted emerald green, envisioning herself racing around under cool grey skies in her jewel-toned baby. She recalled sitting at the VW agent's desk, ready to finalize her order, excited to close the deal. Guy had softly but firmly laid his hand on her forearm, offering his contrary advice in a whisper. He was obviously afraid of upsetting her, disturbing the fragile state that characterized many new immigrants as yet unaware of the major shifts in lifestyle that lay ahead. Before she knew what was happening he'd removed his hand, leaned back in his chair, shifted his gaze directly to the salesman and confidently declared their choice as: "white." After all, it was the smartest option for the Middle East where "cool grey skies" were few and far between.

"White doesn't absorb heat."

She'd protested. How could she knowingly contribute one more white vehicle to the thousands already overwhelming the local highways?

"Who are you trying to kid?" She'd asked him, shoving away his hand, rejecting his insinuation about her fragility with excessive conviction. "White or not, the car is almost always an oven."

She'd won out in the end, only to later understand that his suggestion had been a stab at bringing her into the fold – an attempt to help her make peace with her new environment instead of consistently challenging it in an effort to signify her singularity, her eternal distinction.

Victoria pushed her weight off of the car and gathered her items. *Enough! I made this bed. I'll have to lie in it.* It was time to shake off what could have been and step forward. "Time to get this evening started," she pronounced aloud to a random black cat that had jumped off the sidewalk beside her. She was still the only one to have arrived but it was time to go in. She resituated her feet within the wedges, forever hopeful of finding a comfortable position, and crossed the street, stepping between the pools of light cast by the uniformly stationed streetlights.

She grimaced as she made her way up the long staircase. *Why would anyone put their front door on the second floor?* The particular quirks of local houses, such as this elevated entrance, obvious attempts to break their monotonous reliance on the cube, could be annoying. The whole point of living in the suburbs was being able to walk right in, leaving behind those difficult-to-negotiate walk-ups characteristic of cities. Someone hadn't gotten the memo.

Clutching the wine bottle in the crook of her arm she tapped lightly on the door at the top of the stairs. She knew full well that no one would answer; she hadn't seen Evie's car anywhere in front of the house. She knocked a bit more firmly, announcing herself to anyone inside, and, with no hesitation, turned the knob. The door opened right away. She knew it would. No one locked their door here. At least that's the way it always seemed. Maybe this was an idiosyncrasy particular to new immigrants who, having mostly grown up in areas demanding window bars and burglar alarms, raised never to open the door to strangers and to anticipate intruders and predators at every turn, relished the newfound "freedom of fear" in small-town Israel.

This detail of local life was one of those fun facts she liked to cite to her friends back home, confirmation of her original decision to relocate. *I never bother to lock my door. It's really quite a wonderful way to live! No burglars, no interlopers, no fear.* Of course this dreamy image was shattered once the specter of terrorism was raised. Her version of "safer than safe," something that she truly felt, could never quite hold water against those consistently raised and publicized life-threatening events, despite being a chance of one-in-a-million.

"Hey there, Evie!" she called out as she pushed inside, even more unsteady in her wedges as she shouldered the door and juggled her goodies. Inside the house she was met by complete silence, a deeper version of what she'd encountered waiting in the street outside. She continued through the entrance hallway toward the kitchen, eager to unload her cargo. Upon reaching the counter she gently put down the heavy ceramic cake dish and bottle of wine and, now unencumbered, took a moment to look around. The kitchen sparkled: metal surfaces were burnished, counters wiped clean. How very odd it was to think that each and every one of her expat friends lived very much the same life they might have back from wherever they'd come, replete with well-equipped kitchens, gourmet cooking and standard party fare. Relocation to the Middle East hadn't meant a downgrade for any of them, and in some cases, had been a big step up.

She scanned the utility rack to the right of the sink and spotted the corkscrew. Peeling off the wine bottle's wax seal and pushing in the screw, she anticipated the real start of the evening: that first sip of wine. She always enjoyed a drink, but she hesitated to tally how much alcohol she'd imbibed since receiving that call last week. She had spent days shooting for numb. Numb couldn't feel, couldn't cry, couldn't break into pieces. Numb was safe.

Drinking alcohol wasn't all that popular in Israel when she'd first arrived. Way back when, there'd been absolutely nothing to drink at any given function, and she'd quickly figured out that if she wanted to avoid a dry evening she'd have to supply the booze herself. She could still see it: A cluster of new immigrants, most fresh off the plane, circling one long paper tablecloth-covered folding table anchored by a bottle of Fanta and another of Coca Cola or the local Kinley, slipping from one conversation to another.

"Is there anything to drink?"

The guy whose name she was certain to forget within seconds gestured to the soft drinks.

"Really?"

He shrugged his shoulders.

"Maybe it's on the way?"

Another shrug. She recalled thinking him an unnecessary alliance.

And no. As she realized very early on, the much-anticipated alcohol was not on its way. She had obviously landed in Oz. Such "dry" occasions were unthinkable to an American, beyond the stretch of her imagination. Back in the States the teenage years were characterized by that yearning for the magical day one would hit "21" and finally be awarded legal access to the world of spirits. Stuck in Jerusalem with no opportunity to imbibe was beyond disappointing. It was a tragedy.

Good thing the situation had changed since then. Thanks to the fallout of the Russian immigration in the '90s, directly attested to by the predominance of vodka at any given party, and the recent development of boutique, Napa-wannabee wineries encouraged by the dot-com generation of young Israeli professionals, locals had begun to embrace that ultra-Western tendency to get anesthetized whole hog. It was a welcome relief.

She smiled as she eased the cork out of the bottle of Shiraz, raising it to her nose for a brief sniff. It smelled delicious. She chose a glass from those resting at the ready on the dish drain, poured herself some wine and pulled up a kitchen stool. There were a lot of things worse than peace, quiet and a glass of wine. She closed her eyes for a moment and let the blanket of quiet engulf her. Her mind began to settle into a calm mode, one she relished but almost never had. *This is good.* She allowed herself to wallow in the feeling, to embrace the ease that characterized her local life, its multiple comforts. Again, the past week's events, the altercation along the border that had landed Omer in the hospital with shrapnel in his head, the moments that had toppled a local family, one just like hers, flashed through her mind. Maybe the occasional spark of trouble, terror and even loss, were simply part of life, part of any life she might have chosen, unrelated to location.

She peeked out toward the darkness of the garden and was greeted by her own reflection in the spotlessly clean glass of the patio door. Middle-aged but well maintained, bravely holding back the march of time but definitely heading toward an advanced stage, hair shoved into place but not really done-up, classic American jeans (clearly not designer) and a button-down blouse that said hip but not fancy: in most ways she was pleased with what she saw. The woman reflected in the glass, seated in a picture-book kitchen sipping wine, looked very much like the one she'd imagined years earlier, when she'd been with that boy from Scarsdale, no worse for wear and tear, merely transported halfway across the world and inserted into a Middle Eastern suburb.

Explosive laughter broke out on the patio beyond, breaking Victoria's self-indulgent reverie. Just arriving via the driveway behind the house, her friends hadn't yet spotted her inside; she wasn't party to the joke. She hastily took one more sip of wine, put down the glass and hopped off her stool to meet the onslaught of energy already heading her way. That was the end of peace and quiet; there'd be no more this evening. The women filed in one by one, making no effort to contain their spark and tumble. First there was Evie, their hostess. After a quick exchange of hugs and double-cheek kisses she went into action, opening cabinets, drawers and the refrigerator in a seamless flow of action. The combination of her flutter and an up-to-date, colorful blouse likened her to a tropical butterfly. She gestured at her wine. "You took care of that on your own? Good girl!"

Victoria returned her smile of acknowledgement and was about to respond when she noted her hostess's legs, exposed from manicured toe up to the hem of her shorts. "Tell me you didn't wear those to work. I'm not sure they cover enough to be considered shorts."

Although they shared a similar urban, affluent background, and had both arrived in Israel late in life, neither having experienced an angst-driven stint as a teenager, their friendship was a continual surprise. At no point in her previous life, the one she'd dropped without a second thought back in the States, had Victoria ever considered spending time with a fashion-conscious Brit.

"You're so square," floated back at her as Evie swept through the kitchen, taking quick control of this get-together. Victoria sighed. It was so true. When push came to shove it was she, and not her buddy, who was the fish out of water, hopelessly out of step. She'd always been a Levi original-Wallabee type. Girls that dressed like Evie, stylish and sexy, were far off her radar. Yet she truly admired her friend's sense of style. She'd somehow gotten it right. There was no question that what was and was not considered appropriate changed the minute you hit the Mediterranean. The extreme heat of the summer months made open necklines, sleeveless blouses and short shorts de rigueur, at least if one intended to breathe. Buttoned-up anything, even a polo, save during the brief winter, was unthinkable; the environment simply didn't allow for it. Victoria had spent much of her first decade in Israel assessing the locals, judging them harshly for what she considered the local code of "un-dress." Her Pilgrim roots had originally found those who dressed like Evie a bit too sexy, bordering on offensive; her East Coast, feminist education was perturbed at the concept of women selling themselves as provocative instead of smart. Yet one glance at any given cluster of secular individuals confirmed that all that "out there," Evie being a case in point, wasn't about trying to provoke.

In fact, her whole outfit and demeanor spoke poise and self-confidence. It was one of those things that brought her closer to the natives – making her oh-so-Israeli despite her British origin. Victoria's pathetic attempts to attain such standards, such as donning an ill-fitting pair of heels this evening, paled in comparison. She'd give anything to have a modicum of her friend's composure; one little bit of that attitude that would prove that she, too, belonged – that she too, had shed some of the hang-ups of her birthplace and gone "native." And her envy didn't stop there. Continually struggling to find her own niche, Victoria couldn't help but admire how Evie had transformed an early fascination with style and design, encouraged in her native London, into a flourishing career at the main office of Israel's top-of-the-line furniture design company, Tollman's. The relocation inspired by her desire to live in the sun had worked out beautifully. She truly had it all.

Alison stepped in the patio door next, smiling ear to ear. She'd obviously caught the tail end of Victoria and Evie's brief exchange, as her expression was a mix of amusement and agreement. A born and bred Manhattanite from a traditional Jewish background, she too preferred a bit more decorum. Victoria rushed up to greet her, holding on just a bit longer when they embraced. Alison pulled back and scrutinized her closely, her expression segueing quickly from mirth to concern.

Victoria answered her friend's concern: "I'm okay. Just still a bit shaken-up," then abruptly pulled away and stepped back to take another sip of the wine she'd left on the counter. It hurt to look Alison in the eyes. Her very best friend never missed a beat. She immediately identified the shadow of fear that clouded her eyes the minute their eyes had locked.

"Any further news?"

"Nothing."

Alison squeezed Victoria's arm as she moved behind her to help herself to one of the empty wine glasses on the counter. "I'll join you."

Alison had been the subject of Victoria's very first feature article, at least the first one to be published in a well-known newspaper. She'd been so excited to receive that letter of acceptance from *The Guardian*. It was the earliest indication that she might be able to continue her career in journalism from this far, remote corner of the world. Victoria had suggested her as an example of wasted potential among expats. Alison had given up a burgeoning career in banking to stay home and raise a pack of children. And while the information and experience she accessed through her computer from a tiny corner of her house enabled her, vicariously, to keep one steady foot in the world of the living, it was obvious she yearned to get out there and do it herself. What else could explain her minute knowledge of the American stock market, the fluctuation in the Euro and the economic forecast for their own local, Israeli economy?

At the time she'd worried Alison would be peeved at her article, the bold delineation of what was missing, the gaping holes in her life, appearing there in black and white. But she'd surprisingly been enthusiastic, complimenting the way Victoria had put her finger right on the issue and hadn't held back. She'd insisted the role of happy homemaker was only temporary, that soon enough she'd jump right back into the world of finance. Yet Victoria sensed that her reserved demeanor, frequently diminished at get-togethers such as this by a few generous glasses of wine, was a cover for the storm brewing beneath. She was certain that eventually she was going to explode, or maybe better said, implode. There was something too enthusiastic about the way she drank, too suggestive of a volcano just about ready to blow.

On her more difficult days, those when Victoria feared she'd never be able to recreate the kind of career she was certain she would have had if she hadn't junked it all and moved to Israel, she consoled herself with thoughts of Alison's sacrifice. At least she wasn't alone.

Jackie and Susan squeezed inside the patio door last, deep in a conversation about mosquitoes and stagnant swimming pools. To Victoria, they were definitely an odd couple, their clashing accents only the beginning of the story. Jackie's relocation to Israel had been more from necessity than any burning desire to move to the Holy

Land, precipitated by the consistently dwindling Jewish population in Johannesburg. She'd actually been willing to stick it out there, loved her local circle, albeit small and somewhat limiting, but then the local Jewish Day School had announced they'd be closing due to attrition. Her husband, a true Zionist, was convinced there was no place for them but Israel, and she'd agreed to give it a chance on the condition they settle in an English-speaking community. Despite the fact that a decade had passed since her arrival, Victoria sensed that Jackie was still not at peace with her decision, that it was just a matter of time until she eventually moved on to somewhere she felt more comfortable, say, Australia.

Susan's story was markedly different. Unlike Jackie's traditional background, she had no real base in Judaism. Her upbringing had been entirely secular, her maintenance of Jewish tradition based on the exchange of Hanukkah gifts and an occasional Passover Seder at some distant relative's house. Yet her move had been enthusiastic, generated by the excitement of establishing a home with the man she'd met by chance during the semester she'd spent at Tel Aviv University. Starting out without any financial support from their families, they'd actually settled on a kibbutz those first few years. If that wasn't the proof that she was game for anything, Victoria couldn't imagine what was. Communal life with a minimum of luxuries couldn't have been easy to adapt to fresh out of a New Jersey suburb. Of course that experiment hadn't lasted long, and the moment the kibbutz privatized, Matt bought into a small business and moved them to the far more upscale town of Caesarea. Susan seemed the least perturbed by the exchange of one life for the other, and Victoria was convinced she was here for good.

"Have you been here long?"

Victoria stepped back from the action and watched the others occupy this welcoming space from a haze produced by a mixture of muddled thoughts and wine. The tension of the past few days began to dissipate. Decibels were raised and surfaces cluttered as they spread their particular brand of chaos. The dining room refectory table, pristine and empty minutes earlier, showing off its lustrous wood finish, was now covered with a jumble of platters and cutlery exhibiting uniformity neither in material nor offerings – plastic, glass, ceramic and metal haphazardly mixed with culinary offerings that would challenge the appetites of even the heartiest eaters. Yet the hodge-podge of items collected on the table – a goat cheese and beet salad, onion dip, quinoa salad, a plate of peanut butter-sunflower seed cookies and a bowl of steamed broccoli – indicating a brazen defiance of order or design, was the perfect metaphor for the collection of women beginning to settle around it.

Although at times the bond between those gathered here seemed enormously tenuous, based as it was on a constellation of different personalities and alliances, this clique had become an anchor in Victoria's life here in Caesarea. It didn't matter that they might never have found one another in any other walk of life, specifically, in their native habitats, having attended neither the same synagogue, summer camp nor college. Here in the Holy Land, or more precisely in this little seaside town, they'd gravitated to one another – coming together over the course of years to form a real gang. Something about packing up, picking up, relocating half way across the world and landing in the same small town, had provided enough common ground to justify the creation of a genuine bond.

Israelis usually called them "Anglos," lumping them together as a group despite their origins in what could be very far-ranging places, from Canada to South Africa, Great Britain to the United States. It didn't matter that they represented an enormously diverse population and a wealth of different cultures, since they all fulfilled the requirement of being native English speakers transplanted into the Middle East. In fact, what seemed so cohesive to outsiders, was actually quite wide-ranging. To Victoria, a journalist by profession, this clique represented a perfect exemplar of variety on a theme: coming from vastly different socio-economic backgrounds with varying levels of higher education, espousing family traditions that ranged from observant to a-religious and distinctly different interests. A few had arrived in Israel by design, based on a lifetime commitment to the home of the Jewish people, but others were here almost by chance.

Despite these differences, their fusion was made smooth by the many elements that connected them, those beautiful common threads that wove through the burlap of their haphazard union and made everything come together as a whole. In addition to the common variables of having been born in the same decade, having similarly aged children who attended school together and, of course, living in the same town, was that most fundamental common denominator: their common experience as immigrants.

The challenging negotiation of everyday life blurred the significance of what had come earlier, binding them closely. They'd all experienced something of the shock that comes with first entry as well as the continual aftershocks, time-released, that were part of leading a life here in Israel. Adapting to a foreign culture was a struggle even in the best-case scenario. This experience, one that infected every pore, invaded every nook and cranny, had been enough not only to bring them together, but furthermore, cause them to cling to one another, refusing to separate. They'd become their own organism, taking on a life of its own and continuing to develop.

Victoria leaned forward to help herself to the salad, appreciating the serenity supplied by her friends, finally able to shelve the tension she'd been carrying around for days. She'd known this evening would work its magic, provide the levity she sought after so many heavy days. As her friends joined her around the table, helping themselves to the abundance of platters before them, a wave of warmth and calm engulfed her.

It was then that the ear-splitting crackle of gunshot rang out. All chatter and movement, in abundance just a second earlier, stopped instantly. Everyone froze where they were, serving utensils in hand, leaning across the table, mid-sentence. Another shot followed the first, ripping a gaping hole in the charmed atmosphere that had reigned so supremely moments before. The resonance was so piercing and loud that it sounded as though the shots had been fired right off the terrace. All of the bonhomie dissolved and a joint frisson of fear moved through the group.

Chapter 6

Susan was the first to break through the icy fear that had gripped them, laughing, or rather simulating a laugh. Although the sound she emitted was somewhere between a half-chuckle and a nervous cough, it did the trick, immediately warming up the mood in the room. A wave of sighs, brief exclamations and shrugs of relief was accompanied by an immediate resumption of attention to the various serving dishes on the table. Well-versed in the idiosyncrasies of life in their corner of the Middle East, these women were used to cycling quickly from horror to relief, anxiety to acceptance.

"When are they going to stop this nonsense?"

"How do you live so close to this crap?" Jackie had a short fuse for local peculiarities, unconvinced of the life she'd adopted and continually running up against and vocalizing yet one more reason why it had all been a mistake.

"Do you think they've ever managed to kill anybody?"

The gunfire that accompanied celebrations in the neighboring Arab town of Jisr az-Zarqa was a well-worn subject of discussion. "We never get used to it." Evie picked up the theme with an exasperated tone. "We're so close to them. It's only a few hundred meters to the first houses, just over the wall. I think there's a wedding site just down the road." She gestured with her head. "There's no time it doesn't stop us in our tracks, make us shudder. I'm convinced it's the reason for my elevated blood pressure." She glanced nervously around at the others and then, eager to alleviate the tension in the room, in her home, reached for the bottle of wine and quickly changed her tone. "But you know, it's harmless; simply a sign of celebration. Not one we would adopt, a bit too barbaric, but...well...it is what it is."

Victoria didn't spend a lot of time thinking about her Arab neighbors. To her they were no different from neighbors in the various Jewish towns surrounding Caesarea, an integral part of the local scenery that extended beyond the confines of her little town. True, their children didn't attend school with hers and celebrated different holidays. Most recently she'd come to understand that they didn't serve in the army. That wasn't something she'd thought about until Ben was approaching conscription. And then there was the matter of their village. She could count the times she'd actually driven there. Although there were a few grandiose villas, similar to those in Caesarea, the general appearance of the village was squalid. The majority of the houses were quite broken down, as if on the verge of collapse. Most alarming was the trash, piled up along the roads and in the empty lots between the structures. The sanitary crew that worked so hard to keep Caesarea pristine and spotless obviously didn't make their way to Jisr az-Zarqa.

With all that, the Israeli Arabs were completely integrated into the local scene. They voted in the same elections, shopped at the same supermarkets, went to the same ice cream parlors and stood in line for the same doctors. They weren't part of the political conversation occupying not only her own household, and those throughout the country, but much of the world. They had nothing to do with the Palestinian Arabs about whom so much ink was spilled in the international press. In fact, they too suffered from the political stalemate that threatened to stretch toward a century, the same as the Israeli Jews – both populations frustrated by the inability to simply find a way to live in peace, to move on and live their lives free of terror.

Victoria had been drawn to Arab culture from the moment she'd arrived. She'd loved walking through Yaffo with Guy, stopping at that little hummus place where fresh chick peas floated in a pool of oil, like water lilies on the surface of a pond. And although some of her friends found the muezzin's early-morning call to prayer annoying, she considered it romantic, a daily reminder that she lived in a place rich with a multitude of cultures and wasn't burrowed into some ultra-monolithic American suburb.

But this particular evening the sound of sporadic gunfire had rattled her completely. She felt raw, her nerves still on edge from last week's trauma. No matter how hard she tried to shake it, the image of that young man, lying in a hospital bed with his head bandaged, remained at the forefront of her mind. Although she adamantly refused to draw the line that connected his horrific situation with Ben's, that round of gunfire had sliced through this sheath of denial, leaving her shaky.

"It's unbearable," she whispered. Everyone turned her way. There was complete silence. "There's different. I appreciate different. In some ways I crave it. That's why I'm here!" She smiled hesitantly. It *was* the reason she was here. But then the feeling of terror returned and her facial features drooped. "But then there's insane. This is a bit too close to that."

There was a brief cessation of action around the table as the others paused in their assault on the various serving dishes. Susan cleared her throat and, in a determined and noticeable manner, poked around in her purse. "So maybe this is a good time to talk about this book." She made a big show of pulling the paperback out of the black hole that contained all her necessaries and slapped it on the table with a thud. The others seemed almost relieved. It was time to get on to the main purpose of their gathering.

Victoria reached for her own bag, hoping no one would notice the tears that had sprung into her eyes. She need not have been concerned; everyone seemed equally eager to move forward.

"I could never live in a place like that." Susan gestured toward the book and then looked around the table, waiting for what she assumed to be full agreement. "So fraught with controversy."

Victoria smiled. This might actually be fun. "But you do! If you hadn't noticed, it takes place in Israel – *our* Israel!"

"That is not *my* Israel. Never will be. In fact, I really don't want anything to do with it!"

"I second that."

Comfortable with their general consensus, they resumed eating. "Forget the politics. It's so remote!" Evie's comment was met with a round of laughter. She was such a city slicker. It was hard to imagine how she'd made the decision to trade in cosmopolitan London for the Middle East; it had something to do with her search for eternal sunshine, but imagining her stuck in a far-flung corner of the West Bank was unthinkable. "Why would anyone choose to live in the middle of nowhere?"

"Frankly, it's probably about the same driving distance to Tel Aviv, save the time needed for the checkpoints."

They all looked at Alison. As Victoria recalled, she had quite a bit of family in the Territories. She always mentioned those cousins whose constant invitations for barbecues she'd politely decline, never eager to make the drive there. Although only an hour or so away, she'd once explained that it felt like braving the Wild West. She'd reserved the few trips she had made, fueled by an artificial sense of courage, to major events like bar mitzvahs. Victoria herself had never been over the Green Line. There'd been no reason. "Don't you have cousins somewhere out there?"

Alison laughed. "No. Well, yes, but not exactly. Not in a place like the one described in the book. My cousins live in a large, very established town in the West Bank. They have nothing to do with the kind of pop-up settlement described here. Those outposts, frequently established on land whose ownership is questionable, are usually populated by zealous pioneers." She took a sip of her wine. "I've been to my cousins' house and there's nothing 'frontier' about it. Looks like something straight out of Scarsdale."

"Well, as far as I'm concerned," Evie picked up the thread of conversation, "he didn't manage to make the place at all appealing. Gavron. He probably lives in Tel Aviv. There's something about those funky little wire-frame glasses. Did you check out his picture?"

Victoria flipped over her copy of the book and looked at the back cover. She hadn't noticed it before, but the author of the book they were discussing did look rather hip. Evie was probably right. She looked around the table. She loved these evenings. Sitting around and talking about books was something she would have done if she'd stayed back in the States, continued along that expected path – the one for which she was destined. It comforted her to recall that so much of her life was exactly what it might have been, that she hadn't swung so far off track.

She smiled to herself, beginning to shake the mood that had stuck to her, creeping under her skin, since last week. It wasn't that she didn't know Ben's life was in danger, wasn't aware that soldiers were at risk. But having one of their own, a local boy they all knew, so imperiled, had made it all the more frightening. The fact that this evening, this book club meeting, was working its magic on her, had very little to do with the book itself. In any case these get-togethers were almost an excuse to insure a regular way to get together and laugh, to grasp at those precious, evanescent sparkling shards of diamond in the midst of so much sand. One glance at the table, so cluttered there was virtually no room for the individual copies of the book they'd all brought with them, proved that they were almost beside the point.

Susan slid the popcorn bowl to the left and the crudités to the right, finding a place to open her copy. "Evie, no one could imagine you pitching your tent at such an outpost, but I'm sure it attracts a certain population. Some of the descriptions of the land sounded quite beautiful. When Matt and I first lived on Kibbutz Ma'aleh HaHamisha I couldn't get enough of the local landscape. Every morning I'd be struck anew by the way the sun touched the neighboring hills, waking up the world by changing its palette. It was so much better than one more strip mall."

"I hope it distracted you from all that peach picking. Geez. I'm not sure how you bought into all that kibbutz crap. Once a city girl, always a city girl. You'd never find me stooping so low, except maybe while stepping into a cab." They all laughed with Evie.

"These areas are eternally attractive to the super religious. They can claim they're returning to their biblical roots, restoring a lost heritage. But I don't buy it. I'm certain they could find less backward places to live while still reviving the presence of the chosen people in the Holy Land. What's wrong with Jerusalem proper? I just don't get it."

"And you never will. Without a sense of religious fervor there's no understanding such a decision."

"Actually, that's not exactly the case." They were all surprised by Jackie's interjection. She usually wasn't very vocal about politics, spending most of her time super focused on the travails of her secular, local life. "These families were probably offered a lot of incentives. I'd imagine it's fairly appealing to be able to get that much more for your money. I mean, how much could it possibly cost to set up a home somewhere so remote? It's an absolute fortune to do the same at any mainstream, popular location within Israel proper. Maybe it's the *only* option for certain of those who make aliyah. I can tell you, we never expected it to be so expensive. It wasn't something we calculated right."

"You're cutting them quite a break. It's still a choice. Not everyone has to move to an upscale Anglo neighborhood like swanky Caesarea." They all laughed at Alison's choice of adjectives. "There are so many other places they could go."

"I'm just saying." Jackie looked down for a moment, a bit out of water broaching this subject. "It's not easy. I read the book. It wasn't anything I knew or identified with. At least, most of it. I mean, I never actually intended to come to Israel. But then there was something about those brothers and how they'd both been looking for some kind of refuge. I think that Rob felt that way. And then again, there's what they went through. It's so hard to pack up one life and unpack it halfway across the world. This is complicated business." She looked around the table for confirmation.

"Well, we all understand that. Been there, done that. For certain. But for me?" Evie glanced at the cover of the book, reading the title. "This *Hilltop* of his? It never even entered the equation. I moved here fully cognizant of just how hip Israel could be. Otherwise I wouldn't have considered it." Another bit of laughter.

"None of us can picture you settling anywhere like that, Evie," said Susan, "but I know what Jackie's getting at. There were so many challenges. There *are* so many challenges. Still, after all this time. If it's not one thing it's another. When Matt and I made the decision to come over, well, there were so many things to consider. Expense was at the top of the list. How do you think I ended up picking peaches on a kibbutz? It was the last thing I ever imagined myself doing. But if we'd been offered the right deal? If someone had come along and said they had just the place for us: scenic, inexpensive, lovely people. Who knows? At that point we weren't too focused on finding a place with other English speakers, hadn't even considered finding a group that suited our needs. None of that was a priority, or even something that seemed important. We had to focus on what we could afford and how we could realize Matt's dream of establishing a home back in Israel."

"I loved that phrase Gavron used," Alison interjected, "Accidental settlers. How good was that? Terrific concept. Really does capture the phenomenon."

"It's easy to excuse them, to accept their actions as happenstance. But some of them are there to make a point." Everyone turned to look at Victoria. She hesitated before she continued, aware that her voice had come out just a bit too shrill. "And those people? They're ruining it for all of us. Do you know that Ben has to guard a little 'hilltop' just like the one in the book? A tiny little place with just a handful of houses populated by two handfuls of residents. He and his friends have to sit there, 24/7, and make sure that nothing happens to them. The irony, as he's explained to me time and again, is that the settlers are better armed than the soldiers! Apparently they're all walking around with guns, man and woman alike – ready for whatever may come."

Jackie took an overeager sip of water, choked for a moment on the excess and then cleared her throat. "His descriptions of the zealots, or really, the crazies, got me pretty worked up. Those characters who are making a point by sitting on contested land. The one part of South Africa I was happy to leave behind was its divisive political atmosphere. Living with apartheid was unbearable. I was happy to see the back of it when the law changed. Those nuts in America, the ones fueling the BDS movement, have no idea what they're talking about. And thank God for that! One thing we *don't* have here in Israel is apartheid. Our political struggle with the Palestinians is much more basic, really a question of land rather than rights. So many people don't really understand that."

They were all struck by Jackie's vehemence. So much of her energy was spent denying any connection with her adopted country, let alone expressing a firm opinion, yet here she was vigorously exhibiting her passionate response to the most burning local question.

"Why are you all looking at me? Why so surprised? Just because I pine for Jo'burg, talk non-stop about how much I loved my life there – yes, I'm ready to go back! – doesn't mean I was happy with the forced separation of the races. It was the most compelling reason I agreed to Rob's plan to leave what was, and really will forever be, my home. I'd had enough of living in a country split into two, everything always 'us' or 'them.'"

She turned to Victoria. "I have no idea how you have any patience for the settlers whatsoever. They're endangering our children! The costs of this endless argument are too high. I'm so lucky. Until now it hasn't been personal. But Vic," She reached out and touched Victoria's arm, "I don't know how you bear it. With Adam's conscription right around the corner, just the thought is more than I can stand." She grabbed another carrot from the bowl, angrily plunged it into the dip, and took a bite. "I definitely didn't sign on for all of this."

There was another round of silence. Jackie took a blue corn chip from the bowl in front of her, a few more, and then pushed the whole bowl away. "Could someone remove these from me?"

Susan opened her mouth as if to speak, a small sound attracting the attention of the others and then hesitated. "I really can't imagine what you all go through. It's so different with girls. And now that it's all behind us, now that Lynn's finished her service, it all seems so remote. But those settlers. It all seems so selfish."

"That's the perfect word. Selfish. It's all about *their* faith, *their* beliefs. The fact that their actions may hurt others, may actually cause the death of others, doesn't even enter the equation." The others were struck silent by Victoria's outburst.

She felt hot, a flush brought on by stress beginning to get the best of her. This wasn't a good topic. It was the essence of the book they'd read and she had waited all night for someone to bring it up. When no one did, she'd raised it herself. Better to get it over with even if it pressed all the wrong buttons. Now that she'd said it, she was desperate to move on, to change the topic. "They're comparing Gavron to Franzen, saying his literature offers the Israeli version of Franzen's realistic fiction. I have to say I agree. The story of those two brothers, one who's messed up his family life and seeks refuge on the hilltop, the other who's come to escape after screwing up in New York. His descriptions of their experiences are spot on."

Alison nodded her head in agreement. "He's offered a fairly accurate picture of contemporary life in Israel, not only religious, but also secular. Not just those parts about life on the settlement, but those that take place in the bars of Tel Aviv and on the kibbutzim. I even appreciated the descriptions of those Israelis who've relocated to New York but continue to surround themselves entirely with other Israelis. The ones who've really found their own little Israeli ghetto over there. Franzen seems about right."

"I was actually pleased to find those sections on bourgeois, urban Israel." Victoria shifted in her chair and smiled. "When I first picked up the book I thought it was going to be all about that other side, the Zionism, the sacrifice, the fanatical religious beliefs. That isn't my Israel at all." She raised her glass to Evie. "Right there with you."

"Speaking of new arrivals…" Victoria listened to Jackie begin a new topic, one far removed from the book they'd been discussing, something about a new family living in the house a few streets over, a familiar story: They'd rented the house from a family that had moved to the States ten years earlier, their house being passed from one expat tenant to another, most usually just off the proverbial boat from a mild climate such as California or Florida. Since these stories were par for the course in international communities like Caesarea, they each automatically reviewed the relevant details: number of children, whether there were any matches with their own, age-wise, a bit of information regarding the couple themselves and then, most significantly, a rough assessment of whether the wife might be worth getting to know.

Victoria wondered if way back when, upon her arrival to town, the locals had been equally dismissive of her family: treating them more as a statistic than actual, breathing human beings. She knew the answer. After all, hers had been merely one more familiar tale: Israeli husband, American wife, kids in kindergarten. On the surface it must have seemed neat and tidy. Of course the reality was nothing of the sort.

As the evening wore on she felt herself regress bit by bit from the conversation, felt the edges begin to soften, the words and images before her lose definition. Voices were raised, the clamor around the table loud enough to scare off any outsider (a spouse, children) who might venture into the room. A pitcher of sugary spirits and that first bottle of wine had been dispensed with quickly and they were well into the second. Rosy red cheeks were the norm and everyone's speech was a bit less than sharp, the alcohol blurring the lines of cerebral clarity.

For Victoria, the best part, equally as good as that lovely layer of foam on a fresh cup of cappuccino, was the laughter. These get-togethers with her local pals featured spurts of laughter, that gut-splitting variety that emerged without warning, erupting suddenly and spreading quickly. It was the salve that made everything come together, made their lives, with its daily trials, wash down that much more easily. Twenty-five years into her marriage, with three children teetering on adulthood and a lifetime of trying to establish something concrete in her adopted home, Victoria couldn't get enough of the release it provided.

Things could get so heavy, as they had this past week, almost too heavy to bear. Even in a privileged life, and she knew that's what she had, there was nothing quite as precious as a good dose of levity. She could never pinpoint why the laughter on these evenings was so intense, bordering on hysterical, but figured it had something to do with the chemical reaction created by hinging so many disparate parts to a common, seemingly harebrained experience.

Warm and comfortable, satisfied to the core, having received precisely the medicine she needed to push away the potential of horror that had been eating away at her insides for days, Victoria was startled to find Jackie mentioning the time and beginning to gather her things. The evening was coming to a close. She blinked in recognition. One more night. One more day behind her. Since Ben's conscription she'd begun to count. When she reached a thousand, it would end.

"Um… Everybody…" Susan cleared her throat, a bit more loudly than seemed right for the occasion. "I have something I need to say. There's something I want to tell you." Victoria had been busy trying to find the wedges she'd kicked somewhere under the table, getting ready to go. Now she abandoned that task and looked intently at her friend. The sparkling cheer and air of camaraderie that had reigned in the room only seconds earlier had completely dissipated, like the air of a deflated balloon. This abrupt change in trajectory didn't bode well.

"Sweetie?" Jackie put her hand on Susan's, attempting to ease whatever ailed her.

She cleared her throat again, looking at each of them in turn, making the rounds with her eyes. "We're moving to New Jersey."

There was dead silence as everyone absorbed her announcement. Susan nervously smiled and looked around again, this time starting from the other side of the group, as if carefully collecting the reactions. "It's almost certain. Matt got a job and we're going to relocate." She paused, and then quickly added, "At least for a bit."

Victoria felt woozy. She gripped the edge of the table for support. *Susan is moving to the States? Susan?* She simply couldn't believe it. A stream of thoughts, most those she'd fought to keep out, crashed through her head, unbridled. *How is this possible?* She was stuck here, stuck in this life, the one she forever questioned, while Susan was moving back to the States. She felt desperately jealous. *Why her and not me?*

Within this torrent of emotion, Victoria's distress abruptly spiked. Ben. *How could she consider leaving Ben?* She felt confused, torn between fidelity and desire. She forced herself to focus, to see the situation for what it was. She'd been fretting for a week over something that thankfully had nothing to do with him. She forcibly pushed aside the images that had been haunting her and replaced them with ones decidedly more palatable. Ben was on his base. He was safe and would remain so. Even more significantly, he too would move on. Eventually. There was no reason to hold back the raw, honest feelings now asserting themselves so forcibly.

There were murmurs around the table, questions and comments, a blend of excited energy and nervous hesitation. Victoria couldn't imagine how each of the others was taking this, but she felt as if she'd been punched in the stomach. She'd dreamed about having a chance to do it over, to do it differently, and now it was happening for her friend. *She's so lucky.* As her jealousy overwhelmed her she became absolutely light-headed. She'd considered this eventuality now and again, the thought flitting through her head without warning as the rosy blush of the early years began to fade against the tide of disappointments. She could trace her hesitation back to one particular afternoon soon after her move to Caesarea, that moment she'd began to realize that the local mentality didn't suit her, that she'd never find the right fit; when those nagging feelings she'd been experiencing here and there congealed and she actually began to question her decision to take on life in another culture. But since then she'd managed to continually stymie her disenchantment, to hold it at bay.

No matter how you cut it, living in Israel wasn't easy. Moving back to the States had its appeal. This wasn't a new concept. But until now, the moment it was happening *for someone else, someone close*, Victoria hadn't realized quite how much she actually wanted it. The concept had always been some kind of amusing fancy, one they all bantered about for fun, a meaningless way of venting their frustrations about the difficulties they each experienced living in Israel. But the reality of departure for Susan, one of their own, had suddenly altered its status from pipe dream to possibility.

Firmly buried in a haze of confused and frustrated rumination, Victoria barely noticed that the dishes on the table had magically begun to disappear, lifted away from the table as the others, still actively exploring this dramatic turn of events, firing off question after question, scurried to help tidy up. She tried to regain some of her poise, hide her distress. She daren't let anyone know how she really felt. After all, the image of certainty and confidence she projected to the outside world was crucial to its maintenance. Her actual fragility needed to be carefully hidden away, the best way to deny its existence. Victoria managed to find her shoes under the table and jammed them on. Somehow they no longer pinched. There wasn't room for more pain anywhere else in her body. At that very moment, everything hurt.

She pulled herself to her feet, lifting what felt like a thousand-pound load, and joined the others as they made their way outside, adding an appropriate comment here and there in order to carefully hide her thoughts. *I'll find a way. There's got to be a way.* The fragility of her existence in Israel had, within seconds, been brutally revealed. It had only taken one of her crowd, one part of the puzzle of her local life, to step aside, to threaten leaving the fold, for her to admit to exactly how desperate she was to do the same.

Chapter 7

It was a beautiful summer afternoon, not too hot, just warm enough to enjoy the local playground. Victoria loved her new neighborhood. She and Guy had bounced around a bit since they'd moved to Israel. After finishing her government-sponsored six month ulpan in Jerusalem, they'd spent a few years in Tel Aviv. She'd loved the vibe of the city, so alive and so modern yet continually evocative of an earlier era – tiny pockets of the city refusing to give in to contemporary life. She couldn't get enough of the cafés and night spots, laughter and light spilling out of doorways, more activity taking place outdoors than in; long, broad avenues split by entire parks, their walkways lined with ficus trees whose branches swept so low you had to duck to make your way; streamlined white buildings with their smooth, wraparound corners and ribbon windows jammed right up against crumbling edifices with pointed archways and filigree stonework; the endless stretch of the pale sand and the Mediterranean blue. The scintillating life she discovered in the White City had quickly extinguished any remaining pangs she'd had for New York.

But in the early '90s a run of terrorist bus explosions had changed everything. While many of the locals refused to fold, adamantly continuing their lives, never yielding to fear, she became a nervous wreck. She stopped riding the buses completely and refused to even stand next to one. If a bus pulled up beside her car as she sat waiting for the red light to turn green, she'd count to thirty, one, two, three, four…, the addition of each number marking the safe passing of time, shutting out the wretched potential. Although the attacks were sporadic, and most days were as uneventful as they'd be anywhere else in the world, she couldn't shake the looming threat.

When Ben was born she decided she'd had enough. She needed to find somewhere else in this country that would ostensibly, and hopefully, be unblemished, free of the specters of past attacks that cast their long shadows throughout the city. Although Guy continued to assure her that everything was okay and would continue to be, somehow inured to the occasional horrors which rattled her already raw nerves, he eventually agreed that they move somewhere far out of the fray.

Their decision to choose somewhere with a more international population, where spoken English was par for the course, was prompted by her new motherhood. Since his birth, Victoria had coddled and swathed Ben in English, wrapping him in a warm blanket of her native language and leaving aside the uneven Hebrew she continued to struggle with outside of the house. She began to look ahead, envisioning an expat environment in which she could comfortably raise him as both Israeli and American, and knew a bilingual community was a must.

So far, Caesarea was turning out to be even better than they'd anticipated. It was spotlessly clean and orderly. Endless stretches of emerald green grass lined its byways, with nary a hint at the local water shortage. It held absolutely no resemblance to what she remembered of Israel from visits as a child and of what she'd imagined back in the kitchen in New York when she and Guy had made the decision to build a life there. The charms of crumbling edifices and Eastern detailing she'd found in both Jerusalem and Tel Aviv were virtually non-existent in this pseudo-suburban paradise. The wealthy French Rothschild family had established a modern town on the ruins of Herod's ancient city that could rival any American golfing community, replete with the mandatory eighteen-hole golf course. For Victoria, newly interested in escaping some of the grittier aspects of life in Israel and the jarring realities with which she could never be at peace, Caesarea's harmonious and gentle environment, so distinctly not Israeli, couldn't help but appeal. From the moment they drove through the gatehouse, she'd felt at home.

Victoria smiled as she loaded the kids into the car and headed out of the driveway, really looking forward to meeting her friend Alison. Her growing friendship with this fellow expat, a former city girl fresh from the Mid-Atlantic like herself, had begun to assuage the sadness she felt now and then being far away from her childhood friends. She crept up to the corner and pulled to a stop behind a car waiting to pull out onto the main street. A few seconds passed before she realized that the car had come to a full stop, that the driver didn't seem to have any intention of making the turn. She looked ahead and, not seeing any passing traffic, wondered what he was waiting for. She settled back into her seat. No matter. They were in no rush.

But a few seconds became a half a minute, and Victoria quickly realized that the car wasn't actually going to move – at all. In fact, there was no driver!

"What the…?"

She beeped tentatively. No one beeped around here. It wasn't New York. She took in the parked cars on both sides of the street, trying to figure whether she could somehow bypass the car, scoot around to the side, maybe even go on the sidewalk if need be. But no. She quickly understood that she was stuck. She beeped again, this time with a bit more gusto. Nothing. Not one person popped their head out to see about all the fuss, and there was still no sign of the driver.

Victoria began to lose patience and started beeping persistently, rhythmically, like a crazed woman.

"Mommy, what are you doing?"

The beeping had aroused the curiosity of her kids. They began to jump up and down in the back seat, stretching the limits of their seatbelts as far as they could in an effort to get a better view of what was causing all the ruckus. Victoria was literally sitting on the horn at this point, completely exasperated.

A woman with whom Victoria had only exchanged a handful of words, her neighbor from the house at the corner, assessed the situation – the beeping car, the parked one – and pointed to the house across the street, immediately identifying the culprit. She gestured with her hand that she'd give him a call and went back into her house. Victoria was momentarily appeased.

"Okay guys, we'll be on our way soon." She tapped on the steering wheel and turned on the radio, looking for a decent song. She flipped through one station after another, yet each offered one more dated version of an Israeli ballad or pop song, and nothing, whatsoever, appealed. She began to lose her patience. She opened all the windows and cut the engine. It was no longer a comfortable day. In fact, it was beginning to feel quite hot. This was all a bit too much. Letting out a sound of exasperation she opened her car door and stepped out. "I'll be right back. Whatever you do, wait here. Don't get out of the car."

Victoria snaked alongside the parked cars and peeked inside the offending one, noting that it was piled high with junk, the owner not only inconsiderate but, not surprisingly, a slob. Attracted by the sound of a door opening, she lifted her gaze in time to see a young man step out of the house on the corner. He looked at

72

her for a second and then progressed toward his car, heading right to the trunk. She took a few step backs, assuming a place on the sidewalk, and watched him, perplexed. She couldn't believe that he wasn't going to apologize or at least offer some kind of explanation. But no. Apparently not. With neither a word nor a glance her way he began to rummage around, moving onward from the trunk to the back seat, crouching on the asphalt, reaching under the seats.

That's when it all became clear. He'd lost his keys. The mystery of why he'd parked in the middle of the street in the first place paled in comparison with the realization that she might truly be unable to get her car out of the street. This whole outing had been about fun. Now it was anything but.

"Would you like some help?"

He didn't even look up.

"Maybe I could push your car onto the sidewalk. That way you could take your time finding the keys." She lowered her voice and muttered, "And that way you won't hold up the rest of the world." Inside, she was absolutely livid, fighting not to lose her cool in front of her kids, now eagerly peering out the windows of her car. She glanced behind them, farther back along her street, and verified, as expected, that she wasn't the only one being inconvenienced. They had their very own back-up, right here on this tiny block. She shook her head and went back to her car.

"Mommy. What's going on?"

"Well dear," she started off in an even tone, trying to maintain her cool. "Some very inconsiderate young man has not only inconvenienced us, and many others on our street, but additionally, has absolutely refused to accept help so that we can all be released from this misery."

"I'll help him," piped Ben. Victoria couldn't help smiling. It was so typical of him to want to lend a hand, no matter the assignment.

"Me too," Jonathan and Maia joined in.

Just then they heard a whoop from up ahead and caught the backside of the man as he emerged from the backseat of his car. Within a few seconds they were on their way. But it wasn't that simple. Victoria still couldn't calm down. She drew her lips together in a tight line and shook her head forcefully from side to side as they made their way toward the playground. She simply couldn't get over it. After all that, the inconvenience, the rudeness and the indifferent attitude, he hadn't uttered one word of apology. He'd never once acknowledged that he was holding up a whole street of individuals. Nothing. She felt unnerved and angry.

Where am I?

Steaming with annoyance, wondering how she'd ever agreed to live in a place characterized by such rude behavior – and no, this wasn't the first time it had reared its ugly head – she was startled to find she'd reached the playground. She pulled over as the clamor from the backseat picked up, barely managing to come to a full stop before the back doors popped open and the kids were off and running. Her mood lightened immediately. They loved it here. Victoria stepped out and reached back to close the passenger door, left wide open in the kids' haste to escape the car in which they'd been held captive minutes earlier. She began to relax, enjoying their enthusiasm and energy, and tried to shake off the feeling of disappointment that lingered from this unpleasant encounter. She couldn't get over how rude that young man had been.

Entering the park she spotted Alison sitting on a bench nestled under a grove of trees.

"Vic, come on over! Want some lemonade?" Alison was already pouring her a large cup.

"I'm really steaming. This is great. Thanks."

She sat down on the bench.

"Something more than the weather? What's up?"

She proceeded to tell her what had transpired. Alison listening carefully, all the while shaking her head empathetically.

"Of all the nerve!"

"You said it."

"Did you at least give him a piece of your mind?"

Victoria hesitated and then said, quietly, "No."

"Why, for heaven's sake, not!"

"I don't know. I figured it wasn't going to make the situation any better."

"Yeah, I get that." Alison got up and ran over to the seesaw where her daughter was on the ground, having fallen off. There were sounds of giggles, shouts from the other kids, and before long she rejoined Victoria on their bench.

"Gadi would have a list of suggestions for what you should have done: Make a lot of noise, a whole lot more than you thought appropriate; dress the guy down, make him really feel bad. Call him names, 'tembel,' idiot, something to make sure he knows he's one step above scum."

Victoria looked over at her. "And how, exactly, would that have helped him find his keys?"

"Oh," she paused, "that's not the important part. The main thing would be to make him feel awful for holding you up…you and a whole slew of others according to your story."

Victoria sighed heavily, stretching her legs out in front of her and crossing her arms behind her neck. She leaned her head on the back of the bench. "When did polite become weak?"

The two women sat in silence. They watched the kids climb on the jungle gym, hang off like monkeys, drop to the ground and then start over again.

"Where are we?"

Alison laughed in reply. "Good question."

"I'm never going to survive this place."

"Oh, give yourself more credit than that. You don't need to adopt some of the more questionable native characteristics to survive. 'Outraged' is never going to be a good fit for either one of us. We simply weren't born with an aggressive bent."

"Maybe I should have married an American."

More silence…this one more pregnant than the last. The subjects of life choices, cultural differences, and compromise had popped up early in their friendship, the moment they'd realized they'd tripped on a kindred soul and could begin to let their insides show. Exploring them together had provided a kind of therapeutic catharsis.

Alison tapped her on the arm and handed her another cup.

"I'm set. It's okay."

"No. This is something different. Take a sip and don't offer it to the kids."

Victoria looked down at the drink in her hand. Lemonade. Exactly like the other one. She took a tentative sip. No. Not like the other one. She smiled at Alison as she took a larger sip, her eyebrows raised in collusion. This was perfect.

"I figure we're up to that part of the conversation where we need a bit of fortification."

Victoria lowered the cup, licked her lips and nodded in agreement. "Definitely." She watched the children on the swings, their legs thrusting forward and back as they propelled themselves higher and higher.

An American husband: that definitely struck a chord, opening up a wound that forever refused to heal. How significant was the lack of a cultural baseline over the course of a lifetime? She'd thought about this before; in fact she'd even written an article about it a few years back. It was a hot topic among her best friends, as most agreed that life would, no doubt, have been easier if shared with an American spouse – someone from a similar background who understood their ways and had a similar approach to handling life's mundane and tricky situations. There was not one she knew whose relationship had not been tested by the hardships of adaptation, the continual confrontation with a foreign, "rough around the edges" mentality and the persistent need to negotiate said differences. In many cases these pressures slowly but steadily chipped away at that seemingly solid, overwhelmingly passionate love, and over the decade since she'd arrived, she'd seen marriages stumble, sputter and sometimes even dissolve.

"Remember Sherry? Kind of stocky, blond bobbed hair? Forever dusting that grand piano, cleaning the glass on that display cabinet? The one with her mother's collection of porcelain trinkets. She absolutely refused to admit she was no longer in Jolly England. Couldn't bear the fact that her husband's family would just show up, walk in without knocking and expect her to be ready with tea and cake."

"Didn't she end up taking the kids back to London? She was so excited to enroll them in that Jewish Academy, to squeeze them into jackets and ties, see them march off in a line each morning. She never got used to the T-shirt and sandal culture. There was that trip to Ein Hod, to the Janco Museum. She actually cringed as the children ran from hither to yon in the main exhibition hall, touching the displays. All that untrammeled and unchecked energy freaked her out."

"They were just curious." Alison laughed. "Some call that natural, others impolite. It's all a matter of perspective. My mother-in-law is always chiding me for thanking her when she passes something to me at the dinner table. Different culture, different expectations."

Victoria had understood some of Sherry's reactions at the time. In fact, they weren't all that different from her own. Although back home on the East Coast good manners reigned supreme, here in

Israel the situation was less black and white. Here authenticity came first, even at the expense of politeness. Many expats, at least those she knew, found this local approach abrasive, if not downright rude. Only a native would have dared to excoriate that young man who'd abandoned his car so thoughtlessly in her street. Neither she nor Alison would have considered telling him off, despite the inconvenience. It simply wasn't in their DNA.

"Guy's response would have been exactly the same as Gadi's. He would have expected me to make that young man as uncomfortable as possible – to make sure he knew precisely how wrong he was." Victoria sighed. "He's got this whole theory about being true to your feelings; considers 'passionate' and 'genuine' the most admirable Israeli characteristics. As far as I'm concerned, they boil down to downright obnoxious. I wonder where that leaves us." Her voice petered off.

How could she not wonder how different life would have been if she'd just married an American, how smoothly certain things would have gone. She usually tried to keep that query at bay, constructing a life specifically intended to hold what was foreign, uncomfortable or unsettling at arm's length, to deny these moments of hesitation center stage. Yet here, with Alison, she felt she could let down some of her guard, show a bit more of her uncertainty.

"Life's complicated enough without the constant negotiation of cultural differences." She sighed aloud, feeling defeated.

"No argument there, but you'd probably have found smooth sailing only by marrying yourself, and that wasn't really an option." Alison's smile was gentle. This was a delicate subject for both of them.

"Seriously, think about the things we wouldn't have to explain, justify or excuse if we'd only had that common starting point."

"Agreed."

"Sometimes it feels like an uphill battle. Sometimes, despite a whole lot of harmony, I know the two sides will never meet. That's when I think about that American husband. He definitely would have been a safer choice."

Victoria took another sip of her drink and continued, "You know, I had this boyfriend, way back whenever. Private school, triple Ivy degrees, Reform Jew, multiply degreed professional parents and a preference for urban environments; one hundred percent guaranteed symbiosis!"

"But no chemistry, right? No chemistry means no future. That relationship would be perfect for two seventy-year-olds, not a young couple in their twenties. And yet," Alison cleared her throat, "chemistry doesn't make everything else unimportant. There's a lot to be said for common ground; at minimum, it's always a place to retreat."

"Correct." Victoria sighed. "All the chemistry in the world will never change the fact that one of us comes from a dusty neighborhood carved out of sand and the other from a tree-lined park in a major metropolis."

"Origin is pretty darn important. Take you and me for example: According to the local rules of engagement we shouldn't really have found one another. After all, we have no identically aged children. We've never sat together at a parents' meeting! Imagine all those missed opportunities to hang out, bond, commiserate and moan. Yet here we are, on our way to a bona fide, Israeli born-and-bred friendship!" Alison raised her paper cup in a toast.

"Here's to common ground!"

Victoria broke the toast with a chuckle. "Maybe we should have married one another?"

Alison raised her cup again. "To you and me!"

"*L'chayim!*" Victoria piped back, this time gustily banging her cup into Alison's, sending her souped-up lemonade sloshing.

Alison laughed. "How did we get here? How did two intelligent women with a clear understanding of what's what, make a decision with such dramatic repercussions?"

"Rhetorical question, right? The "how" is actually the simplest part."

They gazed out idly toward their children, watching them work the apparatus. Alison, Victoria and their other expat friends had come to Israel under vastly different circumstances, their original connection with this land ranging from dedicated to tangential. Some had come as teenagers, skipping college in order to work on a kibbutz, hang out on the beaches of Tel Aviv or blend in with the Anglo crowd in Jerusalem. Some had come as children – Israel simply one more destination among many – returning home with a miniature wooden camel and a glass bottle of colored sand by which to remember their journey – certain that would be the end of it. A few had relatives here, distant or close, and others had come on their own recognizance, on a hunch that, at minimum, they'd gain an experience worth having and holding when they resumed their lives back home.

Yet the fundamental reason Alison, Victoria and many of their local friends had stayed was much the same. It was all about love. They had each fallen for a man who came from far across the ocean, whose whole being evoked a world completely different from their own, forever exotic and romantic, yet amazingly willing to extend its arms in welcome. The local magic of Israel had pulled them in and continued to hold on tightly, its intoxicating embrace unyielding and relentless, impossible to wash off or forgo.

"It was all so irresistible."

"Indeed."

"So when did this happen? When did it become resistible?"

"When the kindergarten teacher corrected our Hebrew, or even worse, a passing five-year-old."

"Yes! And while standing in line for meat at the market, when everyone else pushed ahead and we realized we were being punished for being polite."

"And those times we accidentally swerved a bit out of the lane on the highway and received a verbal dressing-down from a nearby driver."

Alison raised her hand and gestured from one end of the playground to another, taking in the tall Eucalyptus trees that bordered one side and the luscious carob trees on the other, the bright red jungle-gym equipment and, most significantly, their children running wild, resplendent. "But, with all that...look at what we have."

Victoria leaned her head back again, bumping against the edge of the bench a bit harder than she'd anticipated. "Alison. Sometimes I can't... I can't help dreaming about another go-around."

Alison shook her head understandingly and turned to Victoria. "So what happens next?"

Victoria shook her head side to side. "I try not to go there." She sighed heavily. "That's a topic I'm unwilling to broach."

Chapter 8

They were out of the house early, on their way to renew their passports at the local office of the Ministry of the Interior. Victoria drove just a bit too fast, feeling off-kilter and out of sorts since Susan's announcement. She wanted to be happy for her friend, excited about this new opportunity, this refreshing change of pace. Instead, she was positively roiling inside, eaten alive by jealousy and frustration. It was getting worse by the hour. She hadn't realized exactly how badly she wanted to go back, to move to the States, to pick up the pieces of the life she'd left behind more than two decades earlier. It was ironic that she'd arranged to renew her passport precisely this morning, securing her way out of here.

Only fifteen minutes away from the sun-kissed houses, palm trees and idyllic seaside that characterized Caesarea, she and the kids were assaulted by the congestion and chaos of the region's biggest city. Chock-a-block with partially crumbled buildings, broken sidewalks, honking cars, a messy web of foot traffic and a general look of decay, Hadera represented everything Victoria found distasteful about the Middle East. It was a wakeup call regarding the true nature of the country beyond the bubble within which she usually hid.

This morning it was really all too much. It was enough to have to deal with her sudden desire to flee, to finally acknowledge that she was genuinely dissatisfied with the life she'd chosen, that she'd been pretending to be content out of some misplaced sense of duty. But having to face its ugliest side, confronted with the seediest of all seedy cities face on, was really a low blow. Eager to get to the Ministry as quickly as possible she turned onto the main street, only six blocks extending east to west, a straight shot to her destination. She glanced up at the street sign on the corner: Presidential Boulevard. *How ironic.* She smirked. There was nothing presidential about it. The choice of names was no doubt an early attempt at a grandeur that never materialized.

Traffic along this thoroughfare was heavy and all movement had slowed to a crawl. The so-called straight shot wasn't going to be a speedy one. Creeping along, bumper-to-bumper, she was able to take in the local scenery, a nutshell summary of exactly how "foreign" local could be. She wondered if Jonathan and Maia, sitting quietly in the car (it was a little too early for them to engage in conversation), felt the same disconnection, felt how dissimilar the life on the streets around them was from their own.

When sudden congestion forced them to a full stop, she glanced over at Jonathan, sitting in the passenger seat with his face peering out the glass window. She followed his gaze up a side street off the main drag to where a large crowd was gathered on the sidewalk. The local souk had spread outward from its alley niche and there was a lot to take in. Every square meter unoccupied by an individual was crammed with stuff, mountains of it. This was the kind of place you bought items by the kilo, whether shoes, tin pans or fresh apricots, most items on offer dumped haphazardly in large metal bins propped up one beside the other. Every item, whether clothing, small appliances, toys or assorted sundries, was some shade or other of grey – coated with grime that suggested it dated back at least one generation. She understood Jonathan's fascination. This wasn't the pristine version of Bel Air they enjoyed in Caesarea.

The car lurched forward again as traffic accelerated to a slow crawl, allowing Victoria an opportunity to take in the scene beyond the souk, the action that stretched out along Presidential Boulevard itself. Everything looked so incredibly tired, the window displays of the stores exuding a general feeling of neglect, an indifference to outsiders that would seem to repulse, rather than entice, shoppers. *How do these businesses survive?*

The general feeling of disregard and decay depressed her. The sidewalks were jammed with electricity poles, parking meters, garbage cans, free-standing billboards and outdoor stands; doorways were plastered with colorful notices of concerts, bargains and festivals as well as black and white ones of funerals and *shivas*, each awkwardly stapled or taped in place, one over the other, sometimes partially ripped.

This wasn't a city looking to attract any attention or garner any kind of reputation. Instead it seemed to nod inward, toward its own. Everything was so obviously pitched to the locals and, true to expectation, they were out in droves to accept and embrace its offerings. The sidewalks positively teemed with individuals pushing in to take a look, check something out, and maybe, after serious bargaining, actually buy.

"Why are so many people awake at this hour?" Jonathan's voice cut through the silence in the car.

Victoria shrugged. "Hard to imagine. Hope they're not headed to the same place as us!"

Focused on her destination and incredibly frustrated by how long it was taking to negotiate a handful of blocks, Victoria tried hard not to form that very Israeli *tsk*ing sound with her tongue, the one that signified impatience. It wasn't easy, as at this point she was beyond irritated. She had no patience for this version of chaos today, and aggressive thoughts zinged around in her head as they crept along.

"Welcome to Israel."

She hadn't meant to voice that thought, which had come out more like an angry bark than a conversation starter, but once she'd let it go she couldn't go back. "Take a look around guys. A trip down this main street at rush hour is the best lesson you'll ever get in the History of Modern Israel." One sweep of the sidewalks revealed representatives of the various waves of immigration: those whose families predated the founding of the modern state as well as those who'd arrived since, refugees and zealous Zionists from any one of a variety of Eastern European, African and Asian countries. The Iraqis, the Moroccans, the Turks and the Kafkazis combined to form a mosaic of skin tones, accents and cultures. In stark contrast to their relatively homogenous Caesarea, Hadera was one seriously mixed bag. "Too bad it's all so very Third World," she mumbled.

For the most part Victoria tried to ignore those aspects of Israel that resembled Mumbai, to forget their existence and stay inside the carefully circumscribed bubble of Caesarea. Errands beyond, such as this morning's, were to be executed in a surgical fashion, as quickly as possible, before hurrying back to the spanking-clean, sanitary environment of home.

There had been a time she'd found this kind of environment appealing, each crumbling surface more charming than the next. Bending down midstride, to pull rubble out of her sandal's outsole, had actually made her smile. The genuine decay of the Middle East was, after all, a big part of its exoticism. She'd been a different person back then, eagerly embracing this alternative world. She hadn't been able to get enough of the smells rising from the hot pavement, the sticky bodies pushing along beside her, the bold clash of colors and textures at every twist and turn. She'd welcomed and even relished the intrigue intrinsic to the grimiest of locations. Back then she would have been thrilled by the souk they'd just passed, with its hodge-podge of offerings, barely registering the level of filth, and wouldn't have turned up her nose at the population crowding the sidewalks.

But that time had long passed, and over the years she'd become inured to these local charms, becoming more intolerant each day. As her world perspective had changed, no longer a young woman soon to be married but a mother with children, no longer a new immigrant taking it all in but a seasoned one struggling to find both a personal and professional niche, she'd begun to prefer a different version of Israel: one far more sanitized and odor-free; one that effectively made this alternative, "genuine" version, unappealing.

Victoria had recently noted how she'd begun to shirk much of what had attracted her in the first place, purposefully stepping right back into any local version of the "West" she could find. An orderly cappuccino, whipped up in her Nespresso machine, had replaced those glasses of Turkish coffee known as *botz* (literally "mud"), flavored with cardamom, that had been an integral part of going "local" those first few years.

The occasional twinge of guilt over the attitude she'd developed was quashed by the fact that it was shared by many of her friends; there's always comfort in numbers. Back home in Caesarea she was surrounded by a community of expats that lived in absolute denial of their geographical location and carefully constructed for themselves some version of what they'd left behind. And of course Victoria was saved from feeling snobbish or superior by the growing number of native under-30s, actual Israeli-born individuals, that exhibited the very same attitude, clinging to local versions of the West and eschewing anything that smacked of former generations. At some point in the '90s the passion for all things American had begun to grow exponentially and now McDonald's hamburgers, Domino's pizza, Adidas sneakers and American sit-coms were considered mainstream, even within the Israeli population. The growing embrace of a cleaned-up, Americanized version of the Middle East was further proven by any visit to one of the newer department stores, with their polished surfaces, neatly organized displays, and an appreciable nod to the client – this latter bit the polar opposite of the storefronts along Hadera's main drag. This city, definitely a holdout, was a reminder of what Victoria had long ago forsaken as a bad fit.

With a great sigh of relief Victoria finally reached the end of the main street and pulled into the parking area closest to the building housing the Ministry office. This part of the city heaved most hours of the day, but the volume at this hour was at its peak. She squeezed her car in between the others vying for spots, nabbing one directly in front of a bakery specializing in *bourekas*. These delicious pastries, composed primarily of phyllo and butter, packed with evil fats and having absolutely no nutritional value whatsoever, were officially banned in their own. That, of course, didn't negate their appeal, and the heady smell of baking dough and grease that entered the car via the cooling vents made all their mouths water.

"Maybe we can stop at the bakery on our way home?" Maia piped up from the backseat, voicing what everyone else was thinking. Her children's attachment to popular street food was visceral and unfettered by cultural hang-ups. *Lucky for them.*

"We'll see," Victoria replied dismissively. She was exhausted by what had gone from a simple errand to a long trek and was desperate to finish up quickly. On top of the greasy *bourekas* she was already picking up the smell of spiced lamb coming from the shawarma stand and that of pure cooking oil from the falafel kiosk at the corner. Barely eight in the morning and this busy intersection was fired up and ready for customers, bombarding the locals with olfactory enticements. Victoria craved only the odor-free environment awaiting her back home.

She glanced in the rear-view mirror and discerned the glassy eyes of her children, gazing out at the multiple offerings. "No distractions! Run in and get in line. I'm sure there'll be tons of people there."

Jonathan gave her a sleepy "I can't be bothered" look, unfolded his long legs and lazily pulled himself out of the car.

"Come on," she urged, "you need to grab a good spot before they open." Maia was already outside, impatiently tapping on the hood of the car, waiting for her brother.

Victoria watched from inside the car as they made their way across the teeming street. She checked the car clock: 7:50 a.m. Astounding. Although siestas were fairly unheard of these days, yet another sign of the Western world needling its way into the dusty infrastructure of the Middle East, the early start had remained. It was simply an accepted part of life in the Levant – beating sun and all. Everyone and everything got moving at daybreak. Maia and Jonathan had groaned momentarily when she'd woken them – what teenagers wouldn't? –but they hadn't really protested getting up. And from the look of what she was witnessing right here, first hand, a sea of individuals streaming through this hectic traffic circle, the same could be said for the rest of the country.

Victoria was in no hurry to go inside. The kids would nab a place in line. She took a few calming sips of coffee from the thermos she'd prepared that morning, jammed it back into the drink dispenser and slowly hoisted herself out of the car with a sigh of resignation, ready to make her way through the bedlam to join them.

It was her very first visit to the Ministry office. She was going to register her first official residence, her local address, and she couldn't have been more excited. Setting out that morning, a mini-excursion to a place she had yet to discover, in this new country, Victoria hadn't thought for a moment about what she'd find. It wasn't even important. She knew this was going to be a special day, a wonderful day. *A registered home! Here in Israel!*

But things didn't go exactly as she'd expected, and by the end of the day she'd picked up one of the very first tales in what would grow to be a collection describing some of the more unnerving aspects of life in the Middle East. The building in which the office was housed had been something between a shock and a disappointment. It was located right off of the main street of Hadera, a city that looked nothing whatsoever like anything she'd ever come across back in the States; more like something out of a novel about the twisted back streets of Bombay by Mistry or Gosh. She'd reached it via a narrow alley, approaching tentatively as she left behind the comforting sea of traffic, unsure whether she was headed to the right place.

Dead-ending at a small, non-descript courtyard, she'd double-checked the scrap of paper on which she'd written the address, certain she'd made a mistake. The one-story building before her looked on the verge of collapse, its stucco veneer crumbling, cinderblocks exposed in a pattern that spoke of neglect. The ground around the entrance was covered with an assortment of trash, a wealth of cigarette butts and an occasional errant chicken. *Chickens?* She'd felt repulsed, her earlier excitement immediately dampened. She must have the wrong place, must have made a mistake. There was no way such a run-down building could be the site of such important business. She began to perspire, anxiety raised.

But the crowd by the doorway, so jammed that it was impossible to see inside, suggested that she had, indeed, come to the right place. Victoria wanted to turn around and run. What lay ahead obviously wasn't going to be pleasant and, worst of all, was going to take a lot of time. She'd never been good at waiting. She had no idea how to progress, how to cross the morass of bodies gathered immediately within range of the door jamb, pouring both inward and out, a heaving diaphragm of humanity. She crept forward timidly. The jumble of obstacles, men, women and children of all ages, buggies, pushcarts and bicycles, was daunting. A heady mixture of perspiring bodies, disorder and heat assaulted her senses. This gathering of Eastern Europeans, North Africans, Indians, Iraqis and Russians may have been her very first experience of the real melting pot that was Israel.

Where am I?

She stood on her toes to get a look into the office, blocked by this mass, and spotted her target: an old rickety number dispenser jammed in between the doorway and the window-lined exterior wall of the main hall. She exhaled a large breath of air in exasperation. The distance she needed to gulf to grab a coveted number seemed far beyond her reach. Something brushed her leg. A stray cat had successfully worked its way through the gathered throng and was on its way into the building. *She's got the right idea.* An errant thought crossed her mind. Maybe, if she closed her eyes and tapped her heels together three times, she could escape this nightmare, end up back home in Kansas. No. There was no easy solution.

Faced with a "do or die" situation, Victoria thrust herself straight into the knot of gathered bodies and snaked her hand toward the dispenser, somehow managing to grab one of the precious call numbers before being figuratively expelled by the crowd *into* the coveted room. It was a miracle. She'd made it. She'd reached the Promised Land.

Her relief and delight were momentary, soon to be replaced by a sense of desperation. The inside of the office exhibited the same squalor she'd found so discomfiting outside, and there was virtually no sign of governmental authority save the sad, ratty flag wedged behind the number dispenser. The atmosphere was stuffy and steamy to the point of suffocation, despite the fact that the large windows along the sidewall were thrust wide open and multiple ceiling fans worked at top speed, thwacking away at the stagnant air.

"May I?" She gestured toward an empty chair next to an older woman, mumbling her request in English. She wasn't sure what to speak since she didn't yet feel confident in Hebrew.

"*Lo panui.*" She didn't understand the response but the intent was clear. The heavyset woman sitting in the next chair picked up a satchel from the floor and swung it onto the empty one Victoria had had her eye on. A few more efforts and she gave up. Her energy for this whole pursuit had seriously waned. One gaze around the room made clear that gaining entry into this desired chamber had merely meant exchanging one form of chaos for another. The flurry of activity at each help desk, each swarmed by a group of people talking all at once, trying to be heard, indicated that her mission was far from over.

Victoria had been so excited as she'd set out that morning, registering her place of abode, her first real home in Israel! Getting on that plane, getting married, looking for a job – they were all big deals, but a home! A home was proof that she was here to stay, that she'd put down stakes. Today was meant to have been about being a part of something new, and instead, jammed in between this United Nations of peoples with whom she felt no affinity whatsoever and wanted nothing to do with, she'd come to realize that she didn't belong at all.

She'd known this wasn't going to be easy, that becoming an insider was going to take work, yet looking around that room she couldn't envision ever finding a place for herself. She'd been prepared for "different" and "foreign"; after all, this was the Middle East. But she hadn't been prepared for distasteful. And right there and then, at the Hadera Ministry of Interior, on the cusp of the new millennium, her fantasy about the alternative life she'd chosen began to disintegrate. She felt slightly sick, and for the first time since her arrival, she genuinely wondered why she had chosen to ditch First World, USA – wondered how she had ended up in a country where a government office resembled a back-alley barn house.

~~~

This place is so creepy.

Victoria awkwardly made her way up the non-functioning escalator, taking exaggeratedly large steps and grasping the stiff, unyielding handrail. The new Ministry office occupied the second floor of what looked very much like an abandoned mall. It bore a disturbing resemblance to one of those post-apocalyptic ones featured in the *Mad Max* movie she had watched years ago. The only illumination came from the natural light that flooded in from the skylight above, picking up gigantic clouds of dust hovering directly overhead. The air felt stale, noticeably not circulated. Most of the store spaces fronting onto this central space, dispersed between two levels, were empty; no wares displayed, no sign of what had been or what might be.

One of the few occupied ones sported a pile of random items: chairs, ladders, sheathes of fabric, large plastic fans and a few pairs of shoes. The general disorder and randomness of its display defied any understanding of specialty or focus, and accordingly, was not benefiting from the active commerce going on just outside. By the doorway, she'd passed a Domino's pizzeria. Ben and his friends sometimes stopped here for take-out on their way home, its intimation of Americana guaranteeing its continued popularity despite the undesirable location. At this early hour it was closed up tight.

Victoria spotted Jonathan and Maia seated along the concrete ledge of the escalator well, waiting for the Ministry office to open.

"How'd we do?"

"Number 7."

"Terrific. Good job guys."

She didn't have a chance to sit down. There was a sudden surge, and the crowd began to file through the security arch and into the office. Although there wasn't any pushing, there was a definite sense of urgency among those who'd taken care to arrive first thing. A few steps forward and they found themselves in a brightly lit, spacious, air-conditioned room, the complete opposite of what Victoria had expected on the heels of the eerie, forgotten aura of the mall outside. There was total calm. In fact, even the clamor of the waiting crowd had dissipated completely, replaced by a soothing occasional *bing* as the numbers on the electronic customer service board changed. They filed into one of the back rows in the hall and sat down to wait their turn.

Feisty and on edge since this morning, really since the previous night, Victoria was almost startled by the civility of the office. She'd been bound and determined to see everything local as black, disappointing and backwater this morning, had been ready for a fight, yet instead she found only order and calm. She was almost disappointed. She didn't want anything to lighten her rotten mood, set on stewing over the black hole in which she'd been abandoned.

She wiggled back in her chair, gently resting her head against the cool ceramic tiles of the back wall, and gazed up at the fluorescent lighting above. Her eyes closed and she began to drift off, lulled by the general hum of the cooling system. *This is good.* She'd recalled her earliest journey to the ministry on her way in this morning. This experience was quite different.

Suddenly she was startled by Maia's insistent voice, "Mom… *Mommy!*"

She must have nodded off for a few minutes. She banged her head as she opened her eyes to find Jonathan and Maia standing in front of her. "Come on, Mom." Their number had been called. She rubbed her eyes a second, trying to get her bearings. *Where am I?*

The vision before her was nothing like that first Ministry office. This room, full of well-dressed individuals seated quietly and waiting their turn, absent of sticky bodies, chickens, and smells, was quite First World.

Maia was insistent. "Mommy, come on. The woman's waiting for us!"

Things moved along smoothly from there: paper work was exchanged, signed, stamped and sent out for registration. Before they knew it, mission accomplished and they were on their way, negotiating the immobile escalator and heading into the sunlight. Soon enough their new passports would arrive in the mail. The whole process had been smooth as silk, so very unexpected.

But Victoria's delight and surprise were muddied by last night's revelation. This simple act of renewal, something she'd done before and would do again in ten years, took on new significance in light of Susan's announced departure. This official document, the one that enabled her to go back and forth between two lives, never forcing her to choose between them, was actually conveying her friend home. And although she'd never really considered the lives of her expat friends as being better or worse than her own, she was suddenly struck by the overwhelming, and unmistakable, sensation of envy.

As Jonathan rushed ahead (eager to pick up a few of those coveted *bourekas*), Victoria and Maia renegotiated the still-swarming traffic circle, each step forward cut off by either an individual hurrying through, the wheel of a bicycle, a cart full of produce or the occasional bumper of a car whose driver wasn't too interested in slowing for pedestrians. *So much for that glimmer of the*

First World; this town will forever be stuck in the Third. The disorder made her stomach churn. Victoria wanted out. She knew it was all a matter of finding the correct path through the muddle and determined, right there, to let nothing stop her. *I will find a way.*

Chapter 9

A group of people in black tights, brightly colored tops and glow-in-the-dark sneakers milled around the entrance to the parking lot. Everyone was moving: some jiggling around on the balls of their feet, some hugging in greeting and others gravitating to an invisible "start" line – each and every one, at the ready. It was pitch-black and the jittery movement of neon limbs resembled a pack of nervous fireflies. Victoria peeked at the clock on the dashboard as she pulled into a spot: 5:44 a.m. She turned off the engine and jumped out of the car; not a moment too late – the others were already off and running. No one wasted even one minute at this early hour.

"Morning." She leaned over to kiss her running buddy, Naomi, on the cheek in mid-stride.

"Good morning, darling!" Naomi greeted her in English.

There was nothing like a smiling face at the crack of dawn.

"How late did the wedding go?"

Naomi made a face. "Oh, you know how it goes." She switched to Hebrew. "The main course wasn't served until 11:00. Well after my normal bedtime! Good thing I filled up on the starters. We didn't get home until 2:00. I can't imagine what I was thinking, setting my alarm for 5:00."

"You must have wanted to see me!" Victoria smiled.

The two women matched their paces as they moved through the darkness of the local industrial park together, still a good thirty minutes from sunrise. Warming up with a friend was as much about comfort as fitness.

"Hey listen." Victoria turned toward Naomi. "I want to tell you something. I should wait but I can't. It's too exciting. I got a letter from Columbia University, from the School of Journalism. Remember? I sent them an inquiry way back? Well, you won't believe it." She took a deep breath and huffed out the rest. "I'm a candidate!"

Naomi hurled herself at Victoria mid-stride, wrapping her arm around her for a quick hug. "That's wonderful!!!" They hooked arms as they resumed their run.

"No. Wait! I didn't actually get the job. I'm a candidate. I'm one of many candidates. Let's save the celebration for later."

"Hey," Naomi pulled up to a sudden stop, causing Victoria to crash into her. "Are you leaving me?"

Victoria picked up a sad tone in her friend's question. She grabbed her arm and pulled them back to pace.

"Most definitely not. But...Naomi," she paused her words for a moment but realized she couldn't contain her excitement. "Wouldn't this be amazing? Wow, if only it could actually work out. It's exactly what I've always wanted."

"It's across the world."

"Yes. But..." She paused, hesitant to spill how desperate she'd become to find a way out, to figure out a way to get back home. "One step at a time."

"What does Guy say?"

"Well, actually, I haven't told him."

"What?" Naomi interjected.

Victoria continued, "There's simply so much to explore before it even comes close to being a reality. What's the point in rocking the boat early?"

"Sounds right." The two sunk into a brief silence, the only sound the pounding of their feet on the pavement. "And Ben? It's one thing to leave two back in school but…"

They ran for a stretch. Victoria could feel her heart begin to accelerate despite the slow pace. This question was much harder. "His service will end. At some point we're all going to move on."

More silence. Victoria felt Naomi pat her on the back lightly. "So, tell me. What's the next step?"

"Well," Victoria struggled to return to her excitement, to leave her hesitation behind. She took a big breath and continued, "First step: I've got to prove myself. I need to prepare two feature articles indicative of the material I'd be teaching, something capitalizing on the expat angle. I've already chosen the subject of the first. I was thinking of something along the lines of High Tech Nation and Triathlon." She chuckled as she took in Naomi's responsive smile and continued, "Perfect. Right? And all I have to do is base it, start to finish, on what goes on here, in the dark, several mornings a week."

Her friend positively glowed. "You'll certainly have no problem collecting raw data."

The road curved uphill and they stopped speaking for a moment, focusing on the shift in incline. Once it leveled off they picked up where they'd left off, Victoria laying her hand on Naomi's arm to slow her a bit so they could continue speaking.

"So I was thinking about focusing on the creative energy it takes to be in high tech and relating that to the consequential need to channel some of the overflow elsewhere, say, to endurance sports.

I would touch on the kind of personalities that seek out extreme challenges that test limits, whether technological or physical; the fascination with relevant technological innovation in both industries, algorithms and engineering in one, bicycle geometrics and power monitors in the other.

"Then I would bring in the economic side: those who have, spend. Success affords the ability to equip, at any cost. Of course all of this is done with one eye focused on what's happening in North America. Where does everyone look for the most cutting-edge equipment? There's that whole American envy aspect among the local high-tech population." Victoria paused, now breathless. She let out a long exhalation, catching her breath in order to finish. "What do you say? You think I could milk 5,000 words out of this subject?"

"Definitely. I'll help. It'll be fun."

They headed into their second lap of the park. "You know, when I first made aliyah I was afraid to run outside. No one was running outside. I was frantic to stay in shape, part of being American I guess. I used to run back and forth in my tiny apartment and walk up and down the stairwell in order to keep my secret. I even did jumping jacks on the carpet so as not to disturb the neighbors. I really missed the Stepper back at the New York Health Club. Looking back now, it all seems rather pathetic."

They turned the corner and headed up the hill again, pausing before continuing their conversation.

"You and your preconceptions. Why do Americans think they invented the wheel? We used to run through the fields and meadows behind the kibbutz. I have a degree in Phys Ed. The fact that you didn't see people exercising doesn't mean they weren't."

Victoria laughed. "You are so right! We've definitely been raised to believe we're the best – the greatest! And really, I mean, aren't we?" They both laughed. "But honestly, Naomi, I never spotted anyone wearing exercise duds, not once, never heard anyone mention working out, and the local pace seemed to be something between a crawl and a ramble.

"I figured it was a Middle Eastern thing, the inner wiring on this side of the world simply different, tuned to ramble rather than sprint. It was so counter to everything I knew, you know, from living in the City. There was an unstated primer you needed to follow simply to get along: don't stop at an intersection, cross at 'green' no matter your intended direction; step off the corners and walk in the street if pressed for time; jaywalk if need be. People here seemed to drag themselves from place to place. I couldn't relate."

They headed down the other side of the park. This was the easy part, a nice downhill to compensate for the effort expended on the uphill side.

"Was it summertime?"

"Yes, and blistering hot."

"Well, that explains it. The real athletes were probably out long before you hit the streets, carefully avoiding the sunny hours of the day." She paused. "But Vic, wait a sec. Did you actually think you were the only person that donned sneakers? That's crazy."

"It crossed my mind. But I figured they'd found other pursuits. There seemed to be an awful lot of people hiking. Those big bulky boots were everywhere." They approached the end of the second lap. "Oh, come to think of it, there were certain occasions when I saw people shuffling along rather quickly! But they weren't actually going jogging, just hurrying to cross to the shady side of the street. Ha! That was one of those important lessons I learned right upon my arrival, 'At all costs, don't stand in the sun!'"

Naomi laughed. "Yes, well, that's simply a given. It explains why we're out here running around in the dark! But seriously,

Vicki. If you're going to write this article you're going to have to release a bit of that American attitude; you know, the 'we invented the wheel' business. It's tiresome and incorrect. Exactly how long has America been around?"

Naomi straightened herself to full height and smiled, obviously proud of those Mesopotamian roots. Victoria laughed in response. She was used to locals reminding her that America was a nation in diapers compared with the ancient land of Israel.

"You have to view modern Israeli fitness in decades, not centuries. It's a really short story but moves along in leaps and bounds. You start with the first generation: those pioneers who worked so hard to cultivate oranges, clear swamps and establish livable communities. They didn't have a lot of time left to put on athletic shoes and go out for a run. Jump forward another generation and things were far more settled. Despite waging several wars of survival, Israelis entered a more stable period and at the end of the day people finally had a bit of energy left to channel toward leisure time. The interest in fitness was demonstrated officially in Olympic participation but also in local club sports, say basketball, soccer, *machanaim*...even *matkot* on the beach."

Victoria sighed. "I see where you're going. Fast forward one more generation: decreased focus on the country's infrastructure, increased activity in the international communications market, resulting in an upsurge of exposure to world trends through international travel. Presto: Hi-Tech Nation! Plenty of leisure time and enough money to sustain real fitness centers, sport clubs and a hefty investment in top-of-the-line equipment."

Naomi nodded as they approached the last lap of warm-up, now well behind the rest of the group. "It's nice to serve a purpose."

"So, how about this: Takes Crazy to Make Crazy: Triathlon and Hi-Tech."

Naomi laughed. "That would work. But let's see, hmmm: Inspiration, Momentum and Creativity: The High-Tech Industry and Extreme Sports in Israel."

"Too serious! I've got it: The New Israel: Giving Silicon Valley a Run for Their Money – or, alternatively, Just a Run."

"Cute. Maybe: Pushing the Limits – Virtually and Physically."

"Or something racy like: Extreme Sports and Innovation: Natural Bedfellows."

"This is fun!" Naomi chuckled. "It's making all this huffing and puffing that much easier!"

As if on cue, there was a strong surge behind them, a sucking swoosh similar to the one made by a vacuum cleaner, and a group of young men passed them on the right with arms raised in salute. They caught snippets of their conversation as they sped by.

"I can't believe I got a slot."

"Next summer, Frankfurt, boys!"

"There's no going back now."

There was a bit of hooting and an exchange of high fives, completely cliché.

"I can't imagine what Miki will say."

"The expense…"

"The hours…"

"Base your feature on *them*," Naomi said conspiratorially, nodding her head toward the backs of the disappearing Ironmen-to-be. "They're perfect fodder."

They both laughed.

"The only thing, Naomi. My audience back in the States wants to hear about Israel. I'm worried that this story isn't going to sound very 'Eretz Yisrael'! I think they expect something more charming, something more in line with Shoresh sandals – biblical is considered genuine."

"Ah. I see, a little less Southern California." She smiled.

Southern California. Victoria's mind automatically shifted elsewhere. *Strange. Doesn't fit with what I found in Hadera yesterday, but here on this track, it's spot on.*

The two sunk into silence as they approached the end of the warm-up. Although officially winding down in preparation to stop and stretch out, her heart began to race. The potential held by the words she'd found in her inbox earlier that morning had her more winded than the exercise.

Things had begun no differently than usual: the 5:00 alarm, the furry paws on the edge of the bed, the shocking chill of the marble floor and the inky black silence of the house. Victoria had adopted an early-morning regime years ago after joining the local triathlon club. At first it had been nothing less than a nightmare. Why would anyone get up in the dark? And there were those mornings, in the dead of winter, when the weather was unusually cold or stormy, that she wanted nothing more than to stay curled up in bed, toes tucked into the hem of her pajama bottoms, back pressed against Guy's warm body. Responding to her own hesitation, her dog Bama would refuse to go out, standing by the open terrace door and looking up at her with beseeching eyes – questioning the need for either one of them to face the elements. She was an intelligent creature; the darkness and cold really weren't all that inviting.

Yet over the years, the early morning workout had become an excuse. These wake-up calls were a blessing, affording her a few minutes of coveted quiet, time to gather her thoughts, assess her day. With Bama already curled up with Jonathan in his bed, back asleep, she would seat herself in front of the computer, warm cup of coffee gripped tightly in hand, a welcome film of aromatic steam coating her face.

This was the time Victoria felt most in control. With everyone she loved safely tucked where they needed to be, the darkness promised complete protection. She didn't need to worry about Ben because somewhere, elsewhere, he was no doubt sleeping. Even soldiers had to sleep. Until the sun shone she didn't have to consider what he might get into, what unknown dangers lurked. At least this is what she told herself. Victoria wished she could bottle this early-morning calm so that she could take a sip, here and there throughout the day, whenever the need arose. Anything, anything at all, to take the edge off and attain the serenity of those moments, tucked into this pocket of her own design.

The last few weeks of mornings hadn't been quite as dependably comforting, compromised by a storm of tormented thoughts. There was Omer, still up in Haifa. She didn't know his precise condition, only that he wasn't home yet and almost a month had passed since the incident. And Ben. Each morning she wondered what he faced, whether this day would be the one she'd get a call; or alternatively, wouldn't, because most days for him, during this training period, truly were like any other: no eventualities, only stories to be shared come the weekend.

On top of all this there was that bombshell Susan had dropped. Since her announcement, Victoria had found herself trying to cope with the frustrations in her own local life, now magnified out of proportion. Her friend's planned egress had prompted an avalanche of thoughts, an assessment of the angles that would need to be considered in order to execute her own return. There was so much work to be done if she wanted to steer this boat in a new direction. She hadn't stopped to deal with the nagging thought that maybe she was overreacting, trying to redirect her energy in an attempt to suppress her concern for Ben.

This particular morning had begun like any other, but then, almost immediately, spun in an entirely different direction. She'd been sipping that daily cup of coffee and casually scanning through her email when she'd spotted the message from Columbia. She'd stared at the return address in the inbox almost a full minute before opening it, feeling the stars align, the path ahead suddenly clear. After skimming through the mail she went back and hovered over each word, growing ever more excited. She'd wished for something just like this to happen, and now, it just might. The window of opportunity was open and the rest was up to her.

Victoria and Naomi lined up under a row of cypress trees alongside the rest of the group, already bent over in a hamstring stretch, one leg extended forward on the curb. Victoria felt simultaneously energized and exhausted, ready for the interval training sets to come but equally eager to get back to her computer and begin pumping out the project that would set her plan into action.

"Nice sneakers. New?"

Her thoughts were interrupted by the male voice behind her.

She turned her head to meet his gaze. "I love my Asics."

"You probably buy them in the States."

"Guilty."

"Any chance you can bring me a pair next time you go?"

She smiled. *How perfect! More material for my article.* This was going to be a no-brainer. She'd quickly pitch those figurative Shoresh sandals, and any remaining impression that fitness in the Middle East was restricted to riding camels and desert hikes. Instead she'd emphasize how the drive among Israelis to push boundaries, to innovate and to excel, led to the overwhelming popularity of extreme sports and the obsession for the hottest equipment America could offer. There's no question she herself had benefited from this phenomenon by association, being a living example of "Made in the USA." How ironic that the mania for fitness that had distinguished her from her Israeli peers at the time of her aliyah now, decades later, wed her to them.

Victoria stood up straight, shifted her weight onto one leg and pulled the other one up behind her, one in a row of stork look-alikes executing that final quad stretch. The fun was behind them; they were here to work. Twenty eager faces listened attentively as the coach described the scheduled intervals. Victoria looked around her, appreciating the company. Finding similar bedfellows in Israel, people whose drives paralleled her own, hadn't been simple; in fact, it had taken decades. They'd made the difficult task of negotiating the "foreign" that much easier and were, no doubt, primarily responsible for a large degree of her integration.

Integration? Her brow furrowed a bit as she realized that here, at least within one area of her life, she had in fact integrated, perhaps without even knowing it. She sighed heavily, attracting the attention of her friends. "It's going to be a tough one. Right? Five sets, four minutes each, Zone 5."

The others thought she was reacting to the difficult workout ahead and one guy patted her on the back. Her mind clouded a bit. Dumping what she'd established, what she had in hand, what she'd worked so hard and long to achieve: a life, a real life, here in Israel; dumping all that and starting over again back in the States – wasn't going to be all that simple. There were good things right here that she'd no doubt miss, things she wasn't that eager to let go when she really thought about it.

She tried to shake off this uncomfortable realization but couldn't get rid of it. Maybe this was ridiculous. Maybe this whole plan was ludicrous and poorly considered. There were simply too many hurdles to cross, not the least of which one she hadn't begun to even broach: working it out with the people she loved most: Guy, Jonathan and Maia, Ben. Thinking about the whole picture made her head ache.

A flurry of activity, people removing warm-up shirts, activating their watches, taking one last sip of water drew Victoria's attention to the moment. She braced herself. With so many difficulties ahead she'd best gather her strength, hang on tight and be prepared to take them on, one by one. No wars were won without losses. She wondered what price this one would exact.

Chapter 10

No way! Jackie stepped out into the humid morning, laundry basket clenched in hand. *I'm not going to that meeting tonight.* She pulled out a few random socks, grabbed at the pile of clothespins and aggressively started to hang them up.

She hadn't missed one school event back in Jo'burg, whether a breakfast, a talent show or an all-school fair. She'd chaperoned numerous class trips, eager to be an active participant in her children's lives. But here things were different. Here she decisively shunned most events and today's, a lecture to the twelfth-grade parents about army duty, would be no different.

She moved down the line, occasionally looking up at the dramatic view of the Carmel Mountains to the east, and paused, reaching one arm across her body to adjust the strap of her tank top. She loved being able to jump right into a pair of shorts and a tank each morning. Mid-May and there was no need for a sweater of any kind. Perfect weather most of the year.

The early-morning sun glinted along the edges of the range, highlighting its nooks and crannies, a mottled mosaic of blue, purple and brown. Nature right here at her doorstep. *What a ridiculously spectacular backdrop for such an inane activity.* Back in Johannesburg she could never have imagined hanging laundry year-round! The environment didn't allow for that nature's-own, air-freshened smell she adored.

This wasn't such a bad way to start the day. She looked down the clothesline, admiring the neatly hung items: school uniforms, random T-shirts and athletic dry-fit gear – a perfect encapsulation of her family's life. She considered running in to get her phone; this would make a perfect family portrait. Not one sign of the zipped up life they'd led in South Africa, one hundred percent casual. She smiled. That was a nice thought; it almost pushed out the other. Almost.

She shook her head fiercely as she finished up. *What a bummer!* She teemed with frustration the spectacular scenery couldn't mollify. She *wanted* to attend this evening's event. She knew she *should* attend. She knew that although her children didn't seem to mind when she consistently bailed, they probably did. She tried to convince herself, again, that she'd attended enough of these events in the past to cover a lifetime, stockpiled enough credits to get through today's. But she still felt deeply disappointed, in both herself and the situation.

Since moving to Israel a few years earlier Jackie had struggled to learn Hebrew. She was neither unintelligent nor incapable, but it was something that simply hadn't worked out. The main culprit had been her work. As a teacher at the local American School she wasn't required to speak or understand Hebrew. Making matters worse, most people she came into contact with outside of work, whether doctors, teachers at her kids' school, supermarket checkers or neighbors, switched to English the second she started to stutter out a sentence in Hebrew, derailing each and every attempt to actually use the language. While making a bona fide effort to communicate in the local tongue, she'd usually only manage to eke out a syllable or two before they'd cut her off with an assured "English is fine," followed by a litany of reasons for this accommodation: "It's no problem to speak English. My aunt is American"; "Please speak English with me. It's good practice"; "I lived in California for five years. It's okay, let's speak in English."

Three months after making aliyah she'd dropped out of the intense Hebrew education program, known as *ulpan*, where she'd been studying. *What was the point?* If she wasn't going to use the language there was no reason to bother investing the hours to learn it. She was finished. Hebrew simply wasn't happening. Her struggle to communicate in the native tongue had gone the way of all flesh. And now, five years later, she'd pretty much forgotten everything she'd managed to learn, her knowledge regressing to a word or two, thrown in for good measure, at the market. *No matter!* In any case all of her local besties, of which she had more than a few, were all from English-speaking countries.

So no, she wasn't going to attend that meeting tonight. It wasn't that big of a deal. She could always depend on Vicki for the recap. *She* went to everything. Jackie pulled her lips together into a flat line, desperately trying to convince herself that it didn't irk her that she depended on others, that this decision was acceptable. It didn't work; she didn't buy her own story. She felt deflated. She cast a glance down the line where the bed sheets were now hung and flapping in the wind, over to the empty basket, and then headed back into the kitchen. She needed to concentrate on mothering *within* the house. That was an area in which she excelled.

Inside the kitchen the lunch rolls were lined up on the counter like obedient soldiers, ready to be sliced and made into sandwiches, a sign of her competence. At least here, in this insular world, she ruled the roost. Standing ready with the knife, she caught a ribbon of bright colors moving off to her left side and turned to catch her daughter running through.

"Mommy, I don't want a tuna sandwich today. Please, can I have a chocolate one like everyone else?"

"Absolutely not!" Jackie pried open a can of tuna and drained it over the sink. "You know I don't buy into this 'chocolate is nutritional' business. I'll prepare one with cheese and one with tuna. I'm sure they'll suffice. You won't miss the chocolate at all."

Ten-year-old Noa pulled a face and swept out of the room with a loud "*Oof.*" Jackie nodded her head assuredly. That one she understood: the local expression for frustration.

"No, siree," Jackie mumbled, wrapping the sandwiches in paper. She adamantly refused to become one of *those* parents. Just because she lived in Israel didn't mean she had to adopt all of their insane habits. She'd never get used to even the *idea* of chocolate sandwiches, let alone participate. She remembered the kindergarten teacher who'd actually begged her to relent. She'd claimed Noa was staring at all of the other kids' food in a creepy way and arranging complicated swaps, sometimes including costly Playmobil figures.

Her son emerged from the powder room by the front door. "Did you sign the permission slip for the class trip?" He rubbed his eyes, pulled a bowl out of the cupboard and began to fill it with cereal.

"I have it right here, but I haven't signed yet." She slid it over the counter towards his bowl. "Is this the right spot? Here on the bottom, to the right?" At his assent she scribbled her name on the relevant line and returned to wrapping sandwiches. "Is there anything else I should know about the trip? I really couldn't be bothered to read all that." She gestured in the direction of the abandoned paper with its lengthy description of the class trip in Hebrew before heading over to the line of book bags by the front door, all ready to be loaded. "Incidentally," she added, as if an afterthought, "where are you going?"

Pathetic. She didn't even know the destination of her son's class trip. That was usually a given. *What kind of parent am I?* Sometimes this life, the one she'd entered kicking and screaming, really was unbearable. She was so uninvolved, so uninformed, so *not* a part of her kids' lives. Back in South Africa she'd been super mommy, so in-the-know. With a loud sigh she pulled the zippers on the bags shut and turned back toward the kitchen. This language issue had no doubt closed the door on any chance of complete integration. But how much time could she spend regretting? It was a done deal.

There was a tap at the door. She stepped to it quickly and opened up to a man in work clothes. He immediately began speaking, rattling off what she assumed was his purpose in disturbing her at such an early hour. She caught a word or two but, missing most of what he was trying to communicate, remained unresponsive. He gestured toward the driveway and continued to explain himself in Hebrew. "Sweetie," she called behind her, "can you come help me here?" Adam hopped off his stool, abandoning his cereal, and sidled over to the door. He was obviously used to the role of "go-between."

Jackie watched as the two exchanged words, amazed at the mellifluous sounds coming out of her son's mouth. He was so lucky.

"Your car is blocking access to the service path. This guy needs you to move it." The man nodded his head in assent at the translation, polite and apologetic. She continued to stare at the two of them, entranced by the words she couldn't follow, jealous of Adam's fluency.

"Mom! Move your car!"

With that, he returned to his cereal. Jackie was left standing at the door with the workman whose face now wore the kind of understanding smile one bestows on a small child dealing with some minor frustration. She felt completely humiliated. Ditched to fend for herself, she put up her finger in the universal gesture indicating "wait one minute" and went to look for her keys.

A minute later she trundled out of the house, head lowered, horrified by the situation and feeling gloomier by the second. There was no end to the help she needed in negotiating this life, the life Rob had insisted on. After moving the car out of the way and hustling the kids out of the house to school she began organizing herself for the workday. At least this was something she could handle on her own. She cheered up considerably and even managed a smile. She loved her job, absolutely loved it. She'd been so fortunate to find a niche that suited her and a pursuit that made her happy. Teaching at the American School was a dream, even if it meant a class of twenty-five adolescents. She crossed back through the living room to take a quick peek to see that everything was closed up and glanced outside once more at those ever-comforting cliffs. Maybe things weren't so bleak. When she got over the language issue, life was very much like it would have been back in Jo'burg, her cup fairly full. In any case it was a waste to continue to harp on what was missing, what might have been otherwise, how things might be different if she could only communicate. Maybe it wasn't all that important to the bigger picture.

She glanced into Adam's room. The sheets and blanket were pulled half off the bed, clothing abandoned where it'd been shed, shoes left hither and yon. She wondered how he was going to adapt to the order demanded by the military. She shook her head. He would, no question, be a hard case. She smiled to herself as she closed the door behind her. Maybe there was an upside to this army thing she hadn't yet considered. Wouldn't he necessarily have to become a bit more organized? There might eventually be hope for this room! For just that moment, she refused to acknowledge the reality of what military life was all about, forbidding it to cloud her amusement.

Packing up her bag she thought about the kisses and hugs she'd received as the kids filed out of the house. She must be doing something right. Maybe it was enough to merely be a loving, supportive mom – enabling her children to entertain their friends, putting meals on the table, taking them wherever they needed to go and providing what she considered a happy atmosphere in the house. Maybe it didn't matter that she couldn't converse with their teachers, understand what they studied in school or attend those "mandatory" lectures regarding safe driving, alcohol usage and what to expect from the army.

A few years ago she had sworn to do better, learn to understand what was said and find a way to better convey her own sentiments. But over time she'd realized she wasn't making any significant inroads and she'd given up, hands held high, white flag waving. Late last night she'd told Adam she wouldn't be attending tonight's lecture. He'd said he didn't care but she swore his expression had flagged a bit; although resigned to her decision, its ramifications were clear to both of them.

She stepped out of the house, locked the door behind her and headed to the car, trying to shake off the disappointment in her parental performance. *Maybe there's still time.* Despite what seemed like a conspiracy, an effort by all those around her to keep her from speaking Hebrew, perhaps she should grit her teeth and give it another chance. After all, this might very well be the one piece of the puzzle needed to realize her dream. They had a pretty amazing life here save this one, itty-bitty hitch. If she could finally chip away at that language barrier maybe she'd have a shot at the pot of gold at the end of the rainbow.

Tonight offered yet one more opportunity to make this right. She would show up at that meeting at school even if it meant sitting in a fog for the evening. Adam would no doubt be delighted. And her friends? They'd be shocked, counting on her to pass. She smiled as she drove, that thought alone improving her mood greatly. This was going to be a good day.

Victoria walked quickly up the path toward the high school. Dusk had set in and the only light came from a few lampposts topped by spaceship-shaped glass globes. Kibbutz Ma'agan Michael was quiet at this hour, the paths stretching from one building to the next, the unspoken network of communication, empty. Although the high school building itself, with its chipped paint, crumbling concrete and that overall feeling of dilapidation, should have discouraged her, she'd always found it comforting. The general atmosphere of acceptance, community and inclusion embodied within the structures that made up the school, the complete lack of pretense, seemed right, even educational.

She pulled open the glass door and started through the rabbit warren of the main building, trying to find the exit leading to the twelfth graders' classrooms. She knew it was at the end of one of these long, twisting hallways but could never remember which. She glanced at the walls as she made her way farther into the depths. One featured images of safe driving tips, one a row of photographs documenting a robotics' competition and one a series of posters suggesting ways to develop a more environmentally friendly lifestyle. Each added a bit of color to what was otherwise an overall sickly green color scheme made all the more nauseating by fluorescent lighting. At the end of the hallway she found herself in an octagonal space, a cul-de-sac of about six classrooms. It looked like something out of *Alice in Wonderland*: many doors to choose from – what lurked behind each, both mysterious and frightening. She recognized it from one of those parent-teacher meetings and realized she'd taken a wrong turn; this was the wing for the eleventh grade.

She let out a long sigh of exasperation and retraced her steps back to the last fork in the road. No matter how many years she spent roaming through this squat concrete building, she could never truly figure it out. She spotted another long hallway heading off in the opposite direction and decided to give it a chance. A patch of light up ahead held promise. At this point it would be a relief to simply find the way out of this labyrinth.

Walking down this alternative hall her thoughts segued to Ben and that first time he'd taken a suburban train alone in Philadelphia. She'd been nervous about letting him go on his own, but he'd insisted. She'd instructed him to head straight to the closest exit the minute he alit. Negotiating underground tunnels and hallways could be complicated and confusing; once on street level orientation was a lot easier – buildings, street names and other landmarks helped pull everything into place.

Ben. Now he could navigate his way through difficult terrain without the help of such obvious landmarks. *Ben.* They'd spent the previous weekend trying to remove the briars he'd picked up from that last exercise in the Carmel mountain range. No amount of soaking in hot water had helped dislodge all those stuck under the taut skin of his forearms. Some remained resistant. *What girl will agree to take my bumpy-armed child?* Victoria smiled to herself and shook her head clear. She didn't want to think too much about Ben at that moment, to begin to wonder where he was, what he was doing, whether he might be in danger from one threat or another. She was eager for the distraction of this evening's lecture.

And there it was: the long-coveted exit door. She gave it a push and stepped into the courtyard of broken-up tile and pebbles, trying to make up a bit of lost time with loping steps. The twelfth grade building was dead ahead, isolated from the rest of the high school. Although hard-pressed to give credit to the local school system, forever comparing it unfavorably with the American one she'd benefited from back in the States, Victoria had to admit this one idea very clever. Beyond the obvious benefits to the kids themselves, allowing them to bask in that "king of the mountain" mentality inherent to the last year of school, it served the needs of the faculty, reducing their stress by clearly separating the wheat from the chafe, those still in the game from those with one foot out the door.

At the entrance she came to an abrupt stop and peered inside. She smiled. Almost every school building in the area was equipped with some kind of amphitheater, either indoors or out – capitalizing on the ancient symbolism of the well-known Roman theaters throughout the Middle East, and, most germane, the one right there in Caesarea. Ancient was something to be proud of around here.

Light poured out from the space inside, and she could see the back of other parents' heads, already seated, attentively listening to the speaker. She was later than she'd thought. She ducked a bit, hoping no one would discern her tardy arrival, and quietly opened the side door. Nearly no one looked her way; all attention was focused on the man standing behind the lectern, there to illuminate the mysteries of life in the army. Victoria quickly assessed the audience. Although she knew a good portion of those in attendance, she'd never met them in quite this context – bracing themselves for their child's leap into the unknown. There was a bit of déjà vu from a similar lecture she'd attended for Ben. Same combination of those clueless about how any of this worked and stultified by what lay ahead, easily identified by their tentative body language (teetering on the edge of their chairs) and their obvious close attention to what was being said, and those better versed on the subject at hand, perhaps through their own experience or that of an older child, for the most part slouching comfortably in their folding chairs and looking considerably less apprehensive, even somewhat bored.

"Psssst." Victoria looked sharply to the right, to the back row of the hall. Jackie was gesturing wildly to an empty chair directly in front of her. Victoria couldn't believe it. Her friend had insisted she wouldn't attend, yet here she was. She hesitated to move, afraid of drawing even more attention to herself than Jackie's waving hands had already. She decided to go for it, sliding in sideways, clumsily bumping into the bent knees crammed between the crowded rows of folding chairs. *Always better to just rip off the band-aid.*

She settled herself into a squeaky chair in front of Jackie and leaned slightly backwards, almost tipping into her friend's lap. "What did I miss?"

"I have no idea," she answered with a nervous giggle, "but it can't be much. He just began."

The speaker at the front of the hall, dressed casually in polo shirt and jeans, stepped out from behind the lectern and began to stroll across the room, from one side to another. He obviously wanted to engage his audience. One look around convinced Victoria he needn't have tried so hard; the place was packed, and he had the parents' rapt attention. No one wanted to miss a word. Anyone offering pearls of wisdom regarding the army experience had an easy audience with parents of teenagers on the brink.

This evening's presentation, one in a series, concerned the overall absorption of eighteen-year-olds into a system meant to de-individualize teenagers precisely at the stage when they're becoming individuals, a real conundrum. The speaker's aim was to explain how parents could help ease what could, potentially, be a very rocky road. Behind him was a large screen featuring two images set up as a "compare and contrast." On the left was a slovenly, sloppily clad, long-haired, slouching teenage boy, and on the right, a young man standing ram-rod straight dressed in a standard green uniform and sporting a crew cut.

Victoria discerned a distinct feeling of unrest among the audience. Legs shuffled, throats were cleared and a few hands were raised.

"Doesn't this have a lot to do with how we've raised our children?"

"Isn't this a matter of whether or not they're adaptable to change?"

Murmured exclamations of agreement and support were heard here and there throughout the hall. Despite enormous differences in backgrounds, the parents were united. There was an overall "We can do this!" attitude throughout the room.

But then came the whiny moans from that regular handful of stressed out mothers. "How will I be able to deal with this?"

"Why is this happening to me?"

"Not my little boy."

These were mostly met with angry glares. Victoria joined in; this wasn't the time to be wimpy. The way these mothers vocally expressed their fears annoyed her. The concept of automatic conscription was a hard enough concept to grasp for those who hadn't been born into it; the raw fear of the peanut gallery didn't help.

Of course it wasn't that she didn't understand their anxiety. She knew how they felt. Omer had come home last week, miraculously saved, but he had a long road of recovery ahead of him, and head injuries carried the heavy possibility of future complications. There was no denying that this was terrifying business. Since the very first day Ben had entered the service she hadn't been able to fully relax, feeling jumpy and unsettled throughout each and every day, even if she knew deep down that he was just fine. With Jonathan set to join soon, she wasn't sure how she'd ever get any sleep. But surviving this experience, one thousand days for each, was about letting go, assuming that her children would be fine and never giving into hysterical fear. Wasn't that the goal of parenting? Wouldn't it have been the same anywhere – even if she'd stayed in the States? Anticipating the worst was never a good choice; from that stance there was no point of return.

The speaker continued on despite the comments, now suggesting ways parents could support their children through this transition. Projected on the screen was an image of a large fuzzy teddy bear sucking on a pacifier and clutching a blanket decorated with sailboats. Victoria was baffled, amazed that a psychologist would choose such an infantile slide to illustrate such a serious subject. She looked around the room for reactions. No one else seemed perturbed. This was such an unsophisticated audience. A fleeting vision of a bunch of hapless sheep popped into her head unsolicited.

The slide changed. This time it was a picture of two large penguins clustered around a baby penguin in the snowy Arctic, making a stab at the closest thing to an embrace their flippers allowed. The lecturer was smoothly moving from one subject to another. Having started with the subject of parental support, the difficulty of leaving the warmth of home and becoming one in a large unit, he now focused on the cold, brutal world of the military – hence, the appropriately illustrated frozen environs. The audience was silent. The cuddly teddy had been easier to handle. If the lecturer had intended to completely paralyze this crowd, he'd succeeded. The harsh reality of what he was suggesting was inconceivable to most seated in the amphitheater. Those who'd been holding it together with a stiff upper lip before this moment began to unravel, reduced to a group of horror-stricken, whimpering mommies and daddies.

There was a lull, an extended silence wherein everyone seemed to be holding his or her breath. And then:

"Lord Help me."

"Give me strength."

Signs that everyone was a bit more worked up, a good amount of shuffling, chairs, legs and bags rattling, were followed by a wave of consoling comments.

"They deal better than you'd expect."

"It's not that dramatic a change."

Those with older children already in service attempted to alleviate the fears generated by the provocative slides. Victoria casually leaned back again and tilted her head to the right, curious to catch the expression on Jackie's face. Albeit all in Hebrew, she was certain her friend had caught some of the comments being issued throughout the room, at minimum the intonation. Language of concern, bordering on hysteria, was universal. Although they swapped stories most days, Victoria had tried to keep the news about Omer out of their conversations. His injury had sent her completely into a tailspin; she couldn't imagine how Jackie would react.

It wasn't easy for either one of them, hailing from a country where conscription was usually reserved for those from an entirely different background, the polar opposite of here in Israel. Although she didn't hold the monopoly on conquering fears, Victoria did have some experience at tucking them out of the way enough to find a safe space in which to survive those thousand days. She tapped on Jackie's knee to get her attention, or rather, distract her – most certainly to pull her back from that precarious edge.

"Hey."

She gestured with her head at the crowd around them and rolled her eyes in an exaggerated expression.

"Aren't these kids supposed to grow up at some point, encounter a few challenges and leave the nest?" She continued in a whisper, "Where's the slide with the parents reclining on an exotic beach in Thailand wearing skimpy bathing suits and drinking rum?" Jackie's sharp peel of laughter, which she muffled quickly with her hand, revealed a mixture of concern and relief. She was obviously keen to be saved from the worrisome thoughts prompted by the tone of the lecture and the mood of the worked-up parents.

A wave of movement, some parents standing up, some turning to speak to their neighbors and many already shuffling toward the door, provided much needed levity. The lecture was over and it was time to move on to the individual homerooms to meet with the teachers. The feeling of heaviness that had overtaken the room began to dissipate. A cacophony, the running commentary on what had transpired, rose from the crowd.

Jackie and Victoria wound their way between the chairs toward the exit.

"He made me nervous."

Victoria paused and reached out to grab her hand, pulling them both to a stop. She hesitated before she spoke, debating whether her reply should be serious, sarcastic or humorous. Jackie was sensitive; she didn't want to feed her concerns. Light and breezy was best. At least it would allow her another night's sleep.

"Really? I found his comments a bit lame. I mean, going on and on about the difficulty of adapting to wearing army greens 24/7. How difficult could that possibly be? Remember when they imposed a school uniform at the elementary school? Remember that? Everyone was in a panic, worried that it would suppress their kids' individuality. Two weeks later the whole subject was pretty much forgotten, the consensus pure delight. It saved so much time getting everyone organized and out the door in the morning, and everyone appreciated the reduced expenditure on clothing." She paused and then added, "Freedom of expression is so overrated."

Jackie laughed and visibly seemed to relax, and the two continued up the back stairs of the hall toward the boys' homeroom class. "You're only calm because you've done this before. For the rest of us newbies this is really stressful."

"I don't know. I'm not sure how far 'experience' really gets me when it comes to army service. Every day seems to bring something new. There aren't a lot of constants. Why do you think I bothered showing up tonight?"

Since Ben's first day in service there'd been one surprise after another. For starters, she never knew exactly when he'd be home, although it was a lot more frequently than she'd anticipated. She'd merely assumed, once inducted, that his return visits would be few and far between, that he'd be away for long stretches of time like her friends' children back in the States who'd gone off to college. Instead, he seemed to show up every two or three weeks, reentering their lives with a splash – a mixture of exhaustion and exuberance – the contents of his duffel instantly covering every square inch of floor space in his room, the laundry piled high.

There was a running local joke that military duty was actually a three-year stint of laundry duty in disguise, something parents hadn't known they were signing up for. Her regime during those precious forty-eight hours was split between staring at that enormous pile of filth, uniforms so stiff with dirt that they practically stood at attention wherever dropped, and attentively attending to each culinary request, for the most part either steak or peanut butter cookies. While these birds left the nest, just like eighteen-year-olds in the States, in Israel they remained most definitely tangled in its branches. The whole concept of "leaving home" was a lot fuzzier.

Victoria and Jackie entered the boys' classroom together and chose adjacent seats, waiting for the teacher's arrival.

"The audience reaction was actually amusing, at least what I understood of it." Jackie chuckled. "Some people are simply so predictable. Did you hear Irit groaning?"

"She's not quite ready for sonny-boy to leave the comfort of the nest."

"That boy's been a crybaby since day one, an advertisement for redshirting if I've ever seen one." Her comment was quite acerbic. She wasn't a fan. The whole class had had to endure this particular child's tantrums for years – one more budding genius that'd been pushed forward a year and couldn't cope. Bad parenting was a language she understood.

Victoria lowered her voice to a whisper as more parents took their seats: "Remember that time you actually had to ask her to attend Adam's birthday party? Just to keep him in line?"

"Maybe we should have felt sorry for him; he really did suffer."

"Aw, forget it. Don't feel too bad. You know what they say: 'You reap what you sow.' No one pushes kids forward in the States anymore. In fact, if anything, they tend to hold them back." She paused. "Hey, I just realized something. He's a full year younger than our boys! She has one whole extra year to moan and groan, to worry about her prince, before the nightmare of service even begins! And then he'll be precisely like the rest of them: cope or crumble."

A deep, booming voice interrupted their conversation.

"That was so informative!"

They both twisted around in their chairs to check out the source.

"I thought I remembered everything from my army days but I guess…well, a few things might have changed. I don't remember the penguins." David was one of the handfuls of fathers who showed up for these school meetings, most often attended by mothers. The rest were, for the most part, left back home, lurking somewhere in the shadows of active parenting.

The women smiled to one another conspiratorially – this particular father was always a breath of fresh air – and scooted sideways in order to better engage him in conversation. "Come on! It wasn't that long ago!" Jackie tapped his arm and winked with one eye. "I'd assume you, of all people, found that lecture completely useless. I mean, the primary focus was on knowing when to hold on and when to let go. This must be old hat for you." She broadened her smile and batted her eyelashes a bit, subtly peeking at Victoria to make sure she'd noticed. It was nice to have an opportunity to escape the intensity of all those other mothers.

David cleared his throat and scooted his chair forward. There was no sign of the teacher. This was as good a way to pass the time as any.

"Yes. But I don't remember the ins and outs of the process. I can't imagine why they haven't brought in a representative to speak with us before."

Jackie and Victoria both sat up in their chairs, looking first at one another and then back at David. The mood shifted from flirty to sympathetic, borderline patronizing. "David, dare I ask where you've been? This is the third lecture we've had, if not the fourth. I've lost count. The others were far more nuts and bolts, far more useful. This one was a step away from fluff – fairly useless!" Victoria jerked her head upward to emphasize her annoyance, "Teddy bears and penguins – they must think we're emotional basket cases." David's mouth fell open in response. She turned to Jackie, adding for emphasis: "I guess someone isn't keeping up!" They both smiled with satisfaction at making him feel behind the times, secretly keeping to themselves the fact that Jackie hadn't attended any of the other meetings either.

"*Baruchim habaim*," a high-pitched voice sung out from the front of the classroom. Their sons' homeroom teacher had entered and begun to welcome the parents. Almost no one stopped speaking, most still deeply involved in conversation. A low buzz reigned throughout the room. Jackie and Victoria immediately pulled their chairs front-forward and gave her their attention. Quick to judge, Victoria didn't hesitate to cast a scolding glance behind her at one of the offending parents, still deep in conversation with a friend, turning back to Jackie with a knowing shake of the head. They were in agreement. Anglos knew quite a bit about respect. The locals could be so rude.

Forty minutes.

Ben looked at his watch, quickly ticking off the things he could accomplish. He had to take advantage of every minute of this evening break. Shower, organize clothing for the early-morning call, check his weapon, eat, drink, hang out with his friends, maybe check in with his homies via WhatsApp. The list was long. Maybe there'd be time to call his mom. He knew she waited for his calls. He looked down at his uniform, took a good, deep whiff and made his way to the shower area. This was much more urgent at the moment. He really couldn't wait to remove this stench. The phone call would have to wait. In any case, he wasn't sure he had the energy to field her questions. That's what their phone conversations boiled down to lately: questions. She'd obviously figured it was the best way to engage him, and when he thought about it, she was probably right. It was a lot better than hearing a litany of her concerns.

But first things first: he had to rinse off the dirt from this day. They'd been working on terrain conditions for the past few weeks. Most days were spent lurking in bramble and bushes. They hadn't been permitted to talk to one another save when relaying crucial information. That was so much worse than it sounded. Silence wasn't all it was cracked up to be. And the heat! It was so hot. Only May, and summer was already in full swing. He was really looking forward to rinsing off the grime that had worked its way deep into his ears and under his fingernails, stained his naturally blond hair an unfamiliar shade.

He glanced into the shower area before heading into his room to unload his gear. The scene there was already raucous; some of the guys had been quicker than he and had already nabbed spots under the burning streams of water. He looked at his watch again. Time was passing quickly. He decided to wait a few minutes for the crowds to dissipate. This was probably the best time to call home. He bent over to unlace his boots, switching to a crouch to work them off his feet. *What a relief!*

Maybe he wouldn't call after all. It was always a mixed bag. He adored touching base but was never sure which version of his mother he'd reach. He couldn't bear the worried one. He worked so hard to maintain a kind of cool, to keep on an even keel and hold it together. It was so easy to lose it, to come apart at the slightest problem or hitch. And she would pick up on that in a second. He'd learned never to call when he wasn't emotionally on solid ground. Besides undermining his self-confidence, magnifying his own concerns, it transmitted to her a reason not to sleep at night. And he knew she hadn't slept well since he'd entered the IDF.

Boots off, he peeked back into the shower area. "Hurry up in there. *Y'allah.* There's a line!" The others waiting joined in, "*Y'allah, y'allah…*get moving!"

Ben loved these guys. He'd been so fortunate to get a good squad. He couldn't imagine what it was like for those who hadn't. He never felt alone. He knew they had his back.

"Call your mom!" Nadav knocked him solidly on the shoulder as he came through the bunk.

"Why don't you?"

"Going to, as soon as I get out of the shower. She's got some kind of radar. She'd probably pick up on my filth over the line."

Ben took one more look over his shoulder, back toward the crowded shower room, and went over to his locker to find his phone. They hadn't been permitted usage for days; the number of awaiting chat notifications on WhatsApp was out of control. Whoa! He'd never get around to answering them all. He slid around to the other side of the bunk beds and walked barefoot out to the porch, distancing himself from the acoustically magnified hoots coming from the shower area.

He searched his speed dial list and pushed **Mom**, glancing at his watch while he waited for her to pick up. He still had over half an hour. It was 9:30 p.m. She'd be awake.

The call went through. "Hi baby." Her voice was light, expectant but also hesitant. "Hey Mom." His voice sounded flat, emotionless and matter of fact, but it was a lie, he didn't feel any of the above.

"How are you sweetheart?" Her voice softened. It soothed him. It was so obvious she was bracing herself, wanting to make sure nothing difficult was coming, that this call would be as seamless as any other, no hint of disaster.

Ben began to relax. An inexpressible relief moved through him, like that first sip of warm tea on a cold day: embracing, fortifying and reassuring.

"Fine, fine. Everything's fine. I'm here on the base."

Victoria had trained him well. First let us know you're okay – then move on to the news.

"How's your week going?" There it was, a question; safe, familiar.

"We just finished two weeks of terrain training. It was really tough."

"What does that involve?" Another question. He smiled. This felt right. He enjoyed her engagement and her enthusiasm. He understood her need to feel informed. She didn't like mysteries.

He'd tried to accommodate her from day one; anything to make her more comfortable. Her comfort was his comfort.

He began to describe how he'd hacked a path from one designated spot to another, making his way through very tough foliage. The exercise had been timed, so he'd had to hurry. He elaborated a bit here and there, telling her how he'd dug a hole in the sandy dirt beneath a barbed wire fence and somehow managed to wiggle his body underneath, gear and all. And then there was the story about the cows stuck in the briar. He couldn't simply leave them there so he'd taken the time to set them free. That one was almost funny and he hoped it would release some of the tension he knew she experienced vicariously. He didn't want her to concentrate too much on the grimness of his service.

"And you survived all this? Came out in one piece?"

Always questions.

He laughed, "Just barely. It was really difficult: the cutting, the lifting, the thorns working their way into my skin."

"Again!!! Don't you wear gloves?"

"Of course, but it doesn't make much of a difference. Those things are mean sons' of bitches." He looked at his watch. He really had to get moving but he knew an abrupt goodbye would sadden her, leave her hanging.

"I'll be home on Friday, Mom."

"That's fantastic, baby." He could actually "hear" her smile. He let go, allowed himself to feel her warmth; let himself be mothered.

"Gotta go. I love you."

"Bye sweetie. Take good care of yourself."

He hung up quickly. Twenty minutes left. Time was tight. He hoped he'd have a few minutes to shoot the breeze with his buddies before lights out, before everything was silent and he drifted off to sleep.

There was plenty of room in the showers now. He smiled as he peeled off his dirt-encrusted uniform. Good thing he'd taken the time to call home – for him too.

Chapter 11

It was an absolutely perfect day. The sky the bluest of blues. That was a good thing. It might even help. They'd decided to meet at the golf course, she and Guy. This wasn't a conversation for a home audience. Victoria braced herself as she walked up the long path toward the clubhouse café to meet him. So far, things hadn't gone as she'd expected. A few days earlier she'd mentioned the job, or rather, *opportunity* as she'd emphasized, in the car on the way to the market. He hadn't really responded, had simply let her go on and on, reciting various details. She'd almost thought she'd gotten away with laying the groundwork.

But then, while in the market, he'd come out with it.

"You've always wanted a way out."

She'd been perusing the tomato sauces, casually debating whether she wanted something with garlic or basil. She hadn't been prepared for either his words or his tone. She stopped short and turned toward him, caught entirely off guard.

"I get it. We're done." He continued with his hurtful proclamations.

Victoria was taken aback. She took in a quick gasp of air and gripped the handle of the supermarket cart for support, gazing at him with an expression of both fear and confusion.

"What are you talking about?"

"Us. It's over."

She'd frowned. "How did you...?" She couldn't find the right words. She leaned forward onto the cart with more of her weight, hoping the groceries they'd already chosen would provide enough ballast to support her and locked her eyes onto his, trying to find that place they'd always been able to get back to.

"Guy."

"No, really." He'd placed his hand on the side of the cart and inched it forward, steering both of them down the aisle of the market. "I even understand," he'd muttered, almost as an afterthought.

After only a foot or two he stopped up short and turned to her. "There've been so many signs. I know. I've tried to ignore them. I didn't want to take them seriously. But now..."

Victoria had felt distinctly nauseous. She'd worked her fingers into the metal webbing of the cart and closed her eyes. This situation was a nightmare.

Guy had continued. "I guess it was a matter of time. But I never," he'd paused, "I never thought it would actually come about."

Victoria untwisted her fingers from the metal cart and grasped his arm, pulling him slightly off balance for a moment as she transferred her weight onto him.

"Guy." She'd almost gasped out the words. "I don't understand. Is this about the job? How is this about us?" She straightened up a bit more and pulled him closer, forcing him to look into her eyes. "Guy. It's just an idea. A *concept*."

He'd pulled his arm away abruptly and stepped back, almost toppling the cereal boxes on the shelves behind. Victoria had watched them shake threateningly for a second or two: the Cini Minis, the Trix, the Kellogg's Corn Flakes; those reminders of American life whose presence here in Israel had always been so comforting.

"It's merely a possibility, an option." She'd spoken quietly, sweeping her eyes to the opposite side of the aisle, taking in the bottles of Ortego salsa, the Heinz ketchup.

Where am I?

"I thought we got it right." His words came across like a sigh, as if he were speaking to himself rather than her. She followed his gaze, not certain if he was angry or sad. She hoped the latter; that was something she might be able to fix.

Desperate to get his attention, she'd decisively pushed the cart aside.

"Guy. Look at me. Look, here!" She pointed at her eyes. "We did! We did get it right!" She'd looked around, startled at the tone of her own voice, suddenly conscious of her surroundings. Their earlier conversation had been so mild and inconsequential, she'd never anticipated it would go like this. Or maybe, just maybe, she had.

Guy purposefully looked away and, jerking the handle of the cart out of her grasp, continued down the aisle, completely disengaging from the conversation. She'd wanted to shout out, to get his full attention, but the market was full of people she knew. She'd stepped quickly ahead of him, directly in front of the wheels, stopping his advance. He had no choice but to meet her gaze. "Listen to me. This is exciting. This is good. And most of all it's only an idea. I don't know what it means – for us, for all of this." She'd gestured vaguely at the shelves. Somehow this local market was part of their lives.

And then, came that moment – so innocent but so redolent of everything they'd managed to build over decades. Guy had reached behind her, selecting a jar of Skippy peanut butter from the shelf and adding it to their cart. She'd felt a sudden rush of tenderness toward him. He understood her needs, understood what she'd given up, the hardships she'd faced. Everything would be okay.

But no. Guy was shaking his head vigorously.

"I know exactly what this means. You don't go looking for something else if you're where you want to be. Admit it. You've been looking for an out, any out."

Victoria felt panicky. This wasn't what she'd expected. She had to turn this around, make him understand. She grasped the sleeve of his shirt, imploring: "Guy. Please. There's got to be a way to discuss this in a reasonable manner." She lowered her voice in an attempt at some kind of calm. "You know I've never found my niche. That I've been frustrated at the things I gave up when…" She shook her head. "This opportunity…it's simply something I need to pursue. It doesn't mean I'm leaving. I'm sure there's a way…if we just figure it out together."

She'd forced a huge smile, certain she'd win him over. This man had promised to love her forever, no matter what. He'd always supported her, always stood by her side. How could he deny her such a golden opportunity? She'd quickly tried to make sense of this untenable situation. She'd caught him off guard, struck some kind of unforeseeable chord.

"No, Victoria. We're not going to figure this out. We won't have to. If you leave, there won't be anything left to figure out."

She'd been stunned by his inflexibility. "I thought you'd be happy for me." These last few words came out in the form of an anguished, desperate whisper.

"Hah!" His harsh response completely took her by surprise. "Happy to see you choose a life without me?"

"But I'd never…"

But stepping into the Golf Club on this beautiful morning she wondered if he'd been right, if he'd figure out what she'd spent years trying to suppress. Yes, she'd finally found a way to escape, to redress the "mistake" she'd made so long ago. She cringed as she remembered how he'd eventually slammed that jar of peanut butter back onto the shelf, leaving her alone with that cart full of American products.

Maybe he's right.

Victoria stepped into the café and looked around, instantly spotting Guy sitting at a table on the terrace. He was dabbing his face with a towel and smiling widely. He'd come off the course this very moment and was sticky but obviously satisfied. Victoria felt hopeful.

"Good game?"

"Great."

"You love it."

"Yes." Guy ordered two cappuccinos and a cold water from the closest waitress.

"And?"

"Two over par."

She smiled. She needed to play along. This wasn't going to be easy or pleasant. She had a feeling he'd dig in his heels, or worse, go for the jugular.

"It's pretty warm out there."

"Blistering."

She couldn't wait to get through this, to have this conversation behind them.

"So, we need to talk."

"Right." Guy's features, moments earlier natural and relaxed, enjoying the cool temperature of the café after the heat of the golf course, settled themselves into a neutral arrangement, as if awaiting further orders. To Victoria he seemed a bit stiff, sharp around the edges. She needed him to soften up a bit.

"This is a great opportunity for me."

There was a pause as the waitress came over with a pitcher of ice water and poured them each a tall glass. Guy took a hearty slug, and then another, finishing his off. Victoria's remained untouched.

"Guy. What do you think?" The atmosphere had chilled considerably.

"So, no more small talk? We're jumping right in? Well…" He took off his hat, wiped his brow with the napkin, and settled himself back in his chair. "You know exactly what I think. I think it's a bad idea, for us, for the 'greater' us." He gestured around the restaurant with an open palm. "What's going to happen to *this?*"

The waitress arrived with their cappuccinos. Victoria began to feel nervous and a bit angry. Guy was too comfortable, too closed, as if a decision had already been made. She'd have to step up her own game if she wanted to have a chance; gentle wasn't going to work. She opened a packet of sugar and dumped it into her coffee. "Well, frankly, *this,*" she beckoned with her forehead towards the green of the golf course that stretched out beyond the café's terrace, "isn't going anywhere."

They both sipped their coffee in silence. The feeling of animosity at the table was positively tactile. *How did we get here? This isn't what I want.*

Victoria took a deep breath and decided to start again. The conversation needed to be rerouted. There was a goal to be met. The process shouldn't take center stage. "I don't know exactly what this job means to me, to you, to that 'greater' us, as you call it. But I know I want it. Pursuing it is only natural. It means I'm exploring the option." She hesitated a second and then tentatively reached out and touched Guy's fingertips, the ones gripping the coffee cup. She thought she saw a flicker in his eye but he didn't budge. She was startled. Touch had always worked for them, even in the most trying moments. He was obviously resisting her on purpose.

She left her fingers right where they were and modified her tone, made it sweeter, smaller. "Guy, this is important to me. I need to check it out. I don't know all the details. I may not even get the job! All of our concerns about what will happen, how it can work, may be for naught. All I know is that it's exactly what I've been looking for. It's exactly what I need."

He retracted his hand, moving it just out of reach, back to the edge of the table. She felt the chill. Something was terribly wrong. "It's never been enough for you. This life; this beautiful life. Our life. It's never been enough."

She broke in: "But it has. I mean, it is! Don't say that. Don't make this something it isn't."

Guy cleared his throat, shifted in his chair. "Vic, I think it's time. It's time you finally decide. No more games. No more sitting on the fence. No more constant jibes about what's wrong with this life, the shortcomings of this country, how much better things are back in the States. At least admit it, if not to me, then to yourself: You've wanted to leave for years. This isn't about some job. It's an excuse to get out, get away, to finally be on your way."

Victoria looked down at the white tablecloth, spread her spurned fingers wide and moved them over it, smoothing it into place. So many pictures flashed through her head: visions of happy, carefree moments on trips back to the States, admittedly vacations; irritating encounters here in Israel, where the ins and outs of a real life had to be negotiated – all punctuated by occasional outbursts of frustration, exchanges of unkind words. There was more than a kernel of truth to what he said.

Enormous tears sprung to her eyes, threatening to spill over. She blinked them back fiercely. "The fact that I've always had mixed feelings doesn't mean I don't appreciate the good, that I actually want to leave. But this," she paused, "this is the kind of opportunity I've been hoping for, for such a long time. You know that. You've always known there was a piece missing from my puzzle. Guy, it won't come around again."

Guy let out a sigh of exasperation and rolled his eyes to the side, taking in the other diners in the café. The crease on his forehead relaxed, flattening out to smooth. "Vic, you can't have it both ways. Taking this job means leaving, leaving me, leaving the kids. We're not going anywhere. We're staying right where we are. You'll have to do this alone." His tone was steady but Victoria sensed he was softening. Playing hard wasn't easy for him either.

She saw an opening. "I'm aware..."

"No, I don't think you're aware." He cut her off abruptly. "This is a much bigger decision than you realize. Your desperation to cut loose and fly – and don't try to tell me that isn't what you want to do – has major repercussions. Everything you gain will come with loss, loss of a magnitude I'm certain you haven't considered." He pushed away his coffee cup, now empty, and reached out gently and grasped her hands.

That touch! This was their base camp, something they'd always had. It held such magic, such promise; a path back home. Victoria's gaze moved from their hands to his eyes, struggling with the truth in his words. "I'm trying very hard not to get angry. I'm trying to see your point, understand your needs. But I can't but see this as one step toward leaving me."

She pulled her thumbs out of his grasp, rubbing his knuckles, reciprocating his gesture. These weren't the same hands she'd held when they'd first met; these were ones worn with age, ones whose wrinkles and nubs were a record of their lifetime together. How could she do this? Why was it so important? Maybe the whole idea was a mistake.

He squeezed her hands suddenly, getting her attention. "Ben is here. Jonathan is due to start his service soon. And Maia? Every teenage girl needs her mother. It's hard for me to fathom you want to leave them, especially during this time. Impossible, really." He looked straight at her.

That was it. That was when the cogs moved into place and it all became clear. There wasn't a choice to be made. It had been made for her. She stared back into his gorgeous blue eyes, the ones that had won her over with their intensity from day one, compelling her to believe in their love. These were the eyes that had launched her across the world. "We have a beautiful family. It is the most beautiful treasure. You must embrace it. How can you not?"

Victoria looked down at their clasped hands, her attention immediately drawn to the veins in her arms. They were obstinately bulging, pulsing with blood, an undeniable sign of time passed. She wasn't getting younger. Maybe it was too late to look for what was missing. Although her insides threatened to burst, so overwhelmed by her desire to pursue this dream, they were overcome by the sudden calm of acquiescence.

"I don't want to leave you. I don't want to leave the kids." It came out as a whisper, forlorn, defeated and deeply sad. This opportunity wouldn't come around again, but Guy was right. She couldn't have it all. She'd already submitted one of the two articles the search committee had requested. Maybe she'd leave it at that. This whole thing was probably a big mistake. She needed to focus on what she had rather than what was missing.

And Ben. Her heart literally ached. How could she even think of leaving Ben? She needed to give up this plan, tell the university the timing wasn't right. She needed to say no to this golden opportunity. She gulped hard; this pill was critically hard to swallow. But she had no choice. Her hands were tied.

The road ahead, the one that led out one door and right back in through another the one going nowhere, simply staying put, seemed impossible. To meet this challenge she'd have to revamp her attitude, to learn to accept the differences she'd disdained for decades, to swallow the frustrations and the disappointments, to shut out her past and live in the present. If it had been easy she might have already succeeded.

"Shavuot is coming up." It came out so quietly it sounded almost like an afterthought. Guy had moved forward with this brighter tenor, eager to take advantage of the momentum he'd gained by using his most precious ammunition. "Everyone will be there. What do you need me to do?"

They fell into silence. She felt unable to continue. She didn't have Guy's ability to switch tracks so quickly. But then, in an almost robotic fashion, she began to tick off a list of things that needed to be bought, picked up, done around the house. He answered in suit by pulling out his phone, his mood noticeably lighter, and jotting it all down on his notepad. Victoria tried to sound upbeat, to pull herself to another place, to return to their shared space. She knew he was anxious for her to meet him there. His forced joviality was a sign of his desperation to retrieve the territory they'd lost. He too wanted to snuggle back into what they had together, their safe ground – to hold tight. The threat of change, unwanted change, had unmoored him completely. Victoria rattled on, burying herself in preparation and maintenance, forcibly shoving aside the kernel of need that had begun to expand and threatened to pop.

Apparently, she wasn't going anywhere.

Chapter 12

"Steiner."

She whipped her head around. Nothing. But she was sure she'd heard her name.

"Steiner."

There it was again. She looked up. It had come from the direction of the cocktail stand, but the only people there were a group of men she didn't know. Something caught her eye. She quickly searched for her friend Claudine, finding her tucked into the window seat. She crossed the room, checking out the well-appointed apartment. She wasn't sure whose it was, but it was among the nicer ones she'd seen since moving to Paris, nothing like the grim little place with the dubious shower and rickety steps she liked to call home in the Second Arrondissement. Most of the people she associated with, also fresh out of college and living on a starting salary, didn't have such nice accommodations.

"So? What do you think?"

"Nice party. A bit too academic of a crowd." She took a sip of what looked like a *kir royale*, a brilliant ruby color, and nodded over to the bar. "Except of course for that group."

Victoria followed her glance. Again, those men. She didn't know them. They weren't part of their crowd. They didn't even look American. Something about the way they were dressed, the way they held themselves. They seemed so incredibly comfortable in their skin. Her eyes met with those of the one on the end and locked for a long moment. *Was that smile directed at her?* She looked away quickly. *What was that?*

"Do we know anything about them?"

"We know they're good looking."

Victoria took a sip of her own drink, a chilled Chablis, and peered up at the men again, trying not to be too obvious. Boom. There he was. And he was definitely looking at her. That's when she noticed them: those blue eyes. Wow, so blue. She'd never imagined such a thing.

"Should we go and speak with them?"

Victoria leaned closer to Claudine. "No. No way. What's the point?"

"Really? What's the point? Do I have to lay it out for you?"

They giggled. All of a sudden this party seemed a lot more interesting.

"Do you think they're French?"

"Maybe. Definitely not American. Something…well, something exotic." She stood up and tugged down her skirt a bit. "Let's go say hi."

Victoria was uncomfortable. What did she have to do with them? What did any of this have to do with her? She was here to research her dissertation; then she'd be gone. It was temporary. Those men? They were so different. She wouldn't know what to say. Claudine wasn't as hesitant. She'd already walked over. Victoria watched her introduce herself, her body language open, available. She envied her self-confidence. She felt glued to the chair. She twisted her upper body so that she could look out the window, put whatever was happening over there by the cocktail stand out of her head. There was a pretty view down to a gated park.

She took another sip of her wine. *What did it matter anyway?* She was here for the city. She loved every bit of it, whether crumbling or on the edge of collapse.

"Steiner."

She whipped around abruptly, sloshing her wine a bit.

There he was, the man with the blue eyes. He was standing right in front of her. It *had* been him!

"Shall I get you a new one?"

She brushed at the wet mark on her blouse, looked back up and smiled, still hesitant.

"I'm okay. Thanks." She moved her head to the side and peeked behind him. Claudine was at the bar with the other two men.

"I'm Guy." She put out her hand to meet the one he extended toward her, shook it firmly and then let go. But there was a second's lapse, only a second, that they still seemed to be touching. Before she could figure it out, it was over. She looked up into his eyes. Still blue. Maybe even bluer than she'd noticed earlier. And now that he was standing by the window they were picking up the color of the sky. They were incredible.

"How do you know my name?" She couldn't resist asking. It didn't make sense. *Who was this man?* She didn't know a thing about him, save his name. Guy. *Maybe he was French?* He didn't look French.

"I spotted you when you came in." He took a sip from his own glass of wine. "I inquired." They stared at one another. It was a bit disconcerting. She didn't know what to do, let alone say.

"And your first name?" He paused, waited for her to respond. "Remember? I'm Guy and you are…"

"Victoria." He reached out to shake her hand again. There was no question this time. He definitely hung on to hers a bit beyond the expected.

"Mind if I join you?" She didn't respond. He smiled and took a place on the banquette in the window seat beside her. She watched him settle back onto the cushions and then, again, meet her gaze.

She felt it – a beginning.

Chapter 13

Early morning. Blue skies. There was an endless supply of those here in Israel, and it never got old. The streets were fairly empty, part of the calm before the storm associated with a holiday on the threshold. Victoria stood in the doorway and shouted, "Don't forget the challah!" She watched Guy duck back into his car and then, after a brief pause, ventured down the entrance pathway out into the street. She was still in pajamas. Everything was completely quiet. In Israel, that was always a good thing. Quiet meant safe. Quiet meant peace. The collection of parked cars, tall cypress trees and large plastic bins that lined the way looked to be part of some kind of museum diorama; everything staged, fitting a niche – the whole scene characterized by a distinct feeling of stasis. She took a deep breath, happy to grab a few more minutes of this calm before the holiday was upon them.

In only a few hours dinner needed to be on the table, but she wasn't in any hurry to get on with the preparations. It was nice to take an extra minute or two and enjoy the morning. *Erev chag*, the day before a major Jewish holiday, was no ordinary time, but instead, one of the holy of holies that divided up the year. Religious holidays in Israel were characterized by large families and a lot of food; the entire country galvanized into the preparation, or enjoyment, of one celebratory meal. Lines at the supermarket reached gargantuan length, the highways were beset by masses of cars and most conversations gravitated to the subject of what was being served, or alternatively, how much would be consumed. Most everyone she knew was either cooking up a storm, continuing the preparations begun days earlier, or packing up the car on their way to celebrate said feast elsewhere. Whether celebrating at their own table or that of a relative or friend, the entire populace was sucked into a maelstrom of activity, the promise of festivity, gaiety and abundant food generating frenetic energy.

Victoria walked back into the house, closed the door behind her and let her hand linger on the knob, satisfied to take another moment before she returned to the kitchen. After her talk with Guy a few days earlier she'd made a silent decision to make a real effort to embrace their family life, appreciate everything she had. She was hoping this would somehow help her make peace with turning her back on the opportunity at Columbia, denying the unvarying longing for another life.

His accusation that she constantly criticized Israel, that she'd never given it a real chance, had hurt her deeply. She adored her husband, adored her children; she'd invested in them every iota of energy she could muster. She'd always thought that was enough. It shouldn't matter that she wasn't whole hog enthusiastic about every last detail of their local lives. Was anyone? Anywhere?

But Guy had seen through her. He knew she second-guessed that decision she'd made decades earlier, that the wonders they'd built together within the four walls of their house weren't enough. Whether it was the way she followed the US news more closely than events right outside their door, complained about her inability to find a local brand of clothing to suit her taste or raved about the educational system abroad, her disappointment, frustration and sometimes annoyance with her adopted home, and her longing for that she'd left behind, came out loud and clear.

Victoria had high hopes for this particular Shavuot. A holiday weekend was the perfect opportunity to appreciate what she had, to count her blessings. Yet standing in the early morning silence of her house she couldn't shake the sensation of emptiness and knew this holiday was going to have to work some pretty powerful magic to drown out the voice calling her elsewhere, tempting her back.

Maybe if their family were simply a little bigger, maybe then she'd feel more connected to a greater whole, more part of things. This evening they were hosting a few relatives from Guy's side, a handful of individuals to add to their own small nuclear family. Each seat would be taken, the table would be full, but their celebration would pale in comparison with those happening in houses elsewhere. Victoria had had such different expectations. She'd been so certain that moving to Israel would entail the warm embrace of, yes, an entire country, some kind of compensation for the one she'd left behind. The concept of family was a large part of what had attracted her in the first place, having grown up envious of the Roman Catholic one next door. There were always so many cars in the driveway, that cluster of coats and boots by the front door, the clamor of constant interruption as one or another child burst into the house. She'd dreamt of large get-togethers with children running around tables overflowing with food, raucous laughter and heated arguments – a cross between Fellini and Woody Allen.

Family – that was the core, that was what Eretz Yisrael was known for, what it specialized in, what made it magical and worthwhile despite so much of the geopolitical turmoil incumbent to living here. The concept that everyone belonged, that everyone had a part, that everyone – yes, everyone – was somehow related, whether literally or figuratively, had intoxicated her from the start. Yet over two decades had passed since her arrival and, despite adding a few children of her own to the picture, this fantasy still eluded her. The clan model had passed her by completely, and her nuclear family remained as concise and to the point as the one she'd left back in the States. No gain there whatsoever.

Victoria gazed out toward the terrace. The bougainvillea was in full bloom; purple blossoms covered every square inch of the surrounding walls and the branch overlay, effectively shutting out the sunlight. There was no question that what she had here, right at hand, was stunning. But still, somehow it wasn't enough. She let out a long sigh, steeling herself for yet another *erev chag*. One more occasion to feel somehow left out of the action. Guy wanted her to take strength and indeed satisfaction from their family life – indeed he was counting on it to bring her back into the fold – but for her it always came up short. The family unit they'd cultivated in this very house was spectacular but tiny, what little extended family they had was minimal and difficult to corral, even for dinner. Their holiday celebrations were primarily distinguished by the move from the six-seat kitchen table to the one that accommodated ten in the dining room, the addition of a white tablecloth, an extra side dish or two and the occasional guest. It was no wonder that she wanted more.

Victoria returned to the kitchen, bound and determined to provide her children with at least a taste of what they were missing. Dinner would be festive, the table ornate and the food overwhelming in appearance and quantity – come hell or high water. The word "pathetic" would not be uttered out loud, and there would be an effort to feign the presence of a robust family where only the skeleton variety existed. She loaded the ingredients for her quiche crusts into the food processor and pressed the button.

The noise was horrific and drowned out all her thoughts, at least for the moment. Finger on the power button, she discerned a shadow crossing the counter and jumped, startled. She hadn't heard Jonathan approach. His mouth was moving. She turned off the machine.

"What's up, sweetie?" She gestured to the food processor. "So noisy."

"I asked who's coming to dinner?" He grabbed a pita from the breadbox and chewed on it lazily while peering into the refrigerator.

"Well, we have the five of us," she paused, counting off on her fingers for him to follow, "and then your aunt and uncle, Orit and Yoav, with Eden. I think that's it."

She watched his face, braced herself for what she knew was coming. "That's it? Eight? We're going to be eight?" He looked so disheartened.

"Well, it's a family holiday so it wasn't the evening to pick up strays. With Hadar and Or away with the kids for the weekend we're left with a fairly small crew. But you know," she felt herself trying to convince the two of them, "it will still be nice to be together." She smiled at him weakly, hoping her tone had been light enough and that he wouldn't pick up on her disappointment.

"*Ke'ilu* family," he scoffed, sinking into one of the chairs at the kitchen table and digging his pita into the plastic container of hummus he'd pulled out of the fridge.

Victoria placed her hand on his shoulder and squeezed. She knew exactly what he meant. *Ke'ilu* said it all. He'd zeroed in on their mutual frustration with one incisive, Hebrew expression. She'd learned this phrase and a handful of others that spoke worlds about Israeli culture early on in her relationship with Guy, even before she'd immigrated. He'd wanted to pave the way for an easier integration into the local frame of mind.

Ke'ilu literally meant "as if," but its connotations and usage were wide in range, its nuances so subtle that it had taken what felt like forever before she'd considered using it herself. *Ke'ilu* was all about questioning the validity, veracity or genuineness of whatever, or whomever, was being discussed. It suggested that things weren't as they were presented, despite perhaps being authentic in intention; it could encapsulate a frustrated yearning or a feeling of coming up short and not quite making the grade.

Those first few years in Israel, when she still couldn't grasp the local mentality, this frequently used expression was virtually off-limits, yet another sign that she hadn't yet gained entry into local life, the door to acceptance still firmly closed. With no access, even to a common turn of speech, she would forever remain an outsider. Victoria had eagerly yearned for the moment, for that blessed day, when she'd be comfortable enough to adopt the phrase, becoming, albeit tangentially, that much closer to native.

And then, when she'd least been expecting it, it had happened. There'd come a time when she was no longer so green and had finally, perhaps through osmosis, assumed a new Israeli persona. She'd been standing with a bunch of mothers in front of the kindergarten, waiting for the children to be dismissed.

"Who does she think she is?"

"This group has been closed for months."

Victoria's radar bleeped on, her antennae zinged into action, and she leaned inward, towards the source.

"I heard she appealed to the local council with some story about needing urgent care."

"And they bought that?"

"Fact: She's in."

"The nerve."

Although technically lurking on the edges of this conversation, standing in complete silence, Victoria was now keyed up and ready to join in, to participate in the local outrage over another pushy mother.

"*Ke'ilu!*" Her hand shot outward, twisted upward. Emboldened, she continued, "Who does she think she is? The Queen of France?"

At first she'd been startled by her own voice, had had no idea where all that courage and self-confidence had come from, how she'd managed to come out even a teeny bit mean. She wasn't even sure it was she who had spoken. But the enthusiastic nods of agreement among the little group gathered at the gate confirmed her vocalized assessment, and afterwards, back at home, she'd been delighted with herself, even elated. This was it, the proof she'd finally made it: she was an "insider."

After that everything else seemed to go far more smoothly. Victoria's acquisition of this expression, the fact that she could whip it out and use it whenever the occasion warranted, represented one more step toward her desperate goal of being one of the truly "absorbed."

Of course, back then she hadn't really understood the layers of depth intrinsic to this cultural marker. That had taken decades. *Ke'ilu* could mean much more than one person claiming to be something they weren't, or pretending to be better than those around them. It could be an entire institution assuming unearned airs: a two-year college presenting itself as an elite four-year university; a one-room conversational French class claiming to be a full-fledged language school; a Skoda pretending to be a Volkswagon or, in her case, a few straggly relatives claiming to be a real family.

Yes, Jonathan's appraisal was spot on. Rattling off the expression like a native (which, in truth, he was) he'd expressed the fact that their family would, forever, be a shadow of a real family – a wannabee.

With a restrained sigh, she turned to her preparations. She opened the refrigerator and pulled out the ingredients she needed for her salad: glossy red tomatoes, long, bumpy, green cucumbers, bell peppers. She lined up everything on the countertop then turned around to close the crisper drawer. It refused to budge and remained stuck, jammed halfway in and halfway out. "*Lordy!*" She gave it one hard thwack with the palm of her hand, immediately taming it back into place.

"Hey now, it's only a drawer." Jonathan was standing behind her (he tended to do that), ready to help out if she couldn't manage on her own.

"I have no time for this today." She dismissed his worried expression. She realized she must have hit that drawer much harder than she'd intended, enough to alarm him. She was frustrated, more frustrated than felt comfortable. This holiday was supposed to be about refocusing on her family, appreciating what it gave her so that she wouldn't dream of what she was missing. Yet nothing was as it was meant to be, everything was coming up short. How was she going to make peace with what she was letting go of, if she couldn't embrace what she already had?

Victoria lined up the vegetables on the chopping board and readied the knife. Preparing dinner bored her and making that number one staple of local cuisine, an Israeli salad, was high on the list of most tedious pursuits. But she had no choice; no meal was complete without it. And although it sounded simple – after all, what could be complicated about a bowl of chopped raw veggies – she always managed to mess it up. She could never quite achieve the tiny, uniform cubes others' salads always featured. She started off with the tomatoes, flipping them on their sides and pressing them down, trying to tame them into cube-like shapes before tossing them into the ceramic bowl beside her.

Next up: the cucumbers. She picked up the peeler and absentmindedly began to remove their skin; a pile of dark green fleshy strips grew beside the cutting board. Her eyes wandered to the window above the counter as she peeled. This whole holiday thing felt flat. She knew that her children also felt left out, separated from the mainstream. Years ago, after watching her friends spend weekends visiting one cousin after another, attending what seemed like an endless stream of bar mitzvah ceremonies, weddings and birthday parties, Maia had actually asked whether they had any cousins. How ridiculous was that! Of course they had cousins – somewhere; but there were only a few and, spread far and wide, they barely knew them.

"Mommy." Maia swept into the kitchen, hurling herself into the chair next to Jonathan at the table. She reached over, ripped a chunk off his pita bread and took a swipe of his hummus.

"*Dai!* Get your own!" He moved his dish out of her reach.

"What time is everybody coming? I want to go out afterwards."

Victoria stopped chopping and turned toward her. "On a holiday night? Really? Where to?"

"Alison's." She cringed at Maia's mention of her friend. "They're playing Monopoly after dinner. They've got a lot of family visiting and it's certain to be super fun." Noting the disappointed look on her mother's face, Maia continued in a consoling voice: "In any case, you know we'll probably finish up early. There'll be lots of kids there. If you don't mind..." Her voice petered off.

It did sound fun. Truth be told, she wouldn't mind scrapping her own dinner and joining her friend's.

Victoria turned back to the cutting board. This was all her fault. Her own partial isolation, the way she continued to hold herself apart from situations and individuals she deemed incompatible to her background and interests – part of her active resistance to becoming part of what she felt uncomfortable with in the native population – may very well have created another generation of outsiders. She'd never intended that to happen. It was a reality too painful to consider.

Of course, in their recent conversations, Guy hadn't hesitated to blame her, to claim she'd done this to herself, keeping a distance that made integration virtually impossible. There was something to that, yet she was certain it wasn't entirely her fault. The facts spoke for themselves. She'd come from a small family and married into a similarly small one. International from the get-go, most relatives scattered across the globe, large family get-togethers were few and far between. Any shot at one of the classic, overcrowded holiday celebrations she craved would have entailed producing her own gaggle of progeny and waiting a few years for them to multiply into a crowd. That was never going to happen; she could barely contend with what she had. When push came to shove, the disorder, chaos and commotion about which she'd fantasized were entirely unsuited to her personality. And Israel? Her adopted country? She'd never really given it much of a chance. After the first blush of romance had faded she'd begun to criticize things that weren't pretty, to set herself aside from, and sometimes even above, local life. It had never been a perfect fit, and expecting it to step up and fill such big shoes had been unrealistic.

"Oww!" Victoria winced as she nicked her finger with the peeler, gazing down to investigate the tiny half-moon-shaped piece of skin she'd almost entirely excised. She idly played with the flap left hanging, her finger numbed from the pain by her tortured thoughts. There was no getting around it. Ultimately, she was the one responsible for these ultra-intimate holiday dinners; there was no one else to blame. And although she had gotten used to their minimalistic nature, they weren't going to advance her current attempt to dig in and engage, to strengthen her resolve after the conversation at the golf club. The fact that these family celebrations came one after the other, like rapid fire, didn't help matters. No sooner would she get through this one when another would be on its heels, reminding her that *their* table wasn't quite full, that everyone else seemed to be part of something bigger and definitely more significant. She couldn't bare the constant reminder of her deficiency.

She lined up the peeled cucumbers and began to chop. Agitated by her thoughts she continued to pare them down a size until, before she knew it, the chunks had become so small they were almost hard to discern, too minute to be enjoyed, one step away from mush. She picked up the bowl, now overflowing with tiny smidgens of veggies, opened the fridge and shoved aside a few big tubs of plastic to find it a spot. One down, others to go. She wasn't planning on making too many side dishes; her patience for meal prep was wearing thin. Maybe she'd stop with the salad. It would have to suffice. Maybe it didn't matter. In any case, nothing was exactly as she'd thought it would be.

What, exactly, had she thought would be?

⌣⌒⌒

"Vic, it's simply beautiful. I love the pearl-lined bodice."

"It's not a bit too fancy?"

"Not at all. More in the nature of understated elegance." Jen emphasized the last two words and smiled encouragingly. "Suits you perfectly."

Victoria grabbed at the top seam of the bodice and pulled upward. "Maybe it's too revealing."

"Are you kidding? You're allowed to look a wee bit luscious on your wedding day. In any case, everyone's going strapless these days. You can add a little bolero top for the ceremony if you like. Want me to go look for one?"

Victoria turned completely to the right, back to the left and then tugged at the bodice again as she squared herself in front of the dressing room mirror.

"No. Not yet," she murmured, as she made one more full turn in the dress, entranced by the image reflected before her. She'd dreamed of a dress like this but something wasn't right. "Seems too dressy for Israel."

Jen let out a low chuckle. "How would you know what's too dressy for Israel?"

Victoria stepped out of the dress and replaced it carefully on the hanger before picking up the next candidate. She ignored Jen's question. It held more than a grain of truth. She really had very little knowledge of her home to be. Until she'd met Guy she'd assumed that all Israelis were swarthy with brown eyes.

Her friend persisted. "Okay, so basically we're agreed. You don't know a thing about what's too dressy for Israel."

"I didn't say that." Victoria felt exasperated.

"You didn't have to."

She shifted her eyes to the far corner of the three-way mirror and watched Jen recline on the cushy dressing-room couch.

"Don't think you're going to find too many places like this over there. So plush." She stroked the velour covering on the couch. "Everything in this store is probably too dressy for Israel."

Victoria stayed silent, focusing on the next dress. All set, she stood up straight before the mirror and assessed the overall look. This one was pretty; simple, but pretty. And there was something light and unpretentious about it. It seemed more appropriate.

"You're opting for peasant?"

Victoria laughed. She couldn't help herself. "This isn't peasant! It's just pretty!"

"Vic. Seriously. What are you doing? What the heck are you doing? You remember? We left peasant back in the '80s, safely stuck it where it could no longer rear up its ugly head."

She scooted herself back into a seated position and continued, "None of this makes sense. I don't care how hunky he is, how romantic. I don't care about those dreamy blue eyes. Can't you simply date him forever? Why do you have to commit? You belong here, with me, not in a place where 'peasant' makes sense."

Victoria turned around slowly in front of the mirror, admiring the way the dress flattered her figure yet didn't overwhelm it. There was something so appealing about the lack of pretense, the subtlety, the directness. This dress didn't make a statement. It was a clean slate. *It was perfect.*

"You're only upset because you're going to miss me." She smiled at Jen through the mirror.

"Also."

They both fell silent. They'd been friends forever, as long as they could remember. Almost all of their memories were connected and intertwined: grade school, high school, college, their first jobs in the City; they'd done it all together. That made for a hell of a history. The idea of parting, of living across the world from one another, was anathema. But this is where they were and there was little chance of going back.

"This whole thing is out of control. One day you're starry eyed, the next you're moving to the far ends of the earth. How did you overcome so many obstacles so quickly? You didn't even stop to collect $200 on the way."

Victoria tried not to smile at the joke. "It didn't exactly happen overnight."

"Well. Still. It's only hard to fathom how, after a lifetime of indecision, you not only came up with this bold, earth-shaking plan, but worst of all, had the gall to pursue it without getting my opinion! You've always been dreadful at making decisions: hemming and hawing, calling me up for hours on end to moan about whether you should do one thing or another, assessing the fallout and repercussions of the most inane predicaments." She paused before adding, "And now…"

Victoria halted her inspection, sat down on the couch and leaned her head on her friend's shoulder. "This is a no-brainer.

All of those other things, those millions of other things," here she paused, "weren't."

Jenny let out an enormous sigh. "I don't want you to leave."

Victoria swung her arm around her back and gave her shoulders a squeeze. "I'll be back. How could I stay away? Don't worry. And we'll talk. A lot. Nothing is going to change. In any case, most of our communication is over the phone. It won't be too different."

Jenny pulled away a bit and tugged lightly at the lace hem of Victoria's dress. "But this dress. It wasn't what you had in mind. How many times have we discussed what we're going to wear on our wedding day? How many? This simple frock was never one of the options."

"And I never foresaw this particular ending. Never. There were so many other ways I envisioned it. Yet Jen…here I am. This is happening. And for some reason it doesn't seem like such a difficult choice. It's just the right one. I know it. Deep down, down where it's supposed to count, it feels right."

Jen continued to avoid Victoria's eyes, tracing the seams of the cotton wedding dress with her fingers, ironing out the miniscule wrinkles that had cropped up the minute her friend had sat down. "I can't see down the road, not this road. There's nothing familiar here."

"I know. Nor can I. It feels a bit like jumping into an abyss. But Jen, I'm not jumping alone. It's going to be okay. It's all going to be okay. In fact," she stood back up, faced the mirror and gazed at her appearance in the wedding dress, "it's going to be perfect."

Chapter 14

Alison leaned over and opened the oven door. A sharp wave of heat hit her directly in the face causing her to jump back and abruptly let go. The door snapped closed. No matter how many hours she spent in the kitchen she always forgot that blast of searing heat. A thin layer of heat perspiration peppered her forehead and upper brow. She wiped it off with her mitted hand and then bent over to try again. This time she was more careful, approaching from the side in order to remove the casserole dish.

She tapped the oven door closed with her knee and peeked inside to check that the assorted baking dishes, stacked up one on top of the other on the baking racks, hadn't toppled over. She added the heavy casserole to the other dishes already ready on the countertop. *One day I'll have a big kitchen, one with a Dutch oven and endless counter space.* She twisted her mouth into a peeved expression. She knew she was dreaming. That big kitchen was never going to happen; it was one of those things she'd left behind, back in Great Neck. A long time ago she'd been into big money, very big money. But that was way back whenever, when she'd been certain she wouldn't have to put up with sacrifices of any kind, even those as insignificant as an oven.

She pulled off her mitts, laid them on top of the warm dishes already lined up side by side on the counter, partially cooked in preparation for the evening's meal, then slid over to the sink to check the items waiting on the dish drain: a head of freshly rinsed Romaine, a stack of finely diced tomatoes and cucumbers and a small bowl with the dressing ready to go. She glanced up at the clock on the wall. *Right on time.*

Late Friday afternoon, one like any other but dressed up by the fact that it was *erev chag*. Just about everyone, most extended family, was coming for dinner – her parents as well as her husband's family. Although she'd have more than twenty crowded around the table, she was entirely unfazed. She loved festive dinners and prepared one each and every week. It was part of her ritual, officially marking the start of Shabbat. She didn't have a lot going on other than this. This prep ritual added a little spark to her week.

She moved over to the stovetop and gave the green beans in the large saucepan a shake, peeked under the lid of the broccoli pot and turned off the flame. She was keen to keep the vegetables from wilting to grey.

The phone rang. She moved across the kitchen to answer it, keeping a wary eye on her preparations.

"Cooking up a storm?" the voice asked over the line.

Alison smiled. "You betcha! I've got about twelve dishes in various stages of prep here. I think I went overboard."

"Nah. Not you. Not possible."

They both laughed.

"Who's coming tonight?"

"Gadi's family minus one," she peeked at the rice and turned off that flame as well.

"You're lucky; really lucky."

"To be cooking for hours?"

"Yes. Exactly. And don't try to tell me you don't like it, because I know you do."

Alison smiled. Vicki had her pegged. She did like it. She was proud of the fact that hers was the house to flock to, the one chosen for family get-togethers. She'd married into an enormous Moroccan family, which made her nuclear Ashkenazi one a small unit within an entire complex of relatives, some joined at the hip, others held at arm's length, but all, inevitably, intertwined and in touch. Having picked up and moved to Israel alone in her late twenties, she'd been thrilled to be absorbed into such a welcoming tribe. The fact that over time her home had become "the center of the world," the chosen setting for most family affairs, was all the better – the icing on the cake.

Of course there were things that hadn't panned out, sacrifices she'd had to make. Back in the States she'd worked in finance. When the Twin Towers came down she'd felt it more than most of her friends here in Israel, felt the loss of a space she'd actually inhabited. It was like a personal death: there were so many she knew, so many she didn't, and of course, there was that other life, now lost to her forever. Her destiny had been to climb through the ranks of Merrill Lynch en route to becoming a top financial investment advisor. And now? Well, now she ran a household. She reached for a glass and poured herself some wine.

"We're alone this weekend – well, alone plus three." Victoria cleared her throat, there was a bit of a pause. Alison understood that small was the status quo at Victoria's house and a continual disappointment to her. "Maybe you can help me. I'm trying to figure out how to stretch out our dinner. I have trouble keeping everyone at the table for more than an hour; with so few people the conversation can peter out early or simply stall. Before I know it they're peeling off, one by one, and I'm left sitting there alone, still cutting my steak."

"Try a soup course. That adds at least five to seven minutes between the ladling and the slurping." Alison gripped the phone tightly between chin and shoulder and leaned over to check that the potatoes in the oven were still on the golden side of cooked.

"I'd settle for three. Great idea, I'll do it. What kind of soup did you prepare today? Give me some ideas."

"Sweet potato. And it was super easy."

Alison proceeded to explain how to make the soup and Victoria tried to keep up. Whereas Alison was super comfortable in the kitchen, approaching the task with creativity and energy, even enjoying herself, her friend simply seemed to stumble along. Alison waited on the line, pausing here and there to give her time to write down the recipe; Victoria wasn't an ad-libber in the kitchen. She almost felt a little sorry for her, always struggling to put something decent on the table. Maybe if she'd been a bit more interested…then again, she had more serious things to think about. *Journalist or homemaker? Not much of a choice there.* She picked up her glass and took another sip, this time purposefully smaller. She conscientiously peered down into the pool of burgundy red, allowing just a smidgen of wine to touch her lips before setting it back on the table.

Who was she kidding? She'd much rather brag about securing a 20 million dollar transaction than her latest soup. This morning she'd spent an hour masochistically flipping through online business reports, reading up on the biggest and most significant deals of the last twenty-four hours. That was the action she wanted in on. She sighed. *Another life.*

"I won't hold you up. I'll let you know how the soup goes. We'll catch up."

"Absolutely."

Alison hung up the phone and turned toward the stove. Reconsidering, she reached instead for her wine glass and took a much more generous sip. As the wine trickled down her throat she felt the beginnings of a sense of calm. Fortified, she began her final check of the various dishes. She started with the first pot on the stove but had barely managed to lift the lid when the phone again interrupted her.

"Hi, dear."

"Hi, Mom." She returned to her final go-through while gripping the phone, peeking at the carrot mixture, then the vegetable stir-fry.

"We'll be there shortly, there's quite a bit of traffic."

She stepped over to the kitchen cabinet, taking out plates. It was time to set the table. "I can imagine. Don't worry about it. Lihi wants you to watch the new episode of *Dora* with her." She grabbed forks and knives from the drawer, gathering a large pile of cutlery in anticipation of the evening's crowd.

"I look forward to it! I brought a bottle of wine and an enormous watermelon but left the cake on the counter at home. Do you want me to stop and pick one up?"

Alison laughed. "Don't worry. I've got it covered."

She hung up and began to transfer glasses from the cabinet to the kitchen table, one by one. When she'd moved to Israel she'd been the family trailblazer, heading off on her own and leaving her parents behind. It had been such an adventure. Who'd have thought that a semester at Hebrew University would be such a game changer? But from that time forward everything had simply fallen into place, one thing leading to another after she'd met Gadi.

Of course, choosing Israel hadn't been entirely unforeseen; she'd been raised in a traditionally religious family and attended both Jewish day school and overnight camp. Her connection to the Holy Land was well grounded and solid from early on, her move across the world entirely within the realm of reasonable. Still, she knew she had the best of it. She'd been lucky, experiencing what must have been the easiest absorption ever in the history of aliyah after marrying into a virtual clan. Beyond holiday events she could have as much, or as little, "family" as she wanted. There was always a sibling to turn to if she needed one, a mom for advice and a household full of activity, laughter and good cheer. The good got even better a decade after her own move when her parents announced they were coming to join her. Padded by an enormous cushion of family, her life was complete. Like any other trustworthy recipe: Add water and stir.

And yet... Alison reached for her glass, brought it close for another sip. Nothing. She'd already emptied it. She set it down on the kitchen counter and refilled it from the waiting open bottle. The phone rang. *Again!* She looked at her watch, hesitated a moment, then picked it up. "Hey there!"

"I was thinking..." The voice on the other end of the line faded off.

Alison completed the thought seamlessly, "That you'd like to join us for dinner?"

"I'd love to. The only thing I have planned is an evening locked in my room. Sara is having friends over and I'm not allowed to appear – even for a second. It embarrasses her."

"Why do you put up with that?"

A sigh came over the line. "I really can't answer that question."

Alison loved these calls from her high school buddy. They reminded her of what her life might have been like back in the States. Her stories of family and kids in Great Neck sounded mundane, on the verge of dull, but once removed, being about the life she hadn't chosen, taken as the shadow of a ship that had passed, provided great amusement.

"Are you sure you don't want to come over? I've already opened a bottle of wine." Gil dashed in from the garage entrance, soccer ball in hand. Alison held her hand over the receiver and hissed:

"It's Becca. Shhh." He stepped out of his cleats silently, abandoning them on the kitchen floor surrounded by a pile of mud pebbles. Alison frowned at him in dismay.

"I think it's too early to drink. It's not even noon." There was a pause. "On the other hand…" Becca's voice faded away for a second and then came back even stronger than before, "if you're offering something appropriate to brunch, I could be convinced."

Alison laughed and looked at the assortment of silver, ceramic and glass spread out on the kitchen table. It was time to call the kids and have them help set up.

"Your choice. You always have a place here."

"I know, honey. I wanted to check in before I head to the gym. You know, the whole *Shabbat Shalom/Chag Same'ach* thing." There was a rustling of bags on the other side of the line. "Everything okay? How many tonight?"

"Fine, really fine. My parents, Gadi's parents, a few of his siblings and a handful of kids. Same old, same old. You'd really add some color."

"Aww, that's so sweet. I know I would. I've got a better idea. Take off your apron, go upstairs, pack a carry-on and hop on the next flight over. I promise you a fun evening; a glass of wine will only be the tip of the iceberg."

"Boy, does that sound appealing. I wish!"

"Gotta run. Catch you later."

"Bye, Bec."

Alison hung up the phone and took another sip of wine from her refilled glass, this one a bit heartier than the last. Everything was pretty much ready for the evening. She might even have a few minutes to sit down with her book for a quick "sip and read." She loved the holiday prep frenzy but wouldn't mind a small break before things got hectic. She glanced at the clock again, set the glass down next to the sink and firmly pushed that idea out of her head.

This was no time to lose focus. She pulled the remaining covered pans out of the oven and set them on the last section of unoccupied counter space, at the ready.

Becca's invitation was appealing, in fact, *more* than appealing. Although looking forward to another wonderful evening, she'd love to hop on a plane. Amazing that with so much that was right, among so many that she loved, she still craved a life back in the States. She also knew, deep down, that if given a chance, one golden opportunity, she'd drop everything, take her family and relocate.

It wasn't so much about what might be missing; because officially, nothing was. Even the fact that she'd dropped out of the workforce completely in order to raise a family, given up an exciting and lucrative career in investment banking to run carpools, was something she could swallow. She figured she would have eventually done the same if she'd ended up living somewhere within the New York metropolitan area. *Might have.* But that wasn't for sure.

Alison knew her expat friends were envious of what they considered her successful absorption. She'd done it! She'd managed to become part of the whole! She had everything! And yes, her glass was – no question – full to brimming. She dared not let on that things weren't exactly as they seemed, that she desired another reality as much as they, that maybe everything she had, right here, wasn't enough to make up for what she'd given up. She was plagued by the interstices between all that abundance; minute slivers of life that, no matter how complete the picture, remained unattainable; little bits and pieces of cultural comfort that forever eluded her here in the Middle East.

Despite the fact that her family grew bigger and closer every year, becoming ever more solid, its roots extending far under the surface and growing in strength, those absences were becoming more and more glaring. Her yearning for cultural reassurance of the Manhattan variety – the action, the pace, the noise and the intense engagement – had begun to threaten what she'd thought was indestructible. Sometimes the rock-solid embrace of her family, that element that kept everything standing, flourishing, warm and cozy, felt paper thin.

There was a knock on the door. One more peek at the clock. It was time. The first guests were arriving. She guessed it was Gadi's parents, eager to be underfoot and complicate her efforts to get everything onto the table smoothly. She took another glance at the glass on the counter. *Time for another sip?* No. But she'd catch up in a bit. She took off her apron and relaxed her face into a smile. Denial was a pretty effective modus operandi. Questions would have to wait for another day.

Chapter 15

A sharp clap of thunder split the night sky. The house shuddered. Victoria shot out of bed, shaking the sleep off of her. *Rain?* It never rained at this time of year. She leaned back onto the headboard a moment and waited for her heartbeat to slow. She glanced over at Guy, an immobile lump beneath the comforter. He hadn't even stirred. She was so envious of his ability to sleep through absolutely anything and everything while she tossed and turned, startled at every random noise. There was that story he told – the one from when he was in the military – about how they'd moved a sixty-ton tank he'd been sleeping beneath, a massive piece of machinery, without disturbing him. There was little chance a random storm would wake him.

Her heart continued to beat too quickly, off pace with her peaceful house. She tried to remember if she'd been like this ten years ago. Back then, when the kids were young, she'd also been up and down all night – but for other reasons; she'd had different concerns. Now the worries had multiplied tenfold and taken on a more serious nature. It was all about Ben. She wondered where he was, whether he was dry. After an especially bad storm this past winter he'd sent her a picture, a collection of brown and green smears. She'd had trouble making out much of anything at all. Unable to identify even the hint of a recognizable object, she'd finally had to ask him what she was looking at. He'd explained that those smears were the remains of his tent, the barracks he shared with another eleven soldiers – at least had, before it had collapsed and been washed away in the storm. She remembered it from the day they'd visited him: a sturdy one big enough to encompass twelve soldiers, fortified with extendable walls meant to keep out unwelcome elements and a stove to keep them warm. Ben had found the scene in the picture amusing. She hadn't. Quick to allay her fears he'd assured her that they'd been moved to high ground and were now safely housed in indoor barracks, something with real walls. All was well.

But all was never entirely well. There was no end to this. It was part of being a mother. No, it was part of being the mother of a soldier on active duty. This was something she'd never get used to.

The skies rumbled again. The storm seemed stalled directly above their roof. Victoria took a look at her clock but couldn't make out the numbers. *Where's the clock?* She glanced at her cell phone. No messages. That was a good thing. "No news is good news." With a son in the army it wasn't only a cliché. She swung her legs over the side of the bed. Bama was already there, waiting for her – also startled by the noise of the crackling skies.

Victoria was curious about the clock. Something was definitely off. She picked up the landline phone on the bedside table. No dial tone. She slipped her feet into her slippers and moved toward the door, careful not to make any noise. She made her way down the darkened hallway and then stopped short as a flash of lightening lit up the house. She laid a hand on the cold plaster of the wall, hesitating to take another step, bracing herself for the imminent boom of the thunder. It started as a low growl, working itself up into a crescendo of ferocious rumbling.

There was absolutely nothing like an Israeli storm. It never merely rained and barely ever drizzled. If the skies decided to open they opened up wide, dumping buckets of water and soaking everything within seconds. The thunder shook the houses to their frames, cracking open the sky as if sent by the Almighty Himself, a reminder of life's fragility. Each storm was an all-or-nothing deal, and the whole country went on alert the moment one threatened. Meetings were canceled, itineraries changed, errands postponed and outings deferred. The panic among the local populace was in anticipation of the soon-to-be snarled roads and highways, some actually flooded, others only threatening to be. Anyone who actually needed to get somewhere was in trouble, as the whole country went into shutdown.

Victoria kept one hand on the wall as she made her way along the hallway to the front door. It was pitch black. The storm had obviously taken out the electricity. No wonder she hadn't been able to see the clock. She grasped the door handle and opened it wide. The street was also swathed in darkness. She opened the fuse box and ran her hand over the fuses. Everything was where it should be; it was an area power outage.

This wasn't an auspicious start for the day. She was supposed to drive to Haifa in a few hours to interview a friend who lectured at the university. Exhausted by disappointment at the end of the holiday weekend, Victoria had resolved to find a way to change the drift of her life, making a firm decision to at least complete her application for the Columbia position. The material she'd gather later that day would bolster the second submission required for the application, a piece about the significance of family in Israel. How ironic that a weekend meant to pull her back into the fold, to convince her to embrace everything she had and look no further, had instead inspired her to continue on in her pursuit to pitch it all.

It had hit home as they'd sat around the table. Her children, now fully tilting toward adulthood, if not already there, were participating in a conversation about the recent instance of a soldier in the infantry who'd raised his gun from close-range at an ostensibly unarmed Palestinian. The story had caused a sensation not only in the Israeli press but throughout the world, once again making Israeli soldiers look excessively brutish.

"They're tying our hands. It's gotten to the point where we won't be able to do our jobs. We won't be able to protect others, let alone ourselves."

Jonathan, still in high school but eager to join his brother in the IDF, had been furious. "Brass knuckles? The guy had brass knuckles? I would have shoved my gun right in his face. No question. Who the hell does he think he is?"

"*Teraga*. Relax. It's not that simple Jon. The threats are constant. They never stop. My friends that serve on the line in the West Bank are wired 24/7."

She'd watched silently as Guy comfortably entered a conversation she wanted no part in. "Part of your training will be to discern an actual threat that demands a harsh reaction from one meant to be primarily menacing. Just wait Jon. You'll have your turn as well."

"Does this have to do with all those video messages, throughout the web? People, all kinds of people, soldiers too. All holding signs reading '*Ani im Nachwali*' in front of their faces?" Victoria was amazed that even Maia, far removed from the days she'd don a green uniform, had a modicum of information about the incident. "I thought it had something to do with a bird." She continued, giggling nervously, "I didn't get that it had something to do with some kind of army thing!"

They all seemed to visibly relax at her mistake. The conversation noticeably took a turn as Guy set her straight. "*Nachwali*. Not *Nachlieli*! You're right. A *nachlieli* is a little bird with a black-and-white head. They do sound alike; I can see where you came up with that. But *Nachwali* refers to the soldier's brigade. The soldier who was caught on film raising his gun serves in *Nachal*. Just like your brother."

Ben sat back in his seat, a bit more relaxed than a few minutes earlier. "You know, all those posts: the endless number of photographs that flooded the network, all of that support despite the criticism, in the face of the criticism really, all that was really helpful. We're in such a tight spot. There's so much to consider before we react, and we have a split second to do it."

Victoria had watched her children each voice their feelings, the things they were only now beginning to think about, imagining that years from now, as they branched out and extended their circles, their arguments would become even more well-considered, their ideologies representative of wider worldviews. It wouldn't be long before they would leave the nest, their lovely home in Caesarea – before another gaping hole would open in her own life. She needed to insure she didn't fall into the vacuum they'd leave, to keep her cup as full as possible. And there was no better way to do this than to follow her dream.

Victoria sighed heavily as she stepped back inside. Negotiating the roads to Haifa was going to border on impossible. It was so cozy within the walls of her house. Maybe she'd be better off rescheduling. Bama, who'd been cowering at her feet during the worst of the thunder, equally flummoxed by this awkward start to the day, suddenly turned tail and headed to Jonathan's room. She had the right idea. Victoria grabbed one of the mini flashlights stashed by the front door for precisely such occasions and made her way along the hallway. Easing herself silently back into the dark cave of her bedroom, she couldn't help but mumble aloud something about developing countries, electricity and one lousy clap of thunder before placing the flashlight on the bedside table and climbing back into the warmth of her bed, snuggling up to Guy.

"What time is it?"

"Early. Go back to sleep."

"How come I can't see anything?"

"We have no power. It's a neighborhood black out."

"Maybe I'll stay home."

He draped his arms around her, taking advantage of the storm to pull her in tight and close. She relaxed into his embrace. This was good, in fact, better than good. Her mind shifted to her secret, to what she hadn't told him – what she was thinking she might do. She hadn't even mentioned the day's planned excursion. She cringed for a second. She really didn't want to anger him. But there was no way she was going to give this up. She was certain she wouldn't have to. She'd figure it out. There had to be a way to both go and stay.

The skies continued to rumble. If Guy scratched his plans for the day she'd have to consider staying home, putting off plan A. She smiled in the dark. There might be other ways to soften him up. She snuggled under the covers and tried to fall back asleep, but it was impossible. Soon enough she realized that her eyes were wide open, focused on the tiny slivers of grey dispelling the darkness along the edges of the shutters. She wasn't really tired, but since there was no way to get her day up and running without electricity, she decided she might as well take advantage and enjoy this cozy shelter from the storm.

The light seeping through the shutters began to brighten. Her mind shifted gears, running way ahead of her. She began to envision the scene in the houses next door, neighbors preparing for the day's storm by pulling coats and boots out of storage, opening umbrellas only to find them useless, spines broken from a storm months before. Some were probably considering whether or not to wake their children, whether this might be a good day to let them stay home. The turmoil and chaos caused by one stormy day could be greater than that caused by a rocket launched from Lebanon or Gaza – altering lives, sometimes taking a few, and at minimum wreaking havoc on a large percentage of the populace. If enemies of Israel eventually figured out a way to harness the power of one of these vicious local squalls, they'd all be doomed.

A whirring noise cut through the sound of the rain drumming on the bedroom ceiling and halted her stream of thought. Electricity ran through the house restoring dormant machines to operation. The blue numbers on the clock suddenly appeared, casting their eerie light into the now dawn-lit bedroom: 06:15 a.m. With power restored, life could resume. It was time to kick-start this day. Victoria sighed deeply, snuggling back toward Guy for a few extra seconds and then, reluctantly, pulling herself away. Today was about moving forward, looking ahead, realizing dreams. It was time to get started.

Celia packed up her briefcase, glancing up occasionally to watch her students file out of the room. One made his way toward her.

"How can I help you?" She swung her purse over her shoulder, grabbed her case and stepped out from behind the desk.

"I was wondering if I can have an extension on the deadline for the final paper."

They started walking toward the door. Celia glanced over at him once and then faced forward, continuing out into the main reading room.

"What's up? Does it conflict with another deadline?"

"No. Not really. It's simply that my relatives from England will be in that week and I think it's going to be hard to concentrate in the house."

Celia was always amazed at exactly how many of her students, most post-army, aged twenty-two and up, still lived at home. For most it was an economic consideration, staying home in order to save money on accommodations. But since part of going to college for those she knew back in the States was the actual "going," leaving their parents and living their own life, she was convinced that this detracted from the experience. College in Israel, in effect, was just one more step – not the huge, life-transforming one it was for her generation back home. Maybe that wasn't bad, but it was definitely different.

"I don't really understand the problem. I assigned the paper the first week of class. This is something you've known about."

"True, but it kind of dawned on me this morning. I'm pretty sure I won't be able to turn it in on time in any case. An extension would really help."

Celia sighed. This was such an old story. Every other week she came across one or another instance of how her students' lives weren't necessarily about attending school. The excuses for missed classes ranged from the legitimate – illness, traffic caused by a sudden storm, reserve military duty – to the inane – the previous evening's late wedding, a broken printer. The litany of excuses was endless and tiresome and gave her a headache. She continually wondered how they weren't embarrassed to come up with one reason after another to explain why they couldn't uphold their commitments.

"How much of an extension do you need?" They were walking down the stairs of the library toward the exit and she was eager to move on.

"Another week."

She stopped short. "Another week? Listen." She started out in her head: *Despite the fact that I find your reason lame, at best...* She daren't say that. "I have no problem giving you the extension. That being said, I think you need to organize your time better so that you can honor your commitments. I assigned the paper three months ago and we've talked about it off and on almost every week since. Leave it in my box by noon on Sunday."

The young man shifted his book bag from one shoulder to the other and smiled. "Terrific. Thanks a lot. *L'hit.*" He turned tail and exited the library ahead of her. He'd gotten what he'd come for. Celia realized that a stronger person wouldn't have caved. She followed him out and joined the stream of students flowing toward the office tower and cafeteria. She would love to educate these students in responsibility and accountability. There were times she felt that might be more valuable than anything she could teach them about English literature. She found them incredibly whiny, overflowing with reasons they should be forgiven for assignments not done, tests not aced, required readings ignored. She was continually annoyed by the fact that their exterior lives, those they lived outside of the academic world once they'd left the campus, seemed always more compelling, more significant, and fundamentally, more important.

She wondered how they'd gotten that idea. Back in the United States college studies were the focus of life for a handful of years – the core – a major step forward from the integrated family life they'd left behind in high school. And whether you lived on campus or not, whether an education was handed to you or you needed to struggle for it, it was always something to be valued and respected. Maybe it was the same here, for some, but it sure didn't feel like it.

She stepped through the cafeteria entrance and looked around. She'd arranged to meet her friend Victoria to discuss student life in Israel. Coming off this last exchange she was bound to sound bitter.

"Celia?"

Victoria approached from a nearby table.

"Good morning!" They exchanged a set of kisses.

"How goes it? How long has it been?"

"You'd think Haifa is the end of the world!"

"What's the word from home? Your sister holding down the fort in Boston?"

"First things first. Let's get something to eat. Falafel okay?" Celia looked apologetic. There weren't a lot of options at the university cafeteria, and the falafel stand had the shortest line.

"Absolutely." The two women ordered in turn, each choosing the garnishes that suited their fancy – a smear of hummus, a few crispy fries, cabbage salad or slices of fried eggplant. Once finished, their trays piled high with pitas stuffed to bursting, they made their way to an open table, stopping only momentarily at the condiment stand to add a swirl of *tehina* from a classic squeeze bottle.

"I've really been looking forward to seeing you. We have to do a better job at keeping in touch."

"Agreed. Facebook has made us lazy!"

Celia leaned forward, pita in hand, the corners of her mouth dotted by smudges of *tehina*. "So tell me. This is exciting! Tell me about this job."

Victoria took a sip of lemonade. "Well, at the moment it's only a job *opportunity*. You already know the basics. It's for a teaching position at the Columbia School of Journalism. Celia, *Columbia!* They're looking for voices from abroad, writers who feel that their different perspective has led them to develop different approaches to reporting. I was so excited to be included on the short list. All that's left is to submit two articles, each indicative of directions I would cover in class. Of course, they'll be considered in conjunction with the rest of my publications."

"So you're leaving?"

There was a pause. Both women locked eyes. "I don't know. Boy, everyone jumps right on that. I don't know if I'm leaving. I haven't really thought that far ahead. I simply know that if I were offered this job, with whatever it entails, I'd want to take it. I mean, it's my dream. I've always wanted to branch out into teaching and Columbia…" She paused and looked away toward the long line of students at the food stands. Her voice dropped. "That being said, I can't imagine leaving."

"What does Guy have to say about this?"

"*Oof!* He's impossible. He says that choosing to pursue this dream is choosing to leave the family. I've tried to convince him it's not. He's really pressuring me."

"Men are so primitive!" Celia took a lusty sip of her lemonade, shaking her head. "If the tables are turned, if *they* have an opportunity to do something phenomenal that will advance their career but necessitates leaving for a year, leaving everything behind, they're on the next plane. For us? For the women that choose to do so? Well, we're officially abandoning ship. Absolutely incredible!" Her mind wandered off for a split second to that young man who'd been so sure of himself, her student. He'd known even before he asked that she'd acquiesce to his request. Men were so enabled.

Victoria looked down at her plate. "He's making this very difficult. So difficult. He's laying the guilt on thick. But Celia," she gazed at her intensely, "I want to be *you*! Look at what you have here. You have everything. You're the dream of every person that makes aliyah. You've been able to do exactly what you intended to do when you still lived in the States. I want that. I can't give up the opportunity to find that part that went missing, the piece of the puzzle that will make everything complete." She paused, dropped her eyes to her pita and picked at it, pulling out a slice of eggplant. "I have to do this. I need to do this. At least, I need to *try* to do this. I have no idea what it will lead to. I'm taking it step by step, not looking too far down the road."

"And so you should! I'm completely in your corner. I know how frustrated you've been. Having this career, despite all the personal dramas of the student body, has meant the world to me. It's made it all, well, actually, perfect. Sometimes I wonder if, in fact, it's everything. I mean, if without it…" Her voice petered off. And then, as if the clouds parted, her face broke into a smile. "So, how do I help? I want to help you get there!"

Victoria reached into her bag and took out a big pad of paper and a ballpoint pen. She shoved her plate a bit to the side. "So, this is where I am. I've already finished my first submission. It's an article that follows the interest in extreme endurance sports among the Israeli hi-tech population, over-achieving American wannabees, etc."

Celia laughed, "Well, I expect you had plenty of material for that in your own backyard."

"Exactly. The next piece is about family. It's so important here in Israel. I want to find an angle that will be interesting and new, you know, not merely run-of-the-mill. I came up with the idea to write about student life in Israel. I want to delve into whether there actually *is* such a thing, what with family commitments and all. I'm trying to get a grasp on how it differs from that in the States. I mean, of course there are some surface differences: the fact that the students get a later start, completing army duty first; apply to a specific department of interest, entering directly into their major; and study three years instead of four. But those things are really superficial. They won't garner any interest. I'm looking into a deeper question, something more significant. My sense is that student life differs from the typical American experience because of some kind of empowerment."

Celia burst out, "That's it. You've got it." She immediately regaled her with the story about her earlier encounter and the thoughts it had provoked.

"The student body in Israel is not only more mature, but additionally, has a vaster range of experience. It's not only because of their army service, but that's a big part of it. By the time students matriculate here, they've already held down a full-time job and traveled to far-off places that demanded they live on a miniscule budget and deal with hard conditions. They're extremely hardy." She paused to take another bite of her sandwich. "The fact that they're simply a bit farther along their individual timelines means they're a bit more involved in life – real life – not only their academic one. Plus, primarily due to their army service, they *belong* to something bigger than them, not only a family, but a unit."

"But from what you've told me before, that can be used as a kind of an excuse – a cop-out. Their hyper-involvement, does that justify not upholding commitments? It sounds to me like the students simply don't respect the system." She paused and looked down at her notepad for a moment. "You know, I'm a bit concerned. I'm beginning to get the impression that school comes last within the lives of Israeli youth, and that's going to make this piece awfully negative. I hadn't intended to reveal an ugly underside to the society but that's the vibe I'm getting."

"So let me make it a bit clearer. Students here are as committed to their studies as their peers abroad. What I'm talking about runs much deeper, affecting who these students are when they arrive in class on day one. It's a question of life. These people," Celia gestured around the cafeteria, "have *lives. Real lives.*"

"But so did we!"

"Of course! But for the most part, when we were in college, our lives were one hundred percent about school. Everything else took second chair. Here one's studies have to jostle for attention. Even if education comes first, if going to college is one's number-one occupation, it still has to vie with a larger picture, including family and an extensive network of relationships off campus."

"Then would it be accurate to say that Israeli students don't have a 'pure' academic experience? That instead, their lives on campus are just one part of a larger network of stimuli, responsibilities, and considerations? Sounds to be in line with lower-income students back in the States who live at home while at college and have responsibilities to their families and communities."

"That's pretty much the conclusion I've reached. Once they've begun their studies these students have expanded the concept of what they consider family enormously and are intricately connected to people from all over the country. It's not only about staying in touch with a few friends from high school." Celia poked at a bit of shredded lettuce remaining on her plate with the last dry shard of pita and then wiped the stray *tehina* off her upper lip with her napkin. "Don't forget that family is considered sacred in Israel. You know that better than anyone else. Many operate like clans. Since attending college, in most cases a short ride from home via train or bus, doesn't necessarily entail *leaving home,* neither literally nor figuratively, family continues to play a vital role, sometimes supportive, sometimes demanding, sometimes interfering and frequently all of the above!"

"Do you think all this involvement, maybe even interference, is a *good* thing? I'm the first to admit to family envy, but described this way, it almost sounds suffocating."

Celia lowered her voice a bit and spoke in a measured tone. "My American side says these guys should get over it, stand on their own two feet and move onward. My Israeli side says they're inordinately lucky to be such an intricate part of so many others' lives, to be able to draw on such a large pool of support. These students step into the classroom armed with the riches of an entire unit. Whether that's a burden or an asset is really up to them. You know, had we started as insiders, like our children, you and I, we might very well desire to escape what is probably quite a sticky web. Since we never had that luxury, since we'll always be outsiders, it's definitely appealing. 'The grass is always greener' kind of thing."

"Oh Celia, I'm in. Really. It sounds absolutely dreamy." Victoria put her pen down, closed her notepad and continued, "I don't want to tell you how disappointing Shavuot was, and not only for me. I think the kids felt it as well. Our family is so tiny, so contained. And although their lives are far more intertwined locally than my own, I'm convinced they also sensed something missing."

"I get you," Celia said, leaning back again. "Although I have it a bit better than you in that department, I mean, I have about enough of what I need with Lior's extended family, I'll never know what it means to be one of *them*. Imagine being born and raised in such an environment, growing up secure in knowing the depth of support at your beck and call?" She bunched up her napkin and put it on the table. "Vic, I'm one hundred percent convinced these guys come out ahead."

Victoria nodded her head in agreement, her face breaking into a wide smile. "Ben's the best example. He's got it all. He hosted his squad in our garden this past Saturday. I couldn't help watching them from my bedroom." Victoria paused to raise her right forefinger to her mouth in the universal sign for *Shhhh*. "There was something so easy, so comfortable about the way they related to one another. Whether amused, incensed or excited, they seemed to anticipate each other's reactions, completing one another's sentences and jokes in a way we usually associate with husbands and wives." She lowered her voice to a whisper. "Ben's found a whole new family, right there in his squad. I never foresaw that being a part of his army experience."

The two women sat in silence for a moment, each perhaps thinking about their own absorption or lack thereof: the hits, the misses, the abundance and the gaping holes. Celia watched Victoria fold her napkin, match up its corners and then refold it. She could see she was agitated, definitely on edge. This job wasn't just a professional opportunity; Celia could see it meant much more.

Victoria cleared her throat. "Anyway, sounds like it's pretty frustrating trying to teach this population, making demands, etc. You have to compete with so many other elements in your students' lives. As a lecturer, is it difficult to know you're playing second fiddle?"

"Definitely. But after so many years I've begun to respect the different parameters that guide their lives, to be more flexible about their timetables. And you know? I've come to understand that different – and yes, the college years in Israel are vastly different from those in the US – doesn't necessarily mean worse. Standing on the side, watching the effect of all of this attention-demanding *good* on these kids, makes me wish I'd had a bit of the same."

Victoria let out a long, extended sigh. "You and me both."

The women cleared their trays and headed up to the office tower. Celia was eager to show off the view from the top floor. It was a clear day and they were able to take in all of the Bay of Haifa, the Chalk Cliffs of Rosh HaNikra to the north and the old fortress in Atlit to the south. After a few minutes they stepped back into the elevator for the ride back to Celia's office a few floors below. Anticipating the next stop, Victoria was taken aback when Celia began to frantically shift her body, bending down to peer between the legs of the other passengers and obviously looking for something.

"I don't see my briefcase."

"Did you leave it in the overlook area?"

The doors opened on the nineteenth floor. Celia pushed the hold button. "I don't think so. I can't remember when I last had it. Can you go back upstairs? I'll go down to the cafeteria."

Victoria got off the elevator and took another one back up. Finding nothing, she returned to ground level to look for Celia. She felt awful for her. It was no joke losing one's valuables. The ride seemed to take an eternity. When the doors opened she rushed down the corridor toward the cafeteria, hoping that by now Celia had found her briefcase and all was fine. Upon arriving she was struck by the emptiness of an area that had been positively teeming with students half an hour earlier. Her eyes went directly to the only sign of life. There, in the middle of the space, stood Celia and two men in uniform, and beside them, on a cafeteria table, lay the missing briefcase. She overheard Celia's "I'm so embarrassed" and tentatively approached. One of the men moved to the side and tucked his head down, speaking into the microphone clipped to his shirt.

"Celia?" The quiet and the sudden emptiness of a space always packed full were creepy. "Is everything okay?"

Celia turned at the sound of her voice, her expression relaxing into one of obvious relief. "Vicky, they wanted to detonate my bag! I caused such trouble! That man over there," she pointed at the security agent to the side, "is calling off the robot that executes the controlled explosions!"

Victoria didn't know whether to laugh or to cry. This scene was ridiculous, and terrifying and hysterically funny, all at once.

Celia made the decision for her, breaking into a sudden laugh. "Shocking, right? A few more minutes and my briefcase would have been blown to smithereens! And look at this place! People were really frightened! Little old me emptied the cafeteria!"

A piercing glance from one of the security officials, no doubt put out by this incident, sobered her instantly. "This is really awkward. I've inconvenienced everyone. Can you believe all this fuss? The whole trip down in the elevator I was afraid my things had been stolen, and it ends up that I instigated an actual security incident. Around these parts, thievery is so much lower on the totem pole than terrorism."

Celia finished up with her apologies to the security men, retrieved her case with a guilty expression and steered Victoria out of the cafeteria by the elbow. Students were already flooding back in. An "all clear" meant lunch could resume.

"That was really freaky. This reality is so very different from the one back home."

With the incident behind them, Victoria began to realize that she was truly shaken. This wasn't exactly where she'd seen this day going. She let Celia escort her out but remained subdued, definitely less effusive than before. She no longer felt like talking, her mind shifting back and forth between an acute awareness of the fear factor that was part of life in Israel and the conversation they'd had earlier in the cafeteria. Her plan to exit stage right, originally intended as a means of professional advancement, was turning out just as much to be about reducing stress.

How did I ever accept this kind of life?

There were so many answers to that question but most germane was the realization that somehow she had. And it was then, as she got into her car, that it all seemed so clear. The local manner of clinging together and operating as a clan, precisely what they'd been talking about back in the cafeteria, suddenly made a lot of sense. It was the perfect way to protect themselves. Maybe the atmosphere of potential threats caused families to flock together and hang on tight. Maybe dealing with stress was the generating source of such consolidation here in Israel. As she pulled out of the university lot she considered whether she might have stumbled over the local version of that classic question of the chicken or the egg.

Victoria had worked so hard to push local terror out of reach, safely hidden beyond the protective walls of the bubble of a life she'd constructed, yet sometimes it managed to sneak in. Exactly how long could she live in denial of her surroundings, justify a twisted acceptance of potential, pointless and tragic loss? Winding her way through the beautiful canyon of the Carmel Mountains, the scenery parallel to none, she felt overcome by a mixture of exhaustion and determination. Although she could live with her fears and disappointments – who didn't have a mountain of both after so many years? – she refused to give up this opportunity to change her course. She would write her heart into this final submission, seize the chance to breathe different air. Her resolve to redress a choice that no longer suited, to regain the calmer life she'd lost, had never been stronger.

Chapter 16

Ben met their car as they pulled into the parking lot outside of the base.

"Baby."

"Hi, Mom. Dad." He tossed his head to the side in acknowledgement of his siblings. "Squirts."

Ben leaned in for a hug, his rifle slung behind him. For just a moment, she saw him not as a soldier, but instead, a grown boy. Hers.

She held on for a few extra seconds. She hoped he wouldn't notice. Then she stepped back and watched Guy give him one of those hearty, backslapping hugs.

"Look what your mother prepared for us."

They all leaned into the back of the hatchback, completely jam-packed with a variety of plastic bags and carry-alls.

"I told her she went overboard."

They carried everything over to a large picnic table cemented to the ground.

"Oh, no. I forgot a tablecloth. Again!"

They laughed. Old story. Every time they came to the base for one of these picnics they enviously admired the spreads at the adjacent tables: white paper tablecloths, endless plastics offering a range and abundance of food. Victoria's picnics were more Spartan, never fancy and always missing one thing or another.

"At least I remembered the forks this time."

She caught Ben rolling his eyes and smiled. No, she wasn't great at this. Whatever she laid out was never going to be all that good looking, nor gourmet. But she knew it was enough and always, appreciated.

When she'd first come to visit Ben at the base she hadn't prepared anything at all. She simply didn't know it was expected. Guy had stood in the kitchen anticipating a pile of things ready to be loaded into the car and had been shocked to find she hadn't prepared a thing.

"We have to bring food."

"No one told me that."

"What's the point of the visit if we don't bring food?"

"Don't they feed him there?"

"Of course they feed him there." He'd shaken his head in exasperation. "But the whole point is to bring him something to eat."

"I don't get it. They feed him. They actually have a dining hall with real food. Why would he want mine?"

At that Guy had actually burst out laughing. He'd tried to say something, add a comment, but in the end had simply continued to snicker to himself, opening up the refrigerator and beginning to pull out a few ready-mades.

"You have a point there."

"Seriously. We're supposed to bring food?"

Victoria began to feel frantic. She liked to get things right. How did she get this wrong?

"Like what? What are we supposed to bring?" She stopped speaking and watched him pull out plastics filled with sliced yellow cheese, a package of pita bread, a few cucumbers, a tub of hummus.

"I'll take care of it. Don't worry."

"Guy. Tell me. Please."

"Do we have any shnitzel? That's always welcome." He continued to line up items on the kitchen table.

This was a new regime for the family, the first week Ben was at a base close enough to visit. She couldn't have known. How could she have known? She needed to cut herself a break.

"I'll make shnitzel. I can do it quickly." She looked up at the clock. "Do we have another half an hour? I'll just whip up a batch."

Guy was rummaging through the cabinet above the refrigerator, pulling out plastic plates, forks, knives and spoons. He put them on the table next to the other items and leaned over to give her a kiss on the cheek.

"It's okay. It's all okay. Make the shnitzel. I'll put together a cold pack."

She'd breathed a sigh of relief but simultaneously shifted into gear. Time was running out. She needed to prepare everything as quickly as possible. She briefly wondered if she'd have time to prepare a cake as well. She could do it. She could put together a proper picnic.

She could be a good mommy to a soldier, as good as any other.

And true to her conviction, she'd pulled together a full meal that first time, and every time since – including this particular Shabbat. Car unloaded, table set, Victoria stood back to look at her handiwork. There was quite a spread. In fact, there were so many plastic tubs of food on the table it was difficult to know where to start. Guy and Ben looked on in amazement.

"Mom. It's only me. Who's going to eat all this?"

"I simply wanted to make sure we have everything. I didn't want anything to be missing. It's no big deal. You can take it back in with you for a snack later."

She watched as he and Guy exchanged a look. "Your mother likes to get things right; didn't want to leave anything out. I told her she was overdoing it."

They congregated around the table and the subject changed. Jonathan wasn't eating. He was busy holding Ben's rifle, touching all of the parts, one by one, gripping it in hand, "at the ready," fascinated.

"And what's this for?" The boys sat together, talking about the weapon, while Guy and Victoria continued to eat their lunch. It was a nice day. Not too hot. Victoria loved seeing her sons together, swapping comments, gestures, looks. This was the best. She turned to Maia, idly munching on a potato chip, detached from the boy's conversation. She was busy taking in the random parade of hungry cats that had appeared the instant the food was on the table. "Where do they all come from?" The picnic area was obviously a favorite for the local strays; so many tidbits to pick up.

Victoria got up to add a bit more hummus to her plate, catching Guy's eyes. They were cloudy. Only minutes earlier they'd been clear and bright and blue. She got it. Those eyes had been for Ben. These were for her. They hadn't spoken all that much over the last few days, ever since she'd received the official invitation to fly to New York. She'd assured him it was only an interview. He wasn't buying it.

"Sweetie. Ben." She wiped the corner of her mouth. Fiddled with a piece of pita. "I'm heading to New York for a few days this week."

He looked up from his plate, clearly surprised. "Oh yeah? What for?"

She hesitated, looking over to Guy. His head was buried in his plate. He wasn't going to be any help at all.

"I simply have a few things to take care of. A reunion with a few friends."

Ben returned to his food; seemed completely unfazed.

"And…" Guy wasn't going to let her off the hook here. He was intent on making this as painful as possible.

"Oh, and there are some people at the Journalism School, you know, at Columbia? I'm going to meet them and see if we can collaborate on a project."

Guy coughed but it came out more like a choking sound.

"Dad, you okay?" Ben reached over and slapped his father on the back.

Guy smiled at him. "Just fine. Don't worry about me." He glanced up at Victoria.

"So Ben. I'm meeting with some people at Columbia."

"'Kay. So, great. When will you be back?"

He'd moved on. How simple it all was. As long as she was coming back it didn't matter if she stepped out a bit on her own here and there.

She felt comforted by his nonchalance. He had his own life; it no longer revolved around hers. She looked over at Guy to make sure he'd picked up on that; to make sure he'd heard that Ben was fine with it all. He was glaring at her. She looked away.

"So anyway, I'll see you next weekend. Right? You'll be home by then?"

"Definitely."

"Good. Because I'm closing after that. No one's going home. The whole platoon is going up north for two weeks."

"Want me to bring you anything from the States?"

"I've given Mommy a whole shopping list," Maia piped in, suddenly engaged in the conversation. "She's promised to bring us goodies. I added a shirt or two for you as well as Jonathan."

This was good. Their conversation had leveled out to normal. Victoria felt less stressed, even a bit relieved. This was going to be simpler than she'd thought it would be. She stood up to put her plate back on the table. She lifted her eyes for a second. Guy was staring at her. Well, maybe it wasn't going to be all that simple after all.

Chapter 17

Susan rifled through the workbooks on the shelf, figuring out who needed what for the coming day. She had an elementary school student working on the alphabet, a high school student decoding the varieties of the perfect tense and a young, native English speaker working on "magic e" spelling patterns. She loaded everything into her tote bag, careful to double-check that nothing was missing. This was her daily routine, her raison d'être. She rolled her eyes as she packed. *Who'd have thought it?*

She'd worked so hard to become certified as a speech therapist back in the States, had landed a primo job at one of the better-known clinics in Manhattan and had already begun to gather quite a client base. And then? Well, and then she'd met Matt. It was a total fluke, a party like any other. And after two years together in the States, he'd convinced her that their children were better off being raised in Israel. They'd packed up and moved, lock, stock and barrel.

She carried the tote bag to the front door, checked her purse and walked outside to the car. She really didn't have much to complain about. She was making a very nice living as a private English teacher and, over all, enjoyed the work. After all, she'd always loved working with children. She tried to convince herself that speech therapy, the field in which she'd invested years of study and training, the one she loved, wasn't that far removed from teaching the ABC. But she'd never gotten used to this new occupation, couldn't even stand the moniker; knew that behind that glaze of complacency was the bare truth. She'd wanted to be so much more, had been well on the path to doing so – and now almost none of her friends even remembered that she'd attained all those extra degrees, had been someone else. She was living a lie.

She couldn't believe it last month when Matt told her he'd received a job offer abroad. He hadn't even mentioned it as an option. He'd probably figured she'd get her hopes up, spend time obsessing about the possibility, its ramifications for their family. He was right. But his announcement about the position, managing the establishment of an Israeli factory in New Jersey, had come as a total surprise. The timing seemed odd. After starting out with very little, spending their first years on a kibbutz trying to be a part of a greater whole, they'd decided to go out on their own and try to establish themselves independently. The culmination of these years was the planning, financing and building of a house, their dream house, to which they'd finally moved just a few months earlier. Matt swore they'd be back, insisted that this wasn't going to be a permanent move. When the job abroad was complete they'd return home and have plenty of time to enjoy the fruit of all that labor.

In the meantime, she'd have an opportunity to resurrect her career, the one circumstances had forced her to abandon, and drop the one she'd picked up by necessity. This makeshift business, her job moonlighting (as she liked to call it) as a teacher, was about to be packed up and shelved. This move back to the States, their relocation, was going to be a new start. There was no way she'd muddy it with the dregs of this patchwork career. For that she was, indeed, excited.

But Susan couldn't also help feeling a bit sad. This really was a pretty place. She'd been proud to build a house in Caesarea, put down official roots in such a beautiful place. She'd never dreamed she'd be trading it all for a semi-attached in New Jersey. The thought of what the renters would do to her pristine new home made her cringe. *Forget it. It's a done deed.* And then there was Lynn. She'd be staying in Israel. Susan knew that was for the best, but she'd miss her daughter. She only had the one and they were so close. She forced herself to suppress these thoughts, focusing instead on when she might hear back from the clinics in the States to which she'd been referred. The thought of returning to her original work sweetened the pot considerably.

She pulled into the beach parking lot and spotted Jackie getting out of her car. Again, she felt a twinge. *I'll miss these guys.* It had taken decades to collect a group of true friends. It wasn't likely to happen during their relatively brief stint in the States.

"Great timing," she said, getting out of the car.

"Who doesn't love Election Day?" The two hooked arms. "Definitely tops my Ten Best about living in Israel." Election Day was an automatic national holiday, another Shabbat. "Great opportunity to hang out in the sunshine!"

As they began their walk down the path to the shoreline Jackie lowered her voice. "Do I have something for you!"

"What's going on?"

Susan discerned bright splashes of color down by the water's edge. Alison and Victoria had already begun their stroll south and were standing at the water's edge looking out toward the sea. From a distance they looked like pelicans, their bodies draped in colorful wraps, their heads capped by large sunhats. Since the sun was an anathema, tanning could only occur by default. She followed the line of their gaze and spotted a flash of black neoprene. Evie stepped out of the breaking surf onto the beach and joined them. She and Jackie caught snippets of their comments as they caught up.

"Hey! Our very own mermaid!"

"Finished paddleboarding early. Went in for a quick dip. God, I love it here." Evie shook the water out of her hair and leaned in for a round of hugs and kisses.

"Isn't it magnificent today?"

"We really are the luckiest people in the world."

"Only five minutes from the house." Evie extended her hand toward the sea. "This! Glacier Freeze."

"Excuse me?"

"It's a Gatorade flavor; same gorgeous frosty blue-green shade." There was general assent, a nodding of heads. "Exactly!"

"So Jackie was just about to tell me…"

"Spill."

"I finally met the new English teacher."

"For the fifth and sixth graders? I've heard he's terrible."

"He's not terrible. He's simply fresh off the boat. The children are eating him alive."

They began to walk south toward the towering smokestacks of the local power plant. "Well, I can affirm that they're learning somewhere close to nothing." Susan lowered her voice. She had quite a bit to say on this topic. "I get them in the afternoons and it's like starting from scratch."

"It doesn't help that he's a little weird. For kids that's pretty much the nail in the coffin. They say his *kippah* is constantly falling on the floor. The only phrase they've all learned to say is: 'Your *kippah*! Your *kippah*!' Guess at minimum they'll know their possessive adjectives! But seriously, the joke is at his expense. They make fun of him incessantly." She paused. "Oh, and get this. You won't believe it. To top it all off, he's Canadian."

They all broke into laughter. There was some unspoken agreement among Anglos, forever outsiders, that there had to be an immigrant population even more pathetic than theirs. Canadians, especially those who'd made aliyah, were easy victims.

"And the very, very latest is," she paused for dramatic effect, "that he's asked them to call him Mr. S."

"You're kidding me! Adopting Mrs. B's policy? Funny. He obviously hopes to achieve respect by association."

The only English teacher to garner any respect at the local elementary school was a middle-aged woman who'd insisted on a formal means of address from day one. The kids, used to the informality that characterized most aspects of life in Israel, had resisted. She'd found a compromise of a sort, attaching "Mrs." to the first initial of her last name. Amazingly enough it had worked! A little distance, albeit symbolic, went a long way.

"Exactly! Apparently he's decided that that's what's been hindering his ability to maintain control in the classroom. He's pinning quite a bit of hope on this new title. There might be something to it, but I'm skeptical. I don't think he stands a chance."

"Sounds clever to me. How many times have we covered this subject? I actually cringe each time my students call me by my first name. Last week one of my ten-year-olds whipped out his new iPhone (for the record, a newer version than mine), turned to me with great seriousness and said, "Susan, from now on I'll be the one calling you to arrange lessons. We can leave Mommy out of it."

"Eww. That actually gives me the creeps."

"This 'first-name basis' business is out of control. No wonder our kids have issues with heeding authority; going around calling their teachers by their first names! It's ridiculous! Whatever happened to Miss Peters, Mrs. Hodgkin, Mr. Howell. Everything was so much clearer then."

Susan had found this aspect of life in Israel, the informality emphasized by the primary usage of first names, difficult to get used to. It rubbed against everything she knew from as far back as elementary school. Absolutely everyone in Israel was known by their first name, whether the housekeeper, the bank manager or the prime minister. This created a situation in which the lines between figures of authority and everyone else were dramatically blurred, enabling pupils to feel on par with their teachers and citizens to feel as powerful as those running the country. In light of this "norm," it was hard to convince any one person to accept any other's authority – whether in the classroom, on the highway or even in places as critical as courts of law and the Knesset, Israel's parliament.

"It all stems from that Socialist crap. You know, 'We built this country with a new world order, etcetera…shirking the one left behind in the Old Country, blah blah blah.'"

"It was a pretty good idea at first," Alison offered. "I don't think the original founders of the modern state ever considered that it might lead to a lack of respect."

"You're always the first to defend the status quo over here. They should nominate you official spokesperson. I don't buy it. This whole business leaves us with a mess, struggling to teach our children to respect their teachers – who all, by the way, go by the names Michal, Anat and Nurit. It's absolutely hopeless."

There was another collective nodding of heads. Susan needed to cool down. She turned away from the group for a moment and entered the surf breaking on the shore, letting the water lick her shins and leaning over to pour scoopfuls over her arms. This subject made her broil. As the others joined her in the surf, one by one, she commented, "You know, I actually feel sorry for Mr. S. He probably had an interesting job back in Canada. Now he's teaching a subject he no doubt has very little interest in, to thirty-five preadolescents." She hoped her words had come across in an off-hand manner and didn't reveal her own feeling of having been similarly slighted.

"How do you know he knows nothing about English?"

"Well, for starters, last week's fifth-grade spelling list included words like cat, mat and hat. At that pace those kids won't even be able to get into the false-starters class at the middle school."

"At least he seems to know something about phonetics, or rather, Dr. Seuss. Have they learned any grammar?"

"I heard they had a lecture about adding an *s* to something or other. All the kids remembered was the large S inside a shield that he'd drawn on the board, Superman style. Not one of them knew that it had anything to do with verb declension let alone something as specific as third-person singular present simple."

"Hey," Alison interjected, "that's all Swahili to me as well. Want to explain yourself to the uneducated among us?"

"Uneducated. Right." They all knew otherwise. Attention returned to Jackie. "Has he ever taught before?"

"Apparently he was a high school principal back in Canada – has some kind of science background."

Evie almost choked. "What a major step backward…and this one right into the shit. Bet he has trouble looking in the mirror each morning, let alone actually showing up at work."

"He'll be gone by next year."

They nodded their heads in agreement as they stood gazing westward toward the horizon.

"It must be so degrading for him to have had to accept this job in the first place."

"Don't I know it," Susan added. "Been there, done that and can't wait to move on." Susan waited, thinking someone would take the bait. *Nothing? They're not going to say a word?* She glanced at her cell phone. "Unfortunately I've still got a few more weeks to go. Got to run girls. I'm due to start in an hour."

There was a long pause. Victoria broke the silence. "You're going to get another chance." She lowered her voice, almost as if speaking to herself. "You gave up so much. I know exactly how that feels. I don't think native Israelis appreciate what's involved in making aliyah; how much work it takes to find a satisfying niche."

Susan answered her understanding comment with a warm smile and then, suddenly, frowned. It dawned on her that her relocation to the States might actually have hit a raw nerve. Victoria had also given up a lot in exchanging one life for another. And Jackie? She constantly moaned over one thing or another, hinting at a future elsewhere. Alison never complained, in fact, she raved about her local life; but Susan knew she too had sacrificed earlier dreams. Only Evie, resplendent in that wet suit, seemed completely in her element.

Susan had been so busy with her own preparations, attending to the endless details incumbent to moving from one corner of the globe to another, she hadn't once considered how this might affect her friends. Not sure quite how to handle that thought – the idea that she might have actually stirred a degree of resentment among those that meant so much – she returned to the safe ground of their original line of conversation.

"That's absolutely right. And way too many of us have had to fall into the garbage pail of teaching English." She stepped backwards, out of the water, and turned northward, up beach, toward the car park. "Do you know how many times I've been approached at the supermarket? *I overheard you on the phone…blah, blah, blah. Do you teach English?* I could probably cobble together a whole schedule based only on market pick-ups."

"Why do they assume that anyone who knows how to speak, knows how to teach? I couldn't begin to teach English. I don't think I've ever even had a formal grammar class. You had me lost there with the present simple." Alison stopped to pick up something glistening in the sand and then pitched it back into the water. None of them collected sea shells; the beach was their entire life here in Caesarea, not a "summer" thing like back home.

"That merely means that you have some kind of standard. You have no idea how many new immigrants use it as a kind of default – obviously out of desperation."

"That's right," Jackie added. "The teacher Mr. S replaced was apparently a child psychologist back in the States. She spent more time analyzing the children than teaching them how to read and write. As I recall, she even handed out calling cards advertising her clinic on parent-teacher day. Nuts."

"Hey! I'm really no different. You could throw me into the same pathetic pile."

"Maybe. But you have a real gift with students, chemistry. And didn't you teach back in the States? Grad school? Same difference!"

"That Canadian dude, our infamous Mr. S, probably gave up a 'real' life in order to assume this 'pseudo' one half-way across the world – all in the name of returning to the homeland, Eretz Yisrael. That can't be easy."

"Wouldn't you figure he could find a more lucrative occupation? How is he going to finance his family's integration?"

"Maybe his wife's in hi-tech. We know nothing about them."

"Good point. In fact, let's give him the benefit of the doubt and assume this job is only meant to tide him over and keep him busy during the morning hours while he finds something more substantive."

Evie laughed. "I can't imagine anyone choosing to battle thirty-five ten-year-olds, several times a week, as a means of passing the time. I think he probably needs this job. Susan hit the nail on the head. This whole aliyah business isn't simple. I can't begin to count how many times I've had to recreate myself since I arrived. I spent years trying to remember what I actually did for a living until, of course, I hit the jackpot. I'm not budging from the design industry. Suits me to a T.

"But the language issue? It simply doesn't go away. I've progressed quite a bit. I mean, thank God! But I still can't have an 'intelligent,'" she made a little air-quotation gesture, "conversation in Hebrew. I can talk until I turn blue but what comes out is never really me. Most of the people I meet in the Hebrew-speaking world treat me like a child."

"I totally get that. Years ago Guy attended a talk I gave at that journalism conference in Jerusalem. Remember? The one on Western immigration and cultural adaptation. His only comment, after listening to me speak for forty-five minutes, was 'It's a shame you couldn't lecture in English.'" Victoria gestured to the large collection of flat-topped rocks marking the entrance to the beach. The group followed her lead and each grabbed a seat, all comfortably situated looking out at the water once again. "Sometimes it feels like I'm treading water."

"Well," Jackie said, "as you all know, I've actually given up. For whatever reason, I simply can't learn this language. I understand a lot more than I did when I arrived, but speaking is never going to happen."

"So, okay," Victoria continued, "this is exactly what I addressed in that lecture. It's not about speaking the language – or rather – it's not *only* about speaking the language. I'm sure even Mr. S has figured that out. There are numerous other cultural differences to bridge in order to take a crack at the gargantuan task of establishing oneself within an already intact society. This country is basically one big village. Coming in as an outsider raises enormous, sometimes insurmountable, challenges, foremost among which is establishing a niche. Without it there's little chance of becoming part of the greater whole.

"I remember when I visited here with my parents in the early '70s. The hot subject was Russian immigration. This was soon after the emigration quota there was raised. There was all this propaganda about how happily settled these immigrants were, thrilled to be working as janitors and cashiers even though they'd been doctors back in Mother Russia."

"I wouldn't have been happy cleaning houses. I don't even think my housekeeper's happy cleaning houses," Evie piped in.

"No one's happy cleaning mine!" Victoria smiled sheepishly as the others laughed. They all knew she was a pack rat.

"Why did they have to clean houses?" Susan chimed in sarcastically. "I'm sure even the Russians would have had no problem being hired as English teachers."

The reaction to Susan's acerbic, but not entirely humorous comment, was a raucous round of laughter. Jackie reached up to wipe away a tear of glee. "That's so incredibly sad…and true!" Amid the giddy atmosphere no one noticed Susan had stopped laughing. Good thing. She didn't want them to pick up on how pitiable she felt despite her willingness to make a joke at her own expense.

It was time to get moving. Her lessons were due to start. She looked up and down the coastline, replete with powdery white sand, a bevy of individuals out enjoying the beautiful spring day. She'd developed a fondness for the glamorous, St. Tropez feel of Caesarea and knew she'd miss it when heading to the mall back in New Jersey. She popped up and brushed the sand off her legs.

Evie rose as well. "Most beautiful place on earth. Right here. Right on our doorstep. Nothing like it."

Susan winced a bit at her comment – just what she didn't want to hear at the moment. "Sorry girls but somewhere out there real life awaits."

"Hey, we didn't even talk about the election."

"I'm not really up on the candidates."

"Just make sure to vote *against* the candidate from Shas, the religious party. We really don't need them interfering any more than necessary. As it is they have much too much say over the budget. All those funds that should be directed to medicine and education get funneled straight into the yeshivas."

"Ben told me there's no milk on the base. They can't have milk products because meat is served. Can you imagine? No milk! These are growing children!"

"I'll never forget that dirty swimming hole I had to dip into before I got married. The public mikvah. It was absolutely repulsive. The water looked as if it hadn't been changed in weeks. Reform Judaism never demanded such an outrageously meaningless bit of ceremony."

"It's really unbearable being constantly, at the end of the day, under their control. I completely understand those young couples that forgo all of this pomp and circumstance and marry abroad. Much simpler."

"In any case, I'm heading over to the Center now. Don't worry. I know exactly what I don't want. Is it crowded?"

"You can't imagine. I was there this morning. Let me warn you. The candidates and their goons are swarming the parking lot. Apparently there's absolutely no official mandate regarding maintaining a reasonable distance from the voting booths. Everything's all quite in-your-face." They dispersed as they reached the parking lot, muttering this and that in agreement: everything about this country was "in-your-face."

"Well, I'm not going to complain. At least we got a holiday out of it. When's the last time we met in daylight? This was a treat!"

"One more opportunity not to teach the kids. Just terrific!" Jackie consistently criticized the school system.

Susan headed to her car and then, with a change of heart, ran over to catch Victoria before she pulled out. "Hey. Do you have a second?"

She rolled down the window. "What's up?"

"You know, nobody mentions my relocation. Nothing. Is it such a sore subject?" Victoria turned off the ignition and got out of the car, pulling her friend in for a hug. "We're all really happy for you, Susan. Really. It's simply that," she hesitated, "well, you know, we're all a little envious as well. Maybe even jealous."

Susan looked down, tracing the toe of her flip-flop along the pavement. "Vic, the thing is…it's not as easy to leave as you might imagine. It's not as easy as *I'd* imagined. I'm going to miss this, you, everybody. I'm going to miss all of it. We have so much."

"Oh, please. Sweetie. Don't bother with all that. You need to go back there and pursue your real life, the one that was derailed. I understand that better than anyone else. I think it's fantastic. If I had the same opportunity…" she hesitated, looked away for a second and then back into Susan's eyes. "Well, you know, I'd jump at it as well."

The two parted after an exchange of kisses and another firm hug, and Susan made her way to her first student. She wondered about Victoria. She had everything: a husband who loved her, amazing kids; she was professionally active, publishing quite a bit in well-known magazines back home. It didn't seem like anything was missing. Yet, at the same time, there were these casual comments. Those times she expressed annoyance and dissatisfaction with her life, with Israel; that undertone of itchiness that suggested something lurked beneath the surface. And just now…what was that? Her comment hadn't seemed entirely innocent. Was she actually hinting that she wanted to go back herself?

Susan dismissed the notion as impossible. With one son in the army and another soon to follow it simply couldn't be. That leap would be far too bold to take, truly off the grid. She poked at the air conditioning buttons in her car. Time to gear up for the day. She simply couldn't wait to dump this charade of a life, to get back to her passion, pick up where she'd left off. So many children needed help with their words, both here and back in the States. But here she'd forever been shut out of her profession, appropriately reserved for native Hebrew speakers.

This was going to be great. For sure. And maybe, just maybe, this three-year relocation would stretch into something more permanent. Her mind stopped racing ahead, startled by that last thought. *Permanent?* She hadn't allowed herself to go there. Her brow furrowed a moment, stricken by a passing notion: *What if we don't come back?*

Chapter 18

Ilana peeked out the window of her apartment, squeezing in as close to the glass as possible in an attempt to get a look at the entrance, four floors down. She wanted to see Vicki as she arrived but it was impossible. There was absolutely no way to manage any view of the street, blocked as she was by a number of other buildings and the clunky fire escape. She sighed heavily, turned around and did a quick take of the living room. It was a bit dark and definitely cramped. They'd collected quite a bit of furniture over the years. Although there'd never been quite enough space for it here in their New York apartment, getting rid of some of the more beautiful pieces they'd collected in Europe seemed a shame. She ran her hand over the curved wood molding on the back of the Biedermeier sofa, watching her fingers run a zigzag along the edge of the upholstery. *No matter.* Soon enough they'd move on to yet another residence. One thing that wouldn't be lacking there was space.

She moved through the room, straightening things that didn't need straightening, tidying what was already neat. She wanted everything to look nice. When Vicki had mentioned she'd be in town – *what was it for, some kind of opportunity at Columbia? –*

she'd immediately perked up. She couldn't wait for the chance to reconnect, catch up, to spend a few hours with a real friend.

She stepped into the kitchen to check the tea set she'd arranged earlier on the counter, to still her excitement. She ticked off the items in her head: teapot, tea caddy, cups, saucers, spoons, sugar bowl, milk jug. She peered into the last, still empty; she'd fill it later. Although Ilana knew this posting was considered enviable, after all, who wouldn't want to live in New York City, she'd found it almost lonely. With her husband gone much of the time, traveling around the United States, the charm of the city had waned; raising the children could be done anywhere and that was pretty much all she did these days. Maybe if she'd come here at an earlier stage in her life, or a later one.

She opened the cookie drawer straight into her knee. *Damn. Every time!* She selected a few more cookies and added them to the plate she'd already prepared, arranging and rearranging them into artistic patterns, first a large star, then a flower, finally settling on a kind of domino. She'd begged for this, pled for yet one more posting outside of Israel, but Nimrod wouldn't hear of it. He was ready to return, was eager to settle down. This was their fourth tour abroad, having lived first in The Hague, then Madrid and the last time, Bonn. He thought it would be better for all of them to dig in and finally establish roots.

She, however, couldn't bear the thought. Every stay in Israel had been characterized by dust, oppressive heat and his suffocating family, and of course there were the sporadic attacks of terror that she could never truly get used to. Who could? She'd spent most of their years there, squeezed in between their postings abroad, nagging him to save her; desperate to gain yet another five-year reprieve from what she considered an unbearable, stressful and yes, even dangerous, life in the Middle East.

As a native Norwegian, New York hadn't been a natural fit. In fact, it had been a real challenge after spending most of the last two decades in European capitals. She'd become accustomed to the small scale, the intimacy; several-hundred-year-old brick buildings leaning one against the other, like athletes shoulder to shoulder in a huddle, blocking out much of the light; uneven pavements thick with shiny green leaves impeding anything faster than a slow, loping pace, forcing one to appreciate the charm of decay; endless alleys of oak trees dating back centuries, redolent of Europe's history.

New York had been a shock at first, to live somewhere so enormous and spread out, where life moved at a galloping pace and one had to hurry to keep up. Although it had taken time to get adjusted, she had. After all, in the end it didn't matter where she was, as long as it wasn't Israel. Whether large or small, vast or embracing, it was all blessedly different than what she'd married into. No sand, no endless negotiations, not as many rude encounters; all smiles, calm, order and an abundance of shade. And of course, there was the secure feeling that came from not having to anticipate random terror attacks, flashes of violence that shook her to the bone and reminded her of how much hatred lurked just beyond the Green Line. It was a blessing to be far removed from all that.

But this was it. Nimrod had firmly informed her that this was to be their last tour. There was no chance of another. She'd metaphorically kicked and screamed when she'd heard the news, trying to finagle another year, understanding that once back, there would be no escape. It hadn't gotten her anywhere. It was late May. Reality was beginning to set in: they were returning home this summer.

Ilana resumed her position by the window. *Home.* What did that even mean? *Israel. Was that really home?* She'd pretty much lost sight of where home was over the last decades, recognizing only its most minute and specific manifestation: her miniscule, nuclear family. Everything else had been forsaken by choosing to live their lives abroad for so very long.

She was the first to admit that despite the numerous gains, this peripatetic lifestyle had its downside. While her children's development had flourished – they couldn't help but benefit from the prestigious education they'd received at one or another of the various private schools they'd attended along the way, both in Europe and the States, picking up one foreign language after another – her own had been stymied. She'd been stranded in a black hole of professional stagnation.

Life within the foreign-service communities abroad came with certain restrictions regarding where one could work, live and even with whom one could associate. For the most part her social life was limited to a very narrow circle: a microenvironment including a handful of individuals with whom, for the most part, she had nothing in common. Although there were get-togethers, parties and special events, some for families, some for couples and a few for the wives alone, events intended to encourage a sense of community among those stationed abroad, they were attended by the very same people and held in a limited number of locations: so-and-so's apartment, so-and-so's house. After a cultural splurge at the start of their stay here, they'd retreated to family life, taking little advantage of the lovely local restaurants – they were simply too pricey – and other local riches. Since even babysitters had to come from within the foreign-service community, they were at a premium. In the end, an experience that should have been mind-expanding, exposing her to the world, ended up being unbearably limiting.

The buzzer rang, startling her. She ran to the front door, pushed the intercom button and went out into the hall to await Victoria's arrival. As she stood in the dim stairwell she had a vivid memory of the two of them decades earlier: two foreigners who'd married into the diplomatic corps, sitting alone at each end of a living room crowded with *real* Israelis. Outsiders dying to be let in, searching for the key. Everyone there was so comfortable in their skin, knew who they were, what they were about, what they were doing there. It was so easy for them. Their role as Israelis stationed abroad was clear cut, their routine familiar: they came, they conquered and they knew, after a few years, they'd go back home.

She and Victoria had fallen into this show backwards, by the seat of their pants, totally unprepared for what lay ahead. Their search for an identity had been almost pathetic; they came off as lame as leftovers. No one ever seemed to know exactly how to speak to them, the cultural gulf so obvious, so glaring. Of course, she'd been better off than Victoria, having conquered the language so quickly. She'd almost felt sorry for her new American friend, the only other foreigner in the room. Everyone made an effort to speak English with her, to include her, but that merely made her stick out even more. Ilana had watched as people drifted over, exchanged a few words, and then moved on, akin to checking out a monkey in a cage. She could see that Victoria was suffering but wasn't sure whether to help save her or stand clear. She hadn't wanted to get pulled down into the undertow, her position equally precarious.

The ceiling of the elevator appeared and Victoria moved into sight, head, shoulders, torso and finally legs. "Darling!"

Ilana pulled the metal scissor gate open. "Sweetie!"

They embraced briefly, pulled back to look at one another a long moment and then moved together again, this time for a clingier hug.

"It's been far too long. Wow! You look great! I've really missed you!"

"Well, soon enough you'll have me on your front step."

Victoria hesitated just a moment, and then smiled.

Ilana took her by the hand and led her into the apartment.

"So, this is it? Your New York pad?"

Ilana laughed nervously. "Well, I know it isn't much. And God knows, it isn't big!"

She watched Victoria assess her home, what she realized probably looked like a dimly lit furniture warehouse. She knew it must seem grim compared with the light-filled airiness of her own home. She gestured for her to take a seat in the living room and stepped into the small kitchen. "It's a bit small," she called out to her. "I'll go and bring in the tea."

Victoria wound her way between the various sofas and end tables, taking a seat before what seemed the best candidate for coffee table. "It's so nice to be here. Wow, I was really looking forward to seeing you." They exchanged a few light questions about the children, comments about the beautiful weather; they raved about the city. But the minute Ilana settled herself on the couch, tea tray set before them, Victoria started in.

"So. Tell me. What's going on? I get you're not quite ready to go; not ready to leave, well…" Her voice faded off as she dramatically looked around the room, smiling slyly as if in on a private joke, and then continued. "All this."

"Ridiculous, right? I mean, who'd want to hold on to such a tiny corner of the world?" Ilana giggled nervously. "It's obvious, right?"

"More than a bit. Your mails have been shorter lately, with clipped sentences and spiky adjectives, almost as though you're preparing for a fight."

Ilana sighed heavily. "In some ways I am." She carefully arranged the teacups on their saucers and placed a tiny spoon on the edge of each before grasping the heavy ceramic pot in two hands. A steaming trail of aromatic vapor, rich and sweet, wafted upwards as she poured. "Jasmine," she murmured, and smiled. She glanced up at Victoria for a second, mid-pour, and caught what was clearly a look of concern. She hesitated a moment, lifting the pot a second before tea spilled out into her saucer, and then resumed pouring. She hadn't been aware that her distress was so obvious. She felt like a deer caught in the headlights.

She placed the pot on the table and tried to steady herself but couldn't erase the expression of abject despair that had appeared, unchecked, on her face.

Victoria reached across and laid her hand gently on the one grasping the handle. "You know," she began quietly, "you've never really given it a chance."

Ilana swallowed hard and sat down abruptly on the couch. *I need a distraction.* She reached forward and spooned a large amount of sugar into her cup. She gave it a stir and took a large gulp, letting out a short, startled cough. She hadn't counted on it being so hot.

"Are you okay?"

She nodded yes but realized she'd burned her gullet. She coughed a few times, purposefully, to clear the pain.

"It's hard to give up what I have here, what *we* have here."

"Like…" Victoria led off. Ilana smiled. *That was actually quite funny.* She couldn't help noticing her friend's skeptical expression as they both acknowledged the cramped space and the hint of squalor created by the lack of light. The blinds were pulled half-closed in an effort to shut out the view of the neighboring buildings that, on their own, cut off most of the available daylight.

Ilana forced a smile. "The kids are so happy. They're actually learning!"

Victoria chuckled out loud. "I hope you're not insinuating that they don't learn in Israel! I guess you're not caught up on the latest business news. Last I heard, Israel was number one in innovation."

Ilana ignored her and continued on. "There's nothing like private American schools: the smaller classes, the beautiful facilities."

"And what proof is there that those details make for a better education?"

"They must! All those hours I spend helping them with their homework each afternoon? That must add up to something!"

"It might add up to schizo kids! Whoever said hours of homework make for a better-educated child! It might actually do more damage than good." Victoria took a sip of her tea. Ilana watched her carefully. Victoria looked so certain, Ilana envied her.

"Ilana, your kids have been dragged from school to school. It hasn't all been one big party. They've definitely paid a price."

Ilana looked down. *Yes, they had indeed.* Most of the children they came in contact with at the international branches of the American school, all those years they'd been in Europe, had come from vastly different backgrounds; they'd offered more of a pastime than any genuine camaraderie. Cultural differences were a continual stumbling block. And making matters worse, they'd never truly had the time to develop real friendships. By the time they actually got close to finding a serious buddy, building a relationship, it was time to move on. She'd always felt pretty bad about that.

Victoria's expression seemed determined, even serious. "I repeat: You've never given it a chance."

"I did. I found the whole system impossible to negotiate. It was crowded and uninspiring. The kids studied in makeshift caravans with air conditioning that either froze them or reduced them to puddles of sweat. The teachers yelled at them. The other children cursed them during recess, said they were snobs. Exactly what did I miss?"

"First of all, I distinctly recall that your return coincided with a huge renovation project at the school. That was bad luck! And by the way, I hear they have a beautiful new facility, something quite akin to the modern megalopolis the American Consulate has established in Even Yehuda for their Embassy brats and those stateless types with which you've always been so enamored."

Ilana ignored her. "There was no interest in the children. They were seated too close to one another. They didn't even have their own desks! How could they learn anything in that kind of environment?"

Victoria took another sip of tea, letting her lower lip linger along the rim of the cup before vigorously shaking her head. "I'm sorry, Ilana. I love you. I love having you as a friend and I'll never forsake you. But you've been hell-bent on denying your children any Israeli identity for decades. The minute you returned from one post or another you were itching to get out, move on, pack your bags and leave. That's no way to establish roots!" She set the cup down in the saucer. "You can't appreciate what's right in front of you if you're constantly looking for what's not. Take it from me. I'm a pro at that!"

She picked up a cookie from the serving dish, dipped it into her tea and then popped it into her mouth. "And incidentally," she licked the crumbs that had gathered at the corner of her mouth, "things in Israel have changed dramatically since you first made aliyah; come to think of it, since we *both* first made aliyah. You've spent so much time away you haven't even noticed that Israel has actually made it to the First World!" She picked up another cookie, waved it in front of Ilana's face and energetically announced, "We've come a long way baby!"

Ilana couldn't help smiling, even laughed. "You can't convince me, but keep on trying. It's cute." She settled back into the cushions on the couch, beginning to relax.

"You know," Victoria sat back as well, shifting gears, "I was really jealous of you when we met. Language is such a key part of integration, and it came so easily to you. You really were a bit of a thorn in my side. I mean, you'd *converted* to Judaism; *I* was the genuine article! All things being equal, I was the one who was supposed to naturally fit in! But there you were chatting with everyone, making friends right and left."

Ilana had known Victoria envied her back then. Learning to speak Hebrew had been a real godsend in terms of finding a niche. But in many ways, that had been both the beginning and the end. For her, Israel would always remain backwards, one step above underdeveloped. Early on she'd realized she didn't want to settle there and, indeed, had adamantly refused to do so. This decision had come at an enormous cost. Although each tour had brought incredible experiences and opportunities, it had simultaneously made clear that she didn't belong anywhere, neither in Israel nor abroad. And going back home was out of the question.

"If only that had been enough. There were so many other obstacles…" Ilana was desperate to shake off this funk. "Fact is, jiffy quick I realized you were the *only* one I had anything in common with!" She raised a hand and ticked off on her fingers: "Background, schooling, upbringing and – hey! the fact that you were also an 'import!'" She paused, looking around the room. "Guess that's why we're still in touch after all these years, meeting in this absolutely ridiculously tiny little hovel of an apartment!"

They broke out into peals of laughter, setting the teacups clattering.

Ilana unexpectedly felt a bit lighter. She'd spent the last few months tortured by her anxiety over the upcoming relocation, unable to shake a sense of heaviness and even doom. This conversation with Victoria was such a relief, a lifeline offering a way out of the morass into which she'd sunk. The life she'd chosen, this life abroad, this life away, two decades of continual movement, hadn't been conducive to the development and maintenance of friendships. It felt so good to spend time with a real kindred soul. Maybe there was a silver lining to their return and it wasn't all one black hole. Maybe it was time to go home. She shivered. That errant thought took her completely off guard.

"You know, your hesitation…it's not your fault." Victoria's words interrupted her reverie. "Nimrod exposed you head-on to an aspect of the country that was never going to be a good fit. His family's insistent intrusion into your private lives could never have jibed with your Northern European penchant for independence and personal space." Ilana's eyes were focused on Victoria as she took another sip of tea but her mind's eye flipped through shifting memories: Standing at the butcher shop, her mother-in-law behind her, telling her which cut of meat to choose. Sitting in the car, her father-in-law pointing out the neighborhoods where she and Nimrod might buy a house. Gathered in the kitchen preparing salads for a Friday-night dinner, her sister-in-law going on incessantly about the local preschool teacher. She'd never had a moment alone.

"You couldn't breathe."

Ilana returned to the present, picking up right where Victoria had left off. "Worst of all, Nimrod always took their side. Albeit, probably more out of habit than conviction." Somehow he'd always ended up standing behind his family members, physically indicating where his loyalties lay. The picture couldn't have been clearer. With all that potential for pain, she'd had to escape.

"Don't be too hard on yourself, Ilana! I'm not entirely sold on this Middle Eastern lifestyle either. There isn't a day I don't wonder how I got there and if I'll ever fit in. And although I crave more family, a clan of the type you fell into, I might also have run away if faced with the constant interference you encountered."

"Ending up in Israel was such a fluke!" They both fell silent and Ilana got up and walked over to the window, raising the blind a bit. It had all been so accidental. She'd reluctantly agreed to fly to Eilat with a girlfriend for a four-day getaway from the deep freeze of Norway. He'd been the young man with swarthy skin and broad shoulders playing beach paddleball near her chaise, hurling back and forth after that tiny black ball. Two blinks of an eye and she was jetting back and forth between Oslo and Tel Aviv, eagerly soaking up all of the romance he exuded. The differences between them had only strengthened the attraction. She didn't remember actually making a choice.

"I have a great life here. Even if a tad bit cramped, it's still ultimately cushy and comfortable, so very First World. I'm not ready to go back to middle-of-the-road Modi'in." She turned back to Victoria. "I don't think you really understand. You found an entirely different Israel. The population of Caesarea is so cosmopolitan and international, in some ways even more sophisticated and world-savvy than, say, what I've found in New York!"

Victoria pushed herself off the couch and stepped over to join Ilana, taking her hands in her own. "Ilana, sweetheart. Put your worries aside and move on. I promise you – I *swear* to you – this time it will be different." Ilana stared into her friend's eyes, hoping to absorb some of her certainty. She would need it to get through the gargantuan effort of reentry that lay dead ahead. Whether she was ready or not, her life was about to shift dramatically.

Victoria strolled down Broadway. It had been wonderful to see Ilana after such a long time, but she'd been rather relieved, at the end of the visit, to escape her tiny apartment. She couldn't imagine living in such a small space. And to think, the children hadn't even been home. She couldn't imagine how they managed a rainy day stuck indoors. This was an aspect of life in Manhattan Victoria hadn't considered, didn't really want to consider. She quickly discarded the thought as irrelevant. If she ever got her plan rolling, if the stars aligned and somehow she were here, up the street in Morningside

Heights, it wouldn't be with family in tow. No, Guy had made that very clear. Her mood darkened for a moment. She couldn't imagine how this was going to work out.

She stopped at a traffic light and within seconds found herself in the middle of a large group of others waiting to cross. She looked to the right and the left, and then quickly straight ahead. It didn't feel good being so packed in. She was used to space, air, the line of the horizon. This new life would definitely be a big change. She let out her breath as the group jumped into motion at the change of the light from red to green, thankful to be out of that claustrophobic cluster, eager to take in the crisp spring air. Was it possible she wouldn't enjoy living here? Her fantasy had never involved cramped personal space.

Victoria shook her head firmly, as if convincing herself, quickened her step and shifted her thoughts back to the unusual turn of their conversation over tea. She'd decided in advance to hold back about the job offer from Columbia. That hadn't been easy, especially seeing as their reunion had come straight on the heels of her successful meeting with the dean. But from the moment she'd stepped out of that clackety elevator, she'd understood the fragility of Ilana's mood, understood that the timing was all wrong. Obviously tormented by her forthcoming return to Israel, it would have been unfair for Victoria to unfurl her plan to be in New York. So instead she'd glossed over the reason for her trip to the City, mentioning something about professional networking and the School of Journalism, and focused her energy on helping her friend as best she could, encouraging her to embrace, rather than dread, her family's imminent return.

How ironic that it was she, of all people, stepping in and assuring Ilana that she should actually look forward to life back in Israel, promising that she'd find much of what she'd been looking for abroad all these years, insisting that there was no longer a need to escape. *How ridiculous was that.* Victoria hadn't intended to take such a positive stance, but for each reservation raised by Ilana she'd had an answer; they'd simply tumbled out, one after the other. And although she'd never expected to become a kind of poster girl for her adopted country, it had felt almost natural, even genuine, to step up to the bat in an effort to calm her friend's anxiety.

Back out on the street, the reason she'd tried to allay Ilana's fears became clear. Victoria understood better than anyone why Ilana didn't want to go home, and truth be told, she'd just as soon she stayed here in New York; one more friend for her to spend time with if she, too, ended up here. Yet the scene back in that dinky apartment was all about maintaining an unspoken code between expats, upholding the impression that everything had worked out, that those life decisions that had ripped each and every one of them from their natural habitats and landed them across the world had been justified. Back there, legs crammed behind the coffee table, Victoria's job had been, first and foremost, to do whatever it took to maintain the facade – even if it meant lying. And funnily enough, she hadn't had to do that even once.

As she approached Lincoln Center her phone rang. She stepped out of the stream of foot traffic, letting the crowd of pedestrians pass by, and reached into her purse. *Guy.*

"Hey." Her tone was light, positive.

"So." His was heavier. The opening wasn't a question.

She braced herself. "It was great seeing Ilana. She was…"

He interrupted her. "I don't care about your visit with Ilana, Victoria."

He never used her full name. Or rather, he only used it when he was angry with her. She took a deep breath. She tried again. "The interview went well." She hesitated and then allowed herself to give in to the excitement she'd felt earlier that morning during the meetings on campus. She couldn't help herself. It had been enough simply keeping it in for the past few hours' visit with Ilana. And this was *Guy*. Her partner, the one with whom she'd always wanted to share the most.

The words burst out. "It's such a vibrant community, so well suited to me. It's exactly what I want."

"So you're going to leave." His voice was curt, to the point, completely unyielding. "This is no longer merely an *option*?" That last word came out like arsenic.

Victoria's excitement began to fade; she began to panic. "Guy, I..."

"You can't have it both ways. You know that. I understand you've been planning this for a long time. I get it now. We're not what you want..."

She began to get angry. "That's not true. I love what we have. It's just...it's just that there's something here." Her voice faded off. How could she ever explain it to him? He'd never understand. It wasn't that he couldn't – he simply wouldn't. Worse, he'd cut her off from everything she loved. Postcard images of her children flashed through her head.

"What about Ben?"

That was it. That was the blow she'd been anticipating. Guy wasn't holding back. He knew precisely the effect his words had. His question hung there, unanswered, for at least a minute. Neither one of them spoke. Victoria watched the endless flow of life around her. He was forcing her hand, making her consider the most difficult ramifications of this plan. It's not as if she hadn't done so without his cruel prompt, as if she didn't understand that stepping across the world would mean leaving those she loved, albeit temporarily. But at that precise moment, on a street corner in Manhattan, hordes of pedestrians passing by, buzzing with the potential that waited way up Broadway, it was simply too much. Her head began to swim and she felt she might actually throw up.

She leaned back, pressing her body into the doorjamb of a store, afraid she'd pass out.

"Well?" He wouldn't let up. At that very moment Victoria absolutely hated him. How dare he ruin this for her? She'd given up so much for him, in fact, everything. She'd occupied *his* life for over two decades. Wasn't it time for her to get her own?

But all that resolve couldn't hold out against the tide of her heart. And deep down his thoughts stirred her own misgivings. Although she was desperate to deny it, she knew this opportunity came at a heavy price. Ben was due to come home this coming Friday. She'd be there to meet his train. How could she purposefully step away from those golden moments, give up even one embrace, one life-giving hug? It was all so crushingly unfair.

Guy stared at the phone in his hand. *What have I done?* He sat back down on the couch and tried to focus on the television screen before him. The nightly news, ordinarily riveting, a highpoint in his daily routine, was a blur of imagery and voices. *Is this how our story ends?* He felt sick to his stomach and gripped the armrest a moment for support.

"Dad, was that Mommy?"

Maia's voice drifted into his consciousness but wasn't enough to stave off the wave of nausea or calm his fears. He barely heard her, the voice insisting that this wasn't what he really wanted drowning out everything else.

"Dad. Daddy!" Guy raised his eyes. Maia was standing in front of him looking quite concerned. "Are you okay? What happened? Is Mommy okay?"

He didn't want her to worry, didn't want to add even one more layer to what was already a complicated situation. He pulled himself together enough to blurt out "Mommy's fine."

"When's she coming home?"

Home. She was coming home. Guy needed to focus on that and nothing else; to remember what they had, *how much* they had. To convince himself this wasn't an end.

He looked up and met Maia's questioning eyes. "Day after tomorrow."

"Okay. Good." She spun around and left the TV room.

Guy followed her ponytail with his eyes as it flounced from side to side behind her, echoing the skip in her step. He envied her sense of security. She didn't worry about her mother's love, her devotion. The concept that maybe she wouldn't come home, that she might decide to live elsewhere, that everything might change, never dawned on her. He wished he were so naive but was burdened by knowing otherwise. And at that moment it was abundantly clear that if she didn't return, it would be his fault.

He picked up the remote control and turned down the volume. The news really wasn't all that important tonight; with such a mess right here inside the house, world events faded in significance. He stared at the talking heads on the screen, not even registering their words, then raised the remote again and turned the TV off completely. Maybe this was the first important step. His obsession with the nightly news had been one of the sticking points in their marriage from early on. Victoria saw its timing as a conspiracy.

"Eight to nine. How ironic! Exactly when I need help. Just when I'm forcing vegetable paste on a resistant baby, up to my eyes in bath water and floating toys, struggling to get damp limbs into onesie pajamas and settle down an overtired infant enough to get him to fall asleep. There you are, precisely *then*, glued in front of the nightly news. More proof of exactly how sexist this society can be." Fuming, she'd carefully insisted it to be otherwise in the States. "Back home the whole system is much more considerate of parenting needs: evening news at six or eleven. None of this 'give daddy an *out* at the height of the storm' business."

Guy knew things hadn't turned out exactly as she'd imagined, that he'd fallen short of her expectations on occasion. That was to be expected in a decades-long relationship. But her disappointment in Israel had always been more troubling, something that seemed based on bare truths, not circumstantial. While he could accept the more annoying local idiosyncrasies, and there were more than enough to disturb even the most forgiving, she continually bemoaned them. He'd come to expect a biting comment here or there, but he'd never once, until recently, imagined she'd pick up and leave. Maybe that's why he'd balked from the moment this job opportunity had reared its ugly head. He'd known it was only a matter of the right temptation to tip the fragile balance – and here it was. She'd found a way to leave him. Period.

Guy stared at the black screen, his mind racing over the conversations they'd had since this opportunity in New York had first arisen, the harsh words and the cold shoulder he'd offered again and again. Was that who he'd become? He didn't recognize the shadowy figure reflected in the glass before him, or want to have much to do with him. All his protestations and threats, where had they gotten him? His unbending rejection of her plan had neither slowed her down nor dissuaded her; it was *that* important to her. And just now he was beginning to recognize the signs he'd missed, the ones that indicated this was difficult for her, that she was torn by wanting to take this chance but needing to keep them together.

Now she was there, across the world, right at the threshold of a life that didn't include him. And what had he done? Shut her out completely. He gazed down at his hands, firmly planted on his thighs. Older hands, aged hands. They'd been at this together for a long time. Victoria had been so thrilled on the telephone, her excitement at actually getting the job obvious, even infectious. He loved her, how could he not want her to be happy? But, overcome by his fear, he'd reacted terribly, shutting her down, his words cold as ice. *What an idiot!* He wished he could take them back. She was one foot out the door, and he'd simply shoved her the rest of the way. *What a fool I am!* What had begun as an idea, then become a possibility, had spiraled into a certainty. He was about to lose the thing he loved most.

Guy stood up and walked out to the terrace, drawn directly to the endless sky above. There were so many stars, so many twinkling lights, all those points of beauty. He wouldn't do it. He wasn't going to let the one he had with Victoria get away. He was a bit late. He'd been blinded by his own fears. But now he understood his mistake; he understood that trying to hold on to her by reminding her of what she'd lose would actually result in the opposite. Helping her realize her dreams, sending her the clear message that he was on her side, was the only way to continue their story.

Chapter 19

Susan's oversized front door swung open and Victoria stepped inside ahead of the others, directly onto a sea of newly burnished parquet flooring. Her eyes swept right and left, struck by the vast, unbroken space that opened in both directions. The entrance, living room, dining room and kitchen were all part of one flowing area punctuated by a minimum of furniture and absolutely no doodads or other signs of actual "living." She felt a bit as if she were standing in a showroom, a mock-up of where one might begin when designing a house, before one filled it up with personal items and made it a home. It was a model of uninhabited perfection.

Susan poked her head around the door and giggled nervously. "Can you take your shoes off? I just cleaned the floors." They immediately acquiesced, fully acquainted with their friend's need for spotlessness and order. They lined their shoes up by the door and proceeded to look around.

"It's so pretty, Susan." Victoria praised quickly, not wanting to leave her friend in suspense, and then each headed for a different spot within the large space. One took up a position by the sole couch, another by the glass doors to the patio, another by the dining room table, and all issued the appropriate *ohs* and *ahs*. Susan swiveled to meet each one, basking in their compliments. She and her husband had planned and built this house ground up over the course of years and had just moved in. Her excitement at showing it off, sharing the result of all that effort, was obvious.

"How are you ever going to leave this?"

"I know. Right? We worked so hard to finish it. In fact, it's not even completely finished." That nervous giggle again.

"Finished enough for me. Maybe I'll move in."

There was a general buzz around the room, everyone in agreement that Susan's was now the "choice" address.

"We're only relocating for a few years. We'll rent it out and do all of the finishing touches when we return. Painful, but, whatever. We weren't expecting this opportunity to come along." Victoria noticed Susan's hands, one balled up inside the other as if holding on for dear life. There seemed something hesitant about her behavior, and it dawned on her, for the first time, that maybe jumping on a plane and flying off wasn't exactly what she'd had in mind. A few months back the only thing they'd talked about was this house – their dream come true. And now they were leaving it. *Life definitely worked in mysterious ways.*

"In any case... I want to show you around." Susan half smiled and gathered them together by touching them here and there, one on the elbow, one on the forearm. She turned around and gestured toward one end of the room. "We'll start with the kitchen." Anchoring one end of the large main space was a granite island featuring a stainless steel sink with a tall, skinny faucet. Isolated in the space, sparkling clean and stunningly beautiful in design, it looked more like a piece of sculpture. Victoria squinted to get a better look, maybe a swan.

They placed their purses onto the bar stools tidily stowed beneath the island and watched as Susan opened one grey cabinet after another, revealing the various elements of the "working" kitchen hidden inside. She enumerated them each: "The refrigerator, the microwave, the mixer, the toaster and over here we have shelving for what have you." She pointed to metal baskets filled with jars, bottles, cans and assorted cartons.

When she closed the cabinet doors again, everything carefully put away in its assigned place, there remained no trace whatsoever of an actual kitchen. To Victoria, the whole ensemble felt more like a walk-in closet than a place one might prepare food. She began to have the nagging feeling that, despite the lovely aesthetic of the house, something was missing. She blamed it on disorientation. She'd just arrived back from the States a week earlier and her head was swimming with questions, concerns and contained excitement.

But as they continued their tour, the feeling continued to grow. Victoria couldn't figure out precisely what was bothering her, what felt off. Maybe it was simply so different, so minimal and streamlined when she was used to overflow and haphazard. When they got to the master bedroom Susan shuffled ahead excitedly, waiting for them to regroup. "Guys, look!" She gestured to a completely empty space branching off the end of the room, the lower section of an *L*, with a view of the neighboring houses and the mountain range behind. "This is going to be the reading area!"

Suddenly it was clear. She understood what didn't seem right. A chain of words leaped to her lips but she instantly held back, hesitant to let them fly. Victoria wanted to make a joke but worried that she'd offend. Not everyone appreciated her cynical sense of humor, and she certainly didn't want to hurt Susan. Then again, it was so hard to resist. This temple of emptiness begged comment. She would tread lightly.

She turned around, facing away from the others as if looking around the room and whispered under her breath. "But there don't seem to be any books!"

She might as well have used a megaphone. Apparently they'd all heard. There was a small, stifled gasp from Jackie and then silence.

All eyes turned to Susan, who giggled nervously and quickly responded. "Oh, I made Matt give them all away."

Alison cupped her hand quickly over her mouth to stymie a chuckle, stretching her fingers up quickly to scratch her nose as cover. There was another moment of silence and then Jackie and Evie stepped in, filling the gap with comments about the houses directly across the way. The tour continued.

Victoria pulled away from the rest, lagging behind as they continued on, having finally zeroed in on what had been disturbing her throughout. It was the emptiness. This was a house with empty shelves, no trinkets and no visual memories; a lived-in space without even one book. She wanted to think it couldn't be, that the closets must be piled high with junk, all carefully hidden from the naked eye due to Susan's well-known abhorrence for clutter. But as each and every one was proudly opened for inspection (this was a thorough tour) and they were allowed to peek into these intimate spaces, she was startled to find only a very limited number of items, each neatly arranged within built-in shelves and niches.

Walking through the rest of the house she was stricken by the complete and total absence of cultural markers, what she liked to call "significant junk." And it wasn't incidental, but instead, part of a very carefully thought-out plan. She considered her own closets, absolutely overflowing with the memories of a lifetime: a trail of garments, documents, photographs, ticket stubs and numerous other knick-knacks with which she adamantly refused to part; after all, they were part of her story.

This beautiful exemplar of aesthetic perfection, adamantly concealing any sign of a soul, collided brutally with Victoria's need for association and depth. Running her hand along the smooth plexiglas banister that ran the length of the hallway she considered those parts of her local life that left her empty; considered the effect they had on the whole experience and whether it would be possible to turn the tide on a lifetime of decisions, to redress the mistakes and start again. With a long sigh of regret she trailed her friends, following the calf-level spotlights to the stairwell, and began her descent to the first floor.

She felt enervated, tired of trying to grasp at something that was so far out of reach. An errant phrase passed through her head as she stepped off the landing: cultural compatibility. She stopped. *No. No, it can't be.* She didn't know whether to laugh or cry, stunned by the recognition of her mother's own prescience. This was exactly what she'd harped on from the beginning of this story, the subject she'd been unwilling to drop, the one that she continued to come back to, again and again every time they met. *How come mothers always know?*

The wheels began to click and ping, rotating into action within her head, and an earlier scene began to play itself out, like a slide dropping into place from one of those virtually extinct 35mm carousel slide projectors. There they were, the two of them, sitting at the local café having breakfast soon after her move to Caesarea. Her mother's continued skepticism over her life-choice was obvious, even several years in, and the atmosphere between them was heavy with the unspoken. That morning's topic of discussion was about the friends she'd made since she'd arrived, and Victoria was bracing herself for what might come.

"Where did she study?" Her mother directed her words toward the omelet she was cutting into small, bite-sized pieces.

Victoria's eyes shifted to the area beyond the café's terrace, welcoming the distraction of the local comings and goings.

"Excuse me?"

"I asked," her mother said deliberately, taking a sip of her cappuccino, "where she went to college?"

"Who?"

Her mother daintily wiped her upper lip, removing all lingering traces of foam, placed her napkin back in her lap and looked directly into Victoria's eyes. "That nice young woman with a child Ben's age. The one who flew back recently to the States to visit her parents."

Victoria crossed and then uncrossed her legs under the table, shifted her weight in her chair, situating herself foursquare to cope with what felt like an onslaught. "I have no idea." She realized her voice was flat, emotionless.

The two women sat in silence, busying themselves with the food. One spread a bit of tuna salad on her roll, the other nibbled on her omelet. Neither one of them knew exactly how to progress, how to get out of this roadblock in the conversation. An outsider noticing them probably wouldn't have thought them related.

"Didn't she attend college?"

Victoria tried not to squirm, but her mother's questions weren't innocent. In fact they were specifically aimed at making a point – one Victoria wasn't comfortable with, something to do with her new crowd. At some level the two were in agreement; there'd been an assumed expectation that she would choose friends who were also well educated, who had similar backgrounds. That's certainly the way it was back in the States. But everything was different here. Victoria reached over and speared a cube of cucumber from the salad.

"I guess she did."

Victoria looked down at her plate as she chewed. The fact that one of her good friends may not actually have finished a bachelor's degree, something positively unheard of in her former life, hung over the table like a sopping rag, the detritus of failure.

They continued their meal in silence, carefully making their way through the tiny salad servings – avocado, roasted eggplant, pesto spread, cream cheese and marinated pimentos – in an attempt to anchor themselves on firmer ground. A friend without a pedigree. Victoria had come to understand that it was par for the course in her new life; the friends she'd made here represented a much wider range of backgrounds than those she'd connected with back in college.

Everything there was more clear-cut; you wore your pedigree on your sleeve. Sometimes people even knew where you'd been educated, what neighborhood you'd grown up in, and what your parents did for a living before formal introductions were made. It was part of the weeding-out process prior to any meeting – whether social or professional; the modus operandi of the Eastern Seaboard, or at least that part of the Seaboard she called home.

And of course the establishment of one's pedigree had everything to do with one's eventual choice of friends; it was the first building block laid in the foundation of any relationship. If it wasn't similar, didn't smack of the same privilege, wasn't good enough or have a faint aroma of that Ivory Tower, it was eventually rejected.

So how was it possible that here, in Israel, pedigree played such a minor role – had almost no part in her selection of who to spend time with? She knew how her mother would answer that question. She herself didn't dare have a go at it.

So close to choosing another reality, an academic life in New York that seemed a far more natural fit, the alternative one epitomized by Susan's just recently occupied house, a glowing example of life unburdened by the past, began to pale. Maybe that wasn't fair. Victoria ached to share her news with her friends, to tell them all about the possibility that waited just up ahead. But somehow it felt like treachery, as if choosing something different was a rejection of what they had. Surrounded by a bonhomie that had supported her for over a decade, thankful for the gem of what she'd been able to establish against all odds, she decided to remain silent. Until it was a certainty there was no reason to rock this fragile boat.

Chapter 20

It was a great day, the very best day. Victoria hurled herself into the front seat of her car. A wave of heat engulfed her and she hurried to put the key into the ignition, desperate to lower the windows. The outside air was stagnant but far better than the unbearable stuffiness inside. Getting into a car in Israel anytime after Passover was somewhat like stepping into an oven. This was an old story. Day in and day out, for something in the range of six months, the afternoon heat was overwhelming and inescapable. Yet she smiled as she settled herself on to the sticky seat. It didn't matter. *Today* everything was much more bearable. *Today* she was willing to take it in stride, to not let it become one of those things that peeved her, that provoked that consistent feeling of frustration. Yes, *today* the world seemed like a brighter place.

Upon returning from New York, Victoria had been shocked to find a different version of Guy. The chilly husband she'd left at home when she'd flown to New York, barely speaking to her and when he did, spewing out angry words, exhortations and even a few threats, was gone. In his place was the one she'd fallen in love with decades earlier. She felt it in the way his eyes lingered on hers and his hand touched her back as he whisked through the house.

He'd begun to call her from work simply, as he said, "to check in – no reason." She wasn't certain what had brought about such a dramatic change, but she welcomed it. In fact, it had been an inordinate relief. Sitting on the plane back to Tel Aviv she'd braced herself for what she'd assume would be crippling conversations.

Instead they'd spent that first week discussing how accepting this job might play out, how they could enable it without completely rocking the boat of the life they knew. He'd stunned her with his effort to embrace the possibility he'd earlier been dead set against.

And then, this very morning, he'd come out with it.

"I have it."

She'd been rinsing the dishes, loading the dishwasher and clearing off the kitchen counter. She barely heard him and was more focused on getting Maia and Jonathan off to school than anything else.

"Hmmm?"

"I have it. Victoria. Hey! Look at me! I know how we can make this work!"

He had her attention. She turned around, wiping her hands on the hand towel hanging off the handle of one of the kitchen drawers.

"A summer. A summer semester." He'd hurriedly sputtered out the words, as if concerned they'd otherwise escape him. "In any case, you usually travel to the States in the summer. You'll extend. You'll be there a little longer. Or maybe a bit longer than a little. But no matter. I'll join you at some point and we'll have some time in New York together."

She concentrated on his face and that extraordinary smile. He looked so pleased with himself. She felt a warmth move through her body before she even had the chance to reply, and then she could barely contain herself, wanting to shout out in excitement. This sounded perfect. She hadn't pitched the idea to the dean of the

Journalism School yet; she was waiting for life on the East Coast to wake up a few hours later, but she was certain she'd be able to convince him. This was actually going to happen; she was going to realize this dream. And somehow, she was going to see it through without damaging the fragile web that held her family together.

Since then the whole mood in the house had shifted. After weeks characterized by a stiff, brittle atmosphere, things had returned to the way they'd been. The plan, now far more limited in nature, no longer threatened Guy, and he'd begun to relax. Getting his support instead of his rancor had changed the entire chemistry between them, and she'd felt a resurgence of energy toward the future, their future.

Of course for Victoria it was more than a relief. Now she could concentrate on that last piece of the puzzle, the one that had always been missing. And although she hadn't broached the subject with Guy, in fact wouldn't – the timing wasn't right – she maintained the small hope that this summer semester would eventually lead to something more, that one small stint would lead to a more substantive one. But for now this was a secret, something she'd keep to herself. *One step at a time.*

This morning's errands had included a special trip to the fresh-fruit market. She wanted to find some way to thank Guy for coming through for her, for standing by her side. What better way to express to him how happy she was to return to where they'd begun than trigger a memory of their first walk through an Israeli souk? Nothing spoke louder than a few baskets of fruit. The peaches, wild cherries and mangoes were here on the seat beside her, at the ready. He was going to be thrilled.

Her mind clouded momentarily. By being away this summer, she'd miss out on the season's best offerings, those ripe to bursting purple-green figs she waited for each year. The cellophane-wrapped versions she'd find at Gristedes this coming summer wouldn't be able to compare. She shook it off. She couldn't have everything. Some sacrifices were worth making.

She smiled to herself. This truly was a glorious day. There was no longer any reason to envy Susan, or anyone else for that matter. She, too, had found a way back. "I'm outta here," she stated aloud as she pulled onto the main thoroughfare of Or Akiva, only minutes from home. "I'm on my way!"

But she wasn't. The brakes of the car in front of her flashed bright red and she was forced to come to a screeching halt. "What the heck?" Up ahead, at the front of what she now saw was a line of cars, Victoria could just barely see two men standing by their abandoned vehicles, in the middle of the road, arguing fiercely. This was a fairly typical occurrence here in Israel, where tempers on the road ran to boiling, yet that didn't make it acceptable. She looked behind her. A line of cars, stretching back as far as the eye could see, was dotted by the heads of the drivers popping out to check out the action. Within seconds, the usually smooth flow of traffic along this single-lane road had stopped completely.

Victoria shook her head and tried to wait patiently. She'd been here before, she'd probably be here again. But the waiting stretched on to minutes and there seemed no end in sight. A round of erratic, perturbed beeping from equally annoyed drivers caused her to snap. She'd had enough of always being the patsy, of waiting around for others to behave properly. She stepped out of the car and made her way forward to where the two men were still actively embroiled in an argument.

"*Slichah*. Excuse me," she started, her accented Hebrew making her feel like a ten-year-old. "Would it be possible to move this argument elsewhere so the rest of us can be on our way?"

The two men, embroiled in an argument that had segued from the original sin to a question of who needed to teach whom a lesson and how the emotional damage of the incident was to be rectified, barely came up for air.

"Hey!" she yelled, surprising even herself.

"*L'azazel!* What the hell!" She gestured behind her. "Don't you all see what you're doing here?"

They paused. The picture of this American woman going ballistic was obviously more interesting than their discussion about road etiquette.

"*Dai kvar!* Enough already!" Victoria was stunned by her own voice, amazed that it could reach such decibels. The men, struck silent, stared at her. She considered turning around and fleeing back to her car. After all, she wasn't the confrontational type. Or at least, she never had been. But here, right then and there, she understood she'd become so.

Who am I?

"Go back to your car!" said one of the men in purposefully American-accented Hebrew.

That really pissed her off. She was so sick of having her accent mimicked. This seemed to be a favorite pastime of locals. She'd never really understood the point. Was it supposed to be funny? Was it meant to continually remind her that she didn't belong? That she wasn't a genuine Israeli? That she'd arrived late in the game, after everyone else was already settled? Whether the tone was jovial or condescending the inevitable result was to make her feel rotten.

"Lady, *at metorefet?*"

Victoria's head reeled. These men were the ones holding up all this traffic yet they deigned to call *her* crazy.

She stared the two men down for a moment, emphatically shook her head in disgust and muttered, "*Nimas.*" Over the past decades, she'd picked up a whole litany of Hebrew words expressing disgust. She turned her back to them and marched back to her car. In a matter of seconds the bright red brake lights on the car before hers signaled the resumption of movement. The two culprits had obviously decided they'd done enough lecturing for the day, had their sport, and finally, gotten into their cars and driven off. Apparently no damage, save to an ego or two, done. Within minutes she was on her way back home.

Victoria progressed slowly, distinctly shaken by the experience and perspiring profusely. She'd forgotten about the heat in the midst of her own personal storm but it had been there throughout. Now she felt steaming hot, sticky and damp. She checked that the vents were turned toward her for the umpteenth time, that the air-conditioning was turned to full blast, and took a few deep breaths of the cool, recycled air.

She shuddered at the thought that she'd become just like *them*, that she'd stepped over the edge and become a rude Israeli. The thought sickened her and she realized she was more desperate than ever to get back to a kinder, gentler life. She made her way home in a stupor, the elation of that morning almost completely obliterated by the brutal realities of the world she'd chosen as her own.

Part Two

Chapter 21

The sound of drilling from behind the house alternated with that of a leaf blower in front. Victoria was assaulted from all sides by noises, but the only one that registered was the thin crackle of the newspaper in her hand. She sat motionless at the kitchen table, stunned by the morning's news. There had been a fatal attack on a southern border town resulting in more than one death and several serious injuries, the latest in a succession of scuffles across the border. There was talk of a ground invasion.

Her eyes skimmed quickly through the article summaries next to the headlines. In strong contrast to what was going on outside, it was dead silent in her kitchen. She fingered the corner of the front page, desperate to flip ahead and move on, to push away all of that fear and relegate it to the farthest corner of her mind. But she couldn't. There was no way to avoid it. Things were unraveling.

In the past it had been so easy to shake off these events, explaining to her friends abroad that it had nothing to do with her, that her life was as humdrum and event-free as theirs. And for the most part this was true, especially when they happened now and then, weeks or months passing between each occurrence. The horrors Americans saw splayed across the front pages, the ones they imagined to be part of her daily experience, had absolutely nothing to do with her life. She'd helped to insure that by staying in that part of Israel far from the all-too-controversial territories and the border with Gaza, reducing her time in the country's fabulous metropolises. She knew she was missing out, knew that her cultural appetite would have been happily sated by a bit more of what she avoided, but could not resist the comfort of tucking herself into the safe little bubble of the immediate Caesarea area.

Victoria lifted her eyes from the page and, for a moment, focused on the dust clouds hovering over the kitchen table, delineated by the rays of morning sun coming in through the window. The beeping of the garbage truck backing up the street to make its collection distracted her for a moment, breaking the heaviness of her mood and redirecting her attention to the coziness of the kitchen, this comforting womb. But the quick feeling of warmth dissipated the minute her eyes flickered downward, back to the paper laid flat on the table. She couldn't help herself and continued to scan the blurred pictures of attack scenes juxtaposed to those of the victims themselves – still photos provided by the families after the fact, documenting happier times. This was such a different reality than hers; so close, yet so very far. Although in some ways all about her, it simultaneously had nothing to do with her – a puzzle that could never be solved.

Victoria had worked so hard to exclude local current events, no small feat in a country that specialized in the concept of "never a dull moment." Although it was almost impossible to stay entirely aloof, to disregard snippets of information and updates exchanged in conversations at the market and at school pick-up, she'd done her best to block out the worst. As a rule, she barely even glanced at the morning paper. When Omer had been injured she'd followed through to a point, making sure that Ben was updated as to when he'd been sent home and then, leaving it at that. The horrific would always exist, but its active role in their lives needed to be held at bay.

Of course, despite her endless efforts, there was no way to remain completely indifferent to local events. They were always right there, front and center. Living in Israel meant involvement at every level. Whether or not you knew the person affected intimately, marginally or not at all, were connected via family, work or social circles; their misery was somehow part of yours. Israel was small and, despite its eight million or so population, operated very much like a village. Somehow, in some way, everyone was related. This was the land of the Jewish people and as such there was a distinct sense, despite vast geographic, cultural and socio-economic differences, that everyone had a vested interest. So while what happened in the West Bank, or down in the settlements near the Gazan border, had very little to do directly with Victoria's daily life and that of her immediate friends and family, it managed, at the same time, to have everything to do with them.

Living in what felt like a bubble didn't mean she was untouchable, that bad things couldn't happen. Victoria wasn't that naive. She knew that bad things happened no matter who you were, what you did, where you went and how careful you tried to be. Life didn't come with guarantees. Friends back home, who questioned how she could live with such stress, didn't take into account their own. But this was different.

The dread of serious conflict, or even war, multiplied twentyfold when one had a soldier in the family. Getting on the plane and leaving when things were heating up meant the possibility that she wouldn't be nearby if Ben was involved. And as an outsider, always an outsider, someone who'd grown up never worrying about anything to do with guns or bullets or tanks or troops or positions or military strategies or booby-traps or really anything at all, it was a lot to digest. This was something that would never change, whether the dangers were imminent or remained a distant threat, hovering far away and seemingly irrelevant.

Until these last few weeks, the protective shell Victoria had erected – although threatened here and there by everyday incidents not at all singular to life in the Middle East – had held up beautifully. She'd been excitedly preparing for the seminars she'd be teaching during the summer semester at Columbia, had even begun to tell her friends the exciting news. The sting of Susan's departure had faded with the anticipation of her own plans. How ironic that in the end it was Guy who'd come up with the solution – he who'd been so steadfastly *against* her taking a position abroad, convinced that this was all about something much deeper, certain that she wasn't committed to him, to the children, and worse, had never been committed to her adopted country. All of a sudden the dream of attaining a piece of the life she'd left back in the States, one solid chunk, was clearly in sight. With this new reality dead ahead, their days were filled with plans. Guy had already scheduled his visit. He'd fly over for a few weeks mid-summer so that they could enjoy the City together. Everything was going to work out.

Or so she'd thought. Although she wanted nothing more than to pull the wool over her eyes, to pretend that nothing outside could in any way derail these exciting plans – or, on a more significant level, affect her life's projection – it was becoming increasingly impossible to ignore the world around her. A series of incidents, one after the other, had ratcheted up local tension, and the potential for some kind of large-scale military effort was growing. She could no longer push aside the news as someone else's trouble – horrific, but fortunately not her own. The crinkled sheets of paper on the table held more than a hint that the already fragile situation was going to escalate and that Ben, her Ben, would be involved.

All of Victoria's arrangements, the ones she'd planned so carefully as everything had begun to fall into place, were suddenly broken up by a web of hairline cracks with seriously destructive potential. Paralyzed with the fear of what might be, she remained glued to the kitchen chair. Maybe if she didn't move, didn't allow time to progress, to follow through, maybe then things would somehow be okay. Victoria tried to work through everything happening around her, to sort things out in an effort to make sense of them and alleviate her fears, but she couldn't get over the serious hurdles that had pushed their way into her humdrum life these past few days.

The horror had started last week during a phone call with Guy, one as routine and predictable as any other. Or so she'd thought. He'd been on his way home from work, driving on the main highway that connects Tel Aviv and the North. She'd been in her car, as usual not far from home, maybe on her way back from grocery shopping. For the most part things were as they were meant to be – it was only one more early evening, a long warm day drawing to a close. But then, quite suddenly, it wasn't. Without warning, mid-sentence, she'd heard him mumble indiscernible words.

"*Gjdebajah.*"

"What? I didn't catch that." She'd barely had a chance to respond when the line went silent. Victoria hadn't made much of that; after all, glitches in cellular lines were more the norm than the exception. But when he'd called her back, a handful of minutes later, it was clear that something had gone terribly wrong.

"Well."

That odd conversation starter had been the first clue.

"Did we get cut off?"

"Not exactly."

She'd waited for him to elaborate, didn't understand his hesitation.

"I had to pull to the side of the road."

She was suddenly unsure of where this was going, unhappy with his obvious shift in tone.

"Cars were pulling off the road, right off the highway. It didn't make any sense. And then it did. There was a siren. I simply didn't hear it."

"Just now? Just this minute? I mean, while we were talking? You had to pull off of the highway?" Victoria's tone became frantic, higher pitched. She felt frightened, struggling to get a visual image of how that scene might have looked. How could all those cars, traveling at high speed, suddenly come to a halt? It must have looked something like what she'd seen in photographs documenting the annual sounding of the siren on Memorial Day, images illustrating how cars stopped wherever they were, helter-skelter all over the road, and drivers got out and stood right beside them, heads lowered out of respect for lives lost for the sake of the nation. But this sounded different.

She cleared her throat. "Everyone pulled over?"

"Just about." He paused. "I think some people didn't hear it. *I* almost didn't hear it. I saw others moving to the side before I actually heard the siren. And they weren't simply pulling over, they were getting out of their cars abruptly, leaving doors wide open, valuables spilling out onto the asphalt, and running over to the guardrail. Once there they dropped to their knees and assumed a crouched position, kind of like what they tell you to do on the plane." He lowered his voice. "Vicki, you can't imagine. A whole nation brought to its knees in fear."

Guy sounded angry, frustrated and sad. Victoria's eyes widened but she couldn't respond. She tried to focus on the practical details, to somehow make it all seem like an exercise so it wouldn't feel so real.

"And that's what you were doing all the time I was driving along thinking about how disappointing cell service can be?"

Guy chuckled. "Yes." The atmosphere over the line lightened a bit. "I ended up next to a mother with a small boy. We were one group of many along the side of the road, stretching as far as the eye could see. She covered his body with her own. He was frightened. It wasn't so much the crouching, but rather the noise of that infernal siren. It wouldn't stop wailing."

He'd gone on to tell her how the mother had begun to sing a popular children's song called *"Eser Etzbaot Li Yeish* – I Have Ten Fingers,"* taking her son's hand and pulling on one finger after the other, matching her movements to the words. She was obviously eager to distract him from this strange and scary circumstance. Guy, who was crouched directly next to them, had reached forward to wiggle his own fingers in sync with theirs. The little boy had been amused, eventually smiling at what was beginning to seem more like a game than a scary nightmare.

Victoria had been captivated by the story; except for its association with a horrific situation it was an absolutely charming tale and must have been quite a sight. Sitting there alone in her kitchen this morning she couldn't keep from smiling at the thought of it, purposefully ignoring the potential for danger that triggered the siren as well as that spelled out clearly right there in the paper before her.

The ringing phone interrupted her thoughts.

"You saw?"

"Yes."

"Are you okay?"

"No."

She continued to leaf through the paper while gripping the phone, taking in only the imagery, not the text. "I don't understand what this means."

"I think you do. But don't worry. It'll be okay."

Guy's words rang hollow yet somehow soothed. In any case she was looking for comfort, not truth.

"What does it mean," she paused, "for Ben?"

There was silence on the other end of the line.

"Ben will be fine."

There it was again. That calm she depended on; the reassuring voice that managed to look into the future and return with a smile. She knew he spoke out of genuine belief, the fact that in the end, it would be okay. For her the questions were more about the interim – how to survive it, how to get through to the other side.

"I don't believe you."

He dismissed her comment. "I'm here whenever you want to call."

"Just let me know if this is happening."

"Will do." There was a click. He'd hung up the phone.

Victoria closed her eyes for a moment. She didn't want to go to that dark place: the place where she understood exactly what this meant for Ben – how much danger he could face. It had taken so much to get used to the concept that he carried a gun. At no point during her Quaker schooling back in Philadelphia had there been allowance for guns. They weren't part of her life, or that of anyone around her, and she'd been sure they never would be. Of course, that was back then. One reality had replaced another the minute she'd changed her global position. In this new home, weapons were a necessary evil.

When the boys were young she'd provided them with all of the toy guns they'd requested, convinced that denying them would only strengthen their yearning to grow up and be Ninjas. They'd thankfully never been the types to run around yelling "Bang, bang," waving their toy guns in the faces of strangers, but that didn't mean they weren't fascinated. There were a good few years where the house was full of those Nerf bullets. They still showed up in the oddest places (behind the toilet, under the kitchen sink, in the garden bushes and jammed between the cushions of the couch in the TV room), witness to one well-armed war or another. Just last month she'd found one crushed under Jonathan's bedroom bookcase.

But that phase had passed to a completely different level with Ben's induction. She'd tried to maintain a straight face as he regaled her with explanations of the chamber, the various calibers and the special night sight; tales of how many times he'd hit the bull's-eye at the shooting range; how, soon after the start of his service, he'd been chosen, and yes it was an honor, to carry one of the heavier guns that fired the most bullets per minute. The whole subject gave her chills, yet she'd forced herself to smile and enthusiastically laud his progress. Who was she to deny him the extraordinary pleasure of achieving and receiving official commendation in his new life as a soldier? It didn't matter that all of this took her far out of her comfort zone.

Nothing in her past could have prepared her six months later when he'd called up, his voice giddy with excitement, to report on an update: he had just been given the even more prestigious position of sniper. *A sniper? My son?* He was an excellent shot and this was apparently his commander's way of acknowledging his capabilities. She recalled squeezing out the mandatory, supportive "That's fantastic baby" between gritted teeth, despite quite literally feeling sick. She'd tried to shake off the horrific reality of the post, laughing about it with her friends whenever the subject arose, associating him amusingly with the fox on that children's show *Dora the Explorer*. "Sniper! No sniping!" she'd giggled. She hadn't had a choice. There was simply no other way to digest the gravity of the situation, the destruction associated with the moments when he might actually have to fulfill his duty.

The newspaper, this newspaper, was filled with imagery of amassing tanks, soldiers preparing weapons, rockets exploding in the sky and buildings with partially collapsed roofs. She wondered if that day had come, if she'd no longer be able to avoid making the connection between Ben's small role as a cog in a great machine and the disintegration of an already flimsy stalemate.

This wasn't entirely new territory. She'd experienced other conflicts, and some of them from across the Atlantic. She began to anticipate what that would be like, the onslaught due to come her way once there this coming summer, bombarded with questions, concerns, worries and inquiries. It was never ending. Living in Israel meant binding oneself to a situation as much as a place, a heavy package even before one added the ingredient of world opinion.

She so clearly remembered one exchange in particular, about ten years earlier. At the time there'd been the imminent threat of Saddam's missiles. An elderly woman she knew tangentially through some friends had stopped her on the street during one of her visits to Philadelphia, gripping her forearm with great emotion. The children had paused beside her.

"How can you do it? How can you go back there?"

"What are you talking about?"

"How can you put your children in such danger?"

It had been a windy day and leaves had fluttered around them, almost literally encasing them within this confrontation. Within seconds Victoria had understood where this virtual stranger was going with her comments, what she was getting at. She'd tried to calm her.

"It's okay. Everything's okay."

The children had come in a bit closer, understanding that their mother was somehow being attacked and wanting to offer support. In effect, they were also ducking the leaves that were swirling above and beyond them, distracting them with their whimsical paths.

"How can you do it?" the woman had persisted, digging her fingers deeper into her forearm.

Victoria had reached out with her free hand and patted the woman's arm, hoping to encourage her to release her grip. It had all been a bit scary. She distinctly recalled noticing the part in the older woman's hair where the gray was fading to white. This woman had lived a longer life, experienced the hardships and losses that come with age. She needed to be gentle.

"It's so kind of you to be concerned about us. But really, we're okay." It was essential that the kids not start to worry, and Victoria had quickly realized that this confrontation alone was nothing short of terrifying. "Remember. We're going home. The kids have school. Our lives need to be lived."

The kids had started to peel off to the sides, stepping out of the vortex of leaves. They were getting bored. The attraction of the confrontation didn't compare with the scuffling noise they could make with their feet if they tried to dance between the brittle oak leaves. There was fun to be had.

Victoria had started to loosen up and relax, sensing a way out of the conversation. She'd been well trained by her extensive contact with Israelis, inured to threats after enduring decades of them, fortified by a seemingly endless supply of inner strength – that infamous *ko'ach* – to remain calm. She'd pulled back her shoulders, straightened up and faced the woman's concern directly. "We're not afraid. This is part of living where we live. We believe that we'll be okay; otherwise we couldn't live there." She had glanced to the right and left, vaguely gesturing to her children, now dispersed along the sidewalk, enjoying the shuffling and the crackling. "I really appreciate your concern."

Yes, this was familiar terrain. Victoria had been there before and would be again. It was all part of living in a politically contested hotbed. She'd felt awfully brave at the time, assuring this woman of their safety. After all, what did this have to do with her?

But now everything was different and it had everything to do with her. There was no way to escape the reality spread across the table in black and white and its direct ramifications for her little life. Too many events in too few days had created a situation set to boil over; an already fragile equilibrium had been disturbed.

Ugly potential was wiggling its way through the interstices of her bubble, threatening to damage the delicate overlay by ripping jagged, irreparable holes.

She stood up quite suddenly, the chair making a sharp, screeching sound as she brutally thrust it away from the table. The stale air in the room seemed to dispel, cleared by the clarity of her resolve. Hyperaware of the bigger picture, she felt a desperate need to check in on Ben. She half walked, half ran to her bedroom. "I simply need to hear his voice." Her whisper was eagerly picked up on by Bama, who jumped up and followed her. She grabbed her cell phone and fumbled with it a bit, scrolling back and forth to find his name on the chat list. Her husband's promise echoed in her head: *It'll be okay.* There it was. She typed in an innocuous: "Hi, sweetie!" and stared at the screen, focusing in on those little check marks to the side. A grey one appeared, and then another, the message had been delivered but not yet read.

She panicked for a second and then forced herself to relax, consoling herself with numerous, logical explanations. Ben must not have his phone with him. He was out on a regular drill exercise. He was on guard duty. She took a few deep breaths, filling her chest up with pure oxygen in an effort to assuage her fear and calm her thoughts. This was going to be a long story – not a short one. She'd have to find a way to get through it. The jarring sound of the drilling from next door was even louder here in the bedroom where the windows had been left wide open. Outside of her house life was exactly as it had been hours earlier, days earlier, weeks earlier; inside it was no longer recognizable.

Ben saw his Mom's name pop up on the screen of his phone. He lay it back down next to his bunk. He couldn't answer it. Part of him wanted to, the soft part. But the sane part couldn't. What was he going to tell her? How would she respond? This wasn't a time when he could deal with her emotions, her fears or even her love. That morning they'd been briefed; his platoon was to be mobilized, moved south toward the Gaza border in order to prepare, alongside many others, for a ground troop incursion. He'd felt an immediate wave of frustration; despite having given this land back to the Palestinians, painfully evicting exactly those Israelis who'd succeeded in turning its sandy shores into prosperous agricultural farms, the Israeli government still hadn't achieved the hoped-for peace. Hamas's grip on the locals was strangling all of them. But as others began to move into action, a mixture of excitement and fear quashed his momentary effort to make sense of an impossible situation.

He stuffed a few things in his pack, the most essential of his essentials. Suddenly everything seemed extraneous. What use were extra underwear, T-shirts or shaving gear going to be when he would be fighting for his life, within range of those so willing to take it from him? He checked the rounds of ammo, shoved the magazines into their relevant pockets and slots, checked his protective vest, the battle portion of tuna and beans they'd been given for that first day. Fact is, there really wasn't room for much of anything personal.

He glanced back at the screen of the phone again. It was black. Good. There wasn't room for the kind of personal baggage it symbolized either. He felt on fire, his body buzzing with energy, his legs jiggling side to side, the nervous tick his mother was constantly on him to control gone wild. But today it seemed appropriate, made to order. He was terrified. He wouldn't admit it to anyone, but he felt it in his bones. And that was exactly the reason he wouldn't dare answer his mother's call. It was certain she'd pick up on his anxiety and *her* fear, even if unspoken, even if she restrained herself and didn't issue one word of concern, would dig unwelcome chinks in the armor of adrenaline his body was naturally producing in order to prepare himself for what lay ahead.

He reached over to the phone and turned it off. The "Hi, sweetie" he'd seen on the screen earlier had both swelled and pinched his heart; his mother's love a great comfort but a simultaneous reminder that she could no longer protect him. He'd moved far off her radar.

"Ben. We're moving."

He had to get going. He couldn't speak with her because he didn't want to lie. And they'd all agreed. Each member of his squad had made a unanimous pact to tell their parents that they were far from the action, that they wouldn't be part of what was going on inside Gaza, that there was no reason to worry. It had taken so much of him to squeeze out those words in a neutral manner a few days earlier when it was still true, when they were still safely tucked away on their base. He'd been determined to make sure she didn't pick up on something and figure out he wasn't telling her the whole story. He couldn't risk that now.

Ben gripped the straps of his bag tightly in his left hand and pulled it onto his back. Its weight was greater than he anticipated, but they'd trained for as much. He could handle it. He swung his rifle over his shoulder and moved toward the exit door to join his squad-mates. Another burst of energy moved through his body. He felt alive. Game on.

Chapter 22

This was it. She was leaving in a few days. It was no longer an idea or a possibility, but instead, a fact. She was on her way to the States to assume an esteemed teaching position within an American academic institution. The dream was becoming a reality. Time to pull out the suitcases and pack. Victoria made her way down to the basement, groped for the light switch and then pulled open the heavy door of the bomb shelter. *A bomb shelter.* Hers was one of the genuine ones, not an armored room dressed up to look like an office or a spare bedroom. This shelter was made of steel-fortified cement, walls, floor and ceiling each 40 centimeters in width. It was equipped with an escape hatch as well as a solid steel door that closed with a circular latch, something akin to what one might find on a submarine. Who would believe that Victoria, hailing from Center City, Philadelphia, had a bona fide bomb shelter. Funny, but true. Albeit, the real joke was that this particular bomb shelter was disguised as a storage closet. The walls inside were lined with hanging racks and shelves piled high with dusty boxes holding off-season clothing, spare bedding and old college T-shirts.

She turned on the light, a naked bulb hanging from the ceiling, and looked over the items on the rack: a bridesmaid dress from the

'80s, her wedding dress, a shearling coat from a former life lived in a cold European climate. This one she pulled out of the pack, examining a hole in the shoulder. A shiver ran up her spine and she made a little noise of disgust as she thought of the rodent no doubt responsible. She shoved it roughly back in place and proceeded to run her hand along the edges of the other hanging items, noting the thin strip of dust along the shoulder line that had gathered uniformly down the row. She couldn't imagine wearing any of these things ever again. Every year Guy threatened to throw things out, randomly, with no prior warning. And now and again, true to his word, she'd find a box of clothing alongside the garbage can out by the road, waiting for pickup. Maybe that was a good thing. She didn't like to think about how much junk was horded here.

She advanced to the end of the line, moved aside some of those former remnants of her life as a working girl in New York City and groped in the dark hollows beneath for the big duffel bags. With one big jerk she managed to pull out the first one, stuck between its neighbors, dragging it toward the exit in a cloud of moldy dust. Not having discerned the large dehumidifier planted smack in the middle of the narrow aisle left between the rows of shelving – the one working overtime to preserve the memories stored in this damp room – she pitched forward toward the hatch, cursing as the duffel banged into the shelves and caused boxes to spill their contents, hanging items to slip off their hangers. Guy definitely had a point.

She repeated the same procedure a few times, moving one duffel bag after another out of the shelter until she'd amassed a pile of them by its heavy door. The effort alone exhausted her; she was covered in a layer of unhealthy dust. She brushed some of it off of her and surveyed the scene. It really was pathetic. God forbid they actually needed this room as a shelter. They'd never be able to find enough space to squeeze in among the Miss Havisham-style collection of historical artifacts. This amount of "memories" didn't leave room for even a modicum of comfort.

She recalled preparing for the Iraqi invasion in the spring of 2003 when Israelis were certain Saddam Hussein would attack them with Scud missiles. She'd stocked the shelter with bottles of water, a radio and a few cans of tuna fish. Guy had assured her that if need be, he would drag in mattresses, blankets and pillows, books, games and even a telephone; that a relatively full life could be lived while waiting out whatever threat loomed outdoors. Merely envisioning this scenario at the time had been terrifying enough. Yet nothing had come of Saddam's ranting and raving, and soon enough the emergency alert status had been rescinded.

She pulled aside a row of Laura Ashley dresses, long ago officially vintage, and peeked at a small shelf near the escape hatch; a few spare items were still there at the ready. The water was probably no longer potable. It was time to throw it out. She picked up one of the cans of tuna, looking for an expiration date. She couldn't recall whether tuna actually ever went bad. She turned off the light and tugged the heavy door back into place, discerning movement at her feet. Bama was waiting just outside, tail wagging. She laughed as she bent down to give her a pat.

"No interest in coming back in with me. No way, right?"

A few days earlier the local warning siren had sounded, something that almost never occurred in their neighborhood, far from any urban area and just out of range of missiles launched from either Gaza to the south or Lebanon to the north. She'd forced Bama into the shelter with her, closing the door firmly behind them. There they'd stood, crammed between the coats and boxes, squeezed into what barely counted as ambulatory space, looking at one another. Victoria had actually hesitated before bringing her in, but Bama, never far from her mistress's legs, hadn't thought twice, barreling in behind her before there was time to consider an alternative plan. No harm done. In any case there was no way she would risk losing her to a live explosive; better that she was there by her side.

After only a few seconds Bama had begun to get nervous, alternating between sitting and standing without satisfaction, beginning to pace the miniscule aisle, obviously uneasy within the claustrophobic space. Her curiosity, leading her to sniff around among the dusty piles of whatever, kept her distracted for only a few more seconds and then began to wane. She'd trusted Victoria enough to follow her inside, primarily so as not to be left behind, but soon enough she was eager to get out.

Finding the door closed behind her, with no possibility of escape, she'd appealed to her mistress with glistening, black eyes (could dogs actually cry?) and squeaky noises clearly meant to communicate. *Isn't it time to go? What do we do now? I don't like it here.* Victoria couldn't have agreed more. She'd found Bama's panic almost more unsettling than the chance that something might actually fall on the house. She'd vowed never to bring her in with her again, even in an effort to save her life. With a few deep breaths meant to slow the quickening of her heart rate set off by that first siren, and the concern that they might be within range of danger, she'd begun to count down the proscribed three minutes. Anything actually falling out of the sky would surely land in that amount of time. Soon enough she'd finished. That was it. They were done. She'd swung open the heavy door to their mutual relief. This was one scenario she wouldn't repeat.

Finished in the shelter, Victoria leaned over and grasped the handles of two of the duffels. Despite being thwarted by Bama, who was excitedly jumping on, over and between the bags, delighted by this new opportunity for sport, Victoria managed to make her way toward the stairwell. She couldn't resist. She dropped one of the duffels before starting up the stairs and caught Bama's soft, black head mid-movement in a long caress. Duffels triggered a memory of long absences for this dog. Her hyperactive behavior was a natural response to the fear that her mistress would soon leave her by the wayside, alone, again. There was no question that dogs were human.

"Bama, my sugar. Mommy's prize." In all of her thinking, plotting and planning, Victoria hadn't considered the fact that she'd be leaving behind this faithful friend. She'd really miss her. "Don't worry. I'll be back. I always come back." She gave her one more pat on the head, this one confirming her words, and then resumed her trek upstairs, bags in hand. Left to her own devices, Bama continued her frenzied pursuit, running underfoot as Victoria tried to make her way. The duffel bags banged against the wrought iron handrail on one side, the cement wall on the other, and Victoria dropped her momentary melancholy; with so much commotion it was hard for her to dwell too much on being sad.

Reaching the landing she hurled the bags into the entrance foyer and returned for another load. Just as she finished, the phone rang. She leaped over the amassed pile, delighting Bama (certain this was a new game) and ran into the kitchen to answer it. She dare not miss a phone call. It could be Ben. She picked it up without taking that extra second to look at the screen. The line was dead. They'd already hung up. Her heart dropped for a moment.

Victoria heard a rustling noise in the entrance hall that sounded suspiciously like a rodent or wild animal and hurried to check it out. Maybe one of those creatures that were eating her clothing down in the storage area was stuck in a bag. But no, it was only Bama. She smiled as she watched her teeter atop the pile of duffels, trying to settle herself among the nylon folds and rugged, woven straps. She really was a sweetheart. "You want to come with me, sweetie?"

A sudden loud knock on the door provoked a round of fierce barking. Victoria flinched and a cold chill moved through her as she grasped the doorknob. Bama positioned herself beside her, at the ready.

"Open up Vic, it's me!"

She breathed a sigh of relief. "Hey! What a surprise!"

Bama jumped up straight onto Alison's legs, almost knocking her over, then proceeded to run out the door and down the path of the house, off to patrol the neighborhood.

"I tried to call but there was no answer!" She stepped inside and stood by the pile of duffels.

"Thank God it's only you. All that knocking and…" Victoria's voice faded off. She didn't need to go there right now.

Alison gestured at the pile of luggage. "I see you've begun to pack."

"Kind of. Pulling out the bags was such an effort. I need a break. Want a cup of coffee?"

She closed the door behind her and made for the kitchen, Alison at her heels. An enormous bang stopped them both in their tracks. This wasn't the time for sudden loud noises; nerves were on edge. Victoria ran back to the front door. Behind the lower pane of smoked glass she could discern the black shadow: Bama seated there patiently, waiting to be let back in. This was an oft repeated exercise. The minute she realized she was alone, left without her mistress, she'd hightail it back home, hurling herself against the door, desperate to make her way back into the inner sanctum. Victoria opened the door for her and watched as she immediately struggled to reposition herself on the pile of bags. Yes. There were many costs to this extended trip abroad.

"She's really going to miss you." Alison had come up behind her silently. "No more mommy."

"Yeah, I know. It's hard to leave her."

Victoria led her back to the kitchen and turned on the coffee machine. "What about you? Are you ready to go?"

"It's no big deal for me, only a hop, skip and jump. I'm not dragging myself half way across the world like you."

"I'd love to go to Paris. I'm so envious. You have no idea."

"Oh, come on. You don't need Paris. You're livin' the dream!" Her smile lit up her face. Victoria couldn't help chuckling.

"How long will you be there this time?"

"Only a week. Just enough time to help my sister with the older kids while she focuses on the baby."

Victoria busied herself with preparing the coffee, pouring milk into the frother. "I love Paris. I always thought I'd end up there." She turned to Alison, already at the table. "Yet here I am and it's definitely not Paris." She took a seat across from her. "I must have taken a wrong turn somewhere along the way." She was startled at her own hushed tone, having intended to be a lot breezier. It was hard to suppress what lurked beneath.

"Only one? You're way ahead of the game. Count yourself lucky."

"Can you bring me some kind of smelly cheese? Your choice, whatever suits your fancy."

"Pleasure. Anything else? Chocolates? Croissants? You probably don't eat such sinful things."

"That's simply the impression I like to give. Anything direct from Paris is welcome by me."

"Wait. You won't even be here when I get back!!! Who'll eat it all?"

Victoria paused. She hadn't thought of that. This trip really wasn't like the others. She'd be gone for a few months, busy with a new job, disconnected in a way she'd never really been.

"Wow, I didn't think of that."

An air of melancholy filled the room. The two sipped their coffee, enjoyed the warm foam that tickled their upper lips as the hot fluid went down. "Anyway," Alison began, "I stopped by because I need my tarte tatin pan – the one you borrowed last month? We're heavy into the 'French' theme at home and I've promised to make one for the kids before I leave."

"No problem." Victoria got up and went to the pantry, bringing out the heavy cast-iron pan, gently laying it on the table.

Alison glanced over at the newspaper beside it, an expected kitchen accoutrement, but this morning's featuring a collage of foreboding images. She picked up her cup and casually walked out of the kitchen, toward the patio door.

"Come outside for a minute. It's such a pretty day. Not even that hot."

Victoria followed her. *This is nice.* Another thing she'd miss. Another aspect of her life she hadn't considered these last few months, while she'd been bashing everything local. Golden rays of morning sunlight stretched across the surface of the deck, warming the wooden planks before extending upwards to the tree surround, caressing the lush green leaves. They stepped out to the atrium, the outdoor area tucked in the embrace of the house reserved for summer luncheons and evening cocktails. She loved the fact that she actually *had* an atrium, the word itself dripping with associations of the ancient world, a fascination since grade school. When they'd first moved in she'd found it one of the more redeeming features of her house, the ultimate exotic detail. No, she definitely wouldn't have had one if she'd settled in Scarsdale or somewhere equally innocuous back in the States.

Bougainvillea ran rampant here, covering every square meter of the stuccoed walls, carpeting the ceramic tiles on the ground with its detritus of purple flowers and stifling the air with its twisted mesh of branches. No question about it, she'd found Shangri-La. Her home was a copy of those Provençal beauties she'd loved as a child.

"Standing here it's hard to imagine there's another reality, a different one, elsewhere."

Alison sat down on one of the patio chairs, put her coffee on the woodblock table.

"Hey." Her voice had softened a bit. "Have you heard from Ben?"

They locked eyes a moment and then both turned outward toward the pool. The embrace of the atrium enveloped their silence, making it heavier with significance, dripping with meaning.

"No. Nothing. No news is good news. Right?"

Victoria tried to keep her voice lighthearted but knew she sounded nervous; she couldn't do better. It took so much energy to lead a life, any life, *her* life, without desperately worrying about someone else's. She was trying to hold it together.

"For sure. I'm certain he's fine. They really take care of our boys. Don't worry."

Another charged silence and then Victoria whispered, "I worry about him all the time. I know he's not there, that his platoon isn't going to go in. They haven't finished their training. They aren't ready to be a part of this, whatever *this* is. But still... Until he's home..."

"I can't imagine."

Alison reached across and touched Victoria's cheek for a second before moving to the side and tugging at a strand of her hair. The gesture made Victoria tear up a bit. Her anguish was right there, hanging out for all to see. She appreciated that her friend wanted to lessen her load, refocus her energy.

"I've been thinking a lot about your summer plans, about the fact that you're finally going to have an opportunity to accelerate your career. It's the best thing you've ever done, for everyone." Alison paused as she took another sip of coffee. "Seriously Vic, don't think twice about it. Your life is as valuable as any other. Doing something that's good for you is no question the right thing for the family." She placed her cup back on the table and added, "You're not abandoning anyone."

Victoria looked back out toward the pool, watched a bird alight on a nearby branch, listened to his song. Definitely paradise. How many times had her brother, far away in Philadelphia, on the other end of the phone line, commented about how lovely it was to hear the birds in the background of their conversations?

"I'll still be waiting right here where you've left me, treading water as always. And Guy? Ben? They're all behind you. Don't think for a second that you're in this alone."

Victoria took in her surroundings, this beautiful bubble of her own design, the one she'd carefully arranged to meet her needs. It had always comforted her with its familiarity, protected her from the undesirable that lurked afield. There had been so many choices along the way, so many paths she could have taken, a range of destinations that didn't lead precisely here, with its very mixed and troublesome bag. Her mind shifted; a door slammed shut.

"I was supposed to live in Paris."

Alison laughed at Victoria's abrupt pronouncement, her change of tone. The air thinned, it became a bit easier to breathe within the atrium. "I took every chance I could to be there: summer, vacations, a semester. You name it. There was that little apartment, the one near the Rue Montorgeuil. My last residence there. God, I loved those twisting, claustrophobic streets; the way I would walk and walk, destination unclear, and then suddenly, reach a blinding light, too much light to even take in, and realize I'd come to one of those Haussmannian boulevards, those throughways that stretch into infinity with their well-ordered, uniform facades – those dark, little alleyways left behind."

"My sister lives in one of those little streets. She finds it quaint, albeit inconvenient. There's limited buggy access."

They both nodded their heads knowingly. Victoria continued, "And the markets, those gorgeous local markets with their bustle of colorful characters, each armed with long fresh baguettes; the tiny gated parks, each more intimate than the last – pockets of peace and quiet you would stumble upon without warning; oh, and those *hôtels* with the courtyards, the ones hiding behind closed double-door entrances that offer just a hint of the families and businesses inside, thousands of stories I could only begin to imagine."

Victoria couldn't help herself. This walk through her past, a different part of her story, tumbled out. "Walking along the rue des Francs Bourgeois in the Marais, you know, that main street that leads to the Bibliothèque Historique in the Second, I simply knew that this life suited me. I was so resolved to have it. I wasn't going to let anything foil my plan to hang on to it: the intimacy, the constant sense of discovery, the foreignness. I realized I had to live in a place where I felt open to the elements – nerve endings almost brutally assaulted by exterior stimuli. It was everything I wanted. Yet somehow," she laughed for a second, "somehow, I ended up here! It's simply inexplicable!"

"Didn't you have some writing gig there? Some kind of a column in the local English speakers' gazette?"

"I told you about that? Seems like so long ago now. Yes, I was on my way to becoming the queen of the local expat gossip scene, the official commentator on life in Paris for all those Americans. There are so many of them! It's a huge community. It was a pretty good niche. I would have been happy to stay on and become a features' writer. That was the plan. And then," she paused a moment, pushed her empty coffee cup away, toward the center of the table, "well, and then I met Guy." She smiled. "And that whole plan fell to the wayside. Poof. Gone!" She raised her hand and snapped her fingers once.

"Last Autumn. Remember? When I flew to Paris for a long weekend? Each day I felt it, that overwhelming feeling of what I'd given up. Everything there struck me as extraordinary, special: the glistening pavements, you know they rinse those pavements clean, every one of them, each morning! The whole city sparkles like a diamond. It's just amazing. And running along the Seine I couldn't believe I'd actually made a choice to go elsewhere, to exchange that crystalline sparkle for the constant grit of sand, the kind that covers every surface, invades each bodily cavity, weighs down the air."

She paused, her sudden silence filling the space in the atrium, rich with significance, and then added, "What was I thinking?"

They both smiled, shifting a bit in their chairs. This tale was amusing, kind of – but on the other hand, not that much. Maybe it was sad.

"You know, Ilana's coming home."

"Yes, she has sent me a few panicky messages."

They both laughed. The continuing saga of their friend who had done absolutely everything she could think of to escape life in Israel, provided continual amusement. Yet Victoria's was a bit too high – almost hysterical.

"We met at her apartment in New York and you wouldn't believe it. I actually ended up trying to assuage her fears. Me. Little Miss "Get me out of here, it's better back there" Victoria. Who'd have thunk it?"

They laughed. "Vic, you love your life here. You have a beautiful life here." Alison grabbed Victoria's hand and gave it a squeeze. "You simply don't like to admit it." She rose from the table, picked up her empty coffee cup and added, "I have to get going."

Victoria joined her, walking back into the house. "You've got to get on your way to *gai Paris*!"

After exchanging hugs and a hearty "*au revoir*" with Alison at the entrance, Victoria stepped back outside to the atrium. She scanned her garden, taking it all in: the exotic and the mundane, a romantic fantasy made real every single day. Although the path that had led her here was uneven and unexpected, seemingly without rhyme or reason, it suddenly seemed almost inevitable – simply a series of steps in her life-long search for… for what? For a sprig of bougainvillea: so beautiful, so luscious, so alive.

Back in the house Victoria studied Bama, snoring away peacefully on top of the duffel bags, deeply content in her slumber and no longer worried by the ramifications of all that reinforced nylon. With one heavy heartbeat she felt desperately sad, the thought of what she was leaving behind overwhelming her with its losses, but with the next she began to feel lighter. Jonathan and Maia were coming with her, excited about summer camp. Ben was safe on his base. She knew that. She didn't have to worry about him. And there was no question that the summer before her would be one of her best. It was time to focus on packing up and getting ready to go, to push aside the hesitations, the considerations, the threatening costs and make room for one enormous balloon of an opportunity. She couldn't wait.

Chapter 23

Victoria closed her eyes for a moment, felt the rush of the plane braking against the force of gravity, and then reopened them: *Home.* She gazed out the window, watching the hangars along the runway pass by as they taxied to the gate. *My other home.* Only twelve hours earlier she'd left Israel. Guy was with Bama. Ben was at some military base. But was he? *Ben. Where was Ben?* She forced her thoughts away from that question, it was more than she could handle. She leaned down to put on her shoes and gather the items shoved into the seat pocket in front of her. She touched Maia's hand to get her attention.

"Excited?"

"What time do the stores open?"

Victoria smiled and settled back into her seat. *Some things never change.* Her daughter's mania for shopping never waned and only got stronger as she felt the magnetic pull of the city with its plethora of lovely boutiques. Caesarea was big on sand, sun, sea and palm trees but short on commerce. Maia was about to be released into her element, a kid in a candy store.

She watched as Jonathan and Maia gathered their belongings. They were obviously eager to deplane, to start their summers. She was glad they were getting a chance to spend the summer in the States. It had been a stressful few weeks and wasn't liable to get better soon. Within a few days they'd be comfortably situated in summer camp, safely tucked away in the Poconos, removed from everything happening back in Israel. Being able to account for their whereabouts would make it that much easier for her to make her way up to New York, to take up her position behind the lectern, to finally begin what had seemed like a pipedream several months earlier.

If only... She felt slightly sick in the stomach. If only she knew that Ben was okay – would *be* okay. She couldn't stop obsessing about him. She hadn't heard from him for days, and since that last conversation the world had begun to tip to the side, everything sliding terribly out of place. She was terrified it would flip over completely and he'd be caught in some kind of maelstrom. It took a huge effort to push away these thoughts, to focus on the excitement ahead.

Victoria pulled the disembarkation card out of her purse and scanned down the fields she'd filled in earlier. She came to the line where she needed to fill in her home address and returned her gaze to the view out the window. This was always a tough one. She'd filled in her Israeli address. That's what they wanted. The information requested by the United States government was all about where one paid taxes and electricity bills – the place where actual "living" was done. In this case, there was no question: Israel fit the bill. Yet each and every time she filled in this card she hesitated.

Where is home?

Although it was technically accurate, and simplest, to write down Caesarea, it wasn't the whole story. After all, her US driver's license still identified her as a Pennsylvanian, she still voted in local elections and the minute she stepped out of the plane she knew she was home. She'd spent almost three decades away, yet always and forever, part of her heart remained here. That might be normal, even expected; most people retained some attachment to the place where they grew up. But she knew that her continuous hesitation, the way her pen consistently, time after time, hovered over this field, as if suspended between two very strong magnets, wasn't completely typical.

The occasional, innocent question: "Is it nice to be home?" felt loaded and would send her into a panic, setting off an avalanche of thoughts, deliberations and considerations. And how incredibly odd that, whether on the Atlantic or the Mediterranean, her answer to that query was always a genuine and resolute "Yes!" Both places lay claim to her heart and at this point it was impossible to declare one over the other.

Watching her children collect their items, ready to start their day here in Philadelphia, she realized she'd passed the buck, handing the responsibility for making the choice to the next generation. Having carefully exposed them to two worlds, guiding them to toe the line she'd drawn, she'd left them with the same dilemma – perched between two worlds. Her intention had been to enrich their lives by expanding their horizons. She'd never considered that such empowerment might be a burden.

On the verge of a summer that spoke worlds about the decisions she'd made decades earlier, silent but firm commentary on where she was headed in the future, she recognized that her actions had forever compromised their everyday experience; that, in fact, they would compel them to make difficult choices down the road, some complicated and emotionally costly. The split-sense of national identity they'd inherited undermined their sense of national affiliation, forever compromising any normal sense of allegiance to one or the other. These annual summer trips back to the States, ostensibly all gain, probably hadn't helped; in some ways they were salt in the wound. She hadn't intended any of this, had never anticipated the significance of her vacillation. She felt saddened by the idea that her children might have been shortchanged.

There was a bit of movement from the front of the cabin. People were pulling suitcases out of the overhead compartment, launching themselves into the aisle to get a place in the line to the exit and swinging bags over their shoulders. Victoria popped up to join the fray, her children ducking out from under the overhead panels, ready to stretch their legs. It was 5:00 a.m. Philadelphia time. They'd only managed to sleep a few hours but none of them were tired – in fact the kids positively vibrated with energy. They were all three impatient, waiting for the attachment of the airport sleeve – the opening of the cabin door that would unseal this protective bubble and release them to the elements. Victoria ticked off the final steps of their journey: immigration, baggage claim and the run – bags bouncing on backs and racing along on carts – down the long hallway to the welcome center to meet their grandparents. No, there was no question at all. This wasn't a "what if" or a "maybe." This was home.

Victoria took her time in the kitchen of her mother's apartment, putting away the groceries they had picked up almost first thing, part of their routine each visit. Exhausted from the trip, wracked with emotional turmoil, she appreciated the mundane rhythm of stacking and arranging items in the cabinets. Settling in was perfect for what ailed her, a way to find her comfort zone. She heard her phone buzz somewhere in the apartment. Maia ran out of the room into the foyer and then came back and reported: "Daddy says Ben is fine." Message delivered, Victoria watched her put the phone down on the sideboard and return to flipping through the television channels for the newest episode of some bit of American junk, settling on *Dance Moms*. She smiled. The message was a welcome one. Last time she'd spoken with Ben he'd assured her he was far from the action and would remain so. She believed him. She had to. Otherwise there is no way she could have gotten on the plane and flown across the world. Yet the inevitable ground incursion would involve many others exactly like him, perhaps even a handful she knew personally or through friends. Her momentary contentment was tinged with a nervous feeling of concern.

This was Israel. Everyone was somehow connected, whether directly or indirectly. Each tragedy affected not only a single family but also an *extended* one including blood relatives, friends and acquaintances. As she had come to understand, primarily through experiences like that with Ben's friend Omer months earlier, the whole country was basically one gigantic web of interconnected strands. Each loss (a soldier, a mother, a child) struck like an earthquake, damage to the epicenter causing deep cracks in the ground in every direction, cave-ins and continual aftershocks.

This morning, the official beginning of this promising summer, Victoria desperately wanted to suppress the likelihood of this new threat, to deny it any place in her heart. She wanted to enjoy the crisp air of the American Mid-Atlantic, such a pleasant change from the oppressive heat back home; to enjoy the change of pace provided by merely getting away; to look forward to the summer at Columbia. When this idea, this new reality, had been a passing thought, a distant possibility, the situation had been a different one. Stepping away from her life back in Caesarea then, even with Ben in service, hadn't seemed such a big deal. After all, a thousand days was a lot to commit to staying in one place; it was a long time to arrest the natural movement forward of any life. How ironic, and unfair, that this pivotal and threatening moment in Ben's life coincided with one of the more exhilarating ones in her own; that precisely as she was starting a phase that held the potential of being absolutely magical, a new beginning, Ben was part of a machine hurtling into unknown and terrifying terrain, an area of which she had very little knowledge and upon which she had absolutely no control. Although she'd managed to engineer so much of her children's lives, like any mother, his was presently – and frighteningly – far beyond her reach.

Victoria finished lining the cans up in the cupboard and went over to sit at the desk. Most days were good ones; she wanted to concentrate on those. In any case, if and when the bad ones came, she'd have no choice but to deal with them as well. She smiled. That was Guy's theory. Although she'd dismissed it for years as far too trite a way to lead a life, it presently suited her well.

Maia peeled herself off the couch and came over as Victoria opened her laptop, connecting herself, via Wi-Fi, to the world beyond.

"What'cha doin'?"

Victoria felt her daughter's hands lightly touch her shoulders as she stared at the multitude of news reports and the tickertape of headlines crowding the screen before her. Together they watched a video report of yet another rocket being shot from Gaza only to be repelled by the Iron Dome antimissile system.

"They never stop coming, those rockets. How do kids in the South deal with it? I've never even been inside our shelter!"

Victoria forcibly pushed aside the fear prompted by the horrific reports on the screen and turned to her daughter. It was crucial she pull herself together enough to help her children deal with what was going on back home. With all the focus on Ben she sometimes forgot there were others who needed her attention. Maia's comments were important, and definitely more pressing at that very moment than her worries about him. She needed to allay her fears.

"Nor will you ever be."

It came out unconvincing and flat. Victoria tried to summon up more energy for the task. She hadn't spent a lot of time considering how her younger children were experiencing this. For the most part they mostly avoided the topic. She'd have to do a better job. Shutting out the reality there on the screen, the images and words on the laptop seeping into her soul, would be a good start. *But how?*

"Are we ready to go?" She worked up a small smile.

Maia's mind moved onward, unwilling to linger in uncomfortable territory. In any case, she was eager to start shopping. "Absolutely!"

"I'm ready too." Jonathan's voice drifted in from somewhere else in the apartment.

Victoria had arrived for a long stay and would have preferred to slow the pace of reintegration, but Maia and Jonathan acted as if they were on speed. Their trip was going to be shorter, the time available to enjoy America's "plenty" limited; there was not one moment to spare. They were keen to hit the streets, to get this summer moving like any other. But that was the hitch: it wasn't like any other. Victoria found herself struggling to shift gears, desperately trying to segue to their rhythm.

Maia persisted. "Mommy, I was thinking, maybe we should start down at City Sports and wind our way back towards home."

Victoria's eyes were back on the screen and she offered a distracted "Okay" that came out something closer to *whatever*.

"Mom." She spoke almost sharply, determined to get her mother's attention, to direct it elsewhere. "Ben's fine. Dad said so."

As if shaken from a trance, Victoria rolled back the desk chair, swiveled it around and faced her daughter. She would love to switch places with her for even a few hours. The burden of motherhood weighed so heavily today, making the levity of Maia's life enviable.

"You're right. You're absolutely right." She reached back to snap closed the laptop behind her, waiting for that satisfactory click, and then walked out of the room toward her bedroom. Maybe she should try to loosen up a bit. There was no sign that Ben was involved in what was going on back in Israel, no indication that she *had* to worry. Being a devoted Israeli didn't mean she didn't deserve to disconnect now and then, take a little break and think about brighter things. After all, this was the summer that might change the course of her life.

She paused for a moment as she passed the mirror in the hallway. Something in her face, staring back at her from its reflective glass surface, seemed a fraction less confident than her resolve. "Let's get this show on the road," she called out toward the living room, as much to herself as to the children. She nodded assuredly. *This isn't about Ben.*

Chapter 24

Only a week had passed since she'd landed in the States, but Victoria's entire world had crashed and broken into pieces. Nothing was as it had once been. She was seated at the desk in the tiny apartment the university had provided for her for the summer. It was pitch black outside. Of course it was. It was 3:00 a.m. She hadn't been able to sleep. After a few restless hours, falling asleep only to awaken with a jerk, grab her phone to check for messages and updates and then, hopelessly, try to fall back to sleep, an extraordinarily unrewarding cycle, she'd given up. She'd abandoned her bed and moved to the desk, one step over in this tiny studio, to check the current Israeli news on her computer.

She hadn't turned on any lights, denying the start of a new day. A patchwork of bright colors and flashing lights, reflections of the ever-shifting stories on the screen before her, moved across her face. Squares of red, of yellow, of stark white and grey, all aflicker, mixed together to give her complexion a sickly hue resembling rancid cheese. Her expression was vacant. She felt so beyond afraid she'd become numb. She read through the updates, the headlines and the stories, the information, imagery, innuendo and implications shaking her to the core.

The air in the room felt musty. She was suffocated by fear. Nothing moved save those shifting images and her eyes, scanning left and right, up and down, trying to take in everything at once, frantically searching for any relevant morsel of information. The bottom had dropped out. She was anchorless, floating, desperate to find something to hold on to – a little bit of solace in an enormous stream of dismay.

The last few days had been exhausting, the mixture of amazing and horrific sapping her of all energy. There was the upside. Only days into the semester, in fact, it had taken about one hour, she was already eons more comfortable than she'd been after years of lecturing here and there back in Israel. Everything was as it should be: the students, a language of which she had full control, the atmosphere of old-world academia – it all felt so natural. Was it possible that she'd spent an entire lifetime squeezing herself into the wrong mold? The thought alone was stultifying.

She wondered where she'd gotten the strength, but then again, she knew the answer to that question. She knew it without even searching for it. Years of coping, making do, and even succeeding, in a foreign country had only made her stronger and were responsible for her smooth entry into life here at Columbia. Surviving and eventually thriving had gained her a measure of self-confidence she'd never have acquired otherwise. Maybe she needed to be more appreciative of the convoluted and unexpected path she'd taken, the one that had shocked her family and friends way back when, separated her from everything she knew. Ironically, the harder road might have given her more than it had taken.

She'd moved to the guest faculty apartment the day after dropping off Jonathan and Maia at overnight camp. It had all been so easy. Traveling light, with one large suitcase of summer clothes and a laptop, she'd felt she could go anywhere. She began to think of a new age, one where she'd pick a different campus each summer, make the experience at Columbia only the first, turn over a new leaf and redefine her life. After Guy had agreed to the arrangement once, he'd certainly sign on again; it could become a fixture in their lives. She'd figured it all out. She could have the best of two worlds – both stay and go.

All that positive energy and excitement seemed like a lifetime ago. Now she was living a completely different reality. Two days earlier she'd come to understand that Ben wasn't tucked safely on a base somewhere within the borders of Israel proper, but instead was in Gaza, right in the middle of the action. She'd been sitting in the faculty lounge, deep in conversation about quality journalism and new forms of media. She'd taken quite a liking to this one woman, another faculty member, who happened to specialize in areas she struggled to comprehend, such as Twitter. They'd been comparing approaches. Victoria's telephone, constantly on silent but still able to interrupt with its bone-jarring silenced buzz, had begun to wiggle across the table beside them. She'd excused herself, picked it up and, not quite able to discern what was on the screen without glasses, stepped to a quiet corner of the lounge.

It was a WhatsApp message and she didn't recognize the sender. She'd been added to a new group, one titled with the name of Ben's squad commander. She didn't understand what that was about. She'd called Guy right away for an explanation.

"What is this?"

"It's merely a forum for information. Don't think too much about it."

"Does it mean something has happened?"

"Not at all. Ben's liaison officer opened the group. She'll be able to update us."

"Update us? About what?" She'd felt panicky. Something had changed – and dramatically. "Guy. Where is Ben?"

"Vic, it's very simple. Ben's recon squad was mobilized. They are stationed in Gaza."

She'd been stunned. Her mind had raced immediately to unbearable places. She'd known this was a possibility but had been certain it wouldn't happen. She'd convinced herself that it couldn't. Her shock turned to fury: "How come you didn't tell me earlier? How come I have to learn it now, from this message?"

"The *how* isn't all that important right now." She could hear him taking a deep breath, frustrated by her anger. "It's just the way it went. This is the first I heard of it as well. We were never going to get a call from Ben telling us where he was going. This way is as good as any other."

He sounded so calm. *How is he so calm?* "It's a good thing. Maybe we'll actually get some information now."

At first, Victoria had been appalled by the mere existence of the group, her antagonism toward its formation stemming from its confirmation of a shared nightmare. She'd never dreamed of being part of such a thing and wanted nothing to do with it – wanted nothing to do with any of this. All of a sudden she craved those other chat groups she'd formerly griped about, the ones filled with insane drivel, usually devoted to organizing refreshments for a school event. Life could be so simple, and then, suddenly, it wasn't.

Since that moment, every beep and buzz set her on edge, threatening her with that one little unwanted tidbit of information – the one she feared most. Guy tried to help: *Think about the chances.* He repeated this again and again, like a mantra. *It's all about numbers.* She didn't find those words consoling but appreciated his efforts. There wasn't a lot anyone could do to calm her.

She longed to go home. *Home.* That word had always been so weighted, evocative of two very distinct worlds and her inability to settle in either one of them. But lately the split screen was melding into one, the blur coming into focus. She was beginning to understand where she stood; even more significantly, where she belonged. It was less about geography than she'd originally thought, less about habits, customs, familiarity and expectations. Instead, exactly as that tired old adage claimed, it was about the heart, and her heart was most definitely far across the ocean, a painfully great distance away. Was that the point of this whole summer? Had this whole exercise been part of some grand plan to wake her from her stupor? These thoughts were crushing but not nearly as devastating as the thought of the horrendous cost of this late-in-the-day realization.

So much for Columbia.

She was ready to junk what had seemed like a golden opportunity, no matter how rewarding, convinced that closing the distance would ease her misery. She was certain the dean would understand why she needed to leave, why she wouldn't be able to see through her commitment. In any case, since the establishment of that chat group, the one that made clear that the pendulum had swung far off its point of equilibrium, everything about this place had changed.

This summer, the summer of her dreams, the start of a fantasized future, had turned to a muddled grey. A thin layer of sediment seemed to cover every surface (the buildings, the people, the green of the campus), altering each and every experience, conversation and interchange. Although she was able to fulfill her teaching duties, to hold it together when in the classroom, even to enjoy the stimulation, the rest of her time was spent obsessing about obtaining information, good or bad. During those hours she remained glued to any screen she could find, whether back in her apartment, at a local coffee shop or at the faculty lounge. She had to literally force herself to put away the phone every now and then, to live her life, to focus on the present she'd so desired. It was insane.

Yesterday she'd called Guy to discuss it.

"I'm coming home."

"Why?"

"I need to come home."

"You don't. You need to stay right there."

"But I can't do anything here." She'd felt desperate. She hadn't tried to hide it from him.

"It won't be different here. Believe me. It's just as frustrating here, maybe even more so. Being so close and yet…" His voice had sounded completely lackluster. This wasn't the Guy she knew. *Where has he gone?* "You need to stay there. We arranged everything for you. What you're doing is important to you. It's important for us. You're not leaving." His voice had become firmer, more resolved. He was obviously making an effort, aware that she was looking to him for direction, for strength.

"I don't want to be here."

"Listen. You mustn't change anything. *We* mustn't change anything. Changing plans means admitting the need for change. And there won't be…" His voice faded away. She heard him clear his throat. "There won't be a need for change. Ben will be just fine." He coughed. It sounded as if there was something fairly large blocking his bronchial passage. "Ben *is* fine."

"Hold on," he'd implored before hanging up.

She'd abandoned her plan to come home and refocused her energy on her teaching as a means of keeping that clock, the one that was going to make time move fast enough to see the end of this nightmare, ticking. Unfortunately that tactic wasn't as easy as it sounded. Her heart felt torn into pieces, each one pulling in a different direction, so broken that it could not be made whole.

She spent much too much time scanning the Caesarea community Facebook page, looking for updates from friends, associates, anyone she'd ever heard of, even those she hadn't, wishing she was right there beside them to get them "live." The flood of messages she was receiving daily from friends and acquaintances wasn't making matters easier. Their casual comments made her blood curdle: "Aren't you coming back?" "How can you not come back?" "You need to be here." "You should be here." It was endless. They tugged at her conscience, crawled under her skin, made her second-guess her decision to stay. They ignited the terrible guilt that all mothers suffer, the worry that they're not doing right by their children.

Was there a right move?

She'd never anticipated such a predicament. How was she supposed to know what she was meant to do? But no, Guy had said no. Her rock of a husband, solid, earthbound, had turned out to be superstitious, maybe even more so than she. Going home would cause a reason to go home. No. That was too frightening a prospect to consider.

The one consolation, the one thing that managed to bring her some peace of mind and make this untenable situation a bit more bearable, was the massive, country-wide effort to provide the soldiers with basics they were most definitely running out of. By this point many had been away from home for several weeks, whether in Gaza or on some other base within central Israel. The entire army had been on alert for weeks. They were most definitely short on personal comforts.

Only yesterday she'd been woken by the telephone, a blistering ring that had startled her terribly. Every call did. Alison apologized even before she began to speak. She hadn't wanted to upset or worry her and, in fact, had hoped to cheer her up with news about the shipments being moved south.

"We want to try to find Ben."

"Where are you going?"

"We'll be near Nitzanei Oz."

"I think that's where their company is based. Maybe. You know, I'm not sure. I have no idea." Every one of these phone calls made her feel more helpless and disconnected than the last.

Alison hadn't given in to Victoria's gloomy tone. Her voice came over enthusiastic and energetic. "We've got socks, underwear. There's Bamba, chips, granola bars. All manner of snacks. You can't imagine what's going on here. The whole town has flocked to the school. There are people here I haven't seen for over a decade; they've simply materialized. Remember Carol? I actually thought she'd moved away. But there she was! In any case, this is it. This is the time. People understand it's now or never. Some are busy collecting, driving around neighborhoods for prearranged pick-ups, others organizing bulk shopping excursions. We've got people sorting through everything. You know," she lowered her voice and laughed, "some of it is really inappropriate. Vic, there's something creepy about the pink underwear."

Victoria smiled and let out a small giggle, unsure whether it was okay to step away from the horror of the situation for a moment and let go; she was desperate to do so.

"And really, I've never seen so many socks in one place!" She paused. "Oh, and let's see. There's more. Susan is still here. She was in the packing room yesterday. She loves putting things in order. It's right up her alley! Anyway, you'd be astounded by what we've managed to collect. We've got boxes upon boxes, stacked all the way up to those ugly ceiling tiles. It's mind-boggling."

"I don't think you'll be able to find him." Victoria's sadness dampened the call.

"Vic, we'll find someone, someone like Ben. That's all we want to do. In any case we're not sure how close we can get. They're keeping civilians far from the borders."

"Thank you." It came out far too thin. It wasn't enough. She didn't know how to express her gratitude, not only to her friend but also to the community, to the country at large. She felt like a child. Everyone was doing something for her, for *hers*, her own hands tied.

"Oh wait. There's something else. This is really sweet. I want to tell you about the children. Many of them aren't in camp. Some actually closed up, temporarily of course. There was no point keeping them open with so many parents, the nervous ones, keeping their kids at home, within eye contact. We've got them decorating the packages with stickers, magic markers and more Smileys than you've ever seen. The older ones are writing letters. Things like: *We love you. Thank you. We want you to come home. Thanks for protecting us.*" She paused. "Really whatever they feel like writing – anything to raise morale. Of course, they're not writing to anyone in particular. Oh, and lots are in English! I'm not exactly sure how many English-speaking soldiers we have down there but we've got 'em covered! It's good. It gives them something to do, keeps them busy. With everything else going on, childcare has moved to the back burner."

"Jackie told me they're flying off next week."

"Yes, they're going to some Greek island, just far enough away to escape the tension. With Adam due to join up in a few months, this is hitting a lot of raw nerves. I think she needs to step back, to remember that that's not *all* this place is about."

Another silence. Victoria couldn't help herself. Although she didn't say it aloud, she wondered whether that was, indeed, what Israel was all about. She kept this painful thought to herself.

"I should be there."

"No. You should be *there*. Guy's right. We're all here, exactly where you left us. And we'll all be here when you get back. Well, except for Susan." She hesitated for a moment and then resumed her update. "We're considering organizing a pseudo book-club gathering right at the school; a kind of bon voyage event. We're there most of the time anyway, and there are plenty of tables and chairs. It'll be a bit cramped, what with all the socks and underwear, and there's the minor issue that no one has had the heart to actually read a book lately, but that won't stop us. A little vino and we're set!"

This time their laughter was more ebullient. Victoria embraced the momentary levity and let herself go. It felt so good.

"Vicki, you're doing something. Precisely like we're doing something. Wow, if I actually had somewhere else to be or something else to do... Just keep going. It's all going to be over soon, so soon. We're all sure of it."

It was so obvious that Alison hadn't wanted her to worry. The media was flooded with stories of community effort all over the country, each part of a grand national endeavor that had even spread to the international community. In this way, albeit far removed, Victoria was doing her part. Instead of cultivating professional relationships among the other faculty members working in the Journalism School, a part of her preconceived master plan to insure that this summer stint would lead to something more permanent, she'd found herself spending a great deal of time contacting New Yorkers and Philadelphians, encouraging them to donate to pop-up fundraising projects. It wasn't the kind of networking she'd had in mind, but it was enormously satisfying. She'd been relieved to find some way to be involved, albeit by remote.

The magnitude of this collective effort, its significance for herself, as a parent and a citizen, and for her son, as one of the many whose needs would hopefully be met, was clear even here, across the ocean, in a dark room, in the middle of the night. This extraordinary act of togetherness, this communal embrace, overwhelmed her with its generosity, gratitude and appreciation. For years she'd witnessed, even written about, this unique aspect of Israel, its emphasis on family, an undefined entity that went well beyond blood and incorporated a heavy dose of involvement and responsibility. She'd desperately wanted to be a part of that and now, through this calamity, she realized she was.

The buzzing of the phone on the desk jolted her; the momentary peace she'd found instantly disintegrated as if it had never been. She reached over and peered at the lit screen. Messages moved down and then disappeared, one replacing the next in a flood. This was different. Certain words stood out, as if in bold, but she couldn't catch the gist, they were popping up and moving off too quickly. An icy fear gripped her as she paged backward, against the avalanche of updates, desperate to find the original message. It wasn't the middle of the night back in Israel, but rather the middle of the day – the local population was keyed up and available. Suddenly she stopped. There it was. There'd been an update from the liaison for the squad. **The boys are fine.** She breathed out an enormous sigh of relief. Her head pounded with the increased blood flow caused by the sudden coursing of adrenaline.

A number of parents had written in with words of thanks, gratitude, prayers and appreciation. All was sprinkled with a panoply of emoticons: hearts, flowers and praying hands. There was a hefty portion of blessings and thanks to God. This pious response, representing the "religious" (as they call it in Israel) population of the group, wasn't all that surprising. A good number of the soldiers in Ben's squad were from traditional homes, donning woven *kippah*s and maintaining *kashrut*. Although their home was far less observant, he was respectful of his friends' practices and had regaled her with stories about those singular times he'd joined their prayers, even letting them put tefillin on him. Victoria was grateful for their prayers. Maybe it wasn't such a bad idea to call on all resources, even ones on high, in this situation.

Today's message offered a kind of solace, although limited in nature. The tidbit they'd been given, this one-liner assuring well-being, was benign and meaningless for the most part, clearly based on old news. The group liaison, sitting in a base somewhere near Netanya, safe inside central Israel, had received the "thumbs up" from someone who was located in one of the preparatory areas outside of the Strip. As Guy had explained after an earlier missive, this second- or even third-hand source reflected virtually no real-time knowledge of what was happening, merely verifying that at some point, the boys had been just fine.

How is Ben now? How is he at this very moment? This was her main concern. She returned to her screen, working over the concept of "fine," weighing its significance in consideration of its dated status. Fact was, after almost a week of no contact whatsoever, and no other update, it was enough. At this point every morsel of information, no matter how tangentially reliable, was a godsend.

Victoria's head throbbed; a low but consistent ache stretched across her forehead. Her fear was paramount, this cascade of comments having made her even more uptight. Yesterday she'd broken up her early-morning vigil by going for a run, heading out into the darkness of the early hours of the morning when she hadn't been able to sleep, bent on releasing some of the tension wracking her body. She'd pounded the pavement, one step after another, pushing hard. When her breath had gotten short she'd thought of Ben. What was he feeling? How hard were his minutes? Was he afraid? These tortured thoughts led to lighter ones, settling on the possibility that he found the whole experience exciting, exactly like any other. Maybe a nineteen-year-old would see it that way.

Stretching her run past an hour, pushing herself to go well beyond her comfort zone, she'd thought about the load he carried: that enormous bag of supplies he had to lug on his back, the one that lay crumpled on the floor of the laundry room weekends spent home. She'd wondered how he managed it, especially at the height of the summer's heat. She'd wished he could be here instead, running along Riverside Drive at dawn with the lights across the Hudson still twinkling. Guy's words echoed in her head. She had to hold the line, keep on doing exactly what she'd planned on doing – no stepping off the path. She had to be as strong as possible – to transmit that strength to Ben, wherever he was. Mothering had very little to do with location, and everything to do with the heart.

Victoria glanced at the clock on the computer. It was 5:00 a.m. Time was crawling. The tickertape of information running along the right side of the computer screen, reporting altercations, injuries and losses, did nothing to assuage her fear. She tapped her fingers nervously on the surface of the desk. The news, seemingly precise, was actually quite vague: events reported, yet simultaneously glossed over, details of anything truly tragic retained until families could be notified. Guy had assured her that if anything happened she'd know before it was on the news; that she didn't have to worry about something she read; that she needn't spend hours running to check what she might have missed.

But she couldn't help herself. The social networks were flooded with personal updates, some apparently anticipating official ones. She had to maintain a vigilant watch on every form of media that might contain even a smidgen of relevance. His assurance couldn't prevent her from clinging to any information she could obtain; she and so many others – an entire nation's attention turning on the whimsy of the media.

Something inside her snapped. *That's it. I can't do this anymore. I need help.* She pushed her chair back and stepped over to the window. It was still pitch black outside, and a pale, ghostly version of her face, distorted by the light from the computer screen and distinguished by an expression of misery and foreboding, gazed back at her. *What's this face going to look like if…?* The potential for crushing sadness was too great. She choked back an errant sob, tried to move aside what felt like a boulder and get some air. A second sob dwarfed the first. The overwhelming chance of disaster was too much for her to handle.

She picked up her phone and frantically searched through the speed dial.

"Guy," she whispered.

"What time is it there?"

"After 5:00."

"Why are you awake?"

"I can't sleep. How can I sleep?"

"Put your head down and close your eyes. You need to sleep."

"I need a lot of things. Sleep isn't going to happen right now. What's going on?"

"Nothing." She heard him clear his throat. "Everything's okay. Ben is okay."

"How do you know that?" This was a replay of a conversation they'd had several times a day since she'd left Israel.

"I just know. He's *o-kay*," he emphasized the last word. "There was a pause.

"I don't think I can handle this."

"You're wrong. You can handle it. In fact, you're doing exactly that."

"I never signed on for this."

Her husband chuckled. "You didn't sign on for a lot of things. This is only one of them."

"That doesn't make it any easier."

"It's not easy. But it's part of life and it's going to be okay."

"You keep on saying that but I don't believe you."

"Would you rather believe otherwise?"

Victoria's eyes moved back to the window. She espied just the slightest suggestion of pink along the horizon, filtering in around the jagged silhouette of the adjacent buildings. A new day was about to begin.

"Of course not. But I keep on going over the possibilities and each one is more painful than the next."

"Then try to stop the cycle. Your son is doing what he's trained to do. He's very much living in the moment. He'll be home soon to tell us all about it."

She couldn't respond. She couldn't find the words. There was silence on the line. Guy waited patiently.

"I don't think I'm strong enough to deal with this. This isn't something I ever learned how to do. It's not a part of my story."

"Well, it's very much a part of your story right now and you're doing just fine."

Victoria chided herself for being so needy. It was really quite pathetic. Guy had better things to do than provide a pep talk. Good thing Ben wasn't party to this conversation, wasn't aware of her misgivings, worries and dreadful fears. It would be so distracting. She needed to pull herself together specifically in order to assume some of his stress, lighten his load. Since he'd become a teenager that task had become more and more important, one of the more challenging, less tangible obstacles she'd encountered as a mother. But it wasn't more difficult than bearing her own fear; this was turning out to be the most demanding of all.

"Sweetie." Guy's voice was soft and low. It flowed out of the phone's earpiece, wrapping her up protectively like a warm blanket. She felt lighter, the burden of worry momentarily lifted. She peeked outside, watching the world wake up, the hustle and bustle of the day here in Manhattan about to begin. And then there was a whisper: "Our boy is okay."

She moved in closer to the window and leaned forward, placing her forehead gently on the cool pane of glass. That strip of pink had segued to orange. Morning had come. She whispered "Thank you for that" into the phone and hung up.

Victoria climbed back into bed. She couldn't possibly fall asleep so instead she tried to enjoy the soft embrace of the pillow, the way her head sunk into the gulf formed by the feathers. Having finally dropped her guard, that armor of steel she wore to face all difficulties, she felt drained and exhausted – an empty shell desperately in need of respite.

Chapter 25

Victoria was amazed by how quickly colors could fade – how within minutes the world around her could look entirely different. Only a few weeks earlier she'd been overwhelmed by the green of Riverside Park, the palette so welcoming and different from that back in Israel. She'd felt heady with the abundance of moisture in the air, the insistent smell of dew and the omnipresent signs of growth. She hadn't been able to get enough of those pockets of shade around campus, literally speckled with bodies as students took a break between classes, enjoying the summer days. That first week she'd been overwhelmed by this vibrant community, thrilled at being able to flesh out ideas and thoughts that fascinated her in a place where she didn't feel different and wasn't an outsider. It had been such a relief.

And today? Today it all seemed a bit less amazing, less illuminated from inside – the emerald greens of the local foliage fading to lime. The same students who had embodied the ideal of intellectualism, the striving for knowledge, the epitome of academic inspiration, had begun to get under her skin. She drew her mouth into a tight expression of dismay as she headed out the main gate at 116th

Street. That conversation, the one she'd overheard yesterday. She simply couldn't erase the memory of it.

"I'm not comfortable with this war."

"I think it was inevitable. I mean, after that non-stop rocket fire, day in and day out…"

"But it's so uneven. The Israeli response is out of proportion. They have nothing to fight back with!"

"Apparently they do."

There'd been a pause in the conversation. Victoria had frozen in the hallway outside the student lounge, unable to continue on her way, to ignore this exchange.

"The whole thing makes the Israelis look monstrous. They're so much stronger. It's an unfair fight."

"Remember, we're talking about the Hamas. They have their ways. They tunnel, they ambush, they fire back. They're not defenseless. In fact, they seem to instigate."

"Still. The locals. Their homes, their lives. Everything is being destroyed. Israel comes off the bad guy."

"Maybe it always will. But the situation isn't cut and dried. It's not the big bad Israelis against the poor, helpless Gazans. That's far too naive an equation. You can't ignore the havoc being wreaked by the Hamas. They seem to have taken the locals hostage. It's hard to get a clear picture from halfway across the world. As outsiders it's always easy to act as judge and jury."

Victoria had determinedly stepped into the lounge at that point, refusing to cower in the shadows or hide, refusing to run away from a possible confrontation. The two students had looked up as she entered, one casting a quick, nervous gaze at the other.

"Professor Steiner."

She stared at them for a moment, wondering if they knew that her son was serving in the IDF, that he was intricately involved in the subject upon which they were theorizing. She saw only innocence, the expressions on their face reflecting a genuine interest in exploring an idea. She'd let out an audible sigh, understanding this wasn't the time and place to challenge their opinion of the conflict, that it wasn't right to drag them into her personal turmoil.

She'd uttered a quiet "Good morning" and watched as they moved off without a further word.

This wasn't the only instance of the charged atmosphere regarding the conflict on campus. There'd been others. There were endless conversations on the subject with students, other faculty, and of course with acquaintances she met through her friends in New York. It seemed everyone had an opinion. More than once she'd been questioned about her self-identification, her allegiance, and recently, she'd noticed herself blurting out "Israeli" instead of "American" – her former default. She couldn't ignore the subtle shift in her outlook as the summer progressed, as the conflict in Israel waged on, suggesting a sincere alliance with the adopted home she'd been so certain, for decades, she had no part in.

This afternoon she felt a strong need for protein and the strength it promised. She picked up a sandwich at a nearby deli on Broadway and headed out to find a nice place to sit in Riverside Park. After descending the steep steps into the forested part of the park off the Drive, she made her way south, following one of the winding paths. She looked up as she walked, captivated by the density of the trees to all sides, desperate for the kind of consolation only nature could offer.

Victoria felt something vibrate under her arm. It was her purse, or more precisely, the phone inside. She stopped along the path and fumbled around for it, almost frantic. She pushed around the collection of small pouches, her wallet, reading glasses, vials of sample perfume and keys. The buzzing continued. Frustrated, she contemplated dumping the whole lot onto the grass; that was one surefire way to find what she was looking for. But then, somehow, she managed to pull it out of the muddle. She frantically looked at the screen. It was a blur. She fished around for her glasses.

What's the condition of the wounded?

She stumbled backward, her movement stopped short by one of the cement garbage receptacles. She stood stone still and held her breath. She simply couldn't comprehend what that could mean. Why were they speaking about wounded? She stared at her phone. There was nothing else. The message had come in yet another new WhatsApp group, the one the parents of the soldiers in Ben's squad had started in order to discuss the official bulletins they were receiving from the squad commander's liaison – the one where they could express concern, swap tidbits of information and post prayers. She braced herself for the stream of responses. Nothing came. Such a different response than the one that came after reassuring reports. She quickly fumbled around for another source, exiting that chat and finding the long-running one she had with Guy.

What's going on?

His answer was immediate: **Nothing. Don't worry. It doesn't have to do with Ben.**

And then, the phone began to wiggle and buzz in her hand, as if alive and desperate to escape her grasp. Messages popped up one after the other as they had a few days back, like the NASDAQ ticker tape. She could barely make sense of them, the pace at which they arrived so rapid she barely managed to read one before another took its place. She couldn't keep track of which were responses and which conveyed actual, new information. The other parents in the group were obviously equally alarmed, equally desperate to understand the significance of that first alarming message. Names of boys began to appear, sprinkled here and there within the comments, mixed with words of concern and questions. *Those infernal praying hands!* She returned to her chat with Guy.

Something happened. What happened?

It's not about his squad.

It is.

Victoria was frustrated. She needed him to focus on what had obviously become a different reality, a game changer. The calm approach wasn't going to work anymore.

She persisted.

Look at the names. Those guys are in Ben's squad. What's going on? I can't follow it.

Guy repeated his earlier text. **It's not his squad.**

It is. Please Guy. Please.

Okay. Hold on.

Struck with clarity of purpose, a need for concrete facts, she felt the need to sit down and gather her wits. She walked a bit farther and lowered herself onto a bench, leaning back onto the wooden support slats. The phone lay silent in her hand. The flow of messages had stopped abruptly and she still didn't understand what had happened. *Where is Ben?*

She looked around her, begging for a distraction. Park life: diverse and varied, a nutshell summary of all humanity. Life here marched onwards, a constant flow of disparate parts moving on to undefined destinations. Yet her life had come to a complete stop. One buzz of the phone had distinguished her from this crowd and now threatened to hurl her to the edge of the abyss.

She wasn't merely sitting on a bench. In fact, she was glued to it with terror, her thighs firmly pressing onto the seat in an effort to brace herself. A sudden sharp intake of air made her realize she'd been holding her breath. She couldn't begin to make sense of the thoughts rushing through her head, their number so vast, their range so wide, each one more horrific than the next.

Ben.

The phone buzzed. It was Guy.

Take it easy. I'm reading the same messages. I'm following the same chat. I'm trying to get hold of the liaison. Wait a second.

I'm here.

She scooted even further back on the bench. This could take awhile. Communication over the last few weeks had been minimal at best, sporadically arriving in bursts and spurts, detached from real time and sometimes incorrect. This particular item was critical, obviously different from the former assuaging ones. Good thing she had Guy. She could count on him. He'd check it out, report back, and yes, as he'd promised, everything would be okay. She knew it. It had to be.

She gazed at the phone. No change. The screen was black. The sudden break in the stream of messages was unsettling. She needed to find some way to wait this out. She tried to calm herself. Ben's name hadn't been mentioned. She flipped back and forth between the messages, checking again and again. That was good. It had to be. *But what about the others?* Her mind slipped to uncomfortable places, and she began to panic again. She needed another tactic, something to keep her busy.

She composed a mental inventory of the people around her, this microcosm of New York. There were those passing in front of her on the path: two women wearing slacks with precision-ironed pleats and folded paper lunch bags; an older woman, fully made up and stylishly dressed, being pushed along by an attendant; a young man wearing frayed jeans way too low on his hips. The grassy area nearby was covered with picnickers of all ages – young women in sundresses and flip-flops, mothers with infants either in buggies or laid out carefully on blankets, businessmen with ties loosened, leather shoes discarded to the side, and a large range of college-aged men and women. *There's so much life here; so many stories.*

Victoria gazed upward, high above, where the crowns of the great spruce, oak and pine trees met, where nature took over from humanity. These trees dated back centuries and would be here long after she was gone. They didn't know much about personal loss and gripping terror despite being steady witnesses to something in the range of a million dramas a day – the lives that frequented this park infinite and complex. As hard as she tried, she simply couldn't distract herself. Everything came back to fear, horror and blackness. Everything came back to Ben.

Victoria had to focus elsewhere, to concentrate on what she knew. Guy was right. Everything was all right. It had to be all right. How could it not? She focused her gaze on the interstices between the heavy webbing of branches and greenery above: minuscule slivers of blue sky. If she widened her eyes and then squinted, if she focused as hard as she could and tried not to blink, the blue and green sections flattened out into a pattern like stained glass and she could almost imagine she was in a cathedral. Surrounded by so much beauty it was hard to imagine pain.

Victoria wanted to wrap up this place and the feeling it instilled in her and ship it directly to Ben. She almost let herself smile in anticipation of his radiant expression as he opened the package. He would understand the gift; relish in its familiarity, let it cloak him with calm. The thought of being able to provide him with this unwavering beauty, magically, as he waged battle in the blistering heat, among the dust of the desert terrain, made her happy, easing her burden for a moment. He would love it here as much as she. *If only it were possible.*

Victoria sent a quick text with a question mark to Guy and then immediately another one with a row of question marks. He knew she was on edge, frantic for something. He wouldn't dare leave her hanging. True to expectation, he responded after a few seconds:

Working on it.

She couldn't sit any longer. Her sandwich was still in its bag; she hadn't managed even one bite. She needed to move. Maybe that would make her feel better. Although her body felt heavy and very much not her own, she gathered strength, raised herself from the bench and made her way farther south, past the crowds enjoying the sunshine, before cutting off in the direction of the Hudson. Her thoughts were grave and ponderous, filling up every last space in her head. She felt it might possibly burst. She continued to check out the passers-by, wondering which, if any, of the people gathered here were equally tormented today.

This thought alone slammed her right back to reality. She was such a small part of what went on in this world, her story one of more than could ever be counted. With so much potential to love came the equal potential to suffer loss. The sampling of hundreds randomly gathered within her range of vision must include those suffering some kind of trauma, be it personal or empathetic. She wondered how they stood it. A searing pain moved up through her stomach and into her chest. Again she felt short of breath and lightheaded. She gasped dryly, praying that the feeling would pass – that all of this would pass. It was unbearable.

Victoria talked herself through this concept of shared pain, hoping the chatter in her mind would alleviate some of her fright, the fear that her story would ultimately have a tragic end. She tried to find comfort in percentages, turning the words over in her head, one after the other. If she concentrated on the whole, the fear of the specific would have no room to squeeze in; and she didn't want that specific. She didn't want this to have to do with Ben.

All of a sudden she was seized by stomach cramps. She must be hungry. This hadn't been a good week for eating. It was so hard to take the time away from worrying to actually lift whatever was on her plate to her mouth, digesting what she did manage to ingest was no simple matter. In any case most of it tasted like sawdust. Yet life needed to be lived and that included feeding her body. She opened the paper bag, pulled out the sandwich she'd been so eager to eat only one hour earlier, unwrapped the paper at one corner and took a bite. The flavors of the mayo-soaked tuna fish and tomato flooded her system, awakening her dulled senses. The combo probably tasted delicious. It looked delicious. But somehow it came across as bland. Chewing was simply something to do to pass the time, to distract her, if only for a few moments, from the wrenching thoughts in her head.

When the phone buzzed again Victoria was taken completely off guard. The sandwich dropped out of her hand onto the grass. She didn't give it another thought, completely focused on checking the message. She gripped the phone in her hand, jerked it close to her face in order to make out the words she'd been praying for. And then everything went black.

Chapter 26

Victoria leaned back against the bank of windows lining the classroom and watched her students in action, presenting their position papers to one another. They'd been tackling immigrant assimilation these past few weeks, and she'd assigned them the project of actually stepping into said immigrants' shoes. They were utilizing role-play to explore a variety of experiences.

"Why should I bother learning Hebrew when everyone I come into contact with speaks English?"

Emily was the captain of her team, responsible for presenting their position. "As long as I can work, run my household, officially 'function,'" this last word she emphasized with air quotation marks, "I'm doing my job."

"It's not going to be enough. How will you ever be satisfied when you know you're missing so much?"

"I don't see a connection. Who said you have to speak the local language in order to have a satisfactory life?"

The rest of the students wanted to test group one's stance, push them, assess whether their position was valid and could hold water.

"You'll never be part of the community."

"That depends on which community you mean. Maybe I'll never be part of the 'native' community, but I have a ton of friends, work associates, even dance class pals, who all speak English. Same thing I would have had back home. In addition, most of those so-called 'natives,'" again, those air quotes, "speak English."

"You can't divorce language from culture. You're effectively giving up on being absorbed into the larger whole, turning your back on the country you yourself decided to be part of!"

"Why do I have to be part of the whole? I can establish a comfortable niche, make it mine. In any case, I repeat: it's absolutely no different than what I would have done back in the States. There, too, I wouldn't have associated with every part of society, only with those I chose to, those with whom I could communicate."

"Next." Victoria interceded. She wanted the students thinking about a lot of things, flooded with the multifaceted aspect of establishing a life in a new land. She didn't want them to over-focus on one aspect or another. Being overwhelmed was part of the experience.

Steve stood up before the class and shifted his weight from one foot to the other. He looked uncomfortable. "I can't get used to the local mentality. Worse, I actually think it's beneath me." He looked down at his feet for a moment, collecting the self-confidence he needed to perfect the role he was meant to portray, and then raised his eyes and looked straight into the faces of his classmates. "In any case, I've begun to think it's not all that important. Part of life is learning that you can't jibe with everyone you come into contact with, that you can't always find common ground. We all pick and choose what fits best."

There was an immediate reaction within the group of students sitting in front of him. "But that makes you a snob. The minute you limit yourself to one group you take a stance. Who are you to judge others? Different cultures have different modes of behavior."

Another student spoke up. "What makes you better?"

Steve rubbed his hands on his jeans for a moment and seemed a bit less confident than when he'd started to speak. "I didn't mean that I was better. Maybe that was misstated. What I meant is that the rest, everything out there," he gestured vaguely in front of him, "doesn't seem quite compatible. *To me*." He pointed at himself. "It's clear I'll always be different, and I've decided I can live with that. I don't have to adopt the local culture merely because I chose to pitch my tent there. Different should be an option."

Again, murmurs among the audience. "But different is going to make you stand out. You'll never blend in; you'll never be accepted." From the other side of the room came another voice. "You'll always be an outsider."

Steve walked to the board, picked up a marker and drew two circles. "Ah, but that's the point. I didn't make this momentous move with the idea of blending in. In fact, it never dawned on me to do so. Well, maybe for a brief period, but that passed as soon as I realized that very few of the people I was meeting could meet my standards."

"Obnoxious."

"So you *do* think you're better!"

"Listen, it wasn't that I didn't want to find a niche. Of course I did. But when it didn't work out, when I realized that I had nothing in common with the people with whom I came in contact, I just chose a different path. You don't have to mesh with your surroundings to find fulfillment. There's plenty of room here for different types." He pointed to the two circles. "I could continue to add circles to this board, each representing a group. There's room for many more. We're talking about an entire country! And they don't have to intersect. You can live a life that doesn't intersect."

"But then what's the point?" One of the students in the front row rapped his knuckles on his desk to get attention. "Why bother going through all the effort of leaving what works if you're not even going to try and be part of what you've chosen to join?" Another picked up the theme, "And here, in the States, growing up, when you were in high school, college, did you feel part of things? Did you feel like you belonged? Was what you found here good enough? Assuming it was, how did you ever decide to junk it all, to choose a life where you'd never be a part of the whole?"

"At what point did you figure out you were an outsider and simply decide to accept it?"

"Wait. I get it." A student seated at one of the desks in the front row banged his hand on his desk. "It's the classic chicken and the egg! You didn't make this decision. It was made for you! After you arrived you simply didn't blend in. It didn't work. So instead of feeling hurt you decided to find a comfortable spot of your own, on the outside!"

"Okay. Good. Next." Victoria interceded again.

Eric stood up and walked to the front of the class. "I've done everything right. I've learned to speak the language, I'm a member of the local community council, the school PTA, and I actually have a job and work with Israelis, all in Hebrew." Having listed an impressive number of accomplishments, what officially counted for full integration, he looked down at his hands, grasped before him, and paused before adding, "I'm unhappy."

No one in the room reacted. No one interjected a question or made a challenge of any sort. They all waited for him to continue, genuinely surprised by that addendum.

"I'm about in the best position possible. I think some people even think of me as part of the old-guard." He looked over toward his group. One of the other students nodded his head encouragingly. Eric cleared his throat. "But the thing is, I'm not. And after everything I've accomplished, all of the effort I've exerted, I still always feel like an interloper. Sometimes I wonder if I made the right choice; how I live in a place where I'll always be an outsider when there's an alternative choice."

Emily piped up from the front row. "But I don't get it. You've done everything it takes: the language, the job, the involvement. You've succeeded whole hog. How is it even possible that you don't feel part of the whole? I can't imagine why you're unhappy. You've managed, where most have failed." Members of her group uttered expressions of agreement.

One of Steve's group stepped in. "What does it matter? You can pat yourself on the back. You've done enough, you should continue along your own path. Why is it so important to feel part of everything? Can't you simply enjoy your success and accept that you'll always be different?" Steve himself folded his arms over his chest, pushing back confidently into his chair. "There's no benefit gained by being a part of something that was never yours and never will be."

Again, murmurs throughout the room.

"Last group?"

Rachel took over. "I can't get a job." She leaned back on the table at the front of the room. "Well, actually I *can* get a job but it's not the one I want. And the thing is, everything else is perfect. Everything. I simply love my new life, this new country. I have a wonderful extended family. Everything suits me to a tee: the people, the colors, the mannerisms, even the smells. But," and here she looked from one to the other before continuing, "I. Can. Not. Get. The. Right. Job!"

Again, silence. Everyone waited to see what would come next. One of Rachel's team members got up and approached from the side. The two consulted briefly. Rachel continued, "I want to be clear. I'm where I want to be. There have been challenges along the way but most everything has worked out. I got so much more than I bargained for out of this move. I'd never leave. There's nowhere else that makes me feel as embraced, included. I walk around knowing in my heart and soul that I belong. If only," her voice cracked, "if only I could have this last little piece of the pie."

"Maybe it's enough. Maybe it's too much to ask for more. I mean, if you'd stayed in your country of origin, where you were comfortable, where you most probably felt that same sense of belonging, you might have had just as much difficulty finding a professional niche."

"Maybe you need to widen your area of interest. Be a bit more flexible"

There were murmurs around the classroom.

"I don't get it." Steve started in, scooting his chair forward. "You have everything. You're happy. You've attained your dream. I mean, how many of us have ever gotten to the point where they feel a part of their adopted life? You are the envy of this class. It should be enough."

"And it is. Yet..." Rachel's voice faded a bit. "Yet, it's part of the proof that I may not belong as much as I believe, that there's still some barrier that separates me from everyone else. Maybe it shouldn't affect my overall experience, but it does."

"Okay," Victoria moved to the front of the room and took up a position next to Rachel. "Now I want the four of you, Eric, Steve, Rachel and Emily, to rotate groups. It doesn't matter where you go, but don't go back to your original team. You need to maintain your position, your particular stance or, say, situation, in the face of that of the group you've joined and yes, you'll be outnumbered. The others will try to convince you that your issues, or rather, disappointments, aren't as significant as theirs. There will be conflict. You're no longer going to have the backing of your original workgroup.

"Pay close attention to the similarities and differences in experience as well as the accommodations you need to make for one another. All of this will help prepare you for the final assignment: the presentation of this multi-perspectival reality to an international audience. You choose the media: print, video or voice. The format is entirely up to you. The trick is to remember that your audience has no information about the complexity of the issue. They're merely casual outsiders with a passing interest. And although you're the knowledgeable ones, the ones with the answers, your job is complicated by the need to represent different experiences, different challenges, different expectations – to represent more than one angle. The effort to find one voice, a given in convincing journalistic reporting, is going to be greatly complicated."

"Do we need to maintain one position? Like we did in this assignment? Or find common ground?"

"You'll probably end up doing both. Finding common ground is a given since you all have the same ultimate goal, but you'll simultaneously need to accommodate contrary experiences, conditions that satisfy some but not others, situations some can live with and accept while others cannot. You have the rest of the week," she paused to look at her watch, as if assessing whether there'd be enough time, "to synthesize a statement on cultural adaptation among expatriates meant specifically for an English-speaking press: 3,000 words or up to 30 minutes of video/voice time. This piece has to be far more comprehensive and in-depth than, say, a blog entry."

Victoria gazed out the window and onto the Green beneath. It was positively teeming with life. She turned around and addressed her students. "We have a bit of time left. Let's get you started with your new groups. Introduce yourselves again, as if for the first time. Tell your stories. Take your time to be precise about your predicaments; be as clear as possible. Elaborate. This way it will be easier to figure out what's most significant and what might be less so. I'm here if you have questions."

There was a lot of shuffling, dragging of chairs, notebooks were opened, pens uncapped, a laptop or two powered up. Victoria watched her students in action. She loved this. She'd loved it from the start. This is exactly where she wanted to be, doing what she wanted to do, yet..." She turned back toward the windows, this time focusing her gaze upwards, toward the sky. She ached to go home. During the last few days she'd found herself looking at the calendar, again and again; counting the days, exactly how long it would be until she'd see Ben, hold him in her arms.

Since the moment she'd received Guy's message last week her world had dramatically shifted. She felt as though she'd been put through a washing machine: pummeled with water, squeezed, wrung out and then thrown against the walls for good measure. Who could have imagined such a summer? It definitely wasn't the one she'd anticipated.

His words had knocked her for a loop. She'd never thought that a handful of letters, especially those printed on a tiny screen, could have quite so powerful an effect; yet the message had been a life-changer or, better put, a lifesaver.

Ben is all right.

That's all Guy had written, and it had been more than enough. She knew he wouldn't have conveyed this message if he didn't know it to be true. It wasn't like him. Facts first, always, then matters of the heart; especially when it was a matter of life or death. She could still feel the wave of relief that overcame her from head to toe, moving through her like that first blast of warm water in the shower after a cold swim, strong enough to knock her off her feet. Those simple words, said so many times in the past but never with quite as much significance. They were as good as it could ever get. They were everything.

Before she knew it her knees had buckled, her phone had slipped out of her hand and her purse off her wrist. Her hands hit the ground just in time to break her fall, quick to cover for her legs, which refused to keep her upright, completely succumbing to the sudden release of tension that had built up over the previous hour. For a few minutes she'd stayed right where she'd fallen, grasping the strands of grass, digging her nails into the dirt to get a firmer hold, desperate for safe anchor.

Ben is safe. My Ben. My Ben is okay.

The crowds of individuals enjoying lunch hour in the park knew nothing of what she'd experienced, were unaware of the fact that she'd just now crossed from one world to another, leaving the darkest place she'd ever known and stepping, thankfully, back into the light. The leaves, the trees, the grass and the weeds around her regained something of their vibrancy, seeming more shimmery and less flat than a handful of minutes earlier. She couldn't stop replaying those words in her head, the ones that had let her off the hook and released her from the grip of fear.

She'd retrieved the phone from the ground and checked the message repeatedly, over and over, making sure she'd seen right, making sure there was no mistake. She didn't need more, neither words nor information; no further elaboration was necessary. She didn't really care about the details or the how. The end result was more than sufficient.

"Are we supposed to make this a critical piece? To take a stand? Or more of a feature, covering the complexity of the topic but allowing readers to draw their own conclusions?"

Victoria turned back to the class, their enthusiastic faces turned toward her. "That's an excellent question. You'll need to determine that for yourselves as you go along. See where you arrive after accommodating the various different perspectives; see which way the wind blows. Follow them to whatever seems the logical conclusion."

Back on the grass in Riverside Park there'd been a moment when she'd finally felt strong enough to stand, felt that she could actually respond. She'd written back to Guy:

What happened?

He'd called her immediately.

"He's okay." Again, such simple words, but this time issued more like an exhalation of relief than a statement.

They'd both fallen silent, sharing this reprieve, maybe even a prayer. Victoria traced the top of her ear with her fingers as she stood in the classroom, remembering the burning sensation she'd felt there, the phone pressed too close for comfort. The second she'd had him on the line she became desperate to hear more, to hear everything he had to tell. She wanted Guy to clarify precisely how Ben had been saved.

"Where was he? Where is he? Who was hurt? What happened? How do you know he's okay? How bad was it? When can you see him?" There was so much she wanted to ask, so much she wanted to know. One question had led to another. Now that she had a chance to ask, they all came pouring out unchecked. The answers were almost immaterial, beyond the point. None of what transpired in that conversation really mattered after its preface: *Ben was all right.*

Guy's solemn tone brought her back to earth, cut off her hysteria. "He's fine. His squad was inside. They were hit. There were wounded. There *are* wounded." He'd mentioned a few names, more than she'd seen in that first horrific run of messages on the group chat. This was a very big deal: a near miss for Ben. It was clear they should count their blessings. "They'll all be okay. He's okay. He's coming out soon."

The enormity of what had surpassed triggered a sudden wave of nausea, her stomach seemed to flip over and she felt light-headed. Standing in a classroom full of students exactly Ben's age – yes, he could have been here as well, in this arena of sanity, thought, ideas and cool-headedness – she was reminded of the trauma she'd experienced out there in Riverside Park: the fear, the horror, the relief, and then, an indescribable calm. No wonder her head had been aching for days.

It would take weeks before she really understood the condition of Ben's friends, what had actually happened; that, in fact, there had been losses. It was hard to move beyond that one moment she'd come to comprehend that Ben himself had escaped by chance. The "what if," the question of a few meters, the reality of what might have made all the difference – added up to something inconceivable that she'd never forget.

In the end, the story was not so simple. And while inordinately relieved at the knowledge that her son would soon be home, safe and sound, Victoria could only guess at the immensity of the emotional trauma he'd bring with him. Ben had just barely been spared, his friends had been injured, and two had been lost. Guy was especially unclear about that at the beginning; it was something that came out during the retellings, days following the incident. She'd wondered all along if he was holding back but accepted it as part of how he, himself, was dealing with the whole event. She had no idea how this would affect Ben, couldn't imagine how he felt. None of them had experience in this area. There were so many things one prepared for in life, but this wasn't one of them.

"When will Ben come home?"

"I have no idea."

"Why is he still inside?"

"It takes time to regroup, to reorganize. It's not about hopping in a car and crossing a border."

"When can we see him?"

"I'll go down to the meeting ground the minute they're moved out."

"Where will that be?"

"Probably along the northern border. Maybe Yad Mordechai."

"I need you to hold him tight and have me on the phone with you – right there, right then. I need to see him."

"No problem, sweetie."

Guy had relayed the few details he'd been able to gather and promised updates. That conversation had ended basically the way it had begun.

Our boy's okay.

The euphoria Victoria had experienced after that exchange, prompted by relief, was like nothing she'd ever known. She felt like the luckiest woman in the world. Ben wasn't home yet, but he'd escaped an unimaginable disaster. Walking back through the park that day she'd enjoyed a certain lightness of mood, an almost celebratory feeling, and pushed away the thought of what might have been – of what other mothers, exactly like her, were experiencing at that very moment. Tears of elation had flowed from her eyes non-stop. It was impossible not to take pleasure in knowing that her baby was safe. And although it wasn't over for Ben – he wasn't yet home – this gift was enough to sustain her: a true blessing.

Since then she'd been manically checking to see if he had used his phone. This capability of WhatsApp, to record if the user had checked their messages, was quite welcome. She couldn't wait to hear his voice and hoped she'd be one of the first he called. But even knowing he'd returned to the world of the living – her world – and picked up that device that kept him connected, would help. No go. From the date of his last check-in, it was obvious he hadn't held his phone in weeks. He was still inside.

Victoria walked around the classroom, peering over the shoulders of her students, fielding the occasional question, and then took a seat at her desk, drumming her fingers on the closed case of her laptop. *Inside.* That word struck her like a slap across the cheek, one she could have lived without, its connotations frightening and unfathomable. "Inside" meant within the Gaza Strip, outside of Israeli territory proper. Having grown up in America she couldn't help but associate it with the phrase "in country" used to describe Vietnam half a century earlier, both terms suggestive of enemy territory, struggle and warfare – swampy jungles merely swapped for desert scrub. What had once seemed mythical, part of history, far removed from her reality, had come slamming into her life full force. There was no way to beautify this picture.

Although Victoria had resumed her life, gone back to the classroom, she was stricken by a kind of emotional paralysis. All of a sudden this job, the one she'd so desired, the one she'd been certain would complete her life's puzzle, failed to meet her expectations. Instead, its singularity, the fact that it would forever be one piece, couldn't compete with the whole that awaited her back in Israel.

It was time to go home.

Chapter 27

Susan picked up her coffee cup and peered out the window. Green. Everything was green. This was something she'd almost forgotten about; on top of everything else, a change of palette. Outside, a child rode by on his bike, a bird alit on a nearby mailbox, a car pulled out of a neighboring driveway. New Jersey. She took a sip from her coffee mug and replaced it on the table. It was so quiet, so peaceful. Almost too much so; somehow it irked her.

She stood up and walked around the kitchen island, its chipped yellow Formica surface pasted onto a butcher-block base, so pedestrian and old-fashioned in comparison with the masterpiece of workmanship she'd left back home. *Home.* She sighed heavily and peered down into the box of newly purchased flatware from Ikea. Nothing else to do; might as well put things away, settle in. She reached in and pulled out first the plates, then a set of bowls, stacking them up on the counter.

Today I'll work on the house. Tomorrow I'll consider what comes next.

She turned toward the cabinets and opened them, one by one. The first door squeaked. The second stuck closed. The one over the sink was hanging almost completely off its hinge. She frowned and felt a sharp pang of longing for the kitchen she'd left behind in Caesarea, the one she'd lovingly designed to suit her every need and desire, the one with the seamless kitchen cabinetry.

She began to transfer the new items into the cabinets, moving them around from shelf to shelf, searching out the most streamlined solution. She experienced a feeling of déjà vu. This was truly ludicrous. Just six months earlier she'd moved into her just-completed dream house in Caesarea and now she was stuck making do with someone else's throwaway. And her own palace? They'd found renters. She only prayed they wouldn't abuse her lovingly crafted designer shelves, stick on doodads that couldn't be unstuck, clutter her flawlessly empty counters. She couldn't bear the thought of it.

The cost of returning to the States was high. She'd known that the minute their plans had jelled. She picked up the phone from the counter and paged through to the picture she'd received that morning. Lynn had sent a selfie from the hip Sheinkin neighborhood where she'd been breakfasting with some friends. The image was all sunshine, smiles and good times. Susan smiled at it, puckered her lips, and blew her daughter a lusty air kiss. She didn't blame her for not wanting to join them. She'd begun her studies at Tel Aviv University a year earlier and was comfortably settled into a shared apartment in Florentine. She had no interest in picking up and joining her parents abroad. This was their adventure, not hers. Besides which, her life was good; it positively blazed with pleasure. Why would she want to leave all that?

Susan put the phone down on the counter and went back to the window. It was so hard to start again. She'd known it would be, had thought about that off and on even after they'd made their decision. But now that she was here, settled into an unfamiliar house that paled in comparison with her gorgeous new one, in a neighborhood to which she had no connection at all, with no local friends, it was

315

beginning to truly sink in. Leaving her daughter was only a part of the story, even quite natural as she began to make her way, to figure out what she wanted to do, where she wanted to be. But leaving her friends, relationships she'd spent decades developing, was another thing all together. If only it weren't so quiet.

She went back to her phone again, flipped impatiently through the numbers and dialed.

"Well, hello!!! What a surprise! I didn't expect to hear from you!"

Susan breathed a sign of a relief. *A voice! A friendly voice!*

"Thought I should check in, show a sign of life."

"Tell me, tell me: How is life on the other side?"

"You know. Quiet. Green." Susan paused a moment and then added, "Event-free."

"Well that must be a very nice change of pace!" Alison laughed. "Here you know the protocol: every minute something new. Absolutely *never* boring."

Boring. That was the word she'd been looking for. But Susan didn't dare express it out loud. "I'm setting up. It's like playing house."

"Sounds kind of fun. Back here it's 'same old – same old.' Have you been in touch with Vicki?"

"Yes. I spoke with her. We're going to meet up before she leaves. I have to see when I can get to the City. There's so much to do here." Susan looked around her. Actually, there was almost nothing to do. Filling up the kitchen cabinets was about the tallest order she had going.

"I'm so envious. A new beginning. That must be so much fun. And wow, after such a dreadful summer. What a relief! So good to get away and breathe different air."

"Well, yes; and a little bit, no. I miss Lynn. It was such a tense summer. I know it's over. I know she's fine. But leaving her there…"

316

"Oh, don't give it another thought. We've got her covered. This is great for you. Hey. What's the plan? Have you had any bites on positions? I'm planning on living vicariously through your success. Here it's Thursday and I'm only beginning to figure out what I'll put on the table for dinner tomorrow night. A big, whopping ho-hum."

Susan took a seat at the table, picked up her coffee and took another sip. It was cold. She let it clatter back onto the table – nothing appealing there. "I have a few interviews, mostly local clinics. I don't want to have to travel too far to work. I'm pretty nervous. It's been awhile."

"Oh sweetie, you'll be fine. This is a great opportunity. Talk to Victoria, she'll give you a little incentive. I know she had a tough summer, or rather, a dreadful one, but even she managed to enjoy a bit of the home-style life she'd been craving. Go for it!"

Susan promised to update Alison and hung up. She had thought speaking with her friend would energize her, cheer her up, but instead she felt even worse. She needed to shake off this mood. How had she ever thought starting over, at almost fifty, was going to work out? What was so bad about teaching little kids the ABC? She looked up at the clock on the wall. Matt wouldn't be home for hours. After working day and night in an effort to relieve the soldiers, worrying about friends' and neighbors' children non-stop, closing up one life and moving to another, she'd been thrilled to finally get on the plane and fly away. Who wouldn't have been? This summer in Israel had been awful as bad as it could get. Maybe it wouldn't be so bad to live in a place without sporadic terror attacks, one whose mere existence wasn't continually an issue.

Yet here she was. And despite this pretty little house with the lace curtains and the green lawns, the trimmed hedges and pebbled driveway, she couldn't help but feel lost, almost at sea. This slice of American suburbia, the one she'd convinced herself she'd missed when Matt's job had popped up, suddenly seemed uninteresting, even lame. She wiggled out of her flip-flops and rested her feet on the plush carpet. They didn't have any carpet at all in their new home, only beautiful wood flooring, shined to a luster, warm to the touch. She rubbed her feet back and forth, working her toes into the long threads of yarn. She made a face. It was scratchy and unyielding, fake and synthetic, not nearly as soft and welcoming as she'd imagined. It really wasn't all that nice. She sighed and put her flip-flops back on. So much for that. She'd have to find other ways to embrace this alternative world, to suppress the sense that it felt so empty.

Her phone beeped. It was an email. She looked at the return address: St. Ann's Speech Therapy clinic. This one was in Brooklyn.

"Could it be…?"

One click and she was in: "Dear Ms. Cohen. We reviewed your resume and think your qualifications a good fit for our team. We'd like to meet you next Tuesday…"

Susan's heart took what felt like an extra beat and she clicked her phone closed. This was it. This was what would make the difference. It was what she'd wanted. She'd never imagined having another chance; had buried her hopes and dreams in the construction of a new home to assuage the professional disappointment of decades. But here it was: an opening. She pushed away from the table and marched into the bedroom to look for the dusty box of grad school books she'd kept stored and tightly sealed since first arriving in Israel decades before. Suddenly the fake carpeting wasn't all that significant. Maybe, in the end, what was meant to be a temporary relocation would lead to a life. She smiled in anticipation.

Jackie wiggled her toes into the damp sand at the water's edge, watching them disappear, swallowed up momentarily as the water rushed in, and then just as swiftly reappear as it rushed out. This was so relaxing, the ebb and flow of the tide, the smashing sunset, the warmth of a summer's evening. She'd been yearning for this for weeks as she waded through the sludge and horror of the summer back in Israel. She'd stuck it out and done her part. She'd sorted and wrapped and repackaged.

What did they do with all those socks?

She'd swapped horrific stories at the local grocery store, prayed for miracles, waited for news with her friends and neighbors. And each day she'd given silent thanks for the fact that her son hadn't yet entered this foray. No. Adam wasn't involved this time around. She had no idea how she'd handle it when, or better said "if," he were. Yet his day was coming, just up the road. She couldn't imagine how she would ever survive a summer like this with him in the middle of the action. She was certain she didn't have the fortitude.

She cast a glance to the west. She couldn't see Israel but she knew it was there, just beyond the long stretch of blue. She really hadn't gone all that far, a large hop, skip and jump away from the Israeli shore. When they'd booked the tickets the destination hadn't been important. She'd merely wanted to get away and pretend, for a few days, that she had another life, far removed from the danger and chaos of the one back home.

She'd escaped. There was no other way to describe it. And for that she was grateful. Here on the island of Crete life was a vacation filled with food and frivolity. Everything was easy and carefree, simple and absolutely safe. She was dying to live in a place just like this.

Noa ran toward her down the beach and straight into the water.

"Come in, Mommy!" she yelled over her shoulder as she bounded ahead, into the calm, lapping waves. "It's warm!"

"Yeah, Mom. Don't hang there at the edge. Come on in!"

Jackie watched Adam skip through the shallow water before diving straight into the surf. Ten meters or so out, the two began to splash each other, Noa squealing a less-than-whole-hearted "Stop," but not swimming away – obviously enjoying the game.

This is what summer was supposed to be.

Her eyes filled with tears as she experienced both relief, the difficult summer behind her, and apprehension, concern over those that lay ahead. She blinked them back quickly as a sudden notion popped into her head. Maybe it was possible to alter the destiny of these two completely by simply changing their course. She forcefully wiped away the tears that had managed to pass her eyelids, teetering on her cheekbone, and then stiffened her entire body with determination, digging her toes firmly into the soft sand there on the water's edge. There was no question about it: choices could be made, tides could be turned. There was another option for them, for her children. There was another option for her entire family. She marched back up the beach, resolved to explore it before it was too late.

Ben stepped away from the falafel stand, balancing the overflowing pita sandwich between his two hands and taking a hearty bite. The *tehina* spread across his upper lip, splotching the mustache that had formed and pooling at the corners of his mouth. He stretched his tongue up as far as it would go and tried to lick it off while still chewing. For weeks it had been tuna and bread, cans of beans. This sandwich was as good as it got. Maybe he'd have another later on. He walked over to a group of his fellow soldiers crouching on a cluster of tree stumps and grabbed a seat, not stopping the cycle of eating for a minute: lift, bite, chew, swallow. Begin again.

"*Mashu, mashu. Kama ta'im, nachon?* This is something else, so good, right?"

"*Elohim. Lo yacholti levakesh yoter.* God, nothing could taste better."

At this moment, these simple sandwiches were better than anything they could have prayed for, absolutely gourmet. A few more guys came over. Someone brought a bottle of cold Coca-Cola and a stack of plastic cups. They distributed them between themselves, poured a round.

"I swear!"

"Heaven on earth!"

"Did you see the shawarma stand? Can you believe it? Right here in the middle of nowhere!"

"And there's an ice cream vendor over there!"

"Someone obviously thinks we need to be spoiled."

"The word is *deserve.*"

There were a few grunts of agreement, a round of laughter and the makeshift feast continued. Ben took a slug of his Coke. It was so cold, so sweet. *Perfect. Absolutely perfect. Best thing ever.* He looked over to the many other soldiers spread throughout the clearing. These were such good guys. They were his guys. It was a relief to be hanging here together, eating, laughing and shooting the breeze. It was almost normal. But then, he remembered, that it wasn't.

He made one more sweep, this one more purposeful, counting heads, finding the members of his own squad. Most were here; some were missing. He twisted the toe of his boot into the dirt beneath him, working it under the roots of one of the adjacent tree stumps, upending large clumps of earth. This was hard. He'd never anticipated anything so hard. He planted his boot in the hole he'd managed to make, forcing his foot to assume an awkward angle, his knees jutting up as he crouched. He was here. He wasn't going anywhere. Maybe that was all that mattered.

"Fried's father just drove up."

All heads looked over toward the parking area beyond the forest, watching as their friend loped over to meet his parents. Ben was too far to hear what was said, but he could imagine. He felt a few tears spring into his eyes and quickly wiped them away with the back of his hand, looking around to check that no one was watching. He couldn't let them flow. He wouldn't let go. Some of his friends weren't okay but he was fine. That was what counted right now. It was all part of the game, an ugly game. He had to be grateful and move on. There was no choice.

"You've wiped dirt all over your face."

His friend Nadav banged his own knees against Ben's, smiling quickly before looking away. Ben looked around a second, trying to find a napkin or towel of some sort, and then, without hesitation, wiped at his face with the sleeve of his uniform. He needed to clean up. His dad was coming. He needed to pull himself together. Appearances were important.

He took one last bite of his pita, brushed off his hands and then wiped them on his pants.

"Anyone up for ice cream?" There were a few enthusiastic sounds of assent and then a wave of movement as almost all of them stood up and began to move in the direction of the cart. Passing by a towering pile of their belongings, a mishmash of battle gear and packs, Nadav uttered a dismissive, "*Aiza hara*. What a load of crap!" Ben followed his glance, taking in the crushing load they'd had to carry, now encrusted with weeks' worth of dirt and grime and abandoned in a heap. He couldn't bear the thought of having to hoist his pack ever again, let alone going back in.

"Ben!"

He looked up excitedly, recognizing the voice, and spotted his father making his way toward him through a grove of trees. "*Achar kach*. Catch up with you later," he mumbled quickly to Nadav and hurried off in his father's direction, careful not to burst into an all-out run. No. He was no longer a little boy. This was a new era.

A few large, loping steps and they reached one another, coming together in a tight embrace. Ben hung on. He didn't want to let go. His father's arms, stretching to reach completely around his muscular back, held him firmly. There was nothing like this. Nothing as good. He heard a sniffle but he wasn't sure from where. It could even have been his. The relief of this embrace was overwhelmingly powerful, drowning out everything else, encasing the two in a protective bubble. His father pulled away a bit, stared into Ben's eyes, and then pulled him back in close. They were both teary-eyed. This was new, this show of emotion, something he hadn't known before; another part of the new stage of life he'd entered this summer.

Ben felt awkward, at a loss. What could he say? What was he supposed to say? How was he meant to act when nothing, absolutely nothing, was the same; when his present world was so dramatically different from that he'd known only two months earlier? His father tucked his own arm under his and led him in the direction of the cart. "Let's get ice cream." Ben smiled in eager acquiescence.

Despite the pain – the excruciating pain that had accompanied almost every thought, invading his dreams since the incident, since the sound and light of the end had flashed before him – something about this moment felt extraordinarily right. Things were never going to be the same. No one had to tell him that. It didn't need to be discussed. But he wouldn't be facing this new world order alone. In fact, here with his squad, his guys, his brothers, gripped tightly by his dad, he felt completely protected, sheltered from harm. Truly comprehending the security of home, Ben could almost relax.

Chapter 28

Victoria stepped out of the Journalism School building and paused, an enormous smile on her face. She'd done it. Somehow, despite the trials of the summer, she'd managed to do a good job, to make enough of an impression to guarantee a future. Just now the dean had offered her a position on the faculty. She crossed the Green in great strides, taking in the majestic and formidable buildings to all sides, all that academic splendor she'd dreamed of having a part in. Ducking down the winding path behind Low Library to Schermerhorn Hall she felt lighter than she had in weeks. Confident. A choice had to be made and the answer was clearer than ever.

Ilana was waiting for her at the entrance to the Wallach Art Gallery. The two linked arms and made their way quietly into the exhibition space. A friend of Victoria's from the Journalism School had gotten them permission to view the fall exhibition, still in the process of installation, before the two departed for Israel. The main hall featured a number of large marble busts, sketches of mausoleums and stained glass fragments primarily devoted to memorials.

Ilana tugged her arm. "Maybe we should go. I don't think it's the best timing for this subject."

"For an exhibition on funerary monuments?" Victoria laughed. "Actually it's kind of ironic. And seriously, when exactly *is* the right time to learn about gravestones?"

They both laughed as they stepped in front of a photograph of Woodlawn Cemetery dating to its creation in the mid-nineteenth century. The text panel explained that it was one of the first cemeteries to assume the landscape-lawn style.

Victoria lowered her voice in adoration. "It's beautiful. So peaceful. There's so much grass! Too bad the image is in sepia tones. Can you imagine how green it must have been?"

Ilana moved in front of Victoria. "This doesn't bother you? Stir up difficult thoughts?"

"Not at all. This is part of life. Cemeteries are all about life. I mean, each and every memorial here is testimony to a whole story. No gloom and doom as far as I'm concerned."

Ilana reached out and grabbed Victoria's arm. "Hey. You haven't told me."

"What?" It was Victoria's turn to stop and frown.

"About the appointment with the dean!" She let out a sound of exasperation.

"Oh that. Well," she paused, "he offered me the job!"

"No."

"Yes!"

"And you took it!" She stepped forward and draped her arms around Victoria's neck with enthusiasm.

Victoria welcomed the hug but slowly unwrapped Ilana's arms and stepped back. "No. In fact, I didn't."

"What?? Are you crazy? You've been dying for that job. It's exactly what you wanted! What you've always wanted!"

"Yes, quite so. But that's not enough to... Well, this summer..." Her voice faded off. She moved a bit to the side and gazed at a map of New York with all the boroughs laid out flat, the way the City looked back in the mid-nineteenth century.

"What an extraordinary city this is...."

"But," Ilana completed Victoria's thought, "you want to go home."

Victoria turned to face her. "Yes, that's it. I want to go home."

Ilana laughed. "You and me alike."

It was Victoria's turn to be perplexed. "What are you talking about?"

"I'm ready, Vic. I'm ready to come home."

"Ready?"

"Remember our tea? The jasmine tea we shared a few months ago when you came to visit? That was a very black time. I couldn't imagine..." Ilana's voice petered out for a moment before she resumed. "But this summer. My eyes opened. I noticed something I'd missed. Now everything seems different." She paused to clear her throat. "There's no question. Israel is a challenge for me, a tough fit. It probably always will be. But what I saw, what Nimrod and I saw, even from so far away: the way a whole country could pull together, put their individual needs aside to do unto others. That's something I've never experienced in any of the lovely places I've lived." She paused again. "Life has been wonderful abroad, although I admit that part of the appeal has always been just being far from the Middle East. But I'm ready to be part of something bigger, something beyond what goes on in the four walls of our house."

Victoria stood in silence, absorbing Ilana's words, and then grasped her elbow and led her forward to a large stained glass window mounted as if in situ. They both stared up at its brilliant colors, taking in the depiction of Mary, of angels with their raised trumpets. Their eyes met within the reflection of the paned glass, locked in a pool of the deepest blues.

"You know, the minute Ben started his service things began to change for me. It was like someone shook up the snow dome of my life. Everything I'd had, all the elements of my life, were still there, but they had re-formed and were almost unrecognizable. I had to try to keep up. It was hard enough when he was in training, but this summer…" Her voice petered out for a moment. "I'd love to be able to give it back. Erase it from the books. So much loss." Victoria shook her head slowly from side to side, still firmly locked onto her reflection. "Everything looks a bit different now, a lot sharper, more defined. There was no way I could ever have anticipated the effect of this summer."

She turned away from the glass with determination and stared straight into Ilana's eyes. "It's time to go home." She beckoned to the exhibition exit with her head. "Come on. Let's go rejoin the land of the living."

Chapter 29

Back at the Binyamina train station, Victoria sat in her car listening to the whoosh of the cool air streaming through the vents. The air conditioning was taxing the engine, causing it to overheat a bit, but she didn't dare turn it off. The heat outside was blistering. It was almost September and the start of another school year, yet the scorching heat in Israel stubbornly denied autumn's proximity. A quick check to either side revealed several other people hermetically sealed into their own cooled cars, equally unwilling to step outside into the murky heat.

Of course her air conditioning had to work double time in an effort to combat the explosive combination of the oppressive conditions outdoors and her own elevated body temperature. She was very worked up, her heart racing. She and the kids had arrived back two days earlier. She was still high from the invitation by the dean at Columbia to assume a teaching position. The summer in New York had been a success. The path was clear.

Guy had wrapped his arms around her in the arrival's hall at the airport.

"Happy to be home?"

"You can't imagine." They'd clung to one another. Neither had wanted to break the grasp, so thankful to be able to physically bask in their relief. Hundreds of travelers had streamed around them; carts loaded with baggage zoomed by, welcoming balloons wafted up to the lofty ceiling,

But since then she'd had only one thing in mind: Ben. She simply couldn't wait to see him, to hold him tightly and more significantly hold on tight – truly for dear life. It'd only been two months since they'd last been together – *only eight weeks?* – but it seemed more like a decade. He was sixty days closer to completing his thousand. Time never ceased its relentless march forward.

She tapped her fingers anxiously on the dashboard, regretting having left the house so early. It would have been easier to pass the time waiting at home. At least there she could have found some kind of menial task to occupy her: folding the laundry, rinsing the dishes, pretending to cook. She could have called Alison, shot the breeze, gone over inanities they'd long since covered. Instead, here she was, waiting – the wheels in her head spinning at an impossible rate. It felt like she was in the middle of running a marathon – heart pounding, breath short, desperate for the finish line.

She pushed the seat back as far as it would go, pressed on the recliner lever, laid her head back on the headrest and closed her eyes. She needed to calm down. She'd made it this far; the rest was insignificant. She was the most fortunate woman alive. She began to relax, her thoughts drifting off in different directions, finally released from their singular obsession. *It was the best of times, it was the worst of times.* Dickens had nailed it. Those words pretty much encapsulated these last few months.

Her mind couldn't calm her body. She looked around within the car and then realized fresh air might help. She lowered the windows. One deep inhalation and she understood precisely how oppressive it was outside. She raised them quickly, shaking her head in disbelief. They never got a break around here. Surviving the summer had been so difficult. It would be nice to finally have a break in the temperature, even a breeze. They certainly deserved it.

She peeked at the clock again. Almost there. The train would arrive shortly but she couldn't bear the wait. She opened the door and got out of the car. It was like stepping into an oven. She leaned against the car for a second, thoughtlessly, and then abruptly pushed away. The exterior was burning hot. She looked down at the black tarmac beneath her, thought about that old adage about it being hot enough to fry an egg, and smiled, luxuriating in the realization that it was okay to feel happy. This was a good day. It really didn't matter that this place was an inferno.

In any case, it was *her* inferno.

She thought about how, back when her children were attending day camp in the States, she would wait for their bus to arrive, day in and day out, standing on the street corner anticipating its yellow profile. How there had been that one day, one so hot you could actually see the heat rise from the pavement. The yellow school bus had rolled up in front of her, the door had popped open, and down the steps had tumbled her children: purple-faced, swooning and positively swollen from the heat. She'd grabbed their sticky arms in a half embrace and then tentatively peered into the bus to thank the driver. Her eyes had locked on a tiny rotating fan mounted high above the windshield and tilted downward at a precarious angle before spotting the man himself, or what was left of him – dehydrated, disheveled and downright miserable.

At that moment she'd been thankful for the modern, fully air-conditioned buses back in Israel; at least there they knew how to handle the heat, were relatively prepared and organized to fight back as best as they could. Even then, more than a decade earlier, she'd known that her slapdash, negative assessments of her adopted country as Third World were more fiction than fact, part of a story she told herself.

Hordes of people began to stream out of the station toting duffels, briefcases and backpacks. A glance back to the tracks revealed the red double-decker train she'd been waiting for. She took a moment to admire its beauty, a red slash of modern efficiency invigorating an otherwise simple arrangement of platforms and tracks.

He's here!

The air that had seemed so oppressively heavy only moments earlier shifted a bit, its molecules regrouping into lighter, more breathable formations. She turned toward the station's exit, eager to find the best view possible, to spot her son the second he appeared. Commuters poured out in a continual torrent, cutting right and left – heading to waiting cars, friends and family, making their way toward the local bus stop, crossing the busy street to continue on foot into Binyamina.

And then, a flash of gold and she recognized Ben's blond hair, a glint of light striking his locks, differentiating him instantly from the crowd. Victoria stood frozen to her spot, unable to move. He emerged from the crowd in dress fatigues, squeezing through the narrow exit, growing larger and larger as he walked through the parking lot, looking for her. She waited a few more seconds, waited for that moment when he would catch her eye, would spot her among the throng.

And then, there it was. She watched him smile. This very moment, this precise spot, this exact sensation, were as much home as she'd ever need.

Afterword

Chapter 30

Victoria tugged at the sleeves of her sweatshirt, pulling them down to make sure they covered her wrists as she pulled her legs up onto the couch beside her, bending at the knees and tucking in tight. She reached over to the small, carved wood footstool standing in as a coffee table, and picked up her mug of tea replete with ginger root shaves and a fresh sprig of lemon verbena. She took a few sips. She loved that combination of tangy, spicy and sweet; the dollop of honey she'd added at the last minute smoothing off the mixture perfectly.

She and Naomi were scheduled to compete in a triathlon the following morning in the neighboring Gilboa mountain range. Naomi's sister and brother-in-law, who lived in Ein Harod, one of the kibbutzim in the valley, had kindly offered them shelter. They'd eagerly accepted the opportunity to enjoy a brief getaway and sleep a bit later thanks to the proximity to the race site. Since the visit was mostly about convenience, Victoria hadn't anticipated the extent of the welcome she'd receive, the jewel of a home she'd discover.

She settled herself deeper into the big cushions on the couch, her free hand idly playing with the creases of the velour covering, and lifted her gaze in order to take in the room. One wall was covered with framed artwork, all Israeli originals, many of them embellished with personal dedications to her hostess. Beside her on the corner table was a stack of books sporting bookmarks and a variety of tiny, colored scraps of paper. They weren't only for decoration. This was a home never short of an interesting subject of conversation, brimming with ideas and creative energy and all wrapped up and presented with modesty, warmth and genuine invitation. It was the epitome of her concept of "home."

From the moment they'd made their way from the car park to Nurit and Yossi's house, Victoria had understood that this wasn't going to be your everyday pit stop. As they rolled their bikes down the path, Victoria had been spellbound by the intense beauty of the spot, an area nestled in the shadow of Mount Gilboa, surrounded by beautiful fields of tall corn stalks and sunflowers. Everything seemed bathed in a coppery light quite different from the glaring, sun-bleached one she was used to. It was as if the entire area was covered by fairy dust.

The properties along the walkway had a special aura, almost enchanted, each preceded by winding entryways marked by tiny pebble or wood-chip paths; neatly tended gardens featuring carnations, moonflowers and purple sage; welcome arches made from entwined bamboo and greenery. There were lanterns strung along the walkways, and she had the feeling she'd entered a Buddhist shrine, not the residential area of a local kibbutz. A mixture of magic and spirituality reigned supreme. Something about the quiet – it was extraordinarily quiet – struck her deeply. The only noise seemed to be that she and Naomi made chattering as they strolled and rolled their way to the house, her friend regaling her with the story of the original settling of this valley, the tents, the mosquitoes and the intense struggle to clear and cultivate the land, all an integral part of the very earliest history of modern Israel.

From those first few instants Victoria had realized she'd stepped into a world entirely different from her own, inadvertently happened upon something "primary" whose existence she'd known of but never before experienced. Unlike the usual collection of newbies she hung out with back in Caesarea, most of whom had arrived in Israel sometime during the '90s, her hosts represented "old" Israel, the real McCoy. And from the moment she'd arrived, she'd been made to feel like one of the family.

Curled up on this comfortable couch, as if she occupied it most evenings, deep in a half slumber induced by the intimate atmosphere, she was startled when she realized Yossi had spoken to her directly, was trying to get her attention. She tried to follow his comments, something about the house, and opened and closed her eyes a few times, long, time-lapsed blinks, struggling to pull herself back from her trancelike state enough to respond.

"Did you notice the ceiling?"

She looked up at the wood rafters and then back at him quizzically. She offered a questioning smile, eyebrows raised and waited. There was a lovely sense of time slowed almost to stalling; she knew he didn't expect a quick answer, if any at all.

"The roof slants downward to accentuate the feeling of intimacy. This room actually has the lowest ceiling in the house. I designed it that way. I wanted the family room to be all about embrace, comfort and coziness." He smiled at her and lowered his head, peering at her intensely to make sure she was following his train of thought before continuing. "But for there," he pointed away, toward the adjacent living space, "for the living room, I wanted something entirely different. You see the line?" His finger moved through the air, following an invisible line indicative of the connection between the family room and the living room. As the entire ground floor was one flowing space, she hadn't noticed the subtle shift in flooring between the rooms, one carpeted, the other parquet, apparently part of the grand plan to differentiate between the two. "Do you see what happens?" Victoria strained to figure out what he was referring to and in general, to keep up with the conversation. She was surprised by the tenor of depth and significance in this late-night exchange. Between the aromatic tea, the physical warmth of the house and now, this captivating explanation of its raison d'être, she felt completely intoxicated.

Yossi didn't hesitate long in the telling. "There's an abrupt change of direction – ceiling rafters and all. Over there, once you've left this family room, everything slants completely the other way, upward and outward. The idea is to emphasize that that room is for guests invited for more formal occasions, larger groups of people. That is a room that needs to look outward instead of inward – to accommodate a crowd, not a family. I don't know if Naomi told you, but we have a lot of events here. Our home has become one of the cultural centers of the valley." He glowed with pride, sitting up straight in his recliner. "We sponsor special evenings: concerts, lectures, readings, spiritual get-togethers – you name it. You're welcome to come up and join any time." He reached for his tea and slumped back comfortably into his chair. "You can make it a weekend."

Victoria remained silent, overwhelmed by an all-encompassing exhaustion that spoke not only of this particular evening, but of the entire past summer. "You have a lovely house." She blushed. That was the best she could do.

Yossi continued, "I built it myself."

She understood his pride. This was an extraordinary place. She could move right in; leave her belongings and hordes of junk behind. She was tempted to give up the morning race and spend a few hours after breakfast, accompanied by a cup of coffee, going through the library she'd espied in the study adjacent to the kitchen: wall-to-wall, ceiling to floor shelving filled with books.

This promised to be a lot more enlightening, in addition to fun, than any competition.

Her host didn't pass on the opportunity to probe her inner thoughts, "Victoria, do you love living here?"

Her eyelids, halfway closed seconds before, snapped open. She was suddenly alert. She didn't respond immediately, but the cogs of her mind began to move apace, churning through a sudden inundation of thoughts. There was a long moment of silence. Everyone was looking at her.

"Do you love Israel?" He asked this next question so confidently – as if the answer were clear, the question itself entirely rhetorical.

She smiled. "Well, I might, if I lived *here*." Her answer was far too pat. She knew it wasn't good enough, acutely aware that he sought a genuine answer. For this man, fully entrenched in a charmed life full of natural beauty, family and a wealth of culture, Israel was a dream come true. She didn't want to let him down.

"I'm coming to."

He picked up on her hesitancy. "But…"

"But nothing. It's been a long journey."

Again, "Do you love living here?" He was persistent. No one had ever asked her this simple, direct and ultimately meaningful question – not once since she'd made aliyah several decades earlier. The words felt so heavy, so laden with meaning. Victoria respected her hosts, appreciated their lifestyle, and understood the extraordinary, envy-inspiring life they lived. She didn't want to simply fudge an answer or worse, to disrespect their legitimate interest by giving them one not well considered.

Yossi stood up and beckoned her to follow. She didn't ask questions, merely untangled herself from the clutch of the couch and trailed him, tea in hand, through the living room to the huge glass doors opening onto the terrace. It was cold outside. The condensation on the glass made the thought of stepping beyond the threshold unpleasant. She shivered in anticipation. Her host persevered; he had a plan. He put his hand on the lock, gave it a twist and seconds later they were both standing on the wooden deck gazing toward the mountain range in silence. She gasped at that first blast of chilled air but almost immediately stopped noticing the sudden change in temperature; there was so much more to consider. The star-filled sky opened in all directions, a canopy of twinkling lights. These were echoed by spots of light on the Gilboa range itself as well as the houses nestled beneath, each one suggesting a pocket of warmth and welcome similar to that in which she was comfortably settled for the evening.

"I meant what I said before. I want to invite you to come here for a long weekend, whenever you like. You'll find what you're looking for; I guarantee it. Don't hesitate."

Victoria, choked with emotion, remained silent. She'd so wanted to give him a positive answer, to confidently claim her allegiance to this land. But her recent change of heart was still too new, still too untried. There'd been this past summer's pain, so indescribably awful, and then, unexpectedly, the revelation – the recognition that Israel had become an integral part of her identity without her own intervention, almost despite it. All of this was just beginning to truly sink in, her completely altered perspective just starting to take root.

Standing on that deck, the coolness of the night slicing through her body and forcing her to viscerally experience all that was natural, spread before her, and all that was spiritual, behind, inside this cozy abode, she understood that it might have been otherwise from the start. Instead of carefully controlling her exposure to all that was local – picking through the offerings with a fine-tooth comb, choosing what suited her and pushing away the rest – she might have embraced a more genuine Israel, one tucked far away from the cities and the coast, nestled deeply in a hidden valley; one peopled by those with whom there was a less obvious bond and no common language, a people with a deep commitment to both the land and their community.

This would, of course, have required her to take an even bigger chance – to forgo the easy solution of holding on to what seemed, at least on the surface, to be the perfect fit. Back then, when everything was so unknown, when each step led to entirely new territory, it hadn't seemed a feasible option.

Victoria stepped back inside after Yossi, closing the door firmly behind her. She was delighted with the discovery of all this potential on the heels of that revealed over the summer. Her thoughts shifted to Ben. Since the war had ended, since he'd resumed regular duty, he'd seemed more relaxed, somehow content. His military experience had enabled him to stretch his realm far beyond the limited one she'd provided, to not only acquaint himself with a wider range of the population, but also a wider range of situations. To go far beyond the circumscribed lives most people, like herself, lived. Ben had begun to carve out a niche for himself, to find a real home here, in this land. Although her own passage had been blocked by years spent isolating herself within a circumscribed existence, limiting herself to a predetermined zone of comfort, the door was now open.

Everything she had ever wanted in a home was right there for the taking. She began to count the ways.

Acknowledgments

This novel could never have been conceived without the man who changed my story completely. My husband Rami introduced me to a life I couldn't have dreamed up if I'd tried, opening my eyes to the multitude of choices life offers. For that, and for so many other things, I am forever grateful.

My mother's fascination with culture, her endless thirst for knowledge and her unceasing effort to learn as many foreign languages as possible in order to best acquaint herself with this glorious world, enabled the enormous step I took decades ago when I leaped across the world and began again. My devotion to my children is a direct result of her own.

I owe my passion for words, the importance of picking the right ones for each situation and the understanding of just how powerful they can be if used correctly, to my father. Besides being my chief editor until the day he passed, he was my emotional backbone, steadfast in his belief in my abilities, one hundred percent devoted to my pursuits.

My brother Richard's wry sense of humor and eyes-open approach to humanity has taught me to take much of life with a large grain of salt. Besides picking up the reins dropped by my father and becoming my anchor in Philadelphia, he is an exemplar of how important it is to be the best we can for those we love.

I would not have known quite how to turn my idea into a novel without the guidance of Caroline Leavitt. She taught me everything I know about story: how to shape it and how to give it life. Of course the end is just as important as the beginning, and I owe much gratitude to my fabulously attentive copy editor, Ita Olesker, and the super competent and ever-lovely staff at Mandolin Publishing.

I am extremely appreciative of my very dear friends in Israel and the United States, from childhood and adulthood. Their support and love have sustained me, their own stories have inspired me – without them I would lack the strength to get through the hardest moments; with them on my side everything is that much lighter. I owe very special thanks to Michal Cooper-Keren, as it was she who urged me to finally write this book. I would never have dared to embark on this incredible journey without her.

I've purposefully left my three children for the end. No others have provided me with more joy, more desperation, more delight and more challenges. They've taught me about the bottomless depth of love, the likes of which I could never have envisioned without them. They are the story that I will never complete, its ending elusive, its potential immeasurable.